Z14

ZOMBIE RULES BOOK 2

DAVID ACHORD

Prologue

There was a sprinkle of snow dusting the roads as we turned east onto Old Hickory Boulevard from Nolensville Pike. There were eight of us in three different vehicles. Julie sat in the passenger seat.

"Is it going to snow all day, do you think?" she asked.

"I hope so. It'll make it a whole lot easier for us," I replied.

We knew they were coming. One member of our group, a former corporal in the United States Army, had stumbled upon a large mass of them slowly moving down Bell Road at the Interstate 24 overpass. He had hurried home and told us about it, estimating there were over a thousand of them. They had probably made it to the Blue Hole Road intersection by now.

They were too close to our homes for comfort. It was unacceptable. We decided something had to be done. So, we took a page from Sun Tzu. We were going to take the battle to them.

Their strategy was ingeniously simple; keep walking until you happened upon a food source, and attack it. They had a herd mentality and they followed the path of least resistance (zombie rules nine and ten respectively, in case you've not been keeping up), which made it fairly easy for us, in a manner of speaking.

We drove east on Bell Road until we spotted them. I stopped my truck in the middle of the road, opened my door, and took up a shooting position. The others parked and followed my lead.

"Alright, here they come," I said, pointing out the obvious. "Keep your rate of fire calm and controlled, and remember, we only have four thousand rounds of ammo. When they get too close, we'll pull back a quarter of a mile and do it again."

I heard a few grunts of acknowledgement as I pulled the charging handle on my AR-15.

Chapter 1 – The Captain

Fuel was essential. We hadn't yet acquired the ability to survive without it and we needed it. And, more importantly, we needed a way to transport it.

Hence, the need for us to reclaim the five hundred gallon fuel tanker we recently had to abandon. It wasn't a big tanker hauled by a semi. This type was small enough to be hooked up behind a pickup truck. It was perfect for us, and I assumed the Captain thought the same.

It was a muggy August morning by the time we got going. I sat in the back seat of the dually truck and looked at my two friends. Fred, the taciturn gunslinger, and Howard, a jovial father of two sons, were riding up front. Both of them were old enough to be my father, but I considered them close friends anyway.

Fred took a surreptitious route back to where we had abandoned it the night before. Our plan was to park a safe distance away, sneak up to a suitable spot, and recon the site before any of us went in.

We spotted a burned out house on a side street approximately three hundred yards away from our destination.

"Looks like a good place," Fred said and parked our zombie-proof truck behind the house. It seemed abandoned, and we assumed as much. I mean, why in the world would zombies be hanging out in a burned out house? Alas, you know what they say about people who assume.

"Look out, Howard!" I shouted as he stepped out of the truck. Four of them, two adults and two kids, emerged from the charred remains and set upon him at once.

Howard began running backwards while attempting to bring his rifle to bear. He ended up falling on his ass. The kids were going to reach him first. Howard froze in fear.

Fred calmly stepped out of the truck, drew one of his pistols with lightning speed, and fired four times. The result was four zombies with an extra hole in their respective heads. Howard collected himself, stood shakily, and walked back to us.

"Holy shit, Fred, you sure can shoot!" Howard exclaimed as he caught his breath. I nodded in agreement. Fred was hell on wheels with his six-shooters. I walked over and looked over the zombies. Even though they were horribly decomposed, the kids looked a lot like the adults. I pointed this out.

"They look like a family," I said. "I think these two are the parents to these kids. They've stuck together all these months. And, they were staying inside this house," I frowned. "Why in the hell were they hanging around inside this burned out house?"

"What do you mean, Zach?" Howard asked. "They've got to go somewhere, don't they?"

"It seems odd, Howard. Look at them. Their clothing is not burned or charred, so they went inside the house *after* it had burned. It seems weird to me. I wonder if they lived here at one time. If they did, it means they remembered it somehow."

Howard scratched the small amount of hair remaining on his head. "I think I see what you mean." He stared at the dead zombies for a minute, trying to figure it out in his mind. "How in the hell did they remember this was their house, and why have they stuck together? Yeah, you're right, Zach, it's weird, and it's totally over my head."

I laughed. Fred, as usual, had no commentary on our observations. I guess he had other things on his mind at present. We cleared the house for good measure and then made our way through an overgrown field.

"What do you think, Fred?" I asked.

Fred pulled up the mosquito netting from around his face. The two girls, Julie and Macie, had taken Boonie hats and sewn mosquito netting around them. We all wore them now. They kept all of the flying insects, which were horrendous this summer, out of our mouths, ears, and nose.

Fred stretched. "Well, Zach, we have three possibilities. They found some lug nuts, put the wheels back on and took it with them. They abandoned it. Or, they've got an ambush set up and are waiting for us to mosey right into it."

He was talking about the tanker we had abandoned the night before. It had several gallons of fuel in it and we wanted it back. As I digested what Fred said, I resisted the urge to scratch the scar on the side of my head. It was healed now, nothing more than a linear scar above my ear, but it still itched constantly.

"Let's work our way closer," I suggested. Fred and Howard nodded in agreement. We slowly worked our way through a sparse tree line until we got within a hundred yards. As the tanker came into view, we saw a solitary man sitting beside it in a lounge chair. He appeared to be reading a book. A dusty black four-wheel-drive truck was parked nearby. Two block letters were painted in red on the door: W-E.

"I'd say it's the Captain," Fred whispered. He handed the binoculars to Howard for confirmation. Howard took a short look and grunted.

"Yep, that's him alright," he lowered the binoculars and looked at the two of us. "Are y'all going to kill him?" he asked. Fred shook his head. He and I had already discussed what to do if, and when, we encountered this man. Since Fred was leaving, we agreed it would be better if I tried to work something out with the man, even though we strongly suspected he was a nutcase.

I looked at Howard. "When you first told us about him, Fred and I talked about it at great length. If we kill him, it might eliminate the possible threat, or it may instigate his group to come after us. We're thinking it may be better to form some kind of truce with him. Besides, I'd kind of like to hear what he says," I said.

I pointed toward the Captain. "How about I drive over there and introduce myself. Fred, you can take him out from here I'm guessing?" Fred nodded as he took the protective caps off of the lenses of his rifle scope.

"Howard, is it agreeable with you?" I asked. I remembered how Howard literally shook when he told us of the meeting he had with the Captain not so long ago.Howard shrugged. "It's your funeral, Zach. I hope you know what you're doing."

We worked out the usual plan. If I raised my hands, or if any aggressive move was made against me, Fred would open fire. I had a feeling of confidence because Fred did not miss when he shot a firearm.

I walked back to the truck and drove to the waiting Captain. He looked up from his book as I drove up. It was then I noticed a second chair beside him. He had been expecting this. I parked the truck and exited warily.

"Why, I'm guessing you are the young man who penned the note I found on this tanker. You are none other than the mighty Zach, are you not?" he continued without waiting for my answer. "You're much younger than I imagined. Please sir, come join me. It is my honor to finally meet you."

I walked up to him, all the while looking around with my peripheral vision. There was a teenage boy standing beside the truck. He was short, maybe five-three, and slender. His arms were also very slender, but I could see some musculature. He had dyed black hair which was cut short, dark brown eyes, accented with some black rubbed under them, and his face would have been feminine looking if he wasn't trying so hard to look like the meanest man on earth. He also had an assault rifle hanging from his shoulder in a sling.

He and the Captain were dressed almost exactly alike; camouflage pants, black lace up boots, wife-beater tee shirts, and tactical vests. Both had side arms, and little dude's weapon looked like an M4 assault rifle. Very lethal. I only had a Kimber forty-five secured in a holster on my side.

I walked up to the big man and held out my hand. "You must be the Captain. I've heard of you. I'm Zachariah Gunderson. Call me Zach."

He was as big as Howard had described him. Hell, his tattooed arms were almost as big around as my legs. He stood easily and extended his hand. His grip was like a vise and I had to keep myself from wincing. He held it a moment longer than was necessary, smiled, and motioned toward the empty chair.

"Please join me, Mr. Gunderson," he said warmly. "What was the gunfire I heard a few minutes ago?" he asked.

I nodded. "A couple of zombies back there. Nothing to worry about though, I got them in the head, and I'll burn them later." I repositioned the chair where I no longer had my back to the armed boy and sat down. The Captain sat a moment later as if he had not noticed. The boy remained beside the truck, glaring at me.

"So, Zach. Zach the Zombie Killer. We meet at last."

He made a casual sweeping motion with one of those big arms. "When journeying around this area, I have been seeing signs, a pattern of behavior of which I've not seen anywhere else. Your rules, the FEMA signs painted on houses, the gas caps on vacant automobiles. Oh, and let's not forget the dead, head shots and burned afterward," he held up a finger and waggled it slightly. It looked like an oversized Vienna sausage. "When I observed these things, I knew there was somebody operating out here with an intelligent, orderly mind."

He stared at me a moment longer, then reached for the book he was reading and held it up with a challenging smile. "Have you ever read any poetry by Rudyard Kipling?"

"I've read a few of his works," I said.

"Oh? Which is your favorite, might I ask? I can tell the cut of a man by his favorite poetry."

In truth, I had read them all. As a young boy, I found Kipling fascinating. But I did not say as much. "The first one I ever read was The Thousandth Man. I like most of what he's written, but the first one has always stuck with me."

He smiled again. "The Thousandth Man you say? Ah yes, a very good poem, a poem of unwavering loyalty," he slowly nodded his head as he stared at me. "Yes, I can see it in you."

He motioned at the book. "I just finished reading Young British Soldier when you appeared. I have my own variation of a part of it," he looked out into an imaginary audience and began his soliloquy.

"When you're wounded and left on the Tennessee plains, and the zombies come out to eat up your remains, just roll to your rifle and blow out your brains, and go to your God like a soldier!" he finished with a triumphant pointing at the sky and looked at me questioningly.

"I must admit, I like it. Kipling is probably rolling over in his grave though."

The Captain smiled, pleased at the compliment. "How did you survive the Apocalypse?"

"I had a friend and mentor who foresaw this event and planned accordingly. I suppose you could say he would be a thousandth man."

The Captain arched an eyebrow. "Oh? I would like to meet a man of this caliber."

"I'm sorry to say, he is now only with me in spirit," I said without any outward emotion.

"Ah, sad, very sad. I hope he went to his God like a soldier," he said somberly. I did not respond. Rick died in his sleep, whether or not he died like a soldier could be debated. It was not something I cared to discuss.

"And yet, you have survived," The Captain said.

I gave a slight shrug. "I can only guess I am somewhat immune to the plague, as I would guess you and others are as well. Would I get infected if I were bitten?" I shrugged. "Probably. How did you survive?" I asked.

"A group of us have a compound near Eagleville. When we saw the signs, we gathered together, put up barricades, and waited it out. You look like you have some Viking heritage. Gunderson, that's a Nordic surname, is it not?" he asked.

I nodded. "My father's family is from Sweden. My mom was of British ancestry."

"Ah," he looked at me a moment before continuing. "What is your opinion of this so-called plague?"

I thought it over before responding. "It started with people displaying typical flu like symptoms, fever, jaundice, and ague. A degradation of physical acuity followed, and then they would become extremely violent. The virus, along with the fever, affected the brain somehow. I'd guess the hypothalamus was greatly affected. The infected seemed to have diminished cognitive functions, but their extreme aggression and acute gross motor skills seem to indicate a high level of adrenalin being dumped into the body," I took a breath.

"From the onset of the infection, the body tissue is breaking down and decomposing. It is my opinion that they will eventually die out."

The Captain gazed at me intently during my diatribe. "Die out, you say? Interesting," he pointed at me suddenly. "You should join my group, Zach. You'd fit right in."

I grunted. "I'm getting the impression you and your group do not welcome anyone other than Caucasians."

The Captain shook his head slowly. "No, Zach, we don't. Now don't get me wrong, I have no personal hatred of niggers, kikes, slopes, spics, ragheads, fags, or any other minority, but they don't belong with our group, nor do they have any place in my plans of rebuilding this world."

I shook my head slowly. "We're going to have to disagree then, Captain. In my world, using a disparaging term to label a group of people is just plain wrong." I pointed at his book. "I believe Kipling agrees with the sentiment."

The Captain scoffed and waved the book around before tossing it in the weeds. "Now, Zach, it is nothing but poetry after all. I would assert to you, your rules are far more worthy in today's world than most poetry," he paused in reflection for a moment and looked back at the tanker. Someone had apparently tried to tow it off. All of the wheels had fallen off and it was now sitting on the ground.

"I believe I have something valuable to add to your list of rules," he said. "What number are you up to now?"

"Ten," I said. I had many more in my head and written in my notes, but I had not posted them as of yet.

He held up a finger. "A zombie rule: Zombies have no need for logistics. On the face of it, it is a very simplistic sentence. But, like your rules, there is a deep meaning within. Think about it, Zach. Those things don't require food or water like regular humans. They don't need warmth on a cold night. They don't need sanitary conditions. They don't need medication or sleep. Hell, they probably don't need air to breathe," he pointed at the tanker. "They most certainly don't need fuel."

I looked at the tanker, wondering how I was going to get it back from him if he didn't want to give it back "It's a good rule," I said.

We sat in silence for a long minute. I was wary of the Captain. He was being downright cordial, but I suspected it was a facade.

Plus, I was fully aware the chair he had waiting for me was strategically placed so his boy would be behind me. All I wanted at this point was to get the tanker and be gone.

"Zach, what are your plans?" he asked. I looked at him questioningly. "Your plans, Zach, what are your plans for the future?"

"Well, Captain, I'm all for rebuilding a productive society. I would like to hope we can avoid the mistakes of past generations. There is no need for pettiness, racial strife, or domination of one group over another. The people who have survived this apocalypse have far more important things to worry about."

The Captain clapped his hands once in mock glee. "Spoken like a true idealist." He stood and stretched. "It'll never happen, Zach. People are people, after all. They covet. They harbor grudges and ill will, sometimes for several years. Their petty egos and jealousies will never allow them to be satisfied with the social utopia you envision. I'm thinking you are an avid reader, Zach, have you forgotten all of the history books you've read?" The Captain laughed without mirth. "Ah Mr. Gunderson, your naiveté is somewhat refreshing, but oh so misguided."

I thought about what the Captain was saying. I thought of Leon. I thought of Jason and his boys; men who had behaved exactly how the Captain had said. They coveted what I had, and even tried to kill me for it. "You have a valid argument, but I'm not looking for conquest. I only want a peaceful life."

"What do you think, Andie?" he asked the boy.

"I think he's an idiot," the boy standing beside the truck opined. The Captain looked at me as if I had been challenged. I shrugged my shoulders dismissively. However, there was something in the boy's voice. I looked at him and was met with a defiant glare.

He gestured toward the tanker. "That was very clever, Zach. We had no idea the lug nuts were missing until we tried to drive off with it. Is there any reason why I should give it back to you?" the Captain asked. He was smiling pleasantly, but there was a cold look in his eyes.

"Before I answer you, Captain, please allow me to ask a couple of questions," he waved a hand. "How's your fuel supply?"

The Captain shrugged noncommittally. "It could be better."

"Do you have any tankers like this one?" I asked.

"We have one," he paused a moment. "We also have a storage tank back at the compound. Why do you ask?"

"Bring that tanker to me and I'll get it filled up with gasoline."

The Captain's eyes now piqued with curiosity. "Did you hear him, Andie? Zach here seems to know where a supply of fuel is."

"Bullshit," Andie said.

"So call my bluff then. What do you have to lose?" I challenged.

The Captain laughed. "Oh, I like you, Zach. I've not been amused in quite a while now. But you must tell me, where is this cache of gasoline? Do you have it at your own compound?"

I shook my head. "Nope, it's in a fuel reservoir in downtown Nashville, on the east bank of the river, near the old Titan's football stadium to be specific."

The Captain stared at me in amazement a moment, and then laughed uproariously.

"Zach, it's impossible. There are thousands of zombies in the downtown area. I've seen it myself. I sent in a team a few months ago and they were surrounded within minutes. They didn't make it, Zach. They were annihilated."

I held my hands out, careful not to raise them. "I have a plan. It might even go better if you want to help out."

He looked at me, unbelieving at first, and then with concern. "Do you have a cadre of soldiers, Zach?" he asked quietly.

I did not answer directly. "I'm going to try it out with a small group. If everything goes according to plan, we'll gain access to the fuel. There are a lot of variables, and to be honest, it might not work. But I think we should try. I could use a few people with rifles."

"What do you think, Andie?" he asked.

"I think he's full of shit. He'll probably get eaten or blow himself up," Andie replied.

"Did you hear that? My niece thinks you're full of shit."

I glanced over at her quickly. Ah, so that explained it. He was in fact, a she. I could see the feminine features now. She was very much a tomboy, but yes, definitely a she.

The Captain sat back down and pulled his chair closer. He leaned forward and placed his big meaty hands on his knees. "Alright, Mister Gunderson, you've got my attention. Tell me your plan."

Chapter 2 – A Matter of Trust

"Don't tell me you trust him?" Howard asked. We were standing around, near the burned out house. I told them about the conversation between the Captain and me as Howard gathered some dead wood and debris.

I shrugged. "Short answer, no."

Once I proposed my plan to the Captain, he agreed to assist in the endeavor. He even helped me reattach the wheels to the tanker and shook my hand before driving off. I waited for five minutes before I drove away.

Fred had been inspecting the tanker for any signs of sabotage. "I have to go along with Howard on this one, Zach. He can't be trusted."

I nodded. "I agree, Fred, but in spite of the trust factor, I think we can pull it off. We're going to need the extra firepower if we have any hope of getting into downtown Nashville. Besides, this will give us an opportunity to learn who and what we're up against."

Howard chewed on his lip a moment. "You might have a point, Zach. Know your enemy, that's what one of them war generals said, right?" I smiled and nodded. "You're thinking if the racist bastard sees we're an asset, he won't try to kill us. Like when I fixed his bus. Is that what you're thinking?"

I nodded again. "He has a grand scheme of rebuilding the world. He'll view us as nothing more than minions, but it should be enough for him to not try any nonsense."

"So, he wants to rebuild the world, with him being the king of this new society of course. He has grandiose delusions," Fred said. He stacked the corpses together and Howard began stacking the kindling. Soaking it with some of our newly acquired fuel, he lit it carefully.

I nodded. "Yeah, I suppose. The point is, he claims he wants to rebuild, not go around killing everyone. He may be

Machiavellian, but we can work with it, at least for a little while. What do you think guys?" I asked as we got the bodies burning sufficiently. Both men thought about it as we got in the truck and started toward home.

Fred pointed at the two of us as he drove. "You two decide and I'll help out however I can. I'm leaving soon and I don't know if I'll even make it back. So, I don't believe I should have a vote on the matter."

I looked at Howard, who shrugged noncommittally. "We need fuel, that's a fact," he rubbed his face. "I don't trust him. He's not right in the head, I'm thinking. But, I'll go along with it if you think it'll benefit us, Zach."

We ultimately agreed. We drove back to my farm with Howard chitchatting about the weather. Fred was his usual quiet self.

"It won't be long now," I finally said. Howard glanced at me. I had brought up the subject none of us wanted to discuss.

"Yep," Fred responded. "I figure the day after we get the gas, I'll head out," he looked over from the driver's seat. "You two have been a tremendous help. Zach, you've thought of stuff I never would have dreamed of. Howard, you've got that truck in tip top shape. I actually think I'm going to be able to make it, thanks to you two."

We were getting close to the turn off to the driveway. He suddenly stopped the truck in the middle of the road. I thought maybe he saw some zombies or something and looked around hastily. Seeing no threat, I looked at Fred. He was staring straight ahead.

"Give me a year. If I'm not back by then, and you haven't heard from me, you'll know I'm dead. You'll know what to do," he was quiet then, and then proceeded up the driveway without waiting for a response.

I looked at him a moment and then stared out of the window. I wanted to say something, anything that sounded reassuring, but came up empty. We had planned, prepared, rehearsed, all in secrecy. Fred did not want the girls to know what he was going to do until the day he was leaving. I guess he hated long goodbyes. I watched him as he readjusted the guns on his hips.

"If you're going to keep carrying your pistols, you might want to wear a set of shoulder holsters. Those holsters you're wearing now aren't meant to be worn by someone sitting in a car seat for hours at a time."

Fred nodded. "I believe I have one sitting on the shelf of my closet. Good idea."

I couldn't think of anything else. I stepped out and unlocked our recently installed gate. Fred drove through. We were at the house a few minutes later.

"Uh, Howard?" I asked as we got out of the truck.

"Yeah buddy?" Howard looked at me as he stretched and wiped the sweat off of his brow.

"Our garden is doing pretty good. In fact, we have some extra stuff. Now, please don't be offended, but we grew a lot of watermelons and I was wondering if you wanted any."

Howard looked at me with a serious expression. "Why sure, as long as you don't tell the white folks," he then laughed uproariously. Even Fred cracked a smile. We walked over to the garden and I pointed them out.

"Dang Zach, those melons are big," Howard said as he rubbed his belly.

"Thank Bernie's bees. According to him, melons are dependent on bees for pollination. Oh, and the ample supply of cow manure is a good source of fertilizer."

"Well, they sure look good. How many can I have?" He asked.

I shrugged. "Help yourself. Hell, let's eat one now."

We grabbed one and went to the front porch. Fred pulled out his bowie knife and cut up a bunch of slices. We dug in, and within seconds we had juice running down our chins as we ate. The girls walked outside and gaped at us.

"Look at you three slobs!" Julie lamented. "I'll get some napkins."

She ducked back inside the house. Fred cut Macie a slice and handed it to her as Julie came back outside with a handful of cloth napkins.

"Dig in," he said. "The baby will love it," Macie smiled, sat on the steps and took a bite. She spit out a seed a moment later. It landed at her feet. Howard got up from his chair and sat beside her.

"Girl, you gots to learn how to properly spit out a watermelon seed. Watch the master," he took a bite, chewed a moment, and then spit a seed across the yard. Macie took another bite and mimicked his actions. The seed flew in an arc and landed a foot away from Howard's seed. He gave a deep belly laugh. "There ya' go. You're now an expert seed-spitter."

Macie smiled as she and Howard took turns spitting. Fred and I watched quietly while the three of them laughed in glee.

"I want to spit too!" Julie said laughingly. Fred already had a slice cut and handed it to her. She sat beside Macie and the three of them took turns spitting seeds. Fred looked over at me and smiled sadly. I knew what he was thinking. He was downcast about leaving. After a few minutes of their antics, Howard stood.

"I've got to be getting home or else Lashonda will jump all in my ass. Thanks for the watermelons," Howard said. We helped carry the watermelons to his Hummer and bid our goodbyes.

"I need to get home as well. I'll see all of you tomorrow," Fred said. He started to walk toward his truck. He stopped suddenly and turned around. He walked back to the girls and took turns hugging them. He looked at Macie. "I think you're going to make a wonderful mother," he said before getting into his truck and leaving. Her cheeks turned a rosy red as she muttered thanks.

The three of us ate a dinner of chicken with a mixture of canned vegetables. Our salt and pepper was running low, so we used it sparingly.

"I'm trying to get my head wrapped around your plan," Julie said.

Dabbing at my face with my napkin, I attempted to explain.

"First, we'll recon the objective. If the plan is feasible, I'll call in fire support. That will be the Captain's duty. He'll come rolling in with his bus firing his machine guns, killing every zombie in sight. The trucks with the tankers will be following the bus. We bring them in to the fuel reservoir, fill them up, and then follow the bus back to the rendezvous point," I said.

"And you trust him?" Macie asked.

"Up to a point," I answered.

"Zach, what's stopping him from pointing those machine guns at you and taking the gas? Maybe even killing you to boot?" Julie asked.

"I'm working out the details, but I think I have a way of avoiding that," I said. I finished my food and retrieved my notepad.

"I'm all ears," Julie said. Macie snorted.

I smiled. "It involves you and employing your sniper skills," I turned to the page where I had a hand drawn map of the intersection of Old Hickory Boulevard and Nolensville Pike. The girls peered closer while I explained.

Chapter 3 – Operation Gas

The evening sky was hazy, overcast, and there were inky ominous clouds creeping up from the south. I saw the faint glimmer of lightning and stopped the truck. I had been waiting for three days since the meeting with the Captain for optimal weather conditions for what we were going to attempt, and I believed it was finally here.

Howard Junior, or Lil' H as we called him, looked at me when I stopped the truck. Seeing no zombies, we got out. We were on a bridge on Nolensville Pike. Mill Creek flowed under. I saw lightning again in the distance.

"Listen Lil' H," I started counting off the seconds out loud. I got to the count of seven before hearing the rumble of thunder. "Seven seconds. The storm is about seven miles away. We're going to wait a minute or two and then do the same thing over again. Do you know why?"

Lil' H scrunched up his face in deep thought, and then shook his head.

"We're going to determine if the storm is moving toward us," another flash of lightning illuminated the horizon. "Start counting."

Lil' H counted out loud as I had done. We heard the rumble of thunder when he got to five.

"It's getting closer," he said.

"How do you know?" I challenged.

"Because light travels faster than sound, and when the time between the lightning and thunder gets shorter, it's because it's moving closer." He said. I smiled and nodded.

"Alright, let's check the level of the creek."

The two of us got out of the truck and walked over to the edge of the bridge.

"What are you looking for?" He asked.

I pointed at the water. "I'm looking at the water level of the creek," I pointed. "Do you see the marks on the bridge abutment?"

"Yeah," Lil' H responded.

"I looked at those marks yesterday. The creek is up by about a foot. And, it's going to keep rising, which is good for us," I put my hand on his shoulder and squeezed. "It's going to be raining soon, time to put our plan into action."

Lil' H looked up at me and grinned. "Alright!"

We got back into the truck and drove to the Allen's home, a former tire shop located at the intersection of Nolensville Pike and Old Hickory Boulevard.

Howard and Lashonda listened as I got in touch with Fred on the shortwave radio. He answered after a few attempts. "Rain is heading our way. Operation Gas is a go."

"I'll bring the boats and tell the others. ETA is one hour," he signed off. I rotated the dial on the radio until I found another frequency.

"Come in Captain, this is Zach," I said into the microphone.

"Go for the Captain," a voice responded after a minute. It sounded familiar.

"Andie, is that you?" I asked.

"10-4, what do you want Zach?" her tone was curt.

"Operation Gas is a go. If you guys are still in, be here in two hours."

"I'll relay the information. Stand by," I sat by the radio and waited. Mrs. Allen came in with a cup of coffee and a half a loaf of hard bread. I nodded gratefully, tore off a piece and dunked it in my coffee. It was then I realized Mrs. Allen was standing over me looking very worried.

"I'd like to hear what your planning again and why you need little Howard so badly," she asked.

I put the soggy bread down on the saucer. I had gone over it with everyone more than once, but she was understandably worried.

"Okay, it goes like this. It's a two person operation. Lil' H and I are going to camouflage ourselves and use john boats to traverse down Mill Creek. Mill Creek meanders its way through the south Nashville area and eventually dumps into the Cumberland River.

We're going to plant noisemakers at various points along the river banks and wait. When the noisemakers attract the zombies away from the reservoirs, the others will move in and we'll fill up our tankers. If we're successful, we'll have enough fuel to last through the winter." I finished my bread and drank some coffee.

"What if there are too many zombies? What will you do then?" she asked.

"I'll get on the radio and tell everyone to abort. Then, we simply reverse course. We'll be home in a few hours."

She stared at me pointedly. "Why do you need my son?"

"It's a two-man job. He can swim and he's small. The boats are going to be full of stuff. We're going to need all of the room we can get."

We had found several old style 'boom boxes' at a pawn shop. Batteries were much harder to find unfortunately, so I had rigged them to run off of car batteries. The advantage was they were going to play loudly for several hours.

"When the zombies have moved away, Fred and Howard will come in with their truck and tanker, along with one of the Captain's men in their truck."

Lashonda shook her head with worry. "If my son comes to harm, I'll never forgive you Zachariah Gunderson," she said.

"I believe the weather, combined with dusk, will greatly diminish their ability to see…" I started to say more, but she walked out of the room without another word. I watched her walk out as Andie came over the radio.

"Are you there Zach?" she asked.

"Affirmative," I responded.

"We'll be there. If anything changes, let me know. I'll be monitoring this frequency."

I acknowledged and signed off.

The rain was starting when we arrived at the creek with the boats and equipment. Fred helped me launch the boats and tether them together. Lil' H and I put life preservers on and got in.

"Okay Lil' H, we got oars and a trolling motor. If you see zombies, hide under those blankets. I'll shoot them if I have to."

"How long will it take Zach?" he asked.

The rain was falling harder now and the lightning strikes were closer. "A few hours I think." I hoped. Fred and Howard waved at us as we floated off.

Mill Creek was rising with water quickly now as the rain steadily intensified. Our boats sped along with the current, occasionally using our oars to push us away from the banks. As we passed through the different neighborhoods, all we saw were rotting corpses. Many of them were now mere skeletal remains with some last remaining vestiges of tissue holding the bones together. We passed by one who was stuck in the mud. He turned his head on a rotting neck as we went by it.

There wasn't a living human in sight.

There were other life forms though. Flies, mosquitoes, mice, and rats, to name a few. Millions of them. Without mankind to control their population, they thrived.

As we went under the Murfreesboro Road Bridge there were a few corpses on the side of the creek bank. Suddenly, Lil' H gasped. Those are moving Zach!" he whispered. I peered closer, and when I realized what I was seeing, almost vomited.

"No H, they're not alive," I whispered. The writhing movements of the thousands of maggots made the bodies seem alive though. I explained it to him. He gagged involuntarily, but to his credit he held it down and didn't complain. It looked they had been living in a hobo camp under the bridge before dying of some unknown cause.

I casually wondered what had led to their demise. Was it zombies? Disease?

There were no other surprises as the creek threaded its way through the Donelson community, and soon we were dumped out into the Cumberland River. Exiting the tributary we now had to travel upstream. This was going to be a test. If the Cheatham dam was compromised, the current was probably going to be too strong for a trolling motor, but I did not feel a loud outboard motor was worth the risk. I threw a small chunk of wood out into the river and the two of us watched it.

"What do you think Zach?" Lil' H asked.

"The current doesn't seem to be any stronger than normal, full speed ahead," I said as I looked back at him. He had practically begged me to let him steer the trolling motor and I relented with a chuckle. The look on his face indicated he was thoroughly enjoying our little adventure.

It was dusk now. We placed our first noisemaker on the bank a hundred yards from the creek. We continued this every hundred yards or so, including a few I had rigged so they would float in the water.

Along with trash, logs, and other unknown types of debris, we saw several corpses in the river. They were unmoving and appeared lifeless. We proceeded unmolested. It wasn't until we reached the east bank where we wanted to land when we encountered them. There were approximately a dozen standing around right where we wanted to land.

"Alright H, it's time to see how good of a sailor you are. Keep us in one place while I shoot those bastards," Lil' H nodded, pointed the boat upstream and manipulated the throttle expertly.

I used my Ruger twenty-two with a homemade silencer attached. I only missed once. The small caliber bullets did not make much of an overt impact, the only indicator was a small hollow hole suddenly appearing in their foreheads and then they would slowly fall over. Truthfully, I was surprised there were any mobile zombies left alive.

Finding no others nearby, I glanced at my watch. It read a little past eighteen hundred hours. We were proceeding on schedule.

"Okay buddy, it's time for the signal," I said. Little Howard grinned in a way only a kid could grin. It made me wonder at what age you lost it and when I had lost mine. He reached down in the boat and retrieved a plastic baggie with a walkie-talkie sealed inside.

****

Fred and Howard waited in the security of the dually pickup truck, parked in the middle of the Nolensville Pike intersection of Old Hickory Blvd. The rain was coming down now in torrents. The sky was inky black and only lit up when there was a lightning strike.

"So, you're really going to do it?" Howard asked. It was not the first time he had asked the question.

"Yep," Fred answered, which was the same answer he gave on the three previous occasions he was asked.

"California and back," Howard said, which was probably the third or fourth time he had pointed out the obvious. "That's one hell of a trip, even when the world was normal. You say Zach has a route all planned out?"

"Yep."

Howard grunted. "Zach's a smart kid, isn't he?"

Fred glanced over at Howard and realized he was the type who talked a lot when he was anxious.

"He's smart, capable, and resourceful. Little Howard is safe with him," he said.

"Yeah," Howard said quietly. "I'm just worried is all." Howard took a deep breath. "If it was one of my kids in Los Angeles, I'd want to go and get him, but damned if I know I'd be up to it. I'd be scared to death, Fred." Fred didn't answer.

The radio came to life. "Come in, Zach," it was a distinctive voice with the southern twang.

"That's the Captain," Howard said. Fred picked up the microphone.

"We're at the staging point. Zach hasn't signaled yet. Where are you?"

"Who is this?" the Captain asked in the tone of a demand. Fred looked at the microphone for a second and then looked at Howard.

"This is Fred. Are you close or not?" Fred asked.

There was a moment's pause. "We'll be there shortly. The rain is slowing us down."

Howard chuckled. A short time elapsed and then there was a large glow moving down the street. As it got closer, they recognized the bus.

"They've put a rack of lights on the top of that contraption since the last time I've seen it," Howard said. "They sure are bright."

The bus was followed by a black pickup truck hauling a tanker. Fred counted four men in the bus, the Captain and a tomboy looking girl driving the truck. The two men got out of the truck. Howard got out as well, walked halfway, and waited for the Captain. Fred lingered back, ready to shoot if things went bad.

"Hello, Captain," Howard said and stuck his hand out. The Captain eyed him as if he was looking at a stain on his shirt. After a moment, his expression quickly changed to jovialness and shook Howard's hand.

"I remember you. You're the mechanic. So, you're in cahoots with Zach, huh?" the Captain said as he eyed Fred. "Who's your friend?"

Howard remained cordial. "That is Fred McCoy. We're all with Zach."

"Well now. Your group seems to keep growing. How many of you are there?" the Captain probed.

"Thousands," Fred responded dryly. The Captain looked at him balefully and then chuckled.

"Alright, you two, have any of the plans changed?" he asked.

"No," Fred answered. "Our only problem that we know of is a choke point at the Thompson Lane intersection. There is a bunch of abandoned cars stacked together, but there is a gap approximately ten feet wide. Zach and I reconnoitered the area yesterday. There is minimal zombie traffic on this side of Thompson Lane. Once you proceed further into downtown, the numbers increase."

"And you think we can drive straight down Nolensville Pike into downtown Nashville, killing zombies as we go, hang a right, cross the bridge over the river, and drive right up to those fuel reservoirs?" the Captain asked.

"That's the plan," Fred said.

The Captain looked over at the man accompanying him. Fred sized him up. He was in his twenties, just under six feet tall, lean and wiry. He had a high and tight haircut and kept his shoulders square. He had the look of a man with military training. Fred noticed they all dressed alike, camouflage cargo pants, black boots, and black tank tops.

The radio crackled to life. "Come in, Daddy."

"That's my son," Howard said. He hurried over to the truck and grabbed the microphone. "What's up, little buddy?"

"Zach and I are here. He says it's clear to come in," Lil' H said excitedly.

Howard chuckled. "He sounds like he's having the time of his life. Okay, gentlemen, they're at the reservoir and it's clear. Are we ready to go?"

"Most certainly," the Captain said. He went back to the bus. Fred looked at his watch and glanced over at Andie standing by her truck. When the bus driver turned on the lights, he got a good look at her. Her right eye was black and swollen shut. Andie saw him looking.

"What're you looking at?" she challenged.

"I can't imagine the Captain allowing anyone to hit his own niece. Unless of course, he was the one doing the hitting," Fred said quietly.

Andie did not respond directly. "Are we ready to go?" she asked. Fred nodded.

*****

One of the buildings had an overhang, which kept most of the pelting rain out. I had an idea and grabbed a can of spray paint. I was now abbreviating somewhat, instead of painting out 'RULE 1' I now simply used Z1. Painting them quickly, I added two more rules to the original ten:

Z11: THEY DON'T REQUIRE LOGISTICS.

Z12: THEY'RE CAPABLE OF RETAINING SOME MEMORIES.

After I finished, we quietly unloaded the tools out of the second boat, attached a grounding rod, and got to work. It was a little nerve wracking. I only had a vague idea of how to bypass the safety controls. The lightning strikes were getting very close, and let's not ignore the fact we were in downtown Nashville where literally thousands of zombies were probably still alive and lurking about.

"Zach, do you have any books I can read?" he asked quietly as he watched me work.

I chuckled. "I have lots of books. First chance I get, I'll get you some good ones to get started on. I'll even work up some lesson plans if you're willing."

Lil' H nodded his head eagerly.

*****

The bus moved quickly and Howard struggled to keep up. Fred spoke into the microphone.

"Captain, we're having a hard time keeping up with these tankers in tow," there was a garbled response, but they finally slowed a little. On the first zombie they saw, the two gunners must have put a dozen rounds each into it. Howard glanced over at Fred and chuckled.

The shooting intensified as they neared the inner city. One of the gunners displayed some common sense and was making disciplined, short bursts to the heads of the unwitting zombies. Fred looked back. Andie was following two car lengths behind with her headlights off.

When they started over the bridge, the vehicles had to slow. There were corpses piled up, a few abandoned cars, and a multitude of infected. Even Fred started shooting now. He marveled at the obliviousness of the zombies as their companions dropped beside them.

*****

I started talking about my favorite books, but I was stopped by the sound of distant automatic weapons fire.

"Here they come," I whispered. I worked quicker now. I wanted to have gas ready to flow as soon as the tankers arrived. Lil' H nudged me and pointed. I saw the bright lights on top of the bus as they slowly made their way across the bridge firing at anything moving. The two trucks were following closely behind.

"You hear it, H? They're shooting the shit out of anything and everything," he nodded silently. The convoy steadily advanced and eventually made their way into the entrance. I aimed a flashlight toward them and blinked it several times. The bus parked at the entrance and the two trucks made their way toward Lil' He and me.

"Any problems?" Howard asked when they got out. He walked over to his son and instinctively put an arm around him. Andie exited her truck and followed.

"So far, it's been smooth as silk." I cupped my flashlight, giving us just enough glow so we could see each other. The first thing I noticed was she wasn't wearing a bra. The rain was causing her tank top to cling to her skin and her nipples were poking out. I quickly looked up and spotted the black eye.

"What happened?" I asked. She glared at me before responding.

"What the fuck is it to you?" she retorted.

I shrugged. "Okay, forgive me for caring."

I changed the subject. "Fred, can I get you and Lil' H to stand guard?" he nodded.

"Howard, drive the truck to that set of pipes down at the end, and Andie, follow Howard. Don't light any cigarettes…" I was interrupted by Andie.

"Let's get this over with unless you want to stand around jerking off all night," she said.

Now it was my turn. Her attitude was pissing me off. "Get something straight right now. We do this my way. You do exactly what I say without your ridiculous remarks, or get the fuck out of here. I'm done trying to be cordial with you. This is a dangerous operation we're about to attempt and I'm betting you have no fucking idea what to do," I declared. She attempted to maintain her one-eyed glare, couldn't do it, and acquiesced.

"Fine," she finally said.

"Good," I went over my instructions again. When I was finished, Howard got to work.

The loading platform of the fuel reservoir was designed to fill tanker trucks equipped with bottom loading apparatus. Designed for safety, there were a few of the processes and safety protocols in which we were going to need to bypass. After a long forty-five minutes, we managed to get fuel coming out of the pipeline, and filled both tankers without blowing ourselves up. I kept eyeing my watch, but we were actually ahead of schedule. It took another hour to fill the tankers. I gave the signal and Howard shut the valve off.

"Alright, Zach, I think I'm going to leave everything exactly how it is, so it won't take so long next time." I nodded in agreement, as Andie watched quietly.

I looked around and saw something I missed. "We're done here, almost," she looked at me questioningly. I retrieved the can of spray paint and added my initial at the bottom of the rules before tossing the can back into the truck.

"Well, now we're finished," she smiled before she could help herself.

"Are we ready to head out?" she asked. She had slung her rifle and was holding her arms around her. The rain had cooled things down somewhat of what would otherwise be a hot August night.

"Yeah. We're going to load up the jon boats and will be right behind you. I've got a windbreaker in the truck. Do you want to borrow it?" She quickly shook her head. "Okay, if you change your mind, let me know. We'll be ready in a minute."

She stared at me for what seemed longer than necessary, and then jogged to her truck.

"Alright, Howard, let's get loaded up and get out of here."

We stacked the two boats on top of each other in the bed of the truck and lashed them down, then I gave a low whistle. Fred and Lil' H jogged up and got in the truck with us.

"Look what I found!" Lil' H exclaimed. He held up a black backpack.

"What's in it?" I asked as Howard drove back over the bridge. We opened it up and looked inside. There was a couple of boxes of bullets, toiletries, some canned food, and a spiral notebook. I thumbed through the notebook. It appeared to be a personal journal. I put it back in the pack. I'd read it later.

"How'd it go with the Captain?" I asked.

"A little tense, but otherwise okay," Howard said.

Howard offhandedly pointed in the distance. "Lots of zombies still out there, Zach. We passed a lot of rotting corpses along the way, maybe thousands of them, but the Captain and his crew still killed quite a few."

I nodded. I was certain they would have all been dead by now. Fred offhandedly pointed at the bus.

"He had two men firing those M60 machine guns. One of them had good fire discipline. He shot in tight, short bursts. Definitely ex-military. The other one was reckless, probably shot three times the amount of ammo. I believe the Captain drove. Oh, and there were a couple of them crouched down in the bus. I just happened to catch a glimpse of them, but they didn't do any shooting. Kind of odd, if you ask me, like they didn't want us to know they were there."

"Are we still planning on standing them up at the rendezvous?" Howard asked.

"Damn right," Fred responded. "The man can't be trusted. I wouldn't put it past him to take our tanker at gunpoint and maybe shoot one or two of us just to show us who the boss is."

Howard nodded vigorously and I had to agree as well. I reached for the microphone.

"Come in, Captain," I said.

"Why Zach, is that you?" he responded.

"Yes sir. The op was successful. Both tankers have been filled. How is it on your end?"

"We're having a good old time here. I believe we've terminated over five hundred of them," he said.

"Roger that, sir," I said as I looked at Fred knowingly.

"Those boys of his must have fired over a thousand rounds each," he said. We were hoping they would expend as much ammunition as possible. The Captain's voice came over the radio again.

"Come in, Andie," he said.

"I'm here," she responded. I peered through the heavy rain and saw the outline of her truck a couple of hundred yards ahead of us. It looked like she had stopped in the middle of the street and was waiting on us to catch up.

"Are you good?" the Captain asked her.

"Yeah, we're more than good," she responded. I wondered if there was any code-speak going on. The original plan involved meeting up with the Captain back at Nolensville and Old Hickory Boulevard. The Captain wanted to run a debriefing and then we'd shake hands or something and go our separate ways. The three of us thought this might be an opportunity for the Captain and his crew to take us out. Or at the very least, steal our fuel. We wanted no part of it and came up with our own plan.

We followed at the tail end of the caravan. When we approached the barricade at Thompson Lane, Howard stopped the truck and I quickly exited.

Howard looked out through the mesh of hardware cloth covering the window. "I sure hope he don't get pissed and do something to you."

"I don't think he will," I said. The truth was I had no idea how he would react. Howard was worried. It was plain to see. He nodded, put on the night vision gear and waited. I jogged over to my Ford Ranger, which was nestled among the abandoned cars. I turned my headlights on and Howard immediately turned his off. He drove off, travelling west on Thompson Lane. They were going to take another route back to the farm while I caught up with them and maintained a fifty yard gap.

We arrived at the intersection a few minutes later. I sat in my truck and waited. The Captain and Andie walked up a moment later. He looked at the truck and scowled.

"Where the hell is the tanker and your friends?" he demanded.

"They left."

"Why? I didn't authorize this," the tone of his voice indicated his temper was rising.

I shrugged. "They had other things to do. Why is it so important, Captain? We pulled off a successful mission. You now have almost five hundred gallons of gas. I had hoped you would be pleased."

"Get out of the damn truck," he snarled and reached for the door handle. It was locked.

"Not a good idea," I said.

He paused. "And why not?"

"Because, when I get out of the truck, it is the signal for my friends to open fire. I took the precaution to have a couple of snipers set up, in case you acted the way you are acting right now." His eyes arched in understanding. He started to reach for his sidearm.

"I strongly recommend you keep your hand away from your sidearm, Captain," I said somberly. He stopped and glared at me.

"Captain, I believe it's time for you and me to have a little heart-to-heart. We are not your minions. I would like for us to continue to work together for a common goal, but your behavior right now is giving me second thoughts," I said.

He leaned forward slightly. "You don't think I can kill you before your friends can get a shot off?" He growled.

I nodded slightly. "You could, but then we'd both be dead. What good is that? I'd rather us part on friendly terms, but you seem to have a lopsided perspective of our relationship. Let me edify you, you do not order us around. We do not kowtow to you. If you want a thousandth man, Captain, you must be one in return. I promised you fuel, and we delivered. We don't owe you anything else."

The Captain glared at me a moment longer. He pointed one of his meaty fingers at me a moment and stomped off. He was met at the bus by two of his men and it appeared they had a quiet, but heated discussion. Andie lingered beside my truck.

"He's pissed. Boy is he pissed," she said under her breath.

"Yeah, I suppose. He'll get over it," Andie stifled a chuckle.

"Are you and I going to be enemies now?" I asked.

She bit her lip, as if coming to a decision. "Do you know where College Grove is?" She asked.

"Yeah. Henry Horton Highway runs right through the middle of it, right?"

She nodded. "At the fork, where Horton Highway splits with Shelbyville Highway, there's a store. We cleared it of zombies a couple of weeks ago. It's abandoned now and I don't think anybody goes around there. Would you meet me there in two days? At sun up maybe? By yourself?"

I looked at her a long moment. "Okay, if I can."

She nodded and started to say something else. The Captain yelled for her. She looked at me a moment longer and then ran back to the bus. I waited for them to drive away and then waited ten minutes more. When I was satisfied, I flashed my headlights. Julie emerged a few seconds later with her AR-15. She ran to me and got into the truck.

"It looked like it was going to go bad for a minute. How'd it go?" She asked. I filled her in as we drove home.

Chapter 4 – The Journal

This is the journal of Harold "Boom-Boom" Walsh. I was, at one time, an aspiring medical student. However, due to unforeseen misfortunes, I had to drop out of college, and found myself installed in the occupation of a deputy sheriff when the worldwide outbreak struck the city of Nashville in inexorable force. I watched in helplessness and fear as the inmates became infected. Oddly, three of us seemed to be immune. Two of us had tower duty, locked away from the rest, when they started turning on each other. Other deputies fled for their lives and abandoned us. We managed to separate ourselves from the infected, and were thus safe, safe being a subjective state of mind.

In summation, Sherry (my other c0-worker) and I found ourselves with over one hundred infected inmates. They were confined in their cells, of course, so we were relatively safe. There were so many of the infected roaming the streets of downtown Nashville, we did not dare go outside. We tried several times, but quickly turned back lest we succumbed to a most unpleasant death. We had taken inventory of the food wares and found we had enough to feed us for several months. The water was still running and we had generators. So, instead of seeking escape, we elected to lock ourselves in the jail. It was safer.

I have started this journal on the second week of our self-imposed quarantine. The infected inmates have not eaten food, nor drank any fluids during this entire time. It is at this time when our experiments started.

Almost all of the inmates are infected. We have one inmate who appears healthy. However, he is an intemperate sort. When I tried to check on him, he responded by throwing feces on me. I use a broom handle to slide his tray of food to him. He thanks me by throwing shit at me.

The noises these things make, combined with the putrid odor, are enough to drive one mad. I hated it, but every time we attempted to go outside, the streets were roaming with those things. There were far too many. We were effectively trapped.

Sherry and I broke open the evidence locker last night and found some marijuana. I think the weed in combination with all of the moaning and shrieking were the seeds for our idea. We had no idea why some people became infected and why others did not. There were many unanswered questions. Sherry thought of it first. I think there is an evil streak in her. She suggested we conduct experiments on the infected. She thought it would be amusing and a fun way to pass the time. I reluctantly agreed, but only because I thought it might help me understand this infection better.

We started with sensory experiments. We would make noises at various ranges and at various distances. We would blink a flashlight on and off. We would use various things to induce motion stimuli. We tried to maintain scientific standards, but to be honest we were lax. In summation, the infected inmates seemed to maintain most of their senses. Their sight, smell, and hearing seemed to remain intact with only a small amount of degradation. I've no idea about their sense of taste.

The sensory experiments segued into other tests. We intentionally withheld food and water from them. It did not matter. Three weeks later and they were still alive. When we would slide a tray of food, or a cup of water through the slot, the infected inmates would ignore it and try to grab at us. The second experiment was also initiated by Sherry. I had found the key to the armory and we had armed ourselves. Sherry had a Glock forty caliber which she decided to experiment with. One of the infected inmates was a large, muscular gangbanger in his twenties. Sherry began the experiment by aiming her weapon through the food slot and shooting him in the shins. He seemed oblivious to the pain and repeatedly tried to attack us by slamming against the cell door. She giggled like a schoolgirl as she worked her way up his torso. The test subject finally collapsed when Sherry shot him between the eyes. We left him lying in the cell. He didn't move for several hours. We finally got up the nerve to open the cell door and check on him. We confirmed his status. He was deceased. Our first experiment yielded the following conclusion: a head shot was the fastest method for killing one of these things.

I found myself nodding, and closed the notebook. I was intrigued, but I was also very tired. Julie had pulled a pillow over her head to block out the soft glow of the candle I had on the nightstand. I blew it out and snuggled up beside her. She let out a brief moan and wiggled her butt up against me. I silently thanked God for bringing the two of us together and drifted off to sleep.

I probably slept four hours before awaking during a dream about the journal. I guess my desire to read it had crept into my nocturnal rest and wouldn't go away. I carefully got out of bed, put a pair of jeans on, and went into the den. It was nearing the end of July and it had been a hot summer. We only ran the air conditioner sparingly, so the house was warm and humid. I opened a couple of windows to let some of the cool morning air inside, lit a couple of candles, settled in Rick's old chair, and opened the journal to the page I had dog-eared last night.

Our next experiment of sorts was an attempt to get two infected inmates to attack each other. Sherry and I donned riot gear, armed ourselves with Taser shields and entered a cell. Upon reflection, it was an ill-conceived idea, but an accidental experiment was performed. The Taser shields had no effect on them! We were successful in getting one of them handcuffed and leg shackled, but it was only through sheer overpowering of the test subject, and not the stunning effect of the Taser shock. Sherry pricked her finger and put a few drops of blood on it (the subject is a male, but it seems malapropos to assign gender to these things now), and then we shoved him into another inmate's smell. The unhindered inmate did in fact attack the subject with Sherry's blood on him, but the attack only lasted a few seconds. He aggressively bit our handcuffed subject, and then seemed to lose interest. Handcuffed subject was not aggressive to the other infected inmate, only toward us.

Next experiment: Attempts to stimulate pain. In summation, we tried many things in an attempt to cause pain to the subject. None appeared to have worked. Or, if they did work, the test subjects showed no physical reaction to the pain stimuli.

I will spare the details and for purposes of brevity, simply list the tests:

1.   Burning - We started with boiling water and escalated to a propane torch.

2.   *Cutting - We started with slight cuts, deeper cuts, disemboweling, and dismemberment.*

3.   *Poisoning - The first phase was forcing drain cleaner down the throat of the test subject, and then we injected the same subject in its arm. You could clearly see the caustic effects of the lye burning through the skin. No reaction to the obvious pain was noted.*

We attempted some other, more intense, pain stimuli. None of them produced a physical reaction. Hypothesis: whatever infection this is, it kills or neutralizes the section of the brain which reacts to pain.

When our imagination of pain stimuli was exhausted, we moved on to other experiments. We attempted to drown a subject and locked one subject in a freezer with a supply of dry ice. Both subjects were rendered inert within comparably the same amount of time a live human would. We thought they were dead, but when they were exposed to air, they returned to consciousness within minutes. The test subject we put into the freezer was also frozen stiff. Within an hour at regular room temperature, the subject had thawed out to the point where it was at least partially ambulatory.

It is at this point, where we decided on another experiment. We used the frozen test subject. While it was still moving slowly, we strapped him down on a table. Once it was completely secured, we cut his skullcap off.

Holy shit, I thought. Boom-Boom and his sidekick Sherry were serious about their experiments. I took a break and went into the kitchen. I found a dark roast blend someone had already ground up. During one of our forays, we had happened upon a Starbucks cafe relatively untouched by looting or vandalism. We procured several bags of their products in various blends. It was a wonderful find. I had a coffee percolator rigged to a battery. I got it going, poured myself a good sized mug, and walked back into the den.

Macie had woken up. She made her way to the den and sat awkwardly on the couch. She was wearing a bathrobe, and with her large baby bulge, she was finding it difficult to keep the robe completely closed down below. I pretended not to notice. She still had lines on her face where she had been sleeping, but her hair was freshly brushed. Although her face was a bit puffier now from the weight gain, I grudgingly admitted to myself she was a very beautiful mom-to-be.

"The baby has been kicking for the last couple of hours. I've given up on sleep. What are you doing?" she asked.

"Just a little reading while it's quiet," I looked down at my mug. "Here, I'll fix myself another," I handed it to her and retrieved a fresh mug.

"Thank you," she said quietly when I walked back into the den. I sat back in the chair and pointedly ignored her.

I had been to an autopsy once, back when I was in school. I remembered watching in fascination as the technician cut the scalp and then peeled it back over the face. She then used a small power saw to cut through the skull. I vividly recalled the distinct popping noise when the skullcap was pried off. I tried to repeat the process I had seen, although my tools were limited to a lock-blade knife and a Dremel saw. Although my technique was quite sloppy, I was successful in removing the skullcap without damaging the brain. The test subject remained alive (?) during this process.

What we observed was startling. The brain itself was the color of obsidian, and it smelled like nothing I have ever experienced before. The spidery veins in the brain tissue were literally... undulating? Pulsating? I quickly backed away and put on my gas mask. Sherry laughed at me scornfully.

"Zach?"

I stopped reading and looked up to see Macie looking at me. She had managed to fold her legs in a ladylike fashion, which was good. The last thing I needed was Julie walking in while I was staring at my ex-girlfriend's crotch. "I know you hate me, but I wanted you to know how appreciative I am of living here with you two," she was speaking quietly.

"I don't hate you," I replied in the same quiet tone. I had good reason to hate her though, with every ounce of my being. I was hopelessly in love with her once. Not too long ago, or maybe a lifetime ago, she had dumped me. To top it off, her new boyfriend and his buddies gave me a harsh beating, my house was vandalized, my Facebook page was filled with cruel comments, and she had some critical remarks of her own to say about me. It was not a good moment in my life. Then, the crazy pandemic set in, society collapsed, and our lives were turned upside down.

Months later, we had a confrontation with some unpleasant individuals and I had been shot. Fred and Julie were rushing me home when they happened upon Macie. She was alone, pregnant, and walking aimlessly down the road with nothing more than a suitcase for company. They took her in. If I had been the one driving, I doubted I would have stopped. She was still looking at me. I sighed.

"You hurt me badly, but I don't hate you." She started to speak, but I held up a hand. "I believe I know what you're thinking. You're thinking we should talk this out, resolve our differences, forgive and move forward, all of that daytime television bullshit. Don't bother, I'm not interested." I started to resume my ignoring of her, but decided to say something else.

"Why haven't you ever asked me how Jason died?" I asked.

She looked at me stoically. "Julie told me what happened. I understand why you did it."

I started to shake my head. Julie had not witnessed it. All she knew about it was what I had told her, and I had glossed over a few of the details. I opted not to go into it. "Julie and you have become friends. I'm happy for that. One day, perhaps you'll catch me looking at you and I'll smile. I can't say it will ever happen though, and I would appreciate it if you didn't try to force the issue."

Macie looked at me a long moment before she spoke. "I understand, Zach."

She pushed herself off of the couch and stood. "I think I'll get breakfast started,." She started to say something else, decided against it, and walked into the kitchen. She returned a moment later and refilled my coffee mug. It was a nice gesture, but I needed some space, so I stepped outside. It was getting light out now. I sat in one of the rocking chairs and continued reading.

We poked and prodded at various parts of the brain. We would be rewarded with the test subject displaying various muscle spasms or tics. The test subject would moan in a queer way, but never spoke or screamed. I must admit, we should not have smoked any weed before conducting this particular experiment, but we did.

We got a little carried away with the poking and prodding. At one point, we accidentally lacerated a section of the brain. A strange black colored goo started oozing out. This seemed to amuse Sherry. She giggled as she made additional lacerations. The test subject died approximately fifteen minutes later.

I hung one of them by the neck. I left it hanging for three days. It would sense us when we were near and its face would contort in - primal anger (?) I hung another one by his feet. Same results, although the subject's face turned a dark color as a result of the strange fluids settling.

Two days after dissecting the test subject's brain, I awakened to the sound of gunfire. Sherry had started shooting all of the infected inmates, and even shot Dante, the uninfected inmate. I watched from the control room. I did not try to intervene. She had a strange look on her face, and to be honest, I was concerned she might try to shoot me as well. When she killed the last one, she looked up at me as I watched her through the thick glass. The expression on her face was - frightening. It was not the Sherry I knew. I sat in the control room the rest of the day contemplating what to do. Occasionally, I looked out at Sherry. She stood in the middle of the day room, unmoving.

It is dusk now. I've decided to make a run for it after sunset. Quite frankly, I'm frightened. There is something about Sherry that is not quite right. I think she may have become infected, or perhaps the strain of the situation has driven her mad. All I know is I've got to get out of this place, and away from her, before I'm killed, or worse. I've loaded up a knapsack with as much food and water as I can, along with some ammunition for my Glock. My plan is to sneak by her, exit the jail, and take my chances on the street. My destination is my mother's house. She lives, or I should say lived (I had no delusions, I knew she was dead) in the Five Points neighborhood. At a slow jog, I can get there in less than thirty minutes.

The journal abruptly ended. I closed the spiral notebook and sat contemplating what I had read. There was some insightful information. Had Sherry become infected? She was certainly acting differently from the other zombies. Perhaps Boom-Boom was right. She had simply gone insane.

I looked up when I heard the door open. "What are you reading?" Julie asked.

She had sat in the chair next to me and was looking at the spiral notebook. "It was in the knapsack we found lying in the road." I said. "It looks like a diary or journal written by a jailer."

"What does it say?" She asked.

I shrugged. "I've only read a couple of paragraphs. Seems like he and another jailer intentionally hid out in the jail when the outbreak was at its peak," I set the notebook down. The experiments intrigued me and I was going to reread the journal when I had the opportunity.

I changed the subject. "How are your equestrian skills coming along?" Fred had recently started teaching Julie how to ride a horse.

She smiled. "I'm having a lot of fun. Prancer can be a bit mischievous though. If I'm not careful she'll try to eat my hair, and yesterday the little stinker snuck up behind me while I was bent over picking something up. She pushed me over and then took off running when I scolded her," she laughed.

"She's a handful. I don't know what got in Fred's head though. One day he up and says I need to learn how to ride."

"He's thinking of the future." It wasn't a lie exactly. "Fuel has a limited shelf life. It'll be a matter of time before we'll be like the Amish, depending on horses for transportation and working the fields," and Fred wants you to take care of Prancer after he leaves, I thought silently.

"What about biofuel?" she asked. "Can't cars run on biofuel?"

"Yeah, diesel engines can. There are several restaurants around with grease pits. I'll need to work on a plan. But Fred's right. We need to round up some horses."

It was a lot to think about. I started the generator, went inside and stuck my head in the kitchen. "Fred will be joining us this morning. I think Bernie may even come by. But Fred is the guest of honor today. Could I ask you to cook him a steak?"

Macie looked at me. "Sure. Do you want one too?"

I shook my head and headed off to the bathroom to clean up. The water would still be cold, but I was used to it. I washed up quickly and dressed. Julie walked in the bathroom as I was drying off.

"Aw, I wanted to take a shower with you," she said. I smiled and kissed her.

"Maybe next time. Go ahead and jump in and I'll tell Macie to get in after you. Today's an important day."

Julie was still groggy, but her eyes came open at my statement. "What's going on, Zach?" she asked.

"I'll explain later. I've got to open up the bridge," I said, kissed her again, and hurried outside before she could question me further.

Fred and Bernie showed up about the time I made it to the bridge. We had located a Volvo truck dealership a few days ago and picked one out. It was a black model VNL630, which I understood to be their middle-of-the-line model. We had done some modifications, including a quasi-cattle catcher Howard had fashioned on the front bumper with some scrap steel. It was designed to push cars and zombies out of the way. We had also loaded it up with anything we could think of. It looked like Fred was ready.

"Good morning, Mister Gunderson," Bernie said in his peculiar high pitched voice as he exited the truck. Fred got out and nodded at me.

"Good morning, Bernie, Fred," I said as I looked at Fred. "All set?"

He nodded again. "Bernie brought his bike along. He said he was going to do some riding around."

We went inside to a prepared table. Due to Bernie's oddities, we had been reluctant for him to be around Julie and Macie. We thought he would be the proverbial dirty old man and would be trying to steal their panties when nobody was looking. However, Bernie was always a gentleman around the girls, and in fact was downright bashful.

Fred led us in prayer before we started eating. The conversation was casual while we ate. I caught Julie looking at me pointedly. She knew something was going on. I waited until we were through eating before I spoke.

"Girls, there is something Fred and I need to tell you." Macie and Julie looked at me expectantly. I was about to speak when Fred cleared his throat.

"Girls, I'm going to be leaving for a spell."

It took a couple of seconds before it sunk in. Julie dropped her fork. Macie's jaw dropped and she covered her mouth with her hand.

"Why are you leaving, Fred? Where are you going?" Macie asked.

"I want you two girls to know I have grown quite fond of the both of you. You've been like surrogate daughters to me. Unfortunately, it is a reminder to me I have a daughter somewhere out there. I'm going to find her, and if I do, I'm going to bring her home."

"But she's somewhere in Los Angeles!" Julie lamented. "You've no idea where to find her!" Julie was practically shouting now.

"You're right, Julie," Fred answered quietly. "Beyond knowing she is in Los Angeles, I've not a clue where to look. All I have is the address of her apartment. Nevertheless, I must try."

Bernie hastened a quick glance around the table, and then dropped his head and focused on his breakfast.

Macie looked over at me. "Zach, how far is Los Angeles from here?"

"Approximately two thousand miles," I replied. The two of them were stunned at the answer. It was as if they never knew this tidbit of information before. However, it was understandable. "I've prepared a travel plan for Fred. Hang on," I retrieved a notebook from the den and brought it back to the kitchen table. Fred knew I had been working on it, but had not seen it. He leaned forward. I had a hand drawn map on the first page with bookmarks and checkpoints along the route. "I named the checkpoints after the phonetic alphabet. If you're able to contact us by radio, we can monitor your progress," or lack thereof, I thought. I looked at the girls. "The reason for the code is for security. We don't want someone listening in and determining where Fred is located."

I gestured at the map again. "This is the main route of travel." I looked over at Fred. "I've put an atlas in your truck and marked it with checkpoints. I expect you will encounter possible choke points along the way. The first major obstacle will possibly be the bridge over the Mississippi. It could be clogged with abandoned cars, trucks, you name it." I looked around the table. "I've played around with the variables, and I believe Fred will be capable of averaging two hundred miles a day. This will mean Fred will make it to LA in ten days, and then ten days to make it back, possibly quicker because you'll now be familiar with the route and obstacles. I've given you a timeline of thirty days to search for your daughter. This is a minimum of fifty days. I've rounded it up to sixty days." I pointed toward where the semi-truck was parked outside.

"We've worked hard on the truck getting it prepared," I said, which was an understatement. The doors were stuffed with surplus Kevlar vests we had found at the police academy. There were dozens of them. They were old, which led us to believe they were used for training purposes. We had no idea if they were even effective anymore, but sometimes one must work with what you have.

We had also salvaged some bulletproof glass from the teller's booths at a local bank. We had to jerry rig brackets to hold them in place over the regular glass, but it would provide some amount of safety for him, although it didn't seem like it was going to be very feasible. We also created shooting ports for Fred in case he encountered hostiles. I outlined these upgrades. "We also installed a Ham radio, so we'll be able to communicate," at least, from time to time. There were bound to be dead spots.

Julie was crying freely now. Suddenly, she jumped up and ran out of the room. The front door slammed a second later. I started to get up, but Fred stopped me. I met his eyes and understood. He needed to talk to her. I sat back down and watched him as he quietly walked out.

Bernie cleared his throat. "Miss Julie needs to add some honey in her coffee, it'll calm her nerves."

"Not now, Bernie!" I said.

"Just saying," he muttered under his breath.

*****

Fred found Julie sitting on top of Rick's hill. It was an old Indian mound, but since Zach had buried Rick there, they had informally named it Rick's hill. Fred worked his way up and sat beside Julie.

"The not knowing has been eating at my soul, Julie. My only blood, the last living McCoy, is out there somewhere. I can't sleep, and when I do, I have nightmares. My little girl is in danger and I'm not there for her," Fred sighed heavily. "I'm probably already too late, but I have to try."

"But, we need you," Julie said weakly.

Fred put his arm around her shoulders. "And I need you all. I have confidence you all will be okay. The young man you are in love with is quite capable, in case you didn't already know it. I'll only be gone a couple of months. Y'all will be fine."

Julie sobbed for a couple of minutes. "I know I'm being selfish." Fred squeezed her tightly. "Will you be okay?" she finally asked.

"I'll be fine, baby girl," he said. In truth, Fred was scared. Fred squeezed her again. "I need you to be strong for me."

After a minute, she looked up at Fred. "Okay," she finally said.

*****

I stood in the yard and watched the two of them start walking back from Rick's hill. I hoped he had calmed her fears. I did not want him to leave either. We had grown very dependent on him. He was quiet natured, stoic, a calming force during turbulent times. When he told me what he had in mind, I told him he was condemning himself to a certain death. He asked me what I would do if I were in his situation. I couldn't answer. Instead, I got a fresh notepad and we started planning. Now, here we were. I heard the door open. Macie and Bernie walked outside.

"Is everything okay?" Macie asked.

"It will be. We're going to have to adjust without him being here," I said.

"Do you think he'll be able to find her?" she asked.

"It seems like an impossible feat, but if anyone can do it, Fred can," I said. Bert grunted in agreement.

"A most impressive man Fred McCoy is. Most impressive," he said. He glanced at Macie and then averted his gaze. "I stored a large jug of honey in his truck. It'll help. Honey prevents dropsy you know." Macie stifled a chuckle. I looked at her and almost smiled, but stopped myself.

We waited for them as they made their way back to the front yard. Fred looked at all of us and gave a reassuring smile.

"I guess it's time for me to start off on this journey," he said. Bernie grunted in agreement, Julie and Macie nodded with tears streaming down their pretty faces. I was feeling a little emotional as well. I held back the tears and shook his hand instead. Bernie did as well. Fred hugged the girls and walked over to his truck. He opened the door and looked back.

"I would be most appreciative if all of you would look after Prancer. She's never been alone before and she might get a little apprehensive."

"I promise I'll take care of her," Julie responded. Fred looked at us and nodded. I thought I detected a bit of sadness in his eyes. Bernie untied his bicycle off of the back of the truck and moved out of the way.

Without further ado, Fred got into his semi, started it up, and drove away. The exhaust noise of the large diesel engine concerned me. It was loud and was bound to draw unwanted attention, but there was nothing we could do about it.

We all stood together, waving at Fred as he drove out of sight. The ensuing silence was heavy, awkward. I think we collectively missed Fred before he was even out of sight.

"I believe I'll ride around and see a bit of the countryside on this end of the county," Bernie said quietly. "That's how I met Fred, you know. He's a fine man," he hopped on his bike and pedaled away.

Chapter 5 – Fred's Journey Begins

With no small amount of trepidation, Fred got into his brand new and highly modified Volvo truck, waved to his friends, and headed out. He caught one last glimpse of them in the driver's side rearview mirror before they disappeared from sight, and wondered if it would be the last time he ever saw them.

Surprisingly, Fred encountered very few obstacles, other than numerous potholes, as he made his way to Harding Place. When he got to Bellevue, a once thriving section of west Nashville comprising a rich mixture of commercial enterprise and residential neighborhoods, there was a substantial increase in the number of corpses. They were everywhere, hundreds of them. No, there were thousands of them. They were strewn in the roadways, in the front yards of houses, sitting immobile in abandoned cars. They were in the advanced stages of decomposition now. Even so, the stench was still nauseating. Zach would be hard pressed to fulfill rule number eight (burn the corpses), Fred thought with a wry smile. The big tires of the Volvo squashed a rat as he continued west on Highway 70 and made his way toward the city of Dixon.

It was at the intersection of Sawyer Brown Road when he spotted a group of zombies. There were approximately twenty of them standing in the road. They had massed together, as they seemed to do, and were already working their way toward him. Fred decided this would be a good test for the cattle catcher Howard had mounted on the front of the truck. He slowed to five miles-per-hour and barreled through them. It worked as intended, all of them were pushed to either side of the truck. None was caught under the tires or undercarriage.

Several miles seemed to have gone by quickly. It wasn't until he got to the city of Waverly when he encountered another human.

"Mister truck driver, do you have your ears on?"

It was a voice on the CB radio. It was a deep baritone, as if it was emanating from the diaphragm of a very large man. The strong southern twang left no doubt this man was a country boy. Fred looked at the radio in surprise for a moment, and then hurriedly grabbed the microphone.

"I am, and hello," Fred replied.

"What's your handle?"

"The name's Fred. Fred McCoy."

"They call me Big Country, Mister McCoy, and I am pleased to talk to you. But I have to ask, what are you doing in our neck of the woods?" Big Country asked.

"I'm passing through, sir, on my way to find my daughter." Fred explained about his dilemma with his missing daughter and using side roads in order to avoid the massive traffic jams on the Interstates.

"Yes sir, Interstate 40 is clear here and there for a few miles, and then you have major roadblocks. Mister McCoy, would you like to park a spell and socialize with us? We don't have a lot, but we can feed you."

"I am much obliged, sir, but I believe I'll wait and catch you on the flip side."

"I understand, Mister McCoy. Have you encountered any other survivors?"

"I have," Fred told Big Country about Zach. "If you're ever in the south Nashville or Franklin area, give him a shout on the CB. If he's around, he'll answer. Tell him you know me and he'll take care of you." Fred also gave him the HAM radio frequency they monitored.

"I appreciate that, Mister McCoy. You're going to be good until you get to Huntington. When you get there, you're going to encounter a roadblock. You tell those fine folks you and I are friends and you'll be just fine."

Chapter 6 – An Appointment with Andie

After dinner, the three of us spent the rest of the evening preparing and canning vegetables. The summer had been relatively mild with lots of rainfall. The result was a bountiful crop.

"What time do you meet the dyke?" Julie asked. Macie giggled.

I frowned at the both of them. "Sunrise."

"Are you going to take her a present?" Macie asked teasingly. Julie laughed this time. They ganged up on me frequently these days.

"Yeah, go ahead and yuck it up," I said. We finished canning at around nine and went to bed.

I was snuggled up against Julie. I was comfortable, tired, and about to doze off, but she decided this would be a good time to talk.

She turned around and started kissing me. "Zach," she said.

"Yes, sweetheart?" I mumbled.

"Let's talk about Macie." I opened my eyes now and looked at her.

"You want to talk about Macie right now?" I asked.

"She thinks you're going to kick her out after she gives birth," she said. "Are you?"

In fact, I remember suggesting it not too long ago. "Wasn't that the plan?"

She started rubbing my chest. She knew how much I liked it when she did that. "She has nowhere to go," she said.

I smiled in the dark. "You want her to stay here?" I phrased it as a question, but I already knew the answer.

"Don't you? She's been really helpful and I've seen how you act around her. You're nice to her. You're a little aloof toward her sometimes, but you're nice to her. You don't mind her being here and you know it," she stroked my chest some more. "She's going to need help raising her kid too. Don't you want to be a surrogate daddy?"

I snorted. "With Jason's kid? I'd rather not."

Now she sat up, causing the blanket to fall, exposing her breasts. I always stared at them. They seemed to have a hypnotic spell on me.

"It's not the kid's fault, Zach. Besides, what if it's your baby?"

My eyes widened, and my jaw probably dropped. I lost all interest in her breasts, which I thought would never happen.

Julie put her hands on my shoulders. "Do the math, Zach. You two hooked up in late November, right? Perhaps, about nine months ago?"

I was shocked to the point where my brain was going into vapor lock. I had to count on my fingers, and then counted twice more. "What does Macie say? Does she know?"

"She doesn't know, and she's scared to death of how you may react," Julie said.

Julie lay back beside me and put her head on my shoulder, which caused her breasts to be pressed up against me. Okay, I liked her breasts against me even better than my chest being rubbed.

"Do you want her to stay?" I asked. I felt her head nod. "Okay."

Julie sat up again. "You mean it?" I nodded again. Julie responded with another kiss. "You won't regret it, Zach. Fate has thrown all of us together you know. We're a family now."

She snuggled closer now, kissed me harder, and put a leg over my waist. As tired as I was, I could not resist her wiles. When I finally did go to sleep, I was out like a light.

College Grove was a sleepy little community in between Eagleville and Nolensville. It grew up in a fork in the road, and eventually became the intersection of two state highways. I sat in the parking lot of the old country store watching the sun come up. There were approximately a dozen corpses on both sides of the road. I drove close to a few of them and saw distinctive bullet holes in the head. None of them had been burned though. The putrid stench had all but abated.

I got out, stretched, and waited. Someone had spray painted "W-E." on the front of the store. I peeked inside, and as expected, the store had been completely looted. Andie drove up as I poured a cup of steaming coffee out of my thermos. She parked a few feet away, looked around everywhere, and then stared at me.

She was driving a Jeep Wrangler with a few modifications. There was a rack of large lights mounted on top, a winch mounted on the front, and everything had been spray painted flat black. There were the same letters stenciled on the doors. I saw a couple of radio antennas as well. I waved. She got out and tentatively walked toward me.

"Would you like some coffee?" I asked as she walked up. She was wearing the same clothing she had on a couple of days ago, camouflage pants, boots, black tank top, and no bra. Her breasts were small, but the taut fabric left little to the imagination. At least her face was freshly scrubbed, and without those stupid looking black streaks under her eyes. Her hair was a little longer now. I kept from staring at her pert breasts as I held up my thermos.

"Sure," I refilled my cup and poured a second. She nodded in thanks and was quiet as she blew into her cup and took small sips.

I motioned toward the graffiti. "W-E. What does that stand for, do you know?"

"Ward's Empire. It's the name of our group. The Captain ordered us to start marking our territory," she said. "It's his last name. Ward. Charles Ward. I used to call him Uncle Charlie, but nobody dares call him by his name anymore."

I grunted. Any opinion I had of them claiming territory I kept to myself. I changed the subject and pointed toward the back of my truck. "We got lucky with our gardens this summer. I brought a basket of assorted vegetables and a few watermelons. I hope you brought some stuff as well."

She smirked at me. "Yeah, I figured you'd want something in trade. I brought some reloading equipment and some weed. Do you get high?"

I shook my head. "I don't get high, but I can always use reloading equipment. Fred believes marijuana would possibly be a good trading commodity. How's that working out for your group?"

Andie set her cup down on the hood of my truck, fished a joint out of her cargo pocket and lit it up. She inhaled deeply and offered it to me. I shook my head again. It got a laugh out of her.

"You're such a square," she said and took another long toke.

I shrugged my shoulders. "Yeah, I guess so. C'mon, I'll show you the vegetables."

We walked to the back of the truck and I pulled the tarp off. She picked up a plump tomato and sniffed it. She then aimed for the front door of the store, threw it, and giggled in glee when the tomato splattered all over the door's new markings. I laughed at her antics and walked over to her jeep. She had two large plastic bags full of cartridge casings and primers.

"It's all in twenty-two caliber. I saw the way you were shooting that pistol the other night, so I took this out of the armory. You like?"

"Oh yeah, I like," I said. "Will the Captain miss this stuff?"

"Yeah, probably." She inhaled and held it in as long as she could before exhaling.

"Wait, does he not know you're here meeting with me?" I asked. She shook her head.

"It'll be our little secret," she grinned and took another toke before continuing. "We've not traded anything with anyone. When we've encountered survivors, they're scared shitless of us. They give us what we want or they run and hide. The Captain said you're the only one who has stood his ground. I think he actually admires you."

She smoked some more and smirked. "He was pissed the other night when you guys didn't meet up with him. He thought it was disrespectful."

"Was he going to rip us off?" I asked.

Andie shrugged and chuckled. "Probably."

"Is he the one who gave you the black eye?"

She looked at me sharply. "You're full of questions, aren't you? I bet you want me to tell you everything about us," she looked at me for a moment. I said nothing as she took another toke.

"Yeah. He's the one who hit me." She finished up her joint and tossed the roach on the ground. She walked closer to me, until her body was pressed against mine and then she put her hands on my waist.

"So, you wanna fuck?" she was looking at me coyly now, with a hint of a smile.

I was taken aback, but I recovered quickly. "I don't think my girlfriend would understand. Besides, I'm betting a good looking girl like you already has a boyfriend. Which one is he, one of the dudes on the bus maybe?"

The smile left her face and she turned away. "I don't have a boyfriend." She was quiet now.

Damn, I thought. I sure do have a way of saying the wrong things sometimes. I tried to repair the damage. I fought for the right words.

"If I've hit a sore spot, I apologize."

She leaned up against the truck and didn't say anything for a few minutes. I figured it was about time to leave when she spoke again.

"There are fifteen of us. When the outbreak hit, there were more, but some of the group became infected. The Captain killed them, which left us with twelve men and three women. There were six women at one time, but one escaped and two killed themselves. The men take turns with the women. Except me. The Captain saves me for himself."

I started. "Wait, I thought he was your uncle?" she nodded while looking at something on the ground. "By blood or marriage?"

"He's my mother's brother," she replied. "It's okay, really. If not him, it'd have to be with someone else. Hell, he might have even made me one of the camp whores."

I didn't know what to say. The Captain was somewhere in his forties. Andie was maybe fifteen or sixteen. So, he didn't mind having incestuous relations, and he didn't mind using women as sex slaves. His vision of a new world order was sounding less and less pristine.

I didn't reply. Instead, I leaned up against the truck beside her and decided to change the subject. "Why does everyone call him the Captain? Was he a soldier or something?" I asked.

Andie scoffed. "He was a captain at the Rutherford County Workhouse. He's never been a soldier. There's one dude in our group who was a Marine."

Andie saw me frowning and laughed. "Don't underestimate the Captain though. He's ruthless."

"Oh, I've no doubt," I gestured with a hand. "Why'd he hit you?"

Andie fished another joint out of her cargo pocket. "Because that's what he does," she said, as she lit it. She took a couple of puffs and then inhaled before continuing. "Maybe I looked at him wrong. I've stopped asking. Sometimes asking will get you another backhand, or worse." I could see her eyes watering up. She turned away and dabbed at them quickly.

I was going to ask her more, like if she thought her uncle was a nut job, but I held off. After all, she may still believe in him and was merely being a rebellious teenager when she wanted to meet with me. After a moment, she seemed to have regained her composure.

"So, tell me about your group. Are you the leader?" she asked.

"We're a very small group and we have no hierarchy of leadership. We work together in order to survive, and we have no interest in conquest." I motioned toward the back of my truck. "We're attempting to set up trade networks with the survivors. Which reminds me; you said you guys have encountered other people. Can you tell me about them?"

She shrugged as she smoked her joint. "Yeah, we've only seen a few people. You, the black family at the tire shop, and there's a man with a couple of kids living in a house on Rocky Fork Road. He said his wife is dead, but the Captain thinks she was hid out somewhere. We've been through some businesses in Eagleville. When we've gone back, it's obvious someone else has been there, but we don't know who. They've been doing a pretty good job of hiding from us. George, he's one of the Marines, is going to set up a patrol to catch them."

"What then?" I asked.

Andie shrugged her shoulders. "I imagine the Captain will make them an offer to either join us or pay taxes. If they refuse…" she shrugged her shoulders again and then looked at me. "They've been trying to find out where you live too." I nodded in understanding. Fred and I had already figured as much.

We talked some more about inconsequential issues, mostly about where we went to school and if we had any friends in common. We didn't. Andie noticed me looking at my watch.

"Do you have a date waiting?" she asked.

I looked up. "What? Oh, no. I just have a lot of work to do back at the farm."

Andie looked at me. I couldn't read her face. "Can we meet again in a few days?" she asked.

"Sure. How about a week from today? If either of us can't make it, we can call on the radio."

She shook her head now. "I don't want anyone knowing I'm meeting you."

We ultimately agreed to coming here once a week at sunrise. If the other one doesn't show up within an hour, we'd try again next week. I helped her load up the basket of vegetables and turned to say goodbye to her. She grabbed me and kissed me.

"My real name is Andrea," she said before she got into her jeep and drove away.

Chapter 7 – A Near Ambush

Andie's kiss lingered in my thoughts as I drove, and I paid little attention to the intermittent abandoned automobiles left haphazardly in the roadway. I should have been focusing more on my situational awareness. I also made the mistake of going back the same way I came to College Grove. These transgressions led to what can be described in scientific terms as a royal screw up.

The only roads I've seen with cars piled up were on the Interstate and some areas of the inner cities, like Nashville and Franklin. On this particular stretch of highway, there were cars here and there. Most were parked on the side of the road. Others were left wherever they ran out of gas. I had no trouble maneuvering around them. However, as I neared one particular group of automobiles, I realized there was something different now from a couple of hours ago. My mouth went dry when I realized what I was seeing. Some of the cars had been moved!

Someone had pushed four or five cars together and used them to create a chokepoint. An ambush, I was sure of it. There was no way around it, both sides of the roadway had fencing and there were cars wedged against them. The only way was right down the middle.

I made a snap decision and floored the accelerator. About the time I entered the narrow gap between the cars, a dirty woman wearing a tattered dress of an indiscernible pattern stepped out in the roadway. It was hard to tell her age, but she definitely was not a zombie. I've no doubt whoever set this up assumed I would slam on my brakes and stop before hitting someone so pitiful looking, especially a helpless looking woman. Once I stopped, the ambush would be sprung. The only problem was, I remembered at least two movies with this exact same scene. I never let off of the gas.

Her facial expressions told the story. First, a tale of downtrodden woe, designed to induce pity. It quickly changed to realization, and then, terror as I bore down on her. She was catapulted up in the air and knocked forward approximately twenty feet before landing on the asphalt. I ran over her body as I sped off and leaned down in my seat. A few shots rang out, and I heard a couple of distinct thuds from the impact of the bullets. Another thump and my rear window shattered.

There was no doubt the woman was dead or dying. I was disgusted and angry with myself. When I was about five hundred yards away I slammed on my brakes and skidded sideways to a stop. It was time for long-range work. I grabbed my trusty Winchester and exited the truck.

Macie's late boyfriend, Jason, had damaged the scope on it in an attempt to kill me. I killed him instead. Nevertheless, even though one of the reticles was cracked, I could still use it fairly effectively. I sighted in. There were three of them. One of them was crouched down beside the motionless body. The other two were merely standing there looking at me, guns in hand. No long range rifles though, only handguns.

I shot the one on the left. He was the ugliest of the three. He took the round squarely in the chest and went down as if someone had gut punched him. The other two immediately began running and hid behind the cars. I waited, and could have waited all day, except for one thing.

The putrid stench hit my nostrils before I saw or heard it. I turned around right as it lunged at me. He still had a little bit of his face left, but all I could really discern was it was a short, very fat male. His tee shirt might have been white once. Now it was heavily soiled and stretched to its maximum allowance due to his extremely swollen belly. I sidestepped quickly, and came within a breath of being bitten.

His hands were nothing more than bony nubs. The tissue was all but gone. I raised the rifle and butt-stroked it in the face. The zombie's lower jaw dislodged and he fell with a heavy thud. I guess you'd say I was extremely angry now. I stomped on his head until it cracked open. Black goo started oozing out and got on my boots.

I looked around for any other zombies. Finding none, I put my scope back on my living adversaries. They were making quick peeks from behind one of the cars. I was breathing so heavily I could not aim. I kept looking and saw their car had an antenna.

I thought, why not. I turned my CB radio to channel nineteen and grabbed the microphone. "Are you idiots listening?" I looked back at them through the riflescope. I watched as one of them crawled to the door and opened it. A guttural voice filled the radio's speaker.

"You're a dead man, you cocksucker!" he snarled. I responded by putting a round through their radiator. He screamed more obscenities into his microphone. I put bullets in the other car facing me and shot out the tires of the other two. Either he or his friend figured out the more he cursed me, the more I was going to shoot. He shut up and I reloaded before speaking again.

"I got a good look at your faces. The next time I see you two, I'm not going to be so nice," I said.

"You ran over my woman, you son of a bitch!" One of them snarled.

"That was your fault. You put her in that situation, so you suffer the consequences," I replied tersely. I got my breathing under control and made a decision. As much as I wanted to play with these two mutts, I had a multitude of farm chores to do. Besides, the sounds were going to draw more zombies.

I fired one more round through the windshield of the car with the antenna and drove off. I made a point of running over the zombie as I left. His belly made the sound of a large water balloon bursting.

I was mad, frustrated, and not a little disgusted with myself. I rationalized my actions. If I had stopped, I would have been relieved of all of my possessions and perhaps killed as well. Still, I had just killed a woman. It didn't seem right. I didn't care about the man, he deserved it.

I put distance between us and was out of sight within seconds. Once I was sure I was not being followed, I switched to a sideband channel. "Come in, Saigon," I said. It was my code for Julie or Macie, indicating it was okay to respond.

"I'm here," Macie responded.

"Heading back," I said curtly, but then I realized I wasn't quite ready to go back. I needed time alone in order to decompress. "Check that. I'll be back in about two hours."

"Okay, I mean ten-four," she said.

I drove aimlessly, trying to clear my head. I stuck to the back roads with no destination in mind. My brain almost did not register it. I drove by a house and happened to observe a swing set in the backyard. I backed up and pulled into the drive. I stared looking at the swing set. Whoever had once lived here had kids. We had nothing for a kid, other than a few cases of disposable diapers.

I did my standard approach and entry. I started with driving right up to the front door of the house. After getting no reaction, I got out and knocked on the door. I left the rifle in the truck but had my hand firmly attached to my holstered handgun. After a minute of silence, I tried the doorknob. It was unlocked.

I cleared the house without any surprises. There were two badly decomposed corpses in the master bedroom. It appeared as though they had killed themselves in the bed. The man still had a revolver gripped in his hand. I wrenched it free and then went back to the children's bedroom. Their kids were gone. I had no idea where they were. I found a picture of the family. They were a good looking yuppie couple. Their kids looked to be around two and three. I was hoping the family had not gotten rid of any baby stuff. A search found all of it stored neatly in a spare bedroom. I bet they were planning on having more kids one day.

I loaded the truck with every baby item I could find. Other than a crib, I had no idea what was needed, so decided to let the girls sort through it all. I could always toss out the rest later. When the truck was filled, I walked around the house to see if there was anything else I could use. When I walked out the back door, I saw it then, two small graves in the backyard with simple wooden crosses.

I marked the front door with the FEMA symbol. I briefly debated on burying the parents next to their children. Instead, I got in my truck and headed home.

Chapter 8 – Fred

Fred hit Jackson, Tennessee as the sun was going down. Travelling a few miles, he found a place to park in Cyprus Grove Nature Park. The entrance ended in a cul-de-sac parking lot. There was only one car parked there, and judging by the level of the dust and grime on the exterior, it looked like it had been there a while.

He got out, stretched, and answered the call of nature behind a tree. He walked around the area and spotted an octagon shaped gazebo a few yards from the parking lot, and it appeared there was an unoccupied makeshift hobo camp set up under it. Fred wondered what happened to the person or persons who set it up. He gathered a bunch of dead tree limbs, broke them up, and started a fire in the in the freestanding grill located by the gazebo. There was a coffee pot sitting in the camp. Fred rinsed it out and used it to prepare some coffee.

The coffee was brackish and unsatisfying, but it would have to do. He spotted a rabbit scrounging for something to eat. Fred looked around, and decided it was worth the risk. He drew his revolver, fired, and reloaded before tucking it back in his holster.

He gutted and skinned the scrawny rabbit quickly and put the meat on the grill. Fred knew without any seasoning or proper preparation, the meat was going to be very gamey tasting. He thought back to the delicious meals his wife used to make and his stomach grumbled.

The rabbit meat was about what he expected, but it would fill his stomach nonetheless. His thoughts were interrupted by a car approaching. They must have heard the gunshot, he thought. Fred knew he was taking a risk when he fired, but he was hungry and needed food wherever he could get it. He stood slowly, and waited.

The car was a silver Cadillac, which maybe was brand new when the shit hit the fan, but it had since been run through the mill and back. There were three people in it, a salt and pepper team of young men, and a woman sitting in the back seat. She was either white or mixed race, and they were all grungy looking. The front passenger exited first. He had three teardrop tattoos under his right eye and a spider web tattooed on the side of his neck. Fred thought tattoos, especially on someone's face, were disgusting.

"Hola, amigo!" he said in mock joyfulness. Fred stood there and stared at him with the coffee cup in his left hand. The young man had his own handgun, which appeared to be a Smith and Wesson Sigma, stuck in his waistband. He walked toward the gazebo with a taunting smile. Fred knew there was going to be no joyful outcome in this encounter, but still, he was willing to give them a chance.

"I said hola amigo, don't you fucking understand Spanish?" he asked with an arrogant note in his voice. The driver exited now, along with the woman in the backseat. They were armed as well. They eyed Fred and the truck before walking over. The three of them spread out into what they believed were tactical positions.

"Hello," Fred said. "I've got coffee. If you all have a tough constitution, you might actually find it tasty. I've no extra cups though."

The driver looked back at the truck. "That truck is the tits. You got some bulletproof glass mounted up there, homey? That's sweet," the driver said. The woman laughed. "Is it yours?" he asked.

"Yes, it is," Fred replied. He knew what was coming. They were going to play a little game in which they thought they were going to be very clever with asinine word games they gleaned from watching B-rated gangster movies.

Fred continued, "Unless, someone is lucky enough to kill me for it. Which one of you is going to try first?"

"You have a problem with us, amigo?" the first one asked with a scowl on his ugly face. Fred did not bother responding. The two men looked at each other, and the driver winked at his buddy. They focused their attention back on Fred and squared off. The woman moved out of the way, grinning in glee at what she thought was going to happen to the poor dumb fuck wearing boots and a stupid looking cowboy hat.

"I asked you a question, amigo. I said do you have a problem with us?"

"You might say that. I can smell y'all from here. Although I wouldn't know firsthand, I'm guessing a dog's ass smells better than you three. I have a question for you, amigo," Fred said.

"Yeah, what's that?" the passenger asked with a sneer.

"How much time do you idiots need to get your courage up and try to shoot me? My coffee is getting cold."

The passenger, the white guy snarled and reached for his Sigma. Fred drew, shot, and holstered his weapon in the blink of an eye. He looked at the second man and noticed for the first time, this one had fake gold upper teeth. Fred gestured with his coffee cup.

"Are those gold teeth?" he asked. The black amigo stared at him incredulously. "They look stupid," Fred commented, and sipped some more coffee. Black amigo yelled and grabbed for his gun, also tucked in his waistband. Unfortunately, for him, in his haste to pull his gun, he stuck his finger in the trigger guard and accidentally shot the head of his penis off. He fell to the ground screaming in agony. Fred had drawn his revolver during all of this, but did not bother firing.

Instead, Fred took another sip of coffee.

The girl gasped in confusion. She ran over to her black amigo and saw blood soaking through the crotch of his pants.

"You shot them, you son of a bitch!" she shouted, and grabbed the gun out of her friend's waistband. Fred shot her a quarter of an inch above the spot where he was instinctively aiming. He frowned at his inaccuracy and looked at his revolver before holstering it.

Fred finished his coffee before grabbing the pot with his handkerchief and pouring the dregs over the fire. Gathering up the extra guns and searching their car, he found little of value. Other than an extra magazine for one of the handguns, there was nothing but stale candy, a burnt spoon, and a used hypodermic needle. Fred managed to eat about half of the rabbit, left the rest, and walked back to black amigo.

"Your friends are dead, and it looks like you have a bad gunshot wound. If there are any zombies around, they will have heard the noise. When they get close, they'll smell the blood. They'll be here soon," Fred said.

"Are you going to help me?" the young man asked. Fred looked him over without emotion.

"Would you help me?" Fred asked, walked back to his truck, and drove off.

Fred didn't want to drive at night. He finally found a parking lot a few miles away and stopped in a parking lot. The area was quiet. He didn't even see any zombies roaming around. Satisfied, he stretched out in the sleeper, but sleep didn't come easily. He kept thinking about the three miscreants he encountered and wondered if it was going to be the same in every city he drove through.

Chapter 9 – Julie's Surprise

The girls and Curly met me in the driveway. Julie and Macie marveled at all of the stuff, but then gasped when they saw the bullet holes in the tailgate. Curly was so concerned, he pissed on one of the tires.

"I had a little encounter," I said. "I'm not sure where to start."

I left them standing in the driveway, took my boots off, and went inside. I was feeling anxious, nervous. I washed up, poured a large glass of water and gulped it down. I had a delayed reaction to the morning's events I think. The two of them walked in a moment later and sat at the table with me.

Julie frowned. "Are you okay?" she asked.

I looked at the two of them. "I don't know." I recounted the story as I drummed my fingers on the kitchen table. Well, I told them most of it. I kind of omitted Andie's parting kiss.

"Holy shit!" Julie said. "Do you think you were set up? Were they part of the Captain's group?"

"I don't know. Andie seemed sincere, but I don't know."

Macie got up and refilled my glass. "Thanks." I said quietly, took another gulp, and looked over at them. "Has Fred checked in? He should have passed at least two checkpoints by now."

"Oh." Macie said. "I almost forgot. I got him on the shortwave shortly after you left this morning. He said he had reached checkpoint bravo, but he had to make some detours due to all of the abandoned vehicles clogging the roadways. I haven't heard from him since. I'll try him on the radio now if you want."

I shook my head. "Checkpoint bravo is in Memphis. He's going a lot slower than I had estimated. If we haven't heard from him by dinner time, we'll try to raise him," I finished my water and accidentally burped. "Sorry," I mumbled. They smiled, but didn't pick on me this time.

We unloaded the truck and put everything in the den. It was becoming quite crowded. "We're running out of room," I said. I thought about last night. During our lovemaking, Julie was quite loud. I had no doubt Macie could hear it. We needed more room.

"After the baby is born, maybe we should relocate to the Riggins house," I said. Julie smiled warmly at the suggestion.

"That's a great idea! We can remodel one of the bedrooms for the baby," Julie added.

"It's going to take quite a lot of work, but I think it's doable," I replied with a nod. The girls organized our new items with great delight. I put on a pair of sneakers and went back outside to survey the damage to my Ford Ranger truck. My back window was completely gone. Nothing but remnants of tempered glass remained. The front window was cracked, and the front end had extensive damage where I had struck the woman. There was also dried blood and tissue in the broken grill. It made me sick all over again. I walked back inside and wondered if there was a bottle of whiskey in the house. Macie and Julie were having a good time inspecting all of the baby clothes and accessories. I sat on the couch and watched them enjoying themselves.

"Are you going to see Andie again?" Macie asked.

"Oh, hell no," I replied. I still did not tell them of Andie propositioning me or kissing me. I intended to, sort of, but I couldn't seem to get it out of my mouth.

"You think she set it up?" Julie asked.

I shrugged. "I'm not sure."

"You should ask her," Julie said. "Meet with her again, get there early and set up, like you've done before. If you see other people in the area, you'll know if she's involved. I'll come too, if you want," I shook my head, a little too quickly.

Julie frowned. "Why not?"

"Remember, she told me about the other women in their group being used as sex slaves. Don't think they won't try to kidnap you two if they get a chance."

Macie and Julie looked at each other. "Zach, there's something I need to tell you," Julie said. I looked at her and waited. "I'm late."

I stared at her questioningly. She scoffed when she realized I didn't understand. "I think I'm pregnant, Zach." She waited expectantly for a reaction from me.

"Oh boy," I responded.

Her mouth dropped open. "Oh boy? That's the only thing you have to say?"

I tried to say something else, but it only came out as an unintelligible stammer. Julie went pale, ran into our bedroom and slammed the door. I looked over at Macie. She shook her head in mock disgust, pointed at me, and then pointed toward the bedroom. I took the hint.

I knocked quietly before entering. Julie was on the bed rubbing Curly's belly, and he was grunting contentedly. I sat down beside them and was rewarded with two different responses. Curly wagged his tail. Julie pointedly ignored me.

"Please don't doubt my love for you. You just took me by surprise," I said.

"You don't want me to be pregnant," she said accusingly.

"No, it's not that. I'm worried, that's all."

Julie scoffed and glared at me. "Worried? Is that all you have to say? I guess I'm wondering why you're not saying, why Julie, we're having a baby, that's so wonderful!"

I suddenly had a couple of itches here and there, I could not resist the urge to scratch.

"Julie, of course I'm happy. You caught me off guard. I'm still a little torn up by running over that woman, you know?" I held my hands out pleadingly. "I don't know what else to say."

"Zach, why would it bother you? You're a cold-blooded killer. You're not torn up by another notch on your holster, or your gun, or wherever the fuck you put your notches."

She got up and went back into the den. I watched her backside go through the door and hurriedly followed.

"What in the world made you say such a cruel thing?" I demanded angrily.

She pointed outside. "Remember when we were sitting right outside eating watermelon? We were laughing and having a good old time, and you and Fred just stood there watching. Now Fred is Fred, but you used to be right there laughing with us. You don't laugh anymore, Zach!" Julie was yelling and crying at the same time now. "You're not happy here," her voice drifted off. I tried to touch her but she shrugged me off and walked into the kitchen.

I tried desperately to think up a response. To say something, anything, to make it better. I couldn't. I was too angry. I walked outside. Looking at my watch, I made a decision. I still had plenty of daylight left. I grabbed some gear out of the barn and loaded it up in the back of my little truck. Macie came outside.

"What are you doing, Zach?" she asked.

"I'm going for a ride. Maybe find a replacement for my truck." I drove off while she was trying to say something.

Chapter 10 – Kuru!

It all happened in the blink of an eye.

Let me start from the beginning. After leaving my house in a huff, I rode around aimlessly. I eventually found myself driving through a nondescript blue collar neighborhood off of Tusculum Road.

When I pulled down a side street, I stopped thinking of everything else. I spotted my new love, a replacement truck for my little Ford Ranger. It was a four-door metallic green Ford F150, SVT Raptor edition, and it was beautiful. It was parked in the driveway of a tired looking brick home and stood out like a gem.

I parked in front of the house and checked it out. It had all the accessories, including four-wheel drive and a tow package. It was almost a shame that I was going to remove all of the exterior bling, strip it of brake lights and turn signals, dull the paint job, and put hardware cloth over the windows.

I found the keys on a hook immediately inside the front door of the house. Pocketing the keys, I cleared the house.

It smelled like all of the houses with rotting corpses smelled, but I was used to it by now. Hell, I didn't even gag anymore. There were two of them, lying on the den floor. When it was clear they were not zombies, I ceased inspecting them. I was beyond caring about their demise, and concentrated more on a superficial search of the house. I found nothing of consequence except for a can of pickled herring. I put it in my knapsack, went back outside, and transferred the rest of my gear from my old truck into my new truck.

After transferring the gas out of the Ranger, I stood there looking at it in silence for a few minutes. It was a present from my grandmother on my fifteenth birthday, and it was the last thing I had which reminded me of her. My mind wandered as I recalled some fond memories of my childhood. All of those memories existed because of the love my Grandmother had for me. She was the one who developed my love of reading. At her encouragement, she listened with rapt attention as I read to her every night after supper. She was a good person, and I was eternally indebted to her. I turned to go, and that's when it happened.

My first instinctive reaction was to grab my gun, but whoever had knocked me to the ground had their hand tightly gripped on it and was trying desperately to wrest it from me. We were in a tug-of-war for several seconds. We were face-to-face as we wrestled, and he was breathing heavily. His breath reeked as if he had not brushed his teeth in several days. I got a good look at his face. He wasn't a zombie, but he was still filthy.

I fought as I held on to my sidearm tightly. If he got it away from me, I was certain I would be shot. We struggled on the ground for what seemed like a long time, but in fact was probably only a minute or two. His heavy breathing told me he was getting winded. He was older, and was probably stronger than I was at one time, but I was the stronger one now.

I punched him repeatedly with my left as we struggled. I hit him so many times my fist was starting to ache. His head was as hard as a rock, but I kept it up. I could hear him gasping for air and grunting with the pain of my repeated blows. He was getting tired and his strength was beginning to wane. With a tremendous grunt, I ripped his hand free of my gun and pushed him off of me. He tumbled back and his legs went akimbo. I hurriedly got to my feet and pulled out the Kimber.

He was large framed and burly looking, like a construction worker by day and a bouncer in a seedy bar at night.

I was about to give him a terminal case of lead poisoning, but hesitated when I saw a woman standing in the driveway next door, holding a small kid. She stared at me with dead eyes. Her plaid shirt was dirty and torn. The kid was runty, dirty, and looked downright weird, as if maybe he had brain damage or something. It was obvious neither of them had seen a bar of soap in quite a while. She reminded me of the woman I had run over.

"You broke my nose," I heard my assailant say. I looked down at him in contempt. He was sitting now and holding his bleeding nose.

"Why did you attack me?"

"You were trying to steal my truck," he snarled and then blew a bloody snot wad out of his nostrils.

"Why are you lying?" I asked plainly.

"Are you calling me a liar, you fuck?" he demanded as he struggled to catch his breath.

"Yes, I am. The people who own this particular truck are inside their house, dead as shit. If you call me another disparaging name, I'm going to shoot you in the kneecaps. You won't be able to walk and sepsis will set in. You'll die a slow lingering death. Choose your next words carefully. I'm not in a good mood today."

He glared at me but said nothing. I looked over at the woman and child. They looked awful, dirty and malnourished. The kid looked no older than three or four. He was having these weird, intermittent muscle spasms and his eyes kept rolling back in his head.

"Who are you people?" I asked.

"He's my husband and this is our child," the woman said. The child suddenly burst out in laughter. Just as suddenly, he stopped and his face went blank, except for the spasms in his legs. It was extremely weird. I looked behind her. There, six pathetic, but unfriendly looking men emerged from the back of a house across the street. They were about fifty feet away and steadily making their way toward me. Then it suddenly hit me. I had read about the symptoms the little boy was displaying.

"Kuru!" I gasped in disgust. The men continued closing the distance between us. They were armed with an assortment of machetes, bats, and knives. One of them had an old rusty shotgun. I didn't like it. The one with the shotgun started to raise it and take aim, which sealed his fate. He started to say something, probably a threatening demand for me to drop my weapon, but before he could utter a word, I shot him with the quickness instilled by the tutelage of Mister Frederick McCoy.

I knew at any second they were going bum rush me before I could shoot more than one or two. My survival instincts kicked in.

"Stop where you are!" I yelled. They froze and looked at each other.

"He's just a fucking kid," one of them growled, and in a silent agreement, they started to spread out. I quickly aimed center mass and shot another one. One of them started running toward me. I shot him, and then for good measure, put a bullet in the left knee of the one who originally attacked me. He howled in pain. The little kid burst out laughing again.

This time, they listened and stopped. I walked over and grabbed the shotgun. It was a twelve gauge double barrel, very lethal in the right hands. I started inching my way toward my newly acquired truck.

"I'm right, aren't I? You people are cannibals!" In spite of myself, I shuddered. I stared at the woman waiting for a response. She hung her head.

"Fucking disgusting is what it is," I whispered. I continued aiming my gun at them, put the shotgun in the cab, and got in. They stared at me with lifeless, yet hungry expressions. They may as well have been zombies.

"Well boys," I said as I waved my gun at their dead friends. "It looks like you're going to eat good tonight." They looked at their dead friends as if I'd just served up supper.

"*Bon Appetit,* you sick fucks!" I snarled and squealed the tires as I backed out of the driveway. Unfortunately, I ran over a curb as I sped away.

The curb proved to be my undoing. I had driven less than a mile when I heard the telltale sounds of thump-thump-thump. I had at least one flat tire. I stopped my new truck and got out. My front right tire was completely fucked. Even the rim was FUBAR. A quick check revealed no spare. A look around at my surroundings revealed I was fucked more than just a flat tire.

Somehow, I had driven into a nest of zombies. Oh, they were rotten beyond belief. I had no idea how they were still on their feet. Nevertheless, they saw me, and they were moving in for the kill. There were dozens of them and they were close. Too close.

I grabbed a canteen, the AR-15, and all of the ammo I could stuff in my pockets. Then, I did what came naturally to me. I ran.

I shot as I ran. There were far too many of them. I had to make every shot count. Head shots. Anything else was useless. I cleared a path and headed toward home. I mentally calculated the mileage while I attempted to stick to a steady pace. If I stuck to the roads, it was going to be a fifteen mile trek. I ran for a mile before stopping, but only long enough to reload my magazine, then I started again. I was into my fourth or fifth mile when the sun disappeared beyond the horizon. By the time I reached six or seven, it was completely dark.

I was scared. I felt like I was living out one of my nightmares. I forced myself to breathe deep and clear my head.

I had put distance between the first group I encountered, and thought I was in the clear, but then I caught a scent of the stinking bastards and surmised I'd apparently run into another group. They were close and I couldn't see more than a few feet in front of my face. I literally ran smack into one. Fortunately for me, I kept my balance while it fell to the ground. I stomped on his head a couple of times before putting distance between it and me.

I ran another mile before stopping for a few minutes, and crouched in the ditch beside the road. Once I caught my breath, I tried hard to listen. I heard them moaning. No, moaning wasn't the proper word. Their voices were merely rasps now. I guessed the decomposition affected their vocal chords. It sounded like there were several of them down the road. Right in the direction I needed to go. They sensed me somehow and became distinctively more agitated.

The moon finally made an appearance. It was a partial moon, waxing crescent I think it was called. It helped with my night vision a little. I could discern the faint outlines of structures, but not distinctly enough to tell the difference between a house and a business. Perhaps this was the reason why there were zombies so close. I worked my way in between buildings. If only I could see a street address, anything. I had a vague notion of where I was, but…

I continued working my way through the houses, but had to move slowly. The overgrown lawns and scattered debris made the going difficult. Any misstep caused unwanted noise. I hoped I was maneuvering around them. I bumped up against objects more than once. After several excruciating minutes, I made my way back onto a road. I found the North Star, got my bearings, and started running in the direction I hoped would lead me home.

*****

Julie sat at the kitchen table when she heard Zach's truck start. She sat a moment longer, silently cursing him. Then she got up and ran outside, only to see the little Ford Ranger crossing the bridge and driving out of sight. Macie stood on the porch quietly.

"Did he say anything?" she asked Macie.

"He mentioned going to look for a new truck," she looked at Julie. "He's just scared, Julie. Men are like that."

Julie sighed heavily. "I am too. I guess I should have understood."

They sat in the rocking chairs until nightfall. Then both of them became worried.

"Should we go looking for him?" Macie asked.

Julie shook her head. "Where would we start? Why don't we try the radio?"

They went inside and tried several times, but there was no response. They sat looking at the radio wondering what to do next, when suddenly Macie gasped and doubled over.

"What's wrong?" Julie asked.

"I'm having contractions," Macie responded. "I think I've been having them for about an hour now, to be honest. I didn't want to say anything though. You had other things on your mind."

"Oh shit. Oh shit!" Julie said. "Uh, okay. Let's get you into bed and I'm going to look you over." Julie helped Macie to her bedroom and got her undressed.

"Okay, I'm going to look at you and see if you're dilating or anything," Julie said.

Macie nodded tentatively and then grunted, "Uh-oh."

"Uh-oh? What?" Julie asked, and then she looked down. "Did your water just break?" she asked. Macie looked at Julie and nodded. Julie saw fear in her eyes. "You're going to give birth, aren't you, Macie?" Macie nodded again.

"Okay, we've planned for this, right? We'll get through this, girlfriend. Don't be afraid." Julie tried to sound confident but the two of them heard the tremor in her voice.

*****

It was hard trying to keep track of my headings. I had to leave the road and make detours constantly. I'd take side roads or run through backyards, and then try to get back on the main roadway again, all in total darkness.

Let's not forget the God forsaken zombies. Every time I made a turn, there would be one or two lumbering toward me. I lost count of my shots and had no idea how much ammunition I had left.

On top of it all, I had not done any cross-country running in several months. The lack of training was immediately evident. My throat and lungs burned, but to stop and rest for more than a few seconds meant an almost certain death.

I slowed to a walk only long enough to check my watch. It was a little after twenty-one hundred hours, nine p.m. I resumed jogging and approached an intersection. When I got close enough, I could see the street sign. The name of the street was familiar. I knew where I was now and only a little off track. A quick mental calculation told me I had another five miles to go, more or less. I was winded and my feet were beginning to ache. I worked on controlling my breathing and kept telling myself I was going to make it.

*****

Macie's breathing was labored and she was sweating profusely. Julie wasn't keeping track of time. She only knew the baby was coming and Zach was nowhere around.

"It's getting close now, I think. I need you to keep doing your Lamaze breathing." Julie tried to sound more confident than she felt. She continued talking reassuringly to Macie and occasionally wiped her face with a damp washcloth.

"What time is it?" Macie asked. Julie looked at her wristwatch.

"It's a little after ten. It won't be long now until you start crowning. I'll let you know when."

"I'm scared, Julie. Something doesn't feel right," Macie said.

"Come on now. You have no idea what it's supposed to feel like." Julie wiped Macie's brow again, and then took her blood pressure. It seemed really high, she thought. She inspected again.

"Oh my God, Macie, you're crowning! It won't be long now, start pushing!"

Chapter 11 – A Newborn

It was close to midnight when I crossed the bridge to my home. I was exhausted, drenched in sweat, and my entire body hurt. My feet were sore and the inside of my thighs were chaffed so bad I was having trouble walking normally. I made my way cautiously to the house. The generator was still going, which was odd. I walked around the house, but didn't see anything out of the ordinary. I gave the special knock before entering.

"It's me," I said as I opened the door. I'd learned my lesson. I had full intention of begging Julie for forgiveness. I was willing to do anything to get back the life I had a few hours ago, back when Julie smiled at me every time she caught me looking at her. I called out again and heard something in Macie's bedroom. I walked in slowly. Julie looked up at me. There was sweat on her brow and she was holding something swaddled in a small blanket.

"It's a baby boy. Macie is in trouble. She's hemorrhaging," she said quietly.

I looked all three of them over. They looked awful. Macie was ashen faced and unconscious.

"How's the baby?" I asked.

Julie looked at me solemnly. "He's weak. I'm guessing he was born prematurely, but I'm not sure. He's so small! Please, do something, Zach," she begged.

I nodded. "Okay, I'll take care of Macie. You get the kid in the crib. No wait, you better keep him with you and watch him. He'll need to eat soon I'm guessing. We'll need to feed him formula until Macie is strong enough to breast feed him." Julie nodded.

I lifted the blanket. Macie was pale, listless, and still soiled from the birth. Julie walked in and stood beside me.

"Where is her placenta?" I asked.

"It never came out. She urinated and there was a lot of blood, but no placenta. You need to do a fundal massage," she said, and explained. "Take your hand and place it where her uterus is. Gently massage and push down. You'll probably need to do it for thirty minutes or so."

I did as Julie instructed, while Julie watched. After several minutes, the placenta appeared. I pulled it out gently. Other tissue came out, along with a lot of blood. Julie handed me the baby, and then quickly ran to the restroom. I heard her hurling chunks in the toilet. Wonderful, I thought. I placed the child in the crib, got a wash pan, filled it with warm water, and used a washrag to clean her up.

Macie awakened when she felt the warmth of the washcloth. I gave her a reassuring smile.

"Hi, Macie, don't mind me. I'm just getting you cleaned up, okay?" She nodded sleepily and nodded off. After I finished, I carried Macie to our bedroom and called Julie out of the bathroom.

"I need a maxi pad," I said plainly. Julie looked at me, perplexed. "For Macie, not me."

Julie nodded in sudden understanding, disappeared into the bathroom and came back out with one, along with a fresh pair of panties. She brushed me aside and I watched as she put the panties on Macie and positioned the pad.

"I'm going to keep an eye on the baby," Julie said.

"Okay, I'm going to clean up the mess and put some broth on the stove." I gathered up the bedding, shoved them into a trash bag, and temporarily put it in the cellar. I couldn't simply throw them outside. The afterbirth would attract unwanted visitors. After a few minutes in the kitchen, I came back to the bedroom and gently woke her.

"Macie, I need to get some fluids in you. I've made some broth and I need you to take some sips. Can you do that?" I asked. Macie nodded slightly.

"If you feel like you're going to vomit, let me know and don't hold it back," she nodded again. I fed her slowly, a spoon at a time, and managed to get about a cup's worth in her before she passed out. I spent the rest of the night dripping water into her mouth. I did not know if she was going to live and was surprised at how worried I was.

Sometime during the night or morning, I drifted off. Awakening with a start, I looked at my watch. It was a little after five a.m. I found Julie in the den. She was maintaining her bedside vigil with the baby. She looked up at me with worry on her face.

"How is she?" she asked.

"Sleeping. I got some fluids in her, which is good, but I'm not sure if it's going to be enough," I motioned at the baby. "Did he eat?" I asked.

"A little," she said. I looked closely at the child. He was so small, vulnerable. He had Jason's features. I didn't know whether to be relieved or saddened. If he lived, would I have to tell him one day how his father died?

"Why don't you get some sleep? I'll watch over them."

She smiled at me tiredly. "You look like you need sleep more than me," she sniffed. "You need a bath too. What did you get yourself into?" she asked. I explained briefly. Her eyes widened.

"Wait a minute, you ran all the way home from Tusculum Road?"

I nodded.

"In the dark? With zombies around?"

I nodded again. Her eyes grew wider

"Holy shit, Zach," she said. I expected her to jump all in my ass for such a stupid act, but instead, she stood, and in spite of how badly I reeked, she hugged me tightly.

"I'm glad you're okay, but please don't do that again. I was worried sick," she said. I agreed profusely.

"Listen, I have something to say. I'm very sorry about earlier. You took me by surprise. I was scared and stressed," I said sincerely. She looked up at me and I kissed her on the forehead.

"I want you to know I am so very happy you are carrying my baby. We're going to make it work because I love you with all of my heart." I kissed her again. She leaned up and kissed me back.

"I love you too, Zach, with all of my heart," Julie said. Then her expression changed.

"There's something I have to tell you." I looked at her and she looked at the floor. "During all of this, I started my period. I'm not pregnant," she said and looked up at me with a hint of tears in her eyes. "I guess it was wishful dreaming," she quipped.

"It's okay," I replied and hugged her. "I really want a baby with you. I guess we'll have to keep trying." I kissed her deeply and hugged her again.

"I hope you take a bath before we try again," she said with a smile.

We took turns for the next few days caring for the two of them. Macie's health steadily improved and on day two, she was able to eat a whole bowl of soup. She was too weak to stand for more than a few seconds, so I would carry her to the bathroom and help her bathe.

"You've been good to me, Zach," she said while I helped dry her off one evening.

"Just so you know, when you get your strength back, you'll be getting no more sponge baths from me." She looked at me and smiled. I smiled back.

Her eyes widened slightly. "You smiled at me."

"Yeah, I guess I did." I finished drying her, wrapped her in a towel, and carried her back to her bed.

"I guess I can't keep a chip on my shoulder the rest of my life, now can I?" I said as I pulled the blankets over her and fluffed her pillows.

"How about I brush your hair out before you go to sleep?"

She nodded and smiled at me again. I helped her sit up and as I reached for the brush on the nightstand, she suddenly leaned forward and kissed me on the cheek. I smiled to hide my embarrassment. I quickly brushed her hair and fluffed her pillows again. She grabbed one of my hands.

"When we were dating, you were a naïve boy. You've changed, Zach. You're a grown man now." I looked at her and shrugged.

Julie interrupted anything either of us might have said when she brought in the baby. She had him swaddled in a small blanket. Macie took him in her arms.

"You have a beautiful baby boy," Julie said. Macie looked up and tried to smile, but she couldn't seem to do it.

Chapter 12 – A Death

"What did you call it again?" Howard asked.

"Kuru, it's a disease resulting from cannibalism," I said. "Apparently, the only way to properly eat human flesh is for it to be cooked well-done, and avoid eating the brain."

Howard eyed me. "How in the hell did you know what it was?"

"In ninth grade I did a report for my geography class. Each student was assigned a country in Africa. My country was South Sudan. There is a River in Sudan named the Kuru. I was going to add a few factoids in my paper about the river systems and was doing a Wikipedia search. There were a few hits on the word Kuru. One of them was about cannibalism in New Guinea. It fascinated me so much I looked up videos of it on You Tube."

Howard shuddered. "They had videos?" I nodded. Howard shuddered again. "Eating people. That's just plain wrong, Zach. Just plain wrong."

I nodded silently.

"You sure it's a Ford F150?" Howard asked.

"Yeah, it's a nice one," I said. He already knew this. We discussed it before we left his shop and found a spare tire to fit it, which was sitting in the back of his Hummer. Howard was sort of the opposite of Fred. Where Fred was stoic, Howard was a talker.

"Zach?" Howard asked. I looked over at him. "If you were starving, maybe had a wife and some kids who were starving, and they were looking at you, wondering what you were going to do about it, would you do it?"

"Would I do what?" I glanced over at him. "Eat another human?" Howard nodded and eyed me.

"I don't know, Howard. I know I'd have to be very desperate before I even thought of it as a viable alternative. I guess if I had starving kids and there was no other food source…" I shrugged.

"I don't know," I repeated. "The only thing I'm certain of right now is if I see any of those people again, I'm not going to be very civil with them." We rode in silence for a couple of minutes.

"I've never been a fighter," Howard suddenly said. "I had two older brothers. Both of them were in a gang. My oldest brother was killed in a drive-by. There was no rhyme or reason behind the murder. He happened to be in a rival gang is all. My other brother, he swore revenge. He found three of them in an apartment one night and killed them all. The police arrested him, of course. He got tried as an adult and the jury found him guilty. The judge gave him back-to-back life sentences. He was the same age as you at the time." Howard shook his head sadly before continuing.

"I was thirteen when it happened. My momma was devastated. I don't think she ever recovered. I was pretty devastated too."

"What did you do?" I asked.

"I had an uncle who owned a garage. I started working for him after school and on weekends to help momma pay the bills. It kept me out of trouble and away from the gangs. That's how I became a mechanic."

I nodded thoughtfully and pointed down the road. "There it is." The truck appeared unmoved since I had left it.

"Okay, you're the better shot, I'm the better mechanic. I'll get the tire changed and you keep watch," Howard said. He parked behind the truck and we got out. I made a quick scan of the area and looked in the truck. It was empty.

"They took everything, the bastards," I said.

Howard grunted and crawled under the truck. "The gas tank is still intact. No holes, but I'm betting they drained it as well. Good thing we brought a gas can."

I used Howard's binoculars to scan the area as he got the tire replaced and put five gallons of gas in the truck. I fished the keys out of my pocket and it started right up.

"Good thing you took the keys with you. They'd have taken this truck with them, even with a flat tire," Howard popped the hood and inspected the motor. "Everything looks good, Zach. It's got four-wheel drive, a tow package, and a V8 engine. It'll be able to tow up to six thousand pounds. It even has one of those new lithium batteries. That's awesome," he said as he closed the hood, looked around, and studied me.

"What are we, about fifteen miles from your farm? You say you ran all the way back? In the dark?" he asked. I nodded.

"Holy sheep shit, Zach," Howard said incredulously.

I shrugged. "It was either run or meander along, waiting to be attacked and eaten."

Howard laughed. "I get your point."

I frowned then. Howard saw it. "What?"

"It was the weirdest thing, Howard. For a few of those miles I felt like I was being followed."

"Well, of course it was the zombies," Howard replied.

I shook my head. "No, it was something or somebody else. The zombies stank and they made these awful breathing noises. They sounded like someone using a rasp on a piece of old oak. They were fairly easy to avoid. It was something else. I don't know, but when I was running, I felt like someone was trailing me. I made several detours and cut backs, but I never saw anyone, or anything," I shrugged. "Maybe it was a coyote thinking I would be an easy meal."

Howard nodded, although I don't think he comprehended what I was saying.

"Alright, Zach, where to now?" he asked.

"I'm going to get my property back," I said. Howard's eyes widened.

"You're going to confront those cannibal eating motherfuckers?" he asked.

I nodded. "You can wait here if you want."

"Oh, hell no. I'm not sitting here by myself," Howard rubbed his face. "I'll follow you." He walked to his Hummer.

I drove up to the neighborhood and parked near my old truck. The driver's door was open, as if they were looking for something to loot out of it as well. The bodies were missing. Only some dried blood trails remained. I followed the trails through the yard and to a house one street over. I went back inside the truck owners' home and scrounged around until I found a couple of mason jars. I punctured a hole in the gas tank of my Ranger and managed to fill up two of the jars. Rigging them so they were Molotov cocktails,

Howard and I drove over to the next street and parked about twenty feet away from their house. I saw curtains being pulled aside. They knew we were here.

I exited with my assault rifle, shot out the windows before lighting one of the rags on the jar, and threw it through the broken window.

"You fuckers have five minutes to bring my property back to me," I shouted. "Watch 'em, Howard." He took up a position beside his Hummer with his shotgun. I prepared the second jar.

"Four minutes!" I yelled, and threw it through the other shattered window.

"Zach," Howard whispered. "It's only been about twenty seconds."

I looked at him and winked. There was smoke coming out of the window now. I shot a few more times and reloaded.

"Three minutes!" I yelled and glanced back at Howard. He looked at me and then shot out one of the upstairs windows.

"Two minutes!" he yelled. I nodded.

"I'm going to run around to the back of the house. Stay here," I said as I took off running. The back door was opening a crack as I rounded the corner. I splintered the doorframe with a bullet.

"Do you fuck-tards think we're playing? You better bring my property back A-S-A-Fucking-P!"

The door slammed shut and I jogged back around front. The front door of the burning house opened a moment later.

"Don't shoot!" a woman shouted. "We're coming out!" They nervously exited the house with their hands raised. It was the same crew, even the kid. Hell, they were even wearing the same clothes.

"Where is my property?" I asked.

"It's all inside," one of the men said.

"Well, go get it, you dumbass," I demanded.

He tentatively looked inside. "The place is on fire. It's full of smoke."

"Well then, you better make it fast. You men go in there and help your friend. Otherwise, I'm taking out your kneecaps."

They were certainly slow witted, but a shot at their feet reaffirmed to them I was serious. They turned and ran back inside.

They came out a minute later with their arms loaded and coughing heavily.

"Put it all in the back of my truck," I said. "Make it fast."

They hurriedly complied. As the last one dropped my property into the bed of the truck, he looked back at the house. Flames were visible now.

"You've set our house on fire. What do we do now?" he lamented.

"Frankly, I don't give a shit." I motioned at Howard and we left.

"You want to drive over to the Cool Springs Mall and try some of the retail businesses around there? See if there's anything left over we can use?" Howard asked.

"I need to get some baby stuff, and maybe some stuff for the girls, but I need to make it quick and get back to the farm," I said. We were sitting in front of his home, a former tire store near the intersection of Nolensville and Old Hickory. I hooked my thumb over my shoulder at a nearby Walmart.

"Have you been in there lately?" I asked.

Howard shook his head. "Not lately. I tried back in the spring. Man, it was full of zombies." He shook his head again.

"But, I haven't tried it lately. You want to give it a shot?"

I shrugged. "We can give it a try. If there are too many of them still in there, we'll back out and call it a day." Howard frowned with worry, but went along.

We started at the front doors and slowly worked our way in. We spent the next two hours clearing the super store. Every time we thought we had killed them all, another one would emerge out of a dark corner. The two of us were drenched in sweat by the time we killed the last one.

"My ears are ringing. I should have worn earplugs," Howard lamented.

I nodded. "Yeah, mine too," I made a mental calculation. "I'm counting eighteen dead zeds, does that sound about right?" I asked. Howard nodded in agreement.

I pointed toward the front of the store. There were multiple corpses of what I suppose were healthy people before they died.

There wasn't much left of them. Whatever the zombies didn't chew on, the maggots had finished the job.

"It looks like people came in here thinking they had easy pickings and would get attacked. Even so, this store doesn't have much left," I said. Howard nodded again and took a long drink from his canteen.

"We need to apply rule number eight and burn these corpses," I said as an afterthought. Howard got up and walked down an aisle. He returned a minute later with two pair of cheap gardening gloves. I smiled appreciatively.

"It's like you predicted though. Those zombies are dying off. These ones here," Howard waved his finger at the zombies we'd killed. "They could hardly move."

I agreed. It was a good sign. Once they all died off, it would make it a lot easier for the survivors. We had no problem dragging them outside. The decomposition reduced their body weight by a considerable amount. Stacking some debris on top of the corpses, we watched them burn. When the fire was going sufficiently, we walked back in and then spent several minutes looking around at the small amount of merchandise left.

"Looks like all the food products are gone, but there's still some baby and women's products left," Howard said. "I better get Lashonda some of those female things as well. She'll have my ass if I don't bring her a present." He smiled and wiped the sweat off of his brow before continuing.

"You know, it wasn't so long ago if you brought a woman a box of tampons as a present, you'd get your face slapped." He erupted with his signature belly laugh at his own joke. I had to laugh as well. It was a great stress reliever. We got some shopping carts and with the aid of flashlights soon had them overflowing.

"Have you noticed they can't scream or shriek anymore?" I asked Howard.

"Yeah, they sure sound funny," he said. "You want to come over and visit a while?" He asked.

I looked at my watch. "We better call it for the day. I have a lot of farm chores waiting."

"How are Macie and her baby?"

"Macie's still very weak, but I think she's going to be alright. The baby is another story. He's so tiny. I'm worried about him. Macie has been trying to feed him, but he's lethargic. I may know a lot, but I don't know much about babies. Do you think Lashonda could come over one day and see what she thinks?" I asked.

Howard nodded. "Why didn't you say so sooner? Consider it done." He glanced at the sun. "We still have plenty of daylight. I'll go pick her and the boys up, and we'll be right over." I shook his hand and we parted company.

The four of them came to the house an hour later. I was sitting on the porch when they drove up. Lil' H and Derry ran up, said hi and started playing with Curly.

Howard laughed as he walked up. "You sure got those chores done quick."

I shook my head as I stood and spoke somberly. "The chores had to wait Howard." I looked at his wife. "Hi Lashonda, it's good to see you. The girls are inside."

She looked at me and frowned. "What's wrong, Zach?" she asked.

"It's the baby. You better go inside. We'll wait out here." Lashonda rushed inside. I looked over at Howard and his sons. "The baby died."

"Oh, shit," Howard said.

We sat on the porch for a while and listened to the women cry inside. I stood suddenly. "There is some wood in the barn. Howard, would you mind helping me build a coffin?" I asked Howard.

Howard stood. "Absolutely." Howard, his sons, and I walked slowly to the barn. I tried to make some measurements on the wood, but was all thumbs. Howard told me to have a seat and relax. He took over and had a small coffin built in no time. It looked very nice.

We buried the baby on the mound beside Rick. Even though they had never met, he always seemed to like children. Everyone was somber and spoke in hushed tones. Howard recited the Lord's Prayer and I shoveled the dirt. The boys helped me quietly.

Afterward, I gently picked Macie up and put her back on the ATV. She wept silently on the ride back. Julie kept a reassuring arm around her.

"How about I put you to bed and fix you some tea?" I asked. She nodded absently. She was able to walk for short distances now, but the stress of her baby's death had sapped her strength. I carried her inside, and tucked her in while Julie fluffed her pillows.

"I don't know what I'd do without you two," Macie said softly.

"We're all family now, Macie," Julie said. "We stick together, right?" Macie looked up at Julie and nodded sadly.

She fell asleep within minutes. The rest of us gathered on the porch and talked quietly. When the sun was on the horizon, the Allen family said their goodbyes. Julie and I ate a small dinner and went to bed. At Julie's insistence, we slept with Macie. Julie said she didn't want her to be alone.

I was the sandwich. I had one on each side of me. Julie settled in with her butt snuggled up against me and Macie had her head buried in the crook of my shoulder. I drifted off wondering if this was all going to work out okay.

Chapter 13 – Fred

Fred attempted to save time by travelling on the Interstate. He encountered chronic traffic jams, and at one point had to drive in reverse for over a mile before he could back down an entrance ramp. He finally made it to the outskirts of Memphis when the sun was in his eyes. He spent the night in the sleeper of his truck on the side of Interstate 40, at the base of the bridge over the Mississippi River, known as the Hernando de Soto Bridge. It consisted of six lanes with a concrete barrier down the middle.

Daylight confirmed what he suspected last night. The entire bridge, all six lanes, was a logjam. He realized with great frustration there was no possible way he was going to maneuver the Volvo rig through the gridlock of abandoned and wrecked motor vehicles.

Seeing no other alternative, Fred loaded a backpack, retrieved his favorite rifle, a Winchester lever action, his revolvers, and set out on foot. There were a few zombies on foot, but most of them were stuck in the vehicles.

Fred adeptly avoided most them.

Most of them.

It was a long walk across the bridge. Every time he passed a car or a truck, there was a zombie waiting, lunging, gnashing. He shot sparingly, running past them when he could, shooting only when there was no other choice. It was roughly ten thousand feet, almost two miles, before he reached the rest area on the west side of the river.

To his delight, he found an old Volkswagen Bug. It was bright yellow, dirty, but otherwise appeared to be in good condition, if you didn't count the rotting corpse sitting behind the wheel.

Seeing no other option, Fred broke out the little vent window, unlocked the door, and dragged the corpse out. The keys were still in the ignition and the battery was dead, which was no surprise. That was the beauty of the venerable Bug. They seemed to be almost indestructible. Fred dumped his backpack in the backseat, put it in neutral, and began pushing.

After several attempts and, pushing the little car for almost a hundred yards, it sputtered to life.

Fred hopped in and drove on.

Chapter 14 – Getting to Know Andie

It had been two weeks to the day since my meeting with Andie. I had not planned on seeing her again, but I felt the extenuating circumstances warranted another encounter.

I knew it was risky. If she were a part of those idiots who tried to ambush me, I would be taking a big chance by coming to this location again. Nevertheless, I wanted more information from her. Specifically, I needed to know if they had encountered any doctors. The death of Macie's child troubled me greatly. One day, Julie and I were going to have a child.

I started out well before sunrise. It was cool this morning. The outdoor thermometer read fifty-four degrees. September was here and a change in the weather was close at hand. I packed the truck with a picnic basket and grill. A nice brunch might put Andie in a good mood if she even bothered showing up. I also hid a gun under the seat and added one to an ankle holster, in case she was in a nasty mood or brought friends.

I used the night vision gear to drive, but it was slow going. The recent gunshot to my head, although merely a glancing wound, had nevertheless caused me some issues, one of them being if I wore those things for any length of time I'd get a severe headache. I got about five miles before I took them off and used the headlights. Again, another risky move, but I wanted my mind sharp for the meeting.

The problem was, the headlights tended to attract zombies. There were no massive hordes, but there were more than I was comfortable with. I stopped every so often and would wait for them to approach before saying hello with a head shot. They were starting to all look alike. The decomposition eliminated any identifiable character traits. I assumed what gender they were based on their manner of dress. I killed an even dozen before arriving at the old store.

Killing the lights as I parked on the side of the store, I approached the entrance. Using the night vision gear, I did a quick sweep of the interior; no live people, no zombies. I went back outside and scanned the area. There was an old white wooden building behind the store. It was empty of anything worthwhile. There was no need for the night vision apparatus now, since dawn was fast approaching. I sat on the front steps and waited.

She drove into the parking lot shortly after sun up, made eye contact with me, and smiled. When she got out of her jeep, she looked skinnier than the last time we met, but at least her hair had grown out a little more. It helped make her look more feminine. She ran up and hugged me tightly.

"When you didn't show up last week, I was kind of let down," she said.

I shrugged apologetically. "I had all kinds of crap to do around the farm and I don't have any help."

"You're girlfriend doesn't help you?"

I shrugged again. I was not going to tell her Julie was busy tending to Macie and monitoring the radio in case Fred called. She scoffed. "Well, that's bullshit if you ask me. I'd help you."

"I've no doubt you would. Are you hungry?" I asked. "I brought some food. We can have a picnic breakfast."

She eyed me coyly. "You wanna fuck before or after?"

I chuckled. "You know I can't."

She grinned back at me and responded with a carefree shrug. "Your loss, I guess we'll eat then."

She helped me get the grill set up and we laid a blanket out on the asphalt. We had the steaks grilled in no time. I brought a small skillet and fried some eggs as well.

After we finished eating, Andie laid back, pulled her shirt up, and rubbed her belly.

"I'm stuffed!" she exclaimed.

"How are you guys doing for food?" I asked as I eyed her skinny torso. She scoffed again.

"The Captain eats really well, but the rest of us, not so much. Some of our group had canned a lot of stuff prior to this shit going down, but they fucked it up somehow. Most of it was contaminated. We have some gardens we harvested, but not enough. We've been hitting abandoned houses like crazy. It's hit or miss."

"What about cattle?" I asked.

"Yeah, we have some. We used to have a lot, but coyotes killed some and a bunch of them developed some kind of disease."

"You don't have any donkeys?" I asked. She looked at me questioningly. "A donkey will kill a coyote."

We used to have one at the farm. It died and Rick never replaced him. After coyotes killed our chickens, I found a couple of them one day and transported them to our farm. We haven't had any problems since.

"Oh. Well, we don't have any donkeys," she continued. "The Captain is worried. He doesn't say it, but he's worried. I've known him my whole life, I can tell. Anyway, rations have been cut. He sends foraging crews out every day."

"What area are they concentrating on?"

Andie looked over at me. "They've been working in and around the Eagleville area, but it doesn't mean the Captain has forgotten about you. He thinks you guys are well off. By the way, he's been talking about meeting with you again."

"Did he say what for?" I asked.

"Yeah, he wants to have a poetry reading with you."

I arched an eyebrow. She kept a serious expression for about three seconds, and then she started giggling.

I smiled. "Okay you got me."

"I think he wants to pick your brain about food and stuff," she said.

I nodded and changed the subject. "Have you guys been in contact with any doctors, nurses, veterinarians, anyone like that?" I asked.

She scoffed. "We ran into a doctor and his wife not too long ago. They thought they were the shit for some reason. The doctor's wife demanded the Captain pay for her husband's services," her features darkened.

"What happened?" I asked.

"The Captain took a hammer to her. He broke a couple of her fingers. He thought it would make the doctor fall in line, so we left them at their house. When a crew went back the next day, they were gone."

She looked at me. "The Captain was so pissed that he beat a few of us. We went back to their house and he set fire to it."

"Nice guy," I quipped, and then remembered setting fire to the cannibal's home. I found myself uncomfortable with the corollary.

"You have no idea," she said quietly. She pointed at the sky. "When I was a kid, I'd do this. Lay in my backyard, stare at the clouds, and imagine what the shapes were. Look, there's a horse."

I laid back and looked at the cloud she was pointing at. It looked more like a fat cow to me, with oversized bunny ears.

"I suppose every kid has done this."

"Yeah," she sat up suddenly. "But we're not kids anymore, are we?"

I sat up as well. "Not anymore."

Andie sighed and looked over at me. "You want to ask more questions."

"Yep, where is the compound?" I asked.

She pointed. "Go that way for a few miles. There's a road called Rocky Glade. There is a dead end road that runs off of it called Ward Road. The land has been in the family since the Civil War." She turned back at me and grinned. "Are you going to pay us visit?"

I grinned. "More like I want to know where the Captain lives so I can stay away."

She scoffed. "Oh, I understand all too well. So I have a question for you." Andie turned and eyed me. "Since you won't fuck me, how about a blow job?"

I chuckled. "I can't," I said. "My girlfriend would be very unhappy with me."

Andie rubbed her belly some more. "She'll never know."

I shook my head. "I'm a terrible liar. She'd know. Also, I'm in love with her, so I'd feel like shit if I knowingly did anything to hurt her. You don't have anyone else?"

She shook her head. "Nobody would dare touch me. So, enough about me being my uncle's little whore. Tell me about your girlfriend."

"Uh, well, she's a little taller than you and weighs maybe ten or twenty pounds more. She has dark brown chestnut hair growing past her shoulders." I thought of her hair and how much I loved brushing it after she washed it.

"She has pretty blue eyes and some freckles on her cheeks that really turn me on," not to mention her lithe body, I thought. "All of that is wrapped around a pert and beautiful girl with a feisty disposition. We met after everything happened and fell in love."

"How old is she?" Andie asked.

"Same as me, sixteen. I'm turning seventeen in November."

"I turn sixteen in January," she said. "I know what you're about to ask. Besides the baby, I'm the youngest one of our group. There was one boy my age, but he disappeared."

"There's a baby?" I asked. She nodded. "Were there any problems during childbirth?"

Andie shook her head. "Nope, it just popped right out. It's a little boy," she scoffed. "God only knows who the dad is."

I thought about the baby and wondered how he was doing, if he was going to survive. It also made me think of Macie's baby.

"Okay, one last question. The last time we met, did you set me up to be ambushed?"

Her mouth dropped open. "What? No! You were ambushed?"

I nodded and related the story.

"Zach, I didn't have anything to do with that, I swear. You say two people were killed and one of them was a woman?" I nodded. "We haven't lost anyone since the last time we spoke. Why would you think I'd do something like that?"

I shrugged. "You seem pretty cool, Andie, and I like you, but I hardly know you. And, as Julie has said more than once, I know nothing about women."

She glared at me. "She's right."

Andie insisted I kiss her before leaving. This time, it was not a surprise ambush kiss. I knew what I was doing. She grabbed my butt and pulled me against her when we did it. I instantly became aroused and felt guilty as hell about it as I drove away. She also gave me a present, a picture of her. It was a wallet size photo. It looked like a school yearbook picture. I stuck it under the visor.

"What the hell are you doing?" I asked myself out loud. Julie was the love of my life, and here I was kissing another girl. I could rationalize my actions. There was no tongue involved, but still… Plus, I had to admit to myself that I was rather enjoying the sponge baths I was giving Macie.

"You are a stupid idiot, Zachariah Gunderson," I said and ended my conversation with myself. I put a CD in the stereo and made a point of travelling a different route as I returned home.

Chapter 15 – Rocky Fork

"We've not heard anything from Fred?" I asked. Both Macie and Julie shook their heads.

"It's been three weeks now," Macie said. She was putting on weight again and no longer had the pallor of Casper the Ghost. Still, Julie and I were concerned about her. Since the baby's death, she had not mentioned him once and cried frequently.

We were sitting at the kitchen table drinking coffee. I drummed my fingers absently, and finally looked over at Julie. "You want to go for a ride?" I asked.

"Sure. Where are we going?" She said.

"Andie mentioned a man with two kids living on Rocky Fork Road. I'm betting he doesn't like the Captain. I say we introduce ourselves and see if he'd be a good ally."

Macie held up her hand. "I want to go! I haven't been off of the farm in weeks. I'm going stir crazy."

I looked over at Julie. She nodded in agreement. "Are you strong enough?" I asked. Macie nodded readily. "Okay, let's get ready and load up."

I had Julie drive while I kept watch. Macie was in the backseat. I had her armed with my Ruger twenty-two. When we reached Rocky Fork Road, we drove slowly, looking for any telltale signs of life. Macie suddenly pointed.

"Look! Are those goats?" she asked.

Julie stopped the truck and I looked them over with binoculars. "I think someone lives there. The goats are chained to a post stuck in the ground. Let's pull in. You two stay in the truck and I'll try to make contact."

We stopped at the head of the driveway and I got out. We had our standard plan going. If I was being threatened, Julie and Macie would take action. I walked up to within ten feet of the house.

"Hello!" I shouted and then waited. As I stood there waiting, a scrawny little kid wearing nothing more than underwear ran out from the side of the house. He looked like he was no more than five or six. I waved. His eyes widened and he ran back the way he came, giving me a good view of a fresh skid mark.

A short time went by before a man appeared from the rear of the house. He appeared to be in his mid-thirties, average height, brown hair which may have been cut by an expensive stylist once, and a youthful face sporting a month of whiskers. If I were to guess, I'd say he was a yuppie with expensive suits in his closet along with an assortment of leather shoes.

He was also armed with a blue steel revolver. I immediately held my palms out, but was careful not to raise them over my head. I heard a truck door open behind me and knew one of them was about to shoot.

"Easy now," I said. "We're friendly."

"Who are you and what do you want?" he asked warily.

"I'm Zach, Zach Gunderson." I motioned toward the truck with my head. "They're my friends. We spotted your house and thought we'd say hello. There aren't very many of us left these days, so we wanted to make contact. Oh, and we're not with the Captain's group."

His wariness changed to a quizzical expression. "Are you the guy who has been painting those rules everywhere?" he asked.

"Yep, the one and the same," I replied with a friendly smile. He looked at me a minute in silence and then stared at the girls. He still held the revolver, although it was not pointing at anything.

"Listen, if we're intruding just say so. We'll be on our way." I must have broken him out of his reverie.

"Oh. No." He stuck the revolver into his waistband and extended his hand.

"I'm Toby Eason." We shook hands.

"Please, come join us. It's just my two sons and me. We were about to eat lunch. We don't have much, but you all are welcome to join in." I nonchalantly gave the signal. Julie and Macie exited the truck, walked up, and introduced themselves. Toby grinned broadly as he shook their hands. The two boys had been peeking at us from the side of the house. Finally, curiosity got the best of them. They walked up, stood beside their father and gawked at the two girls. Toby noticed and laughed.

"We haven't seen any women in quite a while, especially not as beautiful as you two." He pointed at the two boys. "The youngest one is Joshua and the oldest one is Caleb."

I shook hands with the two boys. "My name is Zachariah, which is also a name in Jewish history. These two are Julie and Macie."

Toby glanced side long at me. "Are you Jewish, Zach?" he asked.

I shook my head. "I happened to remember Caleb and Joshua being two spies of Moses who urged him to trust in God and enter the land of Canaan." He looked at me oddly.

"I went to school with him," Macie said. "Trust me, he's a genius."

"Oh," Toby said. "Well, I'm cooking a chicken on the grill in back. Please join us." We started to follow him but I stopped suddenly, causing Julie to bump into me.

"Where are our manners?" I said. I looked at Toby. "When is the last time y'all had some watermelon?" I went to the back of the truck and hoisted a couple of big ones out. They were mostly still ripe. Toby and his boys gasped in unison.

When we saw the diminutive size of the chicken, or whatever it was, we begged off.

"I'll be honest, Toby," I said. "The girls fixed up a rather big breakfast. I don't think I'll be hungry again until sometime next week." Julie and Macie readily agreed. Toby saw through my lie, but went along with it. He knew there was not enough to go around.

"You don't mind if we eat while we talk, do you?" He asked.

"Not at all." I carried the watermelons over to a picnic table and carved out some slices. The two boys watched as if I were serving up manna from heaven. I handed each of them a slice and they devoured it. Macie gave them spitting lessons.

I briefly told our story to Toby and he listened intently. He grinned when I told him the history of Macie and me.

"So, let me get this straight. You two," he pointed at Macie and me, "are former sweethearts, and you two," he pointed at Julie and me, "are current sweethearts, and yet, the three of you live under the same roof?"

"Yep," Julie said with a grin. Toby laughed. He cut up the mystery bird for his boys and took a small bite for himself.

"My wife and I moved here when she was pregnant with Caleb. We're both psychologists. Anyway, when things started getting bad, we boarded up the windows, nailed the doors shut and hid out in the basement. We had a lot of food stored up, but it didn't last very long." He nibbled a small piece of meat.

"We'd peek out the windows in between the cracks of the wood and watch the neighborhood. It was tough watching our former neighbors and friends walking down the road with that infection ravaging their body." He frowned. "Since both of us were psychologists, we thought we could handle the mental aspect of being shut up in the house, isolated from the rest of the world. We were wrong. One day, my wife took one of our cars and left while I was giving the boys a bath. She'd had enough, I guess. I haven't seen her since."

"How long ago was that?" Macie asked.

"About six months ago," Toby said. His face briefly clouded up at the memory.

"Anyway, we have plenty of some stuff, and very little of other stuff. Down the road is an overgrown farm the Captain and his crew didn't ravage. It has plenty of corn in the fields, despite the most fervent attempts of the crows and other wildlife."

He looked at us. "Crow meat is not very tasty, just in case y'all were wondering. My scavenging forays have had limited success. I've found some stuff, but I'm worried about my kids, so I don't go far. I don't think I'm getting them the proper nutrition."

He pointed down the road. "There are stray cows running around. I killed one about a month ago, but had no idea how to butcher it. I made a big mess and the coyotes dragged most of it away during the night." The three of us exchanged glances. I nodded.

"Toby, we don't have a lot, but I think we can help out a little bit. And if I may say so, I'm a master butcher."

Julie scoffed. "You can't butcher a cow without my help, Zach Gunderson, and you know it." She threw a watermelon seed at me.

I shrugged. "She's got me on that one."

It was after four when we said our goodbyes and got in the truck to leave.

"This might work out okay," I said. "With Toby's help, we can start rounding up a lot of stray cattle. I wonder if he'd be willing to relocate closer to the farm."

"Well, after the way he ogled Macie and me, I'd bet he'll move tomorrow if you ask him."

She turned onto Rocky Fork Road and the evening sun hit her in the eyes at one point. She adjusted the visor and Andie's picture fell onto her lap. She picked it up.

"What the hell is this?" she asked.

"Oh, it's a picture of Andie," I said innocently.

"Why do you have it?" Her tone was not friendly. She was now alternating between looking at the road and giving me the stink eye.

"She gave it to me. I didn't want to hurt her feelings, so I took it. It's not like I hid it in my wallet or anything," I glanced back at Macie. She was looking out of the window and acting as if there were something really interesting going on out there.

Julie slapped the steering wheel. "Wallet, my ass, you don't even have a wallet anymore. That little tomboy has a crush on you!"

I frowned and scoffed. I started staring out of the window as well. "Zach, look at me!"

I did so, but reluctantly. She was glaring at me now.

"Little teenage girls don't go around giving out their picture to just anyone. She's got a thing for you."

I nodded, as if she was telling me something I was totally unaware of. Julie slowed the truck down to a crawl.

"Has she done anything else?" She asked. I scoffed again, but there was no use. I was had. Minimization goes hand-in-hand with lying. I knew better than to lie.

"She kissed me a couple of times," I said quietly. Julie slammed on the brakes.

"Oh my fucking God, Zach! Were you not going to tell me about this?"

I shrugged my shoulders. "I didn't see the big deal. I didn't do anything with her."

It sounded good in my head, but when it came out of my mouth, it sounded more like I was a two-timing weasel who had just been caught.

"Fuck me to hell," Julie said under her breath. She started to drive again. "If you need to sow your wild oats or something, you can sleep with Macie, you know. I won't mind."

Now my mouth dropped open. I hastened a glance back at Macie again. She was still fixated on something outside her window. "What? No! You don't understand."

Julie stopped the truck again. "Explain it to me, Zach. Make me understand why you didn't tell me this from the get-go."

I gesticulated with my hands, hoping it was having a positive effect. "There is nobody else her age in their group she can relate with, and her crazy uncle is molesting her. She's lonely and her self-esteem is probably in the toilet. If I told her I didn't want to kiss her, or refused to accept her picture, how would she feel then?" I sighed.

"I believed, and still believe, she'll be a good ally and source of information. But you're right. I should have told you immediately. I don't know what I was thinking," I said exasperatedly and braced myself. I would have rather faced a few dozen zombies than her wrath.

Julie was staring at me quietly. It was hard to tell what she was thinking from the expression on her face. She took the photograph and looked it over. I thought she was going to tear it up, but instead, she stuck it in between the windshield and the headliner. Now, Andie's picture was prominently displayed. She looked at me again.

"If the little shit thinks she's going to steal you away from me, she's got another think coming." Then she punched me in the arm. Hard. I didn't protest.

"Guys," Macie said from the back seat. "I don't mean to break up this heart-to-heart, but look outside to your right."

I looked. There was a pack of wild dogs running through the neighborhood yards. They were trailing slightly behind us, as if they were following us. They didn't look like normal dogs. These somehow looked different, more feral, and deadlier.

"Stop the truck. I want to see how they react," I said. Julie slowed to a stop. "Okay, wait a few."

I rolled down the window and got the assault rifle ready. The dogs approached and surrounded our truck. These weren't your average neighborhood puppy dogs, they were hunting. They sniffed around a little, and then, as I watched, they started attacking the truck. One of the dogs attacked the mesh covering Macie's window, sinking his fangs in the mesh and trying to rip it out. She let out a frightened yelp.

"Shoot them!" I urged, as I stuck my rifle out of the hole in the hardware cloth and shot the nearest dog. The girls were slow to react, but when I shot, they joined in. We killed five dogs before the rest of the pack ran off. As they ran off into the neighborhood, one of them stopped and looked back. I took aim and was about to shoot, but stopped. I recognized the dog. It was Moe. One of Rick's dogs he found abandoned on the side of the road a couple of years ago. Moe was my buddy. After Rick died, every time I went foraging I took Moe with me. He was with me when I found Julie. Moe stared at me a moment longer before he disappeared behind a house.

Julie saw him as well. "Let's get out of here," she said quietly.

Chapter 16 – Fred

Fred reached checkpoint delta two days after leaving West Memphis. The outskirts of Oklahoma City were an apocalyptic nightmare. It seemed to Fred every street was blocked with wrecked vehicles, makeshift roadblocks and rotting zombies. There were even burned out buildings. Several had been demolished by unknown means. The rubble was scattered everywhere.

Fred was convinced there may have been groups of survivors here and there, as evidenced by the roadblocks, but they seemed to be gone now.

He parked his VW at one of the entry gates to Tinker Air Force Base and got out. He was almost immediately approached by soldiers.

"Identify yourself! A young soldier challenged while brandishing an assault rifle. He could not have been much older than Zach, and as skinny as Zach used to be. He and his comrades were all armed, and the military insignia indicated they were Air Force.

"My name is Fred McCoy. I'm not looking for trouble, I only need a few provisions and I'll be on my way," he said.

"We're a little short on everything, Mister McCoy. What specifically are you looking for?"

"Food, water, maybe some gas; whatever you have to spare," Fred replied.

Sergeant Fandis glanced at his fellow soldiers. "We can spare some water, maybe some MREs. I don't know about fuel. Fuel access is above my pay grade."

"I'd be most grateful to take whatever you can offer and I'll be on my way."

"Where are you going?" one of the soldiers asked.

"Los Angeles," Fred replied.

"What? There's no way, dude! You'll never make it."

"There are others who would agree with you," Fred said plainly.

"Dude, you're fucking crazy," he said.

"Could be," Fred said and looked around. "Are you guys the only ones around here?"

"We've got about a platoon sized unit. We had more, but we've had multiple firefights over the past year. We've lost a lot of soldiers and civilians." His face clouded over.

"There were thousands of them, man," the other soldier said. His fellow soldiers nodded in agreement. All of them looked no older than teenagers.

"You can only imagine. We had defensive positions set up at strategic parts of the city, but there were too many of them, and they don't die when you shoot them. Almost everyone died, or got infected and turned into one of those things." The one who appeared in charge gestured around. "We are the only ones left. We were in the command bunker with General Shoemaker. It took a couple of weeks to shoot enough to regain control, but we haven't got them all." He gestured toward downtown Oklahoma City. "There are thousands more down there, man. You go through there, and you're going to be eaten alive."

Fred looked at his nametag. "Sergeant Fandis?" the young man nodded. "You seem awfully young to be a sergeant."

"General Shoemaker gave me a battlefield promotion. Don't know what good it does, but anyway, I'm a staff sergeant."

Fred looked around. "Anybody here left alive who can fly one of these planes?" He asked.

Sergeant Fandis frowned. "Yeah, Major Fowkes."

"She's a grade-A bitch," the other soldier added, and his comrades quickly voiced their agreement.

Sergeant Fandis pointed. "She lives in an apartment over in the officer's quarters. Are you sure you want to talk to her?" He asked.

Fred nodded. Sergeant Fandis sighed.

"I was afraid of that."

Chapter 17 – The Loss of Moe

It was the time of morning just before dawn, which I'd grown to love. The sky was still dark, but getting lighter. It was called BMNT in military terms, Before Morning Nautical Time. There was enough of a hint of light in the room that I could see Julie's face as she slept. The mixture of light and shadows only enhanced her beauty. I thought about what she had said yesterday in the truck on the way home. I had mixed emotions. There was no way I was going to risk losing her, but I was concerned she was going to tell me to have no further contact with Andie, even though this was probably the best course of action.

I slid out of bed, put some jeans and a tee shirt on, and got a pot of coffee started. I was startled briefly when I felt something nudging my calf. Turning, I was greeted by Curly looking at me sleepily and wagging his tail.

"I bet someone needs to go outside," I whispered as I petted him. His tail thumped the floor in agreement. I shut the door quietly behind us and waited on the porch while Curly sniffed around in the yard, looking for an appropriate spot. Suddenly, the hair stood up on his back. He ran back up on the porch and let out a soft whimper.

"What is it, boy?" I asked as I pulled my handgun out of my waistband. I peered intently into the morning fog. Was it a zombie? I sniffed the morning air, trying to see if I could catch a whiff of distinctive odors. Then I saw it, a coyote. Only, it wasn't a coyote, it was Moe. He was leaner now. His once well brushed coat was dirty and matted. There were fresh scars on his face. I whistled softly.

"Here, Moe, come here buddy," I tried to coax him, but he only responded with a soft growl. He gave me the look he gave me yesterday, and then disappeared into the morning fog. I got some dog food and waited for thirty minutes, but he never reappeared. Curly sat close and leaned against me for comfort. I could feel him shaking. He was scared of his brother for some reason. It was a sad moment. Curly and I went back inside.

"Zach?" Julie called out.

"Down here. I'll be up in a sec," I said. After the encounter with Moe, I started in on the first task for the day, which began in the cellar. It took me another ten minutes before I was finished. I went upstairs to the kitchen and added the wares in the cabinets to my list while the girls prepared breakfast.

"Next time you go foraging, you better find yourself some more notepads," Julie said. Macie giggled. "What are you doing anyway?"

"Updating our food inventory," I said and sat down at the kitchen table. Julie sat a fresh steaming mug of coffee down in front of me. I nodded gratefully.

"Why?" she asked.

"I wanted to get confirmation of what I suspected."

They looked at me, waiting for me to explain.

"We're running out of food," I said. The two of them looked at me in confusion and I explained. "If it were only the three of us, we'd be fine. Especially with the gardens, the rabbits and chickens, cows, etcetera, but we've been contributing food to the Allen family, and are about to start feeding the Eason family. Ten people total. Bottom line, we can't do it. We'll run out of our canned goods before spring," I finished. Julie gasped.

We discussed the dilemma as we ate breakfast.

"Alright, I think we have to agree at this point. We can't continue giving away food. At least, not right now." I stood and stretched. "I'm terribly behind on my chores, so I'll be busy with them most of the day. What are you two going to do?"

"I'm going to ride Prancer, so I thought I'd ride the fence lines and go check on Fred's house," Julie said.

"I'll clean up the house," Macie said.

"It looks like it's going to be a beautiful day. Why don't you get outside? You can work in the gardens. The sunshine will do you some good," I suggested.

"Yeah, girl, you definitely need some sun," Julie added. "I can teach you how to ride Prancer if you like."

"I think I'll stick with the gardening for now," Macie said quietly. Julie and I looked at each other but did not say anything. I got up and kissed Julie. She stood and hugged me.

"Give Macie a kiss, she needs it," she whispered in my ear.

I looked at her questioningly. She motioned with her head. As I walked out, I gave Macie a quick kiss on the top of her head.

It came to me as I finished planting a crop of winter wheat. It was a viable plan, but I needed to meet with the Captain. My watch read eleven. Perfect. I was going to eat a quick lunch and then I'd call the Captain on the radio at noon. I parked the tractor beside the barn and headed toward the house. Macie was sitting on the porch reading a book. She had shorts on and was sunning her freshly shaven legs. She smiled as I walked up.

"How are you feeling?" I asked.

"Pretty good actually. I fed the chickens and rabbits. We had seven eggs, and I've tended the plants in the greenhouse. I think we'll be able to harvest the basil and mint leaves any day now," she said and sighed. "I'm worn out. I'm getting my strength back but I'm definitely not one hundred percent yet."

I nodded. "It'll come back to you." I sat in the rocking chair beside her. "Nice weather today," I commented.

Macie nodded. "Yeah, I wonder what kind of winter we're going to have."

"It's hard to say. If I were to speculate, I'd guess it'll be colder than usual. Mankind's carbon footprint has been significantly reduced, so there should be a noticeable difference."

"Zach, what do you think you would have done for a career, if all of this had not happened?" she asked.

I shrugged. "I don't know. My options were limited. I would have liked to have gone to college to be an engineer. What about you?"

"I wanted to be a nurse," she said, and closed the book. "You know something, Zach, this apocalypse thing was probably the best thing to ever happen to you."

I arched my eyebrows. She chuckled. "You've thrived, Zach. Most people, the ones who have survived, are having a hard time. I guess a good example would be Jason and his friends. They were on top of the world before, but after, we were hungry most of the

time, and miserable." She shook her head. "I was stupid, wasn't
I?"

"Adversity does not build character, it reveals it," I replied
and grinned at her. "I saw that quote on one of those inspirational
posters once."

"Julie and I are two very lucky girls to have a man like you
around," she said, smiling. "And, I'm betting that brain of yours is
figuring out a way to sustain ten or more people through the
winter."

I smiled. "In fact, I am. I think I have an idea, but it's going to
require meeting up with the Captain and getting him on board." I
thought for a minute. "What do you think is lacking around here?"

She thought for a minute. "It would be nice to have friendly
neighbors, like the Allens for example. I think we need to talk
them into moving into one of the vacant houses nearby." She tilted
her head. "I miss the little things we once took for granted. Cheese,
deserts, oh, and let's not forget an occasional glass of wine."

I chuckled. "I believe we've discovered what will be your new
responsibility," I said. "The grape vines we have didn't produce
this year. Perhaps they need some TLC from a pretty blonde girl."

She smiled. I held up a finger as an idea came to me. "It seems
like all of the liquor stores have been looted, but I'm betting if we
go salvaging in some of the rich neighborhoods we'll find a wine
cellar or two."

"That would be so cool," she said. She then reached over,
grabbed my hand, and we shared a quiet moment together.

"Have you seen Julie lately?" I asked.

"She hasn't come back yet."

"Oh. I guess she's having a good time." I looked at my watch.
"Hey, it's right at noon. Let's see if we can make contact with
Fred." We walked inside and Macie sat in front of the HAM radio.
She made several attempts, but there was no response from Fred,
only static. Macie looked at me with worry.

"Do you think he's dead?" she asked.

"I don't know. He's a tough man, but I don't know. Okay,
move over, I'm going to try calling the Captain." She changed the
radio frequency and we swapped seats.

"You don't want me talking to them?" Macie asked.

"Hell no. Neither you nor Julie," I said. I tried calling several times before I received a response.

"Hi, Zach!" Andie's voice came through the radio loud and clear. Macie goosed me.

"She certainly sounds happy to hear your voice," she whispered. I goosed her back and she let out a yelp.

"Hello, Andie. Would you ask the Captain if he would be receptive to a friendly meeting? I have some ideas I want to talk to him about."

"Okay, standby," she said. After a minute, the Captain's voice came over the radio.

"Hello, Zach, it's been a while," he said.

"Yes sir. I've been extremely busy. I'm sure you have as well."

"Indeed I have. What's on your mind?" he asked.

"I'd like to meet with you. I have a few ideas I've been mulling over and I'd like to discuss them with you. I think they could be beneficial for both of us."

There was a long minute of silence. "Okay, Zach," he finally replied. We worked out the details and signed off.

"That wasn't so hard, was it?" Macie asked.

"You never know with him. It may be a friendly meeting, or he may be planning on killing me as soon as he sees me" I stood. "I'm going to grab a snack and get back to the chores."

I was only in the kitchen ten minutes before I was back at it. I worked the rest of the afternoon, lost in my own thoughts. Macie walked up while I was weeding the garden.

"Zach, Julie hasn't shown up yet. I think something may be wrong."

Damn, I had been so absorbed in my own thoughts I had forgotten about her. I looked at my watch.

"Shit, you're right. Go grab a rifle and meet me in the barn."

She hurried inside. I got our ATV started. Macie came in a moment later carrying an AR-15.

"Great, thanks. You might want to wait inside, just in case," I said.

Macie shook her head. "I want to go with you."

Without waiting for me to respond, she jumped on. I hit the throttle. She instinctively grabbed me around the torso and held on.

We found Julie at the far end of the farm sitting under a tree. Prancer was nearby, grazing contentedly. The saddle had flipped and was hanging under her belly.

"My ankle is fucked," Julie lamented. I could see she had been crying. We got off of the ATV and hurried over to her.

"What happened?" Macie asked.

Julie sighed. "A snake spooked Prancer. She reared back and the saddle came loose. I came flying off and my boot stuck in the stirrup. I don't know if it's broken or not."

I looked her over. I saw no injuries other than the swollen ankle and her scuffed hands.

"Okay, let's get you loaded up on the ATV and Macie will drive you back. I'll take care of Prancer."

Julie agreed and we carefully loaded her up on the ATV. I watched the two of them ride away and turned my attention to Prancer.

"Alright girl, if you're nice, I'll give you a couple of carrots when we get back."

I guess she understood, because she calmly let me fix the saddle and took off at a gallop when I mounted her. We were at the barn within minutes. I walked her to cool her down and then gave her a good brushing before going inside. Oh, and she got a couple of carrots, along with a bucket of water.

I found Julie sitting up in the bed reading a book. She had stripped down to a tee shirt and underwear, and her foot was propped up by a pillow.

"How is it feeling?" I asked.

"It's better now. The swelling seems to have gone down," she said.

I looked at it and poked it gently in various places. Julie didn't scream out in pain, which I took as a good sign, but she winced a little and glared at me.

"Yeah, I think you're right. Hopefully it's only a bad sprain." I kissed her ankle before stripping and getting in bed beside her.

"There you go. It's going to be all better now," I said with a grin.

Julie chuckled. "Your kisses go a long way."

"I certainly hope so," I said.

"You didn't notice it, but when you kissed Macie earlier today, she actually blushed."

I frowned. "Why did she blush?"

Julie slapped me playfully on the chest. "Jesus, Zach, for a man who is like a fucking genius, you know nothing about women."

I sighed. "You keep saying that. So edify me, please."

"You don't get it. Women need attention. They need to feel loved. Macie hasn't had anything even close to love in a long time," she scoffed. "You're probably the last person to actually show her any genuine love, back when the two of you were dating. All you have to do is give her a hug occasionally, maybe a kiss, tell her how pretty she is, and you've made her day."

"But, why me?" I asked.

"Because dumbass, you're the only man around." She paused a moment and her tone changed. "Have you thought about sleeping with her?" She asked tentatively.

I carefully rolled over in the bed and looked at her.

"With Macie?" I asked. I watched her as she nodded her head. I suddenly found myself with several spots on my body in need of scratching.

"No, not really," I said. Julie wrinkled her brow at me. "I mean, I guess I've thought about when we were together that one time, but I'm not going to do anything to betray you. I love you too much."

She smiled at me. "I love you too, Zach. I know you won't betray me." She kissed me and buried her head in her pillow. Then she surprised me. "You'd be surprised to know, Macie loves you as well."

Chapter 19 – Dentistry 101

We decided on the location where we had first met. The same spot where Fred and I were forced to abandon the tanker. The first meeting, he was waiting on me. On this occasion, I was waiting on him. Although it appeared I was alone, in fact I had company.

The night before, I prepared a sniper pit very close to the same spot where Fred watched over me during the first meeting. It was near some trees in between two houses with overgrown lawns. I dug a hole in the ground large enough for a one hundred and ten pound girl to lay prostrate in. Macie was dressed in camouflage clothing, complete with strips of burlap rags tied here and there. I had her flaxen blonde hair tucked into a Boonie hat, and her face camouflaged with a combination of earth colors. I also insisted she wear a diaper. Julie would have naturally been my first choice for this endeavor, but her ankle was still too tender to walk on. Macie quickly volunteered when I had talked about it.

"Alright, you have a canteen of water and some energy bars. They're only a few months past their expiration date, but they're still edible. Howard is going to drive up at noon tomorrow. He's going to park right down the road at the burned out house. His instructions are that you'll walk out to meet him at noon, but he is going to wait at least four hours. Do you think you can handle it?" I asked.

"I think so, but I have some questions," Macie said.

"Ask away."

"Okay, let's see. Why are we here six hours before you're meeting him? Why do I have to walk so far to meet up with Howard when I leave? Why am I supposed to keep my walkie-talkie turned off unless there is an emergency? Oh, and let's not forget, why in the world did you insist I wear a diaper?"

"Those are good questions," I replied. "First, we're here early so nobody sees us put you here. Second, you don't want Howard parked close to you. To do so may increase the risk of giving away your position if the Captain has scouts deployed. We don't have headsets for these walkie-talkies, and there is something about the radio's sound which carries a long way, especially at night. We don't want that." I inhaled.

"Now, as for the diaper, at some point you're going to have to go to the restroom. You are not to get out of your hole and go do your business, because if you do, you run the risk of giving away your location. You may not know this, but professional military snipers just go in their pants. They're men after all. A diaper is better."

I let it sink in for a moment before continuing.

"When it's time for you to leave and go to Howard, it won't be a casual stroll. You need to be quiet and sneak your way to him. Oh, and one other thing. If you encounter zombies, make sure they're actually onto you and not simply walking on by. If your life is in danger, start shooting, I'll come." I looked at her in the darkness.

"Anything else?" I asked. She shook her head and sighed.

"I can't think of anything," she said. I reached out and grabbed her by the shoulders.

"I'm putting my life in your hands. You're a great shot. If I didn't think you could do it, I'd have left you at home," I said. Macie nodded. I was trying to think of anything I had forgotten, and remembered what Julie told me last night.

"You look really cute in camouflage," I said playfully, then leaned forward and kissed her on the cheek. The truth was I could hardly see her in the dark.

"I'll do the best I can, Zach." There was apprehension in her voice. I nodded.

"In you go," I said. She crawled into the spider hole and lay prostrate. I covered her with tree limbs and other debris.

I parked at the meeting spot and tried to grab a couple of hours of sleep, but the stress of the impending meeting prevented it. Instead, I sat there in the dark, thinking about our lives, and found myself thinking of Macie lying out there in a hole by herself. I admitted to myself I was growing fond of her and was a little worried about leaving her out there alone.

The sunrise caused the dew to extract itself out of the ground in a morning mist. It was going to be a nice day. I hoped Macie was not too chilled. The Captain was very punctual and drove up promptly at six. And he was alone, or so it appeared. I stood as he got out of his truck. He was carrying some type of pouch in one hand and a folding chair in the other.

"Good morning, Zach. How are you?" He greeted me in his baritone voice.

"I'm doing well, Captain, how about yourself?" We shook hands. He unfolded the chair and sat down.

"Quite frankly, Zach, I am not doing well and I believe I need your help."

I looked at him questioningly. "I have a toothache. I want you to have a look at it." He opened the pouch. It looked like a dentist's kit. "Would you do me the honor, good sir?"

"You want me to look at the tooth? In your mouth?" I asked with no small amount of trepidation. He nodded.

"Okay. Uh, hang on a second." I went to my truck and retrieved some waterless disinfectant along with a mini flashlight. The Captain watched as I squirted the gel on my hands and rubbed it in.

"You see?" he said. "I knew you were the correct person to entrust in this. I don't think any of my crew would of thought of disinfecting their hands."

"Yeah, well they've not been trained properly then." I turned on the flashlight. "Alright, lean your head back and open wide." The Captain obeyed.

"Which tooth is it?" I asked. He pointed at the back on his right side. I used one of those little mirrors first. I saw a distinct dark spot in the middle of a molar and used a probe to poke it. The Captain jerked and grunted.

"Yeah, I'm pretty sure it's a cavity. Judging from the swollen state of the gums around it, I'd say it's infected too," I declared.

"What do you recommend?" The Captain asked when I pulled my hand out of his mouth.

I sat back down. "Well, sir, a dentist would inject your gum with Novocain. Then he or she, would drill out the cavity and fill it with silver amalgam."

"And if there is no dentist available?" he asked.

"From what I've read, back in the old days, they'd take a pair of pliers and pull the tooth out. Of course, the patient would be drunk or would have ingested a healthy dose of laudanum beforehand."

The Captain frowned and nodded. "I see. Let's defer the topic of my tooth for now. Tell me what your ideas are."

I enumerated with my fingers. "Crop production, cattle production, trade."

The Captain looked me over. "Explain."

"First, there is a lot of land here in this area which is not being farmed. We, and I use 'we' in the vernacular, need to farm this land and sow crops. The overage can be distributed, bartered, or stored in silos. I believe, in the long run, this will help abate any possible food shortages. I don't know about you and your group, but my group is going to be hard pressed this winter." I took a breath and casually looked around.

"Second, there are stray cattle roaming all around. They need to be rounded up and tended to before they're killed off by coyotes and these feral dog packs I've been seeing. This is a very good source of food and trade, which leads to the third idea I have. I think we should set up a trading post. We're inevitably going to have a good harvest of some crops and a shortage of other crops. You may have an abundance of cattle, and I may have an abundance of vegetables. This is where a neutral trading post will be beneficial. You and I both know there are other survivors out there. A central meeting place will establish networks with these people." I sat down in my chair. "I have a comprehensive plan all written out if you'd like to see it," I said.

The Captain looked at me somberly. He was wearing a tight fitting olive drab tee shirt today. His muscles bulged underneath.

"Zach, I have been thinking exactly along the very same lines."

I doubted it, but nodded in agreement anyway. "Much like a Greek agora perhaps?" he asked.

"Yes sir, exactly. A trading hub is much more than just a trading hub, as you well know. When people get together, they talk, and when they talk, they give out information. A trading hub is considered a cornerstone in a basic society. At the moment, we're nothing more than a couple of small bands. We need to expand and grow."

"Did you have a location in mind?"

I shrugged. "There are several possibilities. We want a trading hub close to our respective homes, but accessible to others. I say we go with a pre-existing building, maybe a truck stop. A large parking lot would be beneficial. People would come and camp out. We'll need to harden the building of course."

"Yes, I see where you're going with this. It would be a community gathering place, so you'll need plenty of room," he said.

I nodded. "We start with something small and build from there. We can do it, Captain, if we work together." The Captain nodded while holding his jaw. It was obvious he was in pain.

"Zach, I have this scenario in my head where you and I spend many an evening around the fire, enjoying a fine glass of cognac, and having many interesting philosophical discussions." He leaned forward and lowered his voice. "The people in my group, they're fine people, hard workers, but dumber than rocks." He leaned back.

"When I was a younger man, I worked part time at a convalescent home. It was shitty work for the most part but there was this one highly decorated World War Two veteran. He was a most interesting man. The stories he had!" The Captain stared off into space wistfully.

"So, you and I are about to embark on a great journey in which we rebuild society. In the meantime, what do you recommend I do about my tooth?"

I shrugged. "Take someone you trust, Andie perhaps, go to a dentist's office, and use the equipment to fix it." I pointed at my own mouth. "There is a risk factor of course. If it were easy, dentists wouldn't have to go through so much schooling."

"Zach, there is nobody else, what should I do?" he asked.

I shrugged again. "There's no dentist anywhere around, as far as we know. I'll take my Leatherman tool and pull it out if you want. The extent of my experience is a video I once saw in the Internet. I imagine it will be very painful."

He looked at me. "Do it."

The Captain grunted a few times, but never once cried out in pain. It was impressive. I worked the tooth with my pliers for several minutes before it dislodged. After I extracted it, I packed the hole in his gum with Neosporin and gauze. He looked at my work with a small mirror, inspected the rotten tooth, and nodded in gratitude.

We said our goodbyes and drove away at the same time. I drove a short distance, stopped, turned my radio on, and waited. Howard called me approximately forty minutes later. I answered immediately.

"Do you have Macie?" He answered in the affirmative. I was relieved she was okay and headed home. They were waiting for me when I arrived.

"What in the world were you doing to him?" Macie asked. Howard and Julie looked at Macie questioningly.

"I'm watching them through the rifle scope, and before I know it, Zach is bent over him and has a pair of pliers in the Captain's mouth. It was weird looking."

"I have discovered a skill I didn't know I had," I said smiling and explained what I did. They looked at me incredulously.

"And he didn't scream out in pain or anything?" Howard asked. I shook my head.

"Damn," he said in amazement, and then looked at his watch. "You guys need me for anything else? I'd kind of like to get going." I extended my hand and we shook.

"Howard, you've been more than helpful. Tell Lashonda and the boys hello for us. Oh, I think Julie has a care package made up for you."

Julie limped as she walked into the kitchen and returned with an assortment of vegetables and herbs fresh from the greenhouse.

We stood on the porch and waved as Howard drove off. "Zach, I think you owe me a hot bath." Macie asserted. I readily agreed.

Chapter 20 – Fred

Fred saw her as they walked down the road. She was in front of her apartment on the sidewalk performing an endless series of calisthenics. Fred also noted she was clad only in nylon shorts, running shoes, and an athletic bra.

"That's Major Fowkes," Sergeant Fandis said softly. "She'll probably cuss us or something. She doesn't seem to like anyone."

"I can hear you, Sergeant," she said as she finished fifty push-ups and stood. Sergeant Fandis saluted when she stood, which she ignored. She was lean and muscular. Fred could not help but notice her taut and defined abs. Her hair was cut short and tied back in a very small ponytail. Her features were sharp. She'd never win any beauty contests, but still, Fred thought of her as attractive. If she let her hair grow out, and perhaps some makeup, he saw possibilities. He could not tell how old she was She could have been anywhere from early thirties to late forties.

"What are you gawking at, cowboy?" she asked roughly.

Fred took off his hat. "I apologize, ma'am. Sergeant Fandis here says you are a Major. I guess I was expecting you to be all spit and polish, and in uniform."

She stared at Fred coolly. "Who the hell is this man, Sergeant Fandis, and why did you bring him to me? Are you trying to play matchmaker or something?"

"Oh, no ma'am. I'd never do such a thing, trust me," Sergeant Fandis said, to which she responded with a harsh glare. "I've got somewhere I have to be, Fred. I'll come back and get you in a few." He quickly saluted and ran off before Major Fowkes could say anything.

"Alright, start with your name," she ordered.

"Fred McCoy."

"Where are you from, Fred, and why are you here, bothering me?" She asked as she wiped the sweat off of her face.

"I'm recently from Tennessee. I'm trying to find my daughter. The young sergeant said you're the only pilot left. I want to know if it would be possible for you to fly me to Los Angeles."

Major Fowkes looked at Fred with incredulity and chortled. "You got some balls cowboy," she finished wiping the sweat off, tossed the towel to Fred, and walked inside.

Fred followed after a moment and walked in as she put a tee shirt on. The apartment was Spartan in appearance and furnishings. It looked more like a college dorm room to Fred, without any posters or photographs. There were two beds with desks and wall lockers on the end. There was one bathroom with a sink, toilet, and shower. It did not appear there was any electricity or running water.

"What's your daughter doing in California?" she asked. Fred calmly explained while wondering what to do with the towel.

"So, let me get this straight," the Major said as she started mixing a protein drink with water from a canteen. "Your darling little girl thought she wanted to be the next superstar actress, headed out to Los Angeles, and you've not heard from her since the world went to hell?" Fred nodded. "That's been over eighteen months ago, cowboy. She's dead or a zombie by now. You know that, right?"

"Do you have any children, Major?" Fred asked quietly. She arched an eyebrow and scowled. "Betsy is my only child," he continued. "She's the only family I have left. For the past year, I've been asking myself what kind of a father am I to not go find her. It's something I've got to try."

"Los Angeles is a big town, cowboy. Do you even know where to look?"

"All I have is the address of her apartment."

"You're fucking crazy, you know that?" she asked rhetorically.

Fred draped the towel across the back of a folding chair beside the door. "Probably. Would you be willing to fly me out there? You don't have to stay. I can find my way back."

Major Fowkes finished her drink and set it down. "Fred, you're totally wrong on this one."

"Am I? What would *your* father do?" Fred countered.

"Leave my fucking father out of this!" She suddenly shouted.

Fred looked at the floor, and slowly put his cowboy hat back on. "I apologize for troubling you. I'll find my way back to the sergeant," Fred walked out and was half a block away when he heard someone running up from behind. He stopped and waited for her.

"You're going to try to drive all the way there, aren't you," she phrased it as a statement rather than a question.

"Yep," Fred responded, and then added. "I've made it a thousand miles already. So, I only have a thousand more to go. Unless you know of another pilot around here I could talk to, it looks like I'm going to have to drive."

She sighed and shook her head. "Let's go talk to General Shoemaker."

Chapter 21 – Winter

Winter is supposed to officially begin on the twenty-first of December, the day when the sun is furthest from the planet. Someone didn't get the memo. On the morning of the tenth, the rain began. As the sun set, it turned into an ice storm. It lasted most of the night.

We awoke the next morning to everything coated in a thick layer of ice. I've seen beautiful paintings and pictures of a frozen landscape, with glistening icicles hanging from tree limbs and waterways covered in a shiny sheet of ice. In reality, ice can destroy trees as easily as fire, lightning, or pestilence. It sure did a number on our radio antenna.

We had a few sunny days after, but it was a two-edged sword. The ice would melt a little bit, and then refreeze at night. On the fourteenth, it snowed. Beautiful, heavy snow flakes, almost eight inches worth; not a great deal in the northern states, but quite a lot in Tennessee. The three of us gazed out of the window, looking at the snow-covered fields.

"We're most definitely snowbound," Julie said. I nodded. "I wonder how everyone else is doing,"

"I hope they're okay," Macie replied.

"Yeah, me too. I'm curious how the zombies who are outside are faring. I bet they're frozen solid," I speculated, and retrieved a notepad.

"We should try to go see Bernie and the Allens," Macie suggested.

I shook my head. "When I tried to get out yesterday, there were several trees across the roads and there is a thick coat of ice under the snow." I looked at the girls. "It's too risky to travel right now. We're stuck here."

Macie groaned. "Cabin fever, here we come."

She was right. The first few days we spent all day rounding up the cattle and their newborn. As usual, the change in barometric pressure caused a lot of births. There were eight calves altogether. Julie made an offhanded comment about the only male getting around more than me was our bull.

Other than tending to our livestock and the greenhouse, we passed our off time by having contests of disassembling weapons and putting them back together. I had the three of us practice house clearing drills until they begged me to stop. When the sun went down, we either played cards or read to each other by lamplight.

By the beginning of the second week, we were getting quite bored and irritable. We had built as many snowmen as we cared to, and the snowball fights were getting old. We discussed our options one evening after we had finished dinner.

"We've had a couple of sunny days. Maybe the snow is melting and we can go for a ride," Macie speculated. "What do you think, Zach?"

"The temperature has stayed at or below freezing, so the roads probably haven't thawed out very much. We're stuck here a few more days I'd say. Maybe tomorrow, after we feed the animals, we can try to fix the radio antenna or even get out and saw up some of the fallen trees. The first day it's decent, we'll try to go visit."

Julie sighed. "So what do we do in the meantime?" She asked nobody in particular.

Macie raised her hand. "I know!" she jumped up and went to the cupboard. Julie and I looked at each other questioningly. She closed the door and turned around with a bottle of whiskey.

"Where did you find that?" I asked, pointing at the bottle.

"It was hidden behind some junk on a shelf in the barn," she replied with a grin. I laughed. Rick probably had bottles of whiskey hidden in all kinds of places.

"Oh, I've got one more thing." She opened another cabinet and retrieved a package of stale Twinkies. She took one out, and put a small, well used candle in the center of it.

"So, what is the occasion?" I asked as she lit it.

Macie looked at me as if I already knew. "We've totally forgotten your birthday."

Julie gasped and looked at me. I shrugged.

"When was your birthday, Zach?"

"Last month," I said. I turned seventeen in November. I shrugged again. "It's no big deal." I leaned forward and blew out my candle.

"Oh, my God!" she exclaimed. "I had totally forgotten. I am so sorry."

"I'm sorry too, Zach," Macie said. "Please forgive us."

I held my hands out. "All is forgiven if you give me one of those Twinkies. Besides, we have something more to celebrate."

They again looked at me curiously. I took the bottle of whiskey, Jack Daniels black label, and poured a shot into three glasses. At my cue, the three of us held up our glasses.

"Here's to Christmas Eve," both of them opened their mouths in a silent O. I chuckled and took a sip of my drink. They followed.

"Holy shit, I've totally lost track of the days," Julie said, and sipped some more.

"Me too," Macie said. She downed her whiskey and choked. "This shit is strong," she coughed out. We laughed at her as I stood up.

"Okay. Before it gets too dark out, I have something in the barn I need to get. I'll be right back." Julie started to say something. I held up a finger. "It's a surprise."

I walked back in a minute later carrying a large cardboard box. I set it down and took off my jacket.

"What's in the box?" Julie asked.

I smiled. "Why it's filled with Christmas presents."

The two of them gasped in unison. I set it down, away from their prying eyes.

"I believe I'll have another taste of whiskey." I held up my glass expectantly. Macie quickly poured and I smiled appreciatively.

"Why don't you two sit on the couch, I'll get some wood on the fire, and we'll get started."

They sat down and Julie lit a couple of candles. I dragged the old wingback chair close to the coffee table.

"Okay, the first presents are," I reached into the box, "sports bras and socks." I smiled as their faces lit up and reached for them.

"I'm pretty sure I've gotten the correct sizes. Oops, uh-oh. We've forgotten a tradition. Every time you get a present, you have to take a sip." They readily obeyed. Macie did not cough this time.

"Okay, second present," and on it went. I had stocked up on several female items when Howard and I cleared the Walmart of its stinking guardians. They oohed and aahed every time I pulled something out, whether it was a bottle of shampoo, bras and panties, or a box of tampons. By the time I was down to the last of the presents, the girls were giggling drunk. I was pretty lubricated as well.

"And now, for the semi-grand finale," I announced, and pulled out two pairs of pajamas, the kind with footies and drawings of cartoon characters on them.

"Oh, these are awesome!" Macie exclaimed as she held them up. Julie giggled.

"What, you didn't get us any makeup?" Julie asked after taking another sip of whiskey. "I'm joking, I'm joking. Thank you for all of the presents, sweetheart," she said and blew me a kiss.

I smiled pleasantly. "There is no need for makeup anymore."

Julie started to protest but I held my hand up. "However, never let it be said I'm not learning a little bit about women." I reached into the box and pulled out a small, travel makeup case. They smiled appreciatively.

"And, one more final present for you two. I imaging you'd want to wait until it's a little bit warmer before wearing these." I pulled out two black nighties.

"Now bear in mind, they're from Walmart and not Victoria's secret," I said. The two of them gasped. Julie got up and grabbed me in a hug. Macie followed suit. Julie then grabbed the makeup case and some of the other items.

"Okay, big boy, you stay in here," Julie ordered. "Macie and I are going to fix ourselves up."

Macie smiled and followed Julie into the bedroom, but not before grabbing the nighties and grinning at me. I put another log on the fire before sitting back and enjoying some more Jack Daniels. It had a pleasant burning sensation as it went down my throat. I heard them talking and giggling as I pulled my boots off and placed them beside the door.

They came out twenty minutes later. Both of them had their faces made up, and they were wearing the black nighties, the new panties, and nothing else. I had to admit they looked very seductive and hoped my ogling was not obvious. They giggled as they sat down on the couch across from me.

"Do you like?" Julie asked. I must admit I did. Very much. I stammered out a yes. Macie refilled our glasses.

"Let's do something." She looked at us mischievously. "How about a drinking game?" Julie bounced up and down in agreement, which caused her breasts to jiggle under the nightie.

"Okay, but I can't drink anymore. I'm pregnant remember?" She burst out laughing at her own joke.

"I know," she said, "we can play truth or dare," Macie readily agreed. "You first Zach, truth or dare?" Julie challenged.

And so it started. The three of us, snowed in, each suffering from cabin fever, a bottle of alcohol, a crackling fire, soft candlelight, two gorgeous teenage girls sitting there wearing nothing but nighties and a smile. The rest was entirely predictable.

I was the first one to wake up the next morning. The three of us were an entanglement of arms, legs, nighties, and blankets. My bladder was begging in protest and my head was throbbing. I took care of the bladder first, swallowed some aspirin, and found some of my clothes in the den. Managing to get them on, I went outside and turned the generator on. I sat quietly in the den until I felt the water was hot enough, and then snuck into the shower.

I didn't regret what had happened. Hell, from what I could remember, I had the time of my life. Still, for some reason, I felt guilty. As I let the spray work on my pounding head, I sensed someone getting in the shower behind me, followed by a pair of hands rubbing my back. I turned around and faced Julie. She let the spray hit her in the face, got a mouth full of water, and spit it on my chest.

"I've got a bad case of cock breath," she said. I couldn't help but laugh, which was not conducive to helping my headache. Julie laughed too, and then groaned. "Oh, I've forgotten how bad a hangover feels. We should give up alcohol and only smoke weed when we want to party." She took the soap out of my hand and began lathering me up. When she was finished, she gave the soap back to me.

"My turn," she said. I returned the favor. "Did you have a good time last night?" She asked.

"I must admit I did. What I can remember of it anyway." I looked at her. "So, why do I feel guilty?"

Julie scoffed as she rinsed off. "Because deep down, you're still an old fashioned guy." She turned around, pulled my head down, and kissed me. "Let me help you ease your troubled mind. We're together now, the three of us. One day it may change. In the meantime, you've got us and we have you."

I leaned my head down to Julie's ear. "But I love you. I don't love Macie."

Julie scoffed. "You could have fooled me the way you were last night." She grinned at me and nudged me out of the shower. "I'm going to wash my hair. Wake Macie up and tell her to get in here."

Chapter 22 – Fred

Fred and Major Fowkes were escorted into the General's office by a slender black man wearing thick horn-rimmed glasses. He bore the rank of a Senior Master Sergeant. Major Fowkes stopped in front of a desk occupied by an older bald man looking out of his window. She came to attention and rendered a salute.

"Sir!" she said, all the while holding the salute. The General did not turn.

"At ease, Major," he said, before swiveling in his chair and facing them.

General Shoemaker was in his late fifties, with clear blue eyes augmented by wire-framed glasses. With the exception of the hair growing out of his ears, he was clean-shaven, including his head. He stood briefly and shook Fred's hand before returning to his seat.

"Welcome to Tinker. I'm General Thomas Shoemaker," he said. Fred shook his outstretched hand.

"Fred McCoy. It's pleasure to meet you."

"Are you a citizen of Oklahoma City?" the General asked.

"No sir, I'm from Tennessee,"

The General widened his eyes in surprise. "Oh? All the way from Tennessee, you say? What brings you out here?"

Before Fred explained, Major Fowkes jumped in. "He's on his way to Los Angeles to try to find his daughter. He wants me to fly him."

General Shoemaker eyed them both before responding. "Tell me, Mister McCoy, how is Tennessee?"

"About the same as it is here. There are a lot of dead people, a lot of those infected people wandering around, and a few survivors. There was a National Guard Barracks in south Nashville, but they had a mutiny of some sort. Some of the soldiers were killed as a result, and a lot of them were killed fighting the zombies."

"Ah yes, zombies. It seems to be a popular term to describe them." He turned and pointed out of the window. "At one time, Tinker was home to the 72nd Air Base Wing. The number of our personnel was well over ten thousand. Now, all that is left is twenty-two people, five of whom are civilians."

He swiveled and looked back out of his window. "There was a mass infection of our personnel. Several people died in an attempt to contain them. Then, we sadly realized it was better to kill them, which we did. But, there were too many. Hordes of them would come on post. They never slept, and there were no discernable tactics. They simply – came." He turned back around and faced us.

"We realized later of course they were attracted to the lights, and the noise of the aircraft, so I ordered them grounded. We also lost a lot of lives before we realized shooting them center mass was a wasted effort." He leaned forward. "You have to kill the brain. That is what is infected, the brain."

"Yes sir, we learned that as well," Fred said. General Shoemaker leaned back in his chair and studied Fred.

"The very first thought I had when Major Fowkes said you wanted a plane ride was the cost of the fuel. Aviation fuel is very expensive and I am…was responsible for the operating costs of the base." He rocked in his chair with his hands forming a steeple in front of his face. Finally, he looked over at the Major.

"What do you think, Major Fowkes?" he asked.

"The odds are pretty good his daughter is dead, or worse. But, we've not conducted any aerial reconnaissance since you grounded me, sir," she said.

"You're itching to get some flying in," the General commented.

"We have a C130 set up with video surveillance equipment. It has an auxiliary fuel tank in the cargo hold, so we'll have enough range. Also, the GPS satellites are still online. We might gather some good intel." She glanced over at Fred. "Besides, the fuel is going to go bad eventually. We may as well use it while we can, sir."

General Shoemaker swiveled in his chair and resumed staring out the window. "File a flight plan with the Master Sergeant. Give me a briefing when you return, Major. Dismissed."

Chapter 23 – A New Year

We encountered over twenty trees across the roads leading to Bernie's house. We started with handsaws in order to minimize noise, but there were too many. Reluctantly, we resorted to chainsaws. Otherwise, it would have taken a week to clear them all. We cleared the last tree about a tenth of a mile from Bernie's house.

As I suspected, the noise of the chainsaws attracted some zombies. Not many, only five. They moved so slowly it was easy to forget how deadly they could be.

"Who wants to try their hand with a machete?" I asked.

"I will!" Macie said. She took the machete and approached the one leading the pack. He appeared to be a middle aged, diminutive man, wearing jeans and a flannel shirt. She raised the machete in the air, and brought it down in a tomahawk chop on the top of his head. He dropped to the street.

"It's stuck!" she shouted when she could not pull the machete free. The other zombies closed in on her. She yelped and ran back toward us. I laughed and took out the rest of them with my revolver. We dragged them to the side of the road, got a fire going and stood there, watching them burn

"I'm not used to this manual labor," Macie lamented. "My arms are going to be so sore and I have two blisters." She rubbed them tenderly. Julie concurred. I chuckled.

"I think we caught a lucky break. There have been very few zeds in this neck of the woods, nothing like downtown Nashville."

The girls nodded in agreement with my observation.

"The good thing about it, we're going to have plenty of firewood," then I added a comment, "Besides, I don't want my girls to be wimps with toothpick sized arms. This is a good workout." I got a couple of groans in response.

There were wisps of smoke curling out of the chimney of Bernie's house as we approached. I pointed.

"That's a good sign," I said. Bernie met us at the door as we got out of the truck. He did not look very well. His overalls were hanging loosely on his scrawny frame and they had the appearance of not being cleaned since last summer. He grinned at us with toothless gums as we walked up.

"My gums are hurting too bad to wear my dentures," he explained. I nodded. He was displaying symptoms of nutrition deficiency.

"Have you been sick, Bernie?" Macie asked.

"I have been feeling unfavorable of late," he said before he was wracked with a coughing fit. The three of us looked at each other.

Macie put on a cheerful smile. "Bernie, you and Zach sit down and get caught up. Julie and I will cook up a hot lunch."

"That would be most appreciated, Miss Macie," Bernie said. He walked into his den, shoved some bric-a-brac out of the way, and sat heavily on his couch. It seemed to take the wind out of him. His breathing was coming in phlegm filled, erratic pants. The winter had taken a toll on him.

I looked at him quizzically. "How old are you, Bernie?" I asked.

"I'll be eighty-seven on my next birthday." He paused a minute, as if searching for an elusive memory. "What month is this?" he finally asked.

"It's January," I replied. He looked at me as if surprised, and then nodded. I wondered if he even knew what year it was.

We said our goodbyes and left after lunch.

"Bernie wasn't looking so good," I commented.

"You didn't see the kitchen," Julie said. "It was disgusting. His cleaning habits are even worse than before."

We talked about him as we made our way to the Allen's residence. Every so often, I'd have to stop due to a tree lying in the roadway. We'd get the chainsaws out, cut enough of the tree to move it out of the roadway, drive a few miles, and repeat the process. It was slow going, and took over an hour to make it to the tire shop. Lil' H and Derry ran outside to greet us as we drove up.

"Holy shit, you two are growing quick!" I exclaimed. We all took turns hugging. Howard and Lashonda met us at the door and we all hugged again.

"I brought some steaks," I said cheerfully and brought the cooler in.

"Oh, those look good, Zach," Howard said when I opened the cooler. "We're getting low on meat. Lil' H killed a deer last week and we've done a lot of fishing. If it wasn't for that, we'd have turned vegetarian by now." I laughed.

"You sure are in a good mood. What's got into you?" The two girls burst out in laughter. Derry interrupted when he came running inside.

"Daddy, we got zombies again!" he shouted. Howard and I looked at each other.

"We get about one or two a day," Howard said. "They don't move so well. We had a few of them wandering around when the ice storm hit. They were frozen solid." He pointed outside. "They were standing like statues out in the middle of Old Hickory. It was kind of funny looking. Then, one day they were up and gone. I guess they came back to life when they thawed out."

"Let's go take a look at them," I said. We went outside and Derry pointed them out. There were three of them slowly moving down Nolensville Pike. I got my twenty-two revolver and approached them. Howard and Lil' H followed with rifles in hand.

"Let me do the shooting with this gun. It's a lot quieter."

They nodded in agreement. They were three men of indeterminate age. When I got to within thirty feet of them, I could hear their breathing. It sounded like a phlegmatic embrace of two pieces of sandpaper. They were nothing more than rotting skin hanging loosely over their skeleton. Their eyes were a cloudy blackish color. They turned toward me as I approached. I swear they could see me with those weird eyes. I tried circling them. As I sidestepped, they would turn toward me, and struggle to close the distance. Howard, who was standing several feet away, coughed. They immediately turned toward him. So, they could still hear too.

Okay, enough playing, I thought. I took aim and shot each one in the head. When I was sure they were dead, I walked up close to them. The group, except Lashonda, followed suit.

"Did you see how they acted? They can still see and hear," Julie said.

I looked at them carefully. "The eyes definitely look different from what I've seen before."

While we were standing in the street looking them over, I saw Macie cock her head.

"I hear something," she said.

"I do too," Derry added.

The noise was faint at first, but then it became obvious it was a motor vehicle of some sort. Then it came into view. A vehicle was approaching.

After a second, I recognized it. "I believe that's Andie's jeep," I asserted. She wasn't alone. "The Captain is with her."

"What should we do?" Lashonda asked.

"If you want to take the boys inside, I'd understand," I replied. "I'm going to say hello."

Lashonda agreed and hurried her two sons inside as the jeep approached.

There were four of them. Andie was driving, and there was no mistaking the Captain's burly frame in the passenger seat. There were also two men sitting in the back. I waved as they approached. The Captain exited the jeep last and stood there with an air of owning the entire intersection. Andie stood quietly while taking turns looking at Julie and Macie.

"Hello Captain, Andie. This is a pleasant surprise." I welcomed them with false cheerfulness. It was a lie. I never wanted any of these people to see the girls. I walked toward him and shook his hand. As expected, he squeezed my hand hard enough to let me know he could break it if he wanted.

"Zach, it is so good to see you," he replied warmly with a broad smile. I couldn't tell if the emotion was genuine or superficial.

I turned my attention to the other two men and looked them over. They were scrawny runts in their early twenties, unshaven, rough looking. They looked like blue-collar workers who had gone straight to the bar after a long workweek, tied one on, and then fell asleep in the gutter. I held my hand out.

"I'm Zach Gunderson." The two of them ignored my outstretched hand, brushed by me, and headed straight toward the girls.

"Well, well, well!" the taller of the two of them said. "You two sure are some fine looking fillies. My name is Barry and this is my cousin Eli." He held his hand out to Julie. Julie wrinkled her nose.

"You smell like shit. Get away from me," she demanded. His smile was instantly replaced with confusion, which then quickly turned to an ugly scowl.

"You better learn some fucking respect," he snarled.

Julie's hand lingered by her sidearm. "I have no respect for you. Now get away from me and take your little inbred cousin with you."

Now the two of them were scowling at Julie. Eli, sensing he was the better charmer, tried his tact with Macie.

"Hi! What's your name?" he asked her.

Macie rolled her eyes. "Not interested."

Barry, with his freshly bruised ego, was not finished. "I'm going to teach you some manners bitch," he growled as he stepped toward Julie. His hand was raised as if he was going to backhand her. My hand went for my sidearm. Julie was just as quick. She had hers out in a flash. Fred would have been proud. Barry froze when she pointed the barrel at his groin.

"You wouldn't dare shoot me. Don't you know who we are?" he said menacingly. His hand was slowly moving toward his own sidearm.

The Captain and I were standing together, approximately ten feet away. I glanced at him and then at Andie. He had a small amused smile. Andie was staring intensely at Julie. I think she was secretly hoping they'd kill each other.

"If Julie doesn't shoot him, Captain, I will. I'm asking you to tell your men to stand down."

He glanced at me and frowned. He then smiled amicably and let loose with a loud whistle.

"Mind yourself, Barry," he said loudly. "Zach here is liable to tan your hide if you keep messing with his women."

They stopped immediately at the Captain's command. He walked over to Julie and Macie while I cast a baleful stare at Barry. He returned my glare and spit on the ground.

"Please accept my apologies," the Captain said to Julie. "The boys have been cooped up since that bad ice storm. This is the first time we've gotten out of the compound. We've all been going stir crazy. Right, Barry?"

He spat again before answering. "Yeah, don't mind me," he grumbled as he stared balefully at Julie.

"Everybody calls me the Captain. I believe we've never met," the Captain said as he smiled amicably and held an outstretched hand to Julie. Julie shook his hand reluctantly.

"I'm Julie, this is Macie. Let's clear the air right away. Zach may like you, but I don't." She glanced at Barry. "Especially now that I see the company you keep."

Before the Captain could respond, Julie jerked her hand back and walked over toward Andie. I watched curiously. Well okay, I watched nervously.

"You must be Andie." Julie held out her hand. Andie shook it tentatively. "Macie and I were talking about going shopping over at the Walmart. Do you want to come with us?" She looked over at the Captain, and then me. "Girls only," she said pointedly. Andie glanced over at me again. I nodded slightly.

"Okay," she said.

"We're taking the truck," Julie said and the three of them drove off a moment later without waiting for an answer.

"She's certainly – feisty," the Captain commented.

"Yep," I said, and immediately realized it was the same word I had used when describing her to Andie. I wondered if Andie was telling the Captain about our meetings. "Captain, let's take a look at these zombies. I'm seeing something different."

We walked over and I pointed out the eyes. "Have any of you guys seen zombies with eyes like these?" I reached down, and with my knife gently opened the eyelids of one of them. The Captain crouched down beside me.

"I've not seen this," he looked up at his companions. "Boys, how about it?" They each shook their head. "Is it some type of decomposition, Zach?"

"If it is, it's like nothing I've seen before. Oh, this reminds me. When the girls get back, I have a journal I found on the night we made the fuel run. You might find it interesting. The man who wrote it actually opened up a zombie's skull and inspected the brain. He described it as an onyx black color."

"Oh, yeah? It certainly sounds like an interesting read." He looked at the eyes a moment longer before standing. "Andie has tried to raise you on the radio frequently."

I searched his face for any hidden, double entendre. He looked at me plainly, awaiting an answer. "The ice storm destroyed our radio antenna. I've not yet replaced it. I checked a nearby Radio Shack, but no luck. I was hoping to spot one on a business or home and salvage it. Otherwise, I'll have to make a trip further into Nashville."

"I see," he said. Howard brought out some folding chairs when we walked back.

"I thought we'd sit outside and enjoy this sunny weather," he said, and then looked at the Captain. "Unless, or course, you want to go inside."

The Captain waved him off. "Outside is fine. We can soak up some of the rays, replenish our vitamin D." He sat and smiled pleasantly.

The Captain made himself comfortable and then looked at me pleasantly. "You have seemingly become acquaintances with Howard and his family,"

"Yes sir, we have become very close friends," I said.

"Have you met any other friends?" he asked after a moment.

"We've encountered a few people, how about you?" I asked.

He nodded. "One or two, nobody of note." He looked around. "It is a rather pleasant day out, Howard. Do you think the weather is turning?"

"I'd say it's a false spring," Howard replied. "We have a few more weeks of cold weather coming, I'm thinking."

The Captain looked at him and nodded thoughtfully.

"What crops do you plan on growing this spring, Captain?" I asked.

"We're going to grow seed corn for the cattle and sweet corn for the dinner table. We're going to be making several individual plots for various vegetables. We've got to replenish our stores and then of course we need to build up an ample supply for trading purposes," he looked at me as if he needed affirmation.

"Excellent planning, Captain," I answered. He grinned broadly, his walrus moustache twitching in delight.

*****

"Zach and Howard cleared the store of zombies, but we'll still need to be careful," Julie said.

"Can you two shoot?" Andie asked.

"Oh, yeah. Zach taught us both," Julie responded.

"The Captain taught me," Andie said. "He's a crack shot."

Julie nodded, and stored that factoid for later when she'd tell Zach. She drove up to the front entrance and stopped. She tapped the horn, waited a few seconds, and tapped it again.

"Why'd you do that?" Andie asked.

Macie laughed. "Rule number two."

Andie looked confused. "They're attracted to noise. If there are any in there, they'll come toward the noise." Macie held a hand up. "Well, if the nasty shits can still walk." The three of them laughed. "Is there anything you want to shop for, Andie?"

Andie squirmed. "I need some things. You know."

Julie and Macie looked at each other with understanding. "Us too. Let's grab a shopping cart and head to the women's section."

They loaded up on what was left of the feminine hygiene products. "We'll split this all up. I've no idea what we're going to do when we run out though."

"A sponge works, but it's not very comfortable," Andie lamented. Julie and Macie looked at each other.

"How long have you been doing that?" Macie asked.

"Long enough," she muttered.

"Well, enough of that shit," Macie declared. "We'll get you stocked up."

She smiled reassuringly at Andie, and then glanced at Julie, who was pointing her flashlight up and down the shelves. She suddenly reached out and grabbed a small box. "Did you find it?" she asked. Julie nodded and held it up for Macie to see.

"Do you want to do it here?" she asked. Julie nodded.

"I don't want to go back in a dark restroom and I'd rather not pee on the floor," she said.

Macie giggled. "I bet there's a bucket somewhere around here. You can squat over it."

They found one in the housewares section. Julie opened the package, dropped her pants, and hovered over the plastic pail while she urinated on the plastic device. Macie held a flashlight and peered closely.

"What are you doing?" Andie asked. Julie held it up to the light and smiled.

"We just confirmed it. Julie's pregnant," Macie said with a grin.

"I had a false alarm a short while ago," Julie explained. "My period was late and I thought I was pregnant. I wanted to be sure this time before I tell Zach."

"I may as well check too," Macie said. Julie laughed and took the flashlight while Macie pulled her pants down and squatted over the bucket.

Andie's eyes widened. "Wait, you're sleeping with Zach too?" she asked.

"We're all one very happy family," Julie divulged. "Zach has told us all about you, Andie. We think you're a good person in a bad situation. We'd ask you to come live with us, but we don't think the Captain would be willing to let you leave, would he?" Andie dropped her head and shook it slowly.

"Well, it looks like only one of us is going to be a mommy anytime soon," Macie said as she looked at the results. She looked at Andie. "Do you need to do one?"

Andie shook her head again. "The Captain has had a vasectomy. So, I guess Zach told you about that too?"

"It's okay. We don't like your uncle," Macie said. "But we want to be your friends. Us girls have to stick together, right?"

Andie smiled tentatively. "This is turning out to be a nice birthday," she looked at them, "I turn sixteen today."

*****

"So, tell me, Zach, what hardships have you encountered this winter?" The Captain asked. The five of us, Howard and me, the

Captain, and his two minions were sitting in chairs outside of the tire store. We had been talking for a little over an hour now.

"The usual stuff. The ice and snow kept us hemmed up for far too long. We lost some cattle, not to mention our means of outside communication," I said.

"What'd you do to pass the time, play hide the salami with those two whores?" Barry asked. I glared at him. He responded with a mocking grin.

"At ease, Barry," the Captain ordered, and returned his attention to me. "It was the same with us." He paused in thought a moment. "Have you given any further thought to a trading post?" I nodded. I glanced again at Barry. He still had a stupid grin on his face. I wanted to slap it off.

"A spot in downtown Nashville would be the ideal location, but we both know it's not feasible at this time. So, we have to think of a good secondary location. I've pondered over it and I'd say one of the truck stops on I-24 would be best. There is one at the county line. It is centrally located to where all of us live. I like the idea of a trading post being near the farms."

"Where do you live, kid?" Barry asked.

"None of your business," I replied curtly. His stupid grin turned into a stupid scowl.

"George will find you," he said menacingly. "When he does, maybe we'll come pay a visit."

I shook my head. "I'm afraid not. I've posted no trespassing signs. It's strictly enforced."

Eli seemed to find it funny and guffawed. They were silenced by the Captain snapping his fingers.

"Barry, if I want any more of your commentary, I'll beat it out of you," he said calmly. He then continued speaking as if they were not there. "So, you have a plan thought out."

"Yes. First, make a total sweep of the area. Clear it of all zombies and hostiles. Phase two will consist of preparing the facilities. You'll need to harden the building and build good defensive positions against both zombies and highway men. The place has a big parking lot. It'll hold a lot of people and vehicles. There is a creek nearby where you can distill water. Of course, the sanitation issues will need to be addressed. I'd start with something simple, like outhouses." I was interrupted by Lashonda bringing a tray of coffee. I was the only one who thanked her.

The Captain sipped his coffee and made a hand motion. "Boys, listen to this young man. He's smarter than the both of you combined." They glared in silence. "Please continue, Zach," he said.

"Phase three, send out scouting teams. Have them paint the location of the trading post on every billboard, road sign, and building along the Interstate corridor. This same team will also be looting and salvaging everywhere they go. Set up a radio and have frequent broadcasts. You advertise the trading post with an emphasis on its friendliness and safety. I'd recommend a woman be on the radio. A woman's voice sounds a lot friendlier than a man's. Andie would be a good person for the job. Hell, she could probably run the whole shebang."

I sipped some coffee and glanced at the two idiots. They were listening, but seemed bored. It was time to whet their appetites a little. I leaned forward.

"Guys, the Captain can explain it in more detail, but a meeting place like this will attract all kinds of commerce, including the world's oldest profession." They eyed me in confusion.

"Prostitution, you idiots," the Captain said gruffly.

Eli clapped his hands together. "Now you're talking!" The Captain eyed him. "Sorry," Eli muttered.

"Now some people think the only way to obtain prostitutes is through forcible means, but believe me, there will be women and men who will be more than willing to ply the trade, for the right price," I said. The Captain nodded thoughtfully again, and was quiet for a minute before speaking.

"Who do you propose runs this trading post?" he asked.

I shrugged my shoulders. "In order for it to be run and defended successfully, you'll need at least a squad sized unit. So, you should be the person to run it."

"You believe it could be subject to attack," the Captain said.

I nodded. "Most definitely. Someone will eventually try it. And don't forget, there will be petty issues which will need to be dealt with. In the past, there were cops and the court system. These people will look to you for settling any civil or criminal infractions."

The Captain nodded thoughtfully. He glanced over at his two minions.

"We'll need to get started on this immediately," he said to them. "Zach, I believe you've got it all thought out. Are you going to provide assistance in this endeavor?"

I shrugged. "You've got the manpower, but I'll help however I can. Working out a bartering standard can be subjective, but I think I've got a viable formula." I leaned forward toward the Captain, all the while keeping his two boys in my peripheral vision.

"Now, here's the good part," the Captain arched an eyebrow. "Taxes," I said.

"What the fuck are you talking about?" Barry demanded. "Nobody pays taxes anymore." Howard chuckled. Barry glared at him. "What the fuck are you laughing about, nigger?"

I stood quickly, as did Barry, and I pointed at him. "Your name is Barry, right? Well, Barry, you've worn out your welcome. Get out of here."

"Do you think you're going to make me leave, punk?" Barry challenged. I glanced at the Captain. He shrugged and smiled at me, as if to say, what are you going to do now, boy?

The gauntlet was thrown, and let it never be said I backed down from a challenge. I purposely walked toward Barry. He waited for me to get close and suddenly tried for a roundhouse with his right fist. I ducked under it and responded with a right to his solar plexus. I twisted my hips to increase the effect. The many hours working out on the heavy bag paid off. He grunted in pain and stumbled back. I stayed on him, remembering Rick's tutelage, and dictated the distance. I stepped forward quickly and began peppering him with punches to the head. They were having effect. Barry kept stumbling backward and I kept moving forward.

Then I got over confident. Sensing victory, I let my hands drop down, leaving my head unguarded. Barry seized the opportunity and landed another wild haymaker. It connected solidly with my temple. He followed up with a left to the jaw. It stunned me. I saw a flash of stars and stumbled. I felt my knees buckle and had a sudden flashback to the beating I sustained not so long ago.

The humiliation of that day forced me to recover quickly. I planted my feet as he bore in. I feinted with a right and ducked a punch. He leaned in for another punch, but never had the opportunity. I launched an uppercut and my fist made solid contact with his nose. I felt it crunch as his head snapped back. He fell to the ground in a heap. Before he could get up, I kicked him in the face. He grunted in pain and his eyes rolled back. He was bleeding heavily out of his mouth and nose, and a couple of his teeth lay on the ground beside him. He was done.

I looked him over a moment, and not wanting a bullet in the back, I reached down and took his sidearm. I returned to my seat and sat for a minute getting my breathing under control. The Captain stood when the fight started and watched with gleeful amusement. I kind of believed he may have subtly instigated the whole thing. I waited until he sat back down.

"Now, where was I? Oh, yes, taxes." I set Barry's handgun on my leg, casually pointing it at Eli in case he got any idiotic ideas. "Once word gets out, you'll start to have people from all walks of life drift in. Some of them will be craftsman who will set up shop to ply their trades. This is where the large parking lot will come into play. You can charge them rent for the space, or charge them a tax on their business transactions. This can be either a straight fee or on a commission basis." I looked over at Barry, and noted with satisfaction that he was still addled.

"Now, suppose someone is in need of medical services. You'll need to somehow attract doctors, nurses, dentists." I got a smile from the Captain. "These people, you'll need to be paying them. Their skills are highly specialized, so you'll want to do what it takes to keep them nearby."

Barry slowly regained his senses and moved into a sitting position. Howard walked over and knelt beside him. He pulled out a handkerchief and handed it to him. Barry glared at him with contempt.

"Go on now, take it and hold it on your nose. We gots to get that bleeding under control. Zombies can smell blood, you know."

Barry looked at Howard a moment longer, and reluctantly accepted the handkerchief. Howard stood and looked at us. "I'll get some soap and water. We'll get that blood washed off." He walked inside without a backward glance. I noticed Howard's boys and his wife were watching out of one of the windows. I looked over at the Captain. "Perhaps Barry needs to read Gunga Din," I quipped. The Captain grunted.

We were interrupted by the girls driving up. They were laughing over some inside joke as they got out of the truck. Andie had several plastic bags stuffed with items.

"What have you got there?" The Captain asked Andie as they walked up. She gave Barry a passing glance and stored her stuff in the jeep.

"Female stuff," she answered cheerfully. He arched an eyebrow. Julie and Macie both saw Barry sitting on the ground holding the handkerchief over his nose. They looked at me, saw the scrapes on my face and knuckles, and grinned knowingly. I got the journal out of the truck and handed it to the Captain.

"It's an interesting read. There is something more going on with these zombies than we are aware of. Next time we meet, we can discuss it," I suggested. "I have to get caught up on some chores. How about we meet at the truck stop in two days, maybe at noon? If I can, I'll bring some steaks and we'll throw them on the grill." He nodded in agreement. I unloaded Barry's handgun and tossed it on the ground. Before we left, I saw the Captain leering hungrily at the two girls. My two girls. He saw me looking at him, grinned at me, and walked to his jeep.

Chapter 24 – A Fine Blend

We filled each other in on our respective interactions. The girls were especially interested about the fight.

"So you kicked his ass?" Macie asked. I shrugged. "I am so fucking aroused right now," she said. Julie giggled.

"It wasn't without consequences. I need some ice on my eye. It's swelling shut."

Julie stopped where there was some snow still on the ground under a large tree. I scooped some, wrapped it in a bandana, and held it on my eye while we rode.

"You two need to be on the lookout for a radio antenna," I said. I sat in the back of the truck, holding the compress over my eye. The two girls would look at each other occasionally and start giggling.

"What is up with you two?" I finally asked. They giggled again.

"Why nothing, Dad," Macie said. This caused them to laugh so hard Julie stopped the truck. The two of them looked back at me and smiled warmly.

I think my mouth dropped open. "Are you saying what I think you're saying?" I asked. Julie put the truck in park and climbed into the back seat with me.

"Yep. I'm really pregnant this time." She kissed me as she explained how she confirmed it with the pregnancy test kit. When they described how they urinated in a bucket in the middle of Walmart, there was more laughter.

"Oh, there's more," Macie said. "We poured it into a canteen, set it on a counter in front, and put a Hallmark card beside it. We made it out to Barry and Eli." They laughed again.

"No fucking way. What did you write?" I asked.

"Dearest Barry and Eli, here is a present for you two. It's a fine sixteen-year-old blend we're certain you'll enjoy. Hugs!" Julie said between laughter. I had to laugh as well.

Julie suddenly stopped the truck and pointed to a house at the end of a circular driveway. "Found one!" she said cheerfully. There was a HAM radio antenna mounted on the chimney of the house she was pointing at. It goes without saying I was the one who climbed up on the roof and got it down. I guess it also goes without saying I'm the one who remounted it at our house.

After dinner, the three of us cleaned up the house, cleaned ourselves up, and went to bed before nine.

"How is the charge on the radio battery, do either of you know?" I asked.

"It was fully charged this morning," Macie said. I could hear the fatigue in her voice.

"What do you have in mind?" Julie asked. She was tired as well.

"Now that we have an antenna, as soon as we wake up, I want one of us monitoring the radio all day and trying to make contact with Fred. We may even need to scan all of the low band frequencies. I think we need to visit Bernie too. Hopefully he's feeling better."

I realized I was talking to myself, because both girls were sound asleep. Since I was the last one to use the restroom, I was on the end tonight instead of in the middle. I cuddled up to Julie and was asleep within seconds.

Chapter 25 – Fred

Major Fowkes climbed down the stairs from the cockpit and checked on her crew and lone passenger. The crew's complement was Sergeant Fandis and a stocky woman, also bearing stripes of a lessor rank. She was reading a technical manual. Sergeant Fandis looked at the Major with no small amount of anxiety.

"Have you checked everyone's parachute?" she asked the sergeant.

"Yes ma'am. We're all good to go," he replied. She looked at Fred.

"If you throw up, you better use your puke bag. You'll be the one cleaning up any mess you make," she proclaimed. Fred nodded in silence. "You don't talk much, do you, cowboy?"

Fred shrugged. She walked back to the front of the aircraft and climbed the stairs. Fred wanted to accompany her and watch her fly the plane, but she didn't extend an invite, and Fred doubted she'd respond well to him inviting himself. Instead, he sat on the red nylon troop seat. He watched the two soldiers maneuver a Humvee inside the cargo compartment and used several tie downs to hold it securely. The two soldiers went back outside and he listened as each engine was started. He watched out of one of the windows as they quickly and efficiently disconnected the start cart, pulled out various pins, and removed the chocks. A few minutes later, the two of them wheeled in a contraption and began lashing it down.

When finished, Sergeant Fandis focused his attention on Fred. He picked up a helmet with a long chord attached to it and handed it to him. Fred put it on and adjusted it while the sergeant stuck the chord into the intercom jack.

The speaker in the helmet came to life. "Can you hear me, Fred?" he asked.

"I read you loud and clear," Fred responded awkwardly.

"If we have an in-air emergency, we'll be jumping out of the rear door. Here are the controls to raise and lower it. Watch," he pushed a switch and raised the ramp door. "Don't worry about them unless I'm incapacitated, then it will be your responsibility to lower the ramp and jump out. Have you ever jumped out of an airplane before?"

Fred shook his head.

"It's not real difficult. You hook your parachute opening cord up to this cable up here," he pointed to a cable. "When you jump out, the cord will pull out a small pilot chute, which in turn pulls out the main chute." He mimicked the action with his hands.

"Now, it's really pretty simple until you land. You want to be facing the wind, if you can, keep your legs together and your knees slightly bent. If you lock your knees, you're going to injure yourself. Got it?" Fred nodded. Sergeant Fandis smiled. "The Major is a good pilot, we shouldn't have any problems. Any questions?"

Fred leaned forward before speaking, although he didn't need to. He pressed the microphone switch. "She seems to be a little bit tightly wound."

Sergeant Fandis laughed. "Yeah, she can be a real ballbuster. Alright, there's no need to wear the parachute, but keep it close, just in case." He patted Fred on the shoulder and walked over to his fellow soldier. He sat beside her and kissed her on the cheek. She smiled warmly at him.

Five minutes later, the plane taxied down the runway and lifted off. Fred felt the vibration as the landing gear was retracted. The plane increased altitude.

Fred found himself drifting off, but received another tap on his shoulder. Sergeant Fandis was grinning at him.

"The Major said come join her in the cockpit. What you do is unplug your cord, carry it with you, climb up the stairs, and the cockpit is right in front of you. There will be an intercom jack where you can hook up and talk."

Fred nodded and made his way to the cockpit. Major Fowkes was sitting in the pilot's seat, strapped in with shoulder and restraining belts. There was a kneeboard attached to her right thigh and there were various numbers written on it. She motioned to the co-pilot's seat. Fred moved a map, sat and fastened himself in with the restraints.

"This model is a C130 model E. It's an older model but still a very versatile plane. Normally, I would have a co-pilot with me, but it's only me." She pointed out the various gauges and operational procedures. "Your responsibility will be watching the fuel panel. When that one," she pointed at a gauge. "Gets lower than the right one, let me know." Fred looked at her quizzically. "Keeping the fuel consumption evenly balanced is important to the flying and handling characteristics of the plane."

Fred nodded in understanding at the explanation.

"I'm keeping our cruising speed at a touch under three hundred knots, which will put our flight time a touch over three hours. Our primary destination is Los Angeles Air Force Base, which is located practically next door to LAX. If we can't land there, we'll try LAX, but we'll be burning precious fuel. If LAX is untenable, we're going home. If you like, we can find a spot for you to jump out."

Fred pushed the microphone switch. "Whatever option you think is best," he said.

They were silent for several minutes before she spoke again. "You said your daughter was the only family member you had left."

"That's right. My wife, brother, and mother-in-law survived the initial infection, but then my brother got sick and killed them."

Major Fowkes looked over at Fred, but did not comment. "What about you, Major? Do you have any family?"

She looked at Fred and shook her head. "My mother died of cancer when I was young and my father raised me. He never remarried, and passed away a couple of years ago. I'm not married and I have no kids." She glanced at Fred again. "Right about now is the point where you're thinking I must be gay."

"Your personal life is none of my business. But, I'd certainly like to know your first name."

"It's Sarah," she responded after a moment. "But if you call me that in front of the others, I'll kick your ass. Alright, I'm switching my headset to Los Angeles approach frequency."

He heard an abrupt click as she pulled her jack out of the intercom and plugged it into the radio console. Fred looked at her and smiled, which he realized he had not done in quite a while.

Chapter 26 – The Truck Stop

We drove up to the truck stop before dawn. I put Macie on the roof of a building across the street. She was armed with my trusty Winchester, which I had found a new scope for. After taking a look at her field of fire, I found an out of the way place to park, and waited. I had the two-way radio on with instructions to Macie only to call if there is an emergency. I knew she was going to get cold, but it couldn't be helped.

I felt like I only closed my eyes for a minute, but when my the alarm on my watch went off at five minutes before noon, I realized I had slept for over three hours. Between the hard days of work on the farm and my two beautiful, lustful girlfriends, I found myself needing more sleep to keep my energy up. I started the truck and sped to the truck stop.

The Captain and Andie were awaiting me when I arrived. I shook hands with him and began setting up a grill. "I had a cow that died for one reason or another. I managed to get to her before she rotted, so I have some good steaks. I brought a few extra."

"Zach, you are indeed a valuable asset," the Captain said. Andie stared at me quietly. He looked at her and motioned. "I'm afraid we didn't bring much, it's been a hard winter, but we have a few cans of Del Monte vegetables. Andie brought a saucepan. I believe she can boil them up on the grill."

"It sounds good, Captain," I said with a nod, but I was thinking, two cans? If a couple of cans of vegetables were the only food product they brought, they really must be hard up.

"Oh, and I want you to know, we've been successful in rounding up several head of cattle. We've got them fenced in and they are doing very nicely," he said proudly.

I nodded. "That is awesome. Your group has been busy."

"Yes indeed," he responded. "We have definitely made positive strides in these past few weeks. In addition to the cattle, I believe we have eradicated most of the infected bastards in our immediate area. How about you?"

I dabbed at my face with the sleeve of my jacket. "We've had some small successes. After the coyotes killed our chickens, we've killed most of them off and fortified the coop. I got a smoke house built, and our garden has done reasonably well. Oh, and we've killed some zombies, but we haven't seen very many, lately."

The Captain held up a finger. "That reminds me. We've never discussed the fuel run into Nashville. Did you notice all of the rotting corpses? There must have been thousands of them. There were more dead bodies than there were zombies."

This time, I pulled a handkerchief out of my pocket and dabbed my face before speaking. I explained my theory about zombies dying off.

"Do you really think they are going to die off completely?" Andie asked.

"I do. A human body that is decomposing cannot simply continue to live. Although, I thought they would all be dead by the end of the summer. I was partly wrong, there are still plenty out there, but they are dying off. All of those corpses are proof." I pondered a moment. "I'm wondering now if these zombies we're seeing are the result of freshly infected people."

The Captain nodded somberly. "Food for thought, young Zach. Food for thought. What about all of the rodents?" he asked. "Hell fire, there must have been a dozen rats for every corpse."

"Yeah, they've got a hell of a food source now and there are no humans out there spreading rat poison. They're going to be a problem for a while. It's the same with mosquitos and flies."

We finished our meal in silence. The food was unseasoned and bland. My cooking would never earn a Michelin star, but it was a filling meal nonetheless. After eating, the Captain looked around and grunted contentedly.

"I don't know if it was the fine meal we just had, but I have a good feeling about this place," he said. "What do you think, Andie?" he asked. I thought back to the last time he asked her opinion. She said I was full of shit and an idiot.

"I think it will work," she said as she looked at me. I looked over at the Captain. He noticed it as well. After a minute, he spoke.

"I'm sensing there is something going on between you two. I noticed it the other day as well. Would I be right?" he asked evenly. I spoke first before Andie tried to lie.

I set my plate down. "We have a small confession to make to you, Captain. After the fuel run and the tense situation at the rendezvous, Andie asked to meet with me. I was skeptical, but agreed. We met a few days later and talked at great length. You'll have to ask her, but I believe her intentions were to smooth over any perceived conflict between you and me."

He looked suspicious and stared at me.

I cocked my head. "To be honest, after the fuel run, I was through with you. I got the feeling you were going to try to rip us off, but Andie convinced me otherwise."

His face was without any expression which would give an indicator of his mood. "You thought I was going to steal your fuel? Why would you think that, Zach?" he asked.

I met his stare. "Well Captain, your behavior made me suspicious," I contended.

The Captain looked at me a long moment before slowly nodding. "Fair enough."

I noted he did not try to defend his behavior. I also had not overlooked the earlier comment where he referred to me as an asset rather than a friend.

There was a minute of silence as Andie and I watched the Captain. He sat stoically, fingers interlaced, staring at some unseen object. I was wondering what he was going to do next. Did he have his own sniper hidden somewhere, waiting for the signal to shoot me? He then turned and looked at the expanse of the truck stop. There were abandoned semis and cars scattered throughout the lot. The back lot was completely full of abandoned trucks and there was trash everywhere, along with several corpses.

"Have you been inside?" he asked.

"Nope. I imagine there might be a surprise or two waiting in there." As if on cue, a couple of zombies stuck their rotting faces up against a plate glass window and began scratching at it. Andie pointed and laughed.

"There's the welcoming committee," she joked.

He gave a smile which may or may not have been contrived.

"I've been in here before, back a few years ago. That is a trucker's restaurant right there," the Captain said as he pointed at the window. "Beside it is a fast food restaurant. I always thought that was odd. On the other side is a convenience store. There is a locker room and showers in the rear. The semis park in the parking lot out back." He looked around while scratching his crotch. "It's going to take some work."

His thoughts were interrupted by Andie clearing her throat. She pointed at her watch and tapped it with her index finger.

"Zach, I'm afraid we're going to have to leave. We have a meeting of sorts," he said cryptically. I was curious of whom he might be meeting with, but I knew he wouldn't tell me. Maybe I could meet again with Andie and she'd tell me about it.

"No problem. I think I'm going to look around here some more." I pointed at the zombies. "I'll take care of those. I don't think there are any others. Oh, I have some equipment where I can drill out the locks, so I won't break any of the glass."

"Excellent," he said. "If I'm going to live here I want all of the creature comforts I can get." He smiled pleasantly and glanced at his niece. "Andie, do you have that present for Zach?"

I arched an eyebrow as Andie trotted over to their Jeep. She trotted back a moment later carrying a book. I took it and looked at it.

"It's a collection of short stories and poems by Edgar Allan Poe," the Captain said.

"My favorite is The Tell Tale Heart," Andie added as she stared at me intensely. I picked up on the hint.

I nodded. "I'll enjoy reading it. Thanks, Captain."

We shook hands and they left a moment later. I stood there a few minutes appearing to be interested in the zombies in the window. I was using an old spy trick. At least, it was in every spy book I had ever read, and I've read a lot of them.

The plate glass was acting as a mirror. I used the reflection to scan the area behind me. It was a big parking lot, which limited what I could see. I turned around casually and stretched while checking the area. The only thing I saw of concern was the barrel of Macie's rifle sticking out of the roof scupper. I turned around and pulled my walkie-talkie out of my jacket.

"Come in, Saigon," I said quietly. There was a click of the radio. "Your barrel is sticking out."

I turned back and watched through the window reflection as the barrel slowly retracted out of sight. "Good. I'm going to get inside here, clear the zombies, and have a look around. Watch my six, please."

There was a click of acknowledgement.

When I used the drill to disable the lock, the zombies obliged me by moving toward the door. I dispatched them quickly and dragged them outside. The rest of the building was devoid of any life forms other than an infestation of mice.

The place smelled horribly due to the rotting food from the restaurants. It made me second guess the logic behind using this place. I tied my bandana around my face and went in.

I scored a coup when I found a case of toilet paper sitting on a closet shelf. I carried the box outside and stood there going over the litany of tasks needing to be done to this place. My thoughts were interrupted by Macie's voice on the radio.

"You've got a couple of zombies coming out from behind the building," she whispered. I drew my weapon and met them as they rounded the corner. A quick two shots and we had two additional dead zombies. Adhering to rule number eight, I dragged them to the middle of the parking lot and stacked them together. I made a decent sized pile on top of them with the ample amount of trash lying around, a little gas, and set them on fire. I watched for a minute.

"Okay, I'm heading out," I said loudly into the radio. Macie clicked in acknowledgement once again. I got in the truck and drove away, stopping once I got out of sight. I changed frequencies on the radio and washed up with hand sanitizer while I waited. Macie waited ten minutes before speaking.

"Nobody followed you," she whispered quietly. I clicked the microphone in acknowledgement, started the truck, and headed back.

"Okay, I'm going to paint the rules and we're done here," I said into the radio when I stopped in front of the building she was on. She clicked the radio and I saw a ladder emerge from the top a moment later.

"How'd it go?" she asked.

"Okay, I guess," I said as I painted the rules on the side of the building she had been hiding on top of. "He's going to move in there. If it works out, he'll be a happy camper, king of his own little realm, and we won't have to worry about him paying us a visit with his crew." I looked at my work.

"You didn't sign it," Macie observed.

"Not yet. Time to add another rule." I added the following -

Z13: THEY'RE EASILY DISTRACTED.

"Okay, now I can sign it," I said and added my trademark Z. As an afterthought, I put the initials W-E off to the side. "The Captain will love it."

Macie shuddered. "I don't know why you like him, Zach. He's a creep. He's molesting his own niece and letting the other women be used as whores for Christ's sake. I should have shot him."

I glanced over at her. She looked like she was serious about it and maybe even regretted not doing it. After a minute, she continued.

"No, wait. I think I know what it is. He's like a father-figure to you."

I looked at her and frowned. She continued, "I'm serious. Think about it. Your real father died when you were a young child. The first real man in your life was Rick. He was a good man and took care of you." She paused and pushed some hair behind her ear before continuing. "So, Rick dies. Then Fred comes along. He's been like a father-figure to all three of us. Now, he's gone and God only knows if he's alive or not. Howard is our friend and he treats you with deference, but he's busy with his own family. So what's left is *The Captain*." She had held her fingers in quotation marks and said it in a derogatory tone.

"We should kidnap Andie away from him. There's no telling what kind of emotional damage he's inflicting on her. Did I mention he's a creep?" She shuddered and turned the heat on high.

I stopped the truck. "That reminds me." I fished the paperback book out of my jacket pocket and thumb through it until I found the Tell Tale Heart story. There was a small scrap of paper wedged between the pages.

"What is it?" Macie asked.

"It's a note from Andie. She wants to meet this Sunday. She says it's urgent." I told Macie of the dialogue between Andie and the Captain.

"Who were they meeting with?"

I shrugged. "I have no idea, it seemed odd though. Why didn't he say they've met some people? Maybe Andie will tell me," Macie had been eating while I talked. When she was finished, she let out a small burp and giggled.

"Excuse me," she joked. I smiled. "What are we going to do now, Zach?"

"Let's go check on Toby and his sons," I suggested.

"Okay, but I'd like a favor from you first." I looked at her. "I need to use the restroom and then I want to shoot a zombie with the rifle. I've only ever shot at paper targets with it."

"Right now?" I asked.

"Yes, right now," she said, grabbed a paper towel, and got out of the truck. I waited inside while she did her business. When she got back inside, I handed her the hand sanitizer, and then the two of us drove to the bridge overlooking I-24.

"Alright, here we go. You can start with binoculars or use the scope to find a target. I'm betting there is at least one zombie stuck in an abandoned car out there." I pointed toward the sea of automobiles and tractor-trailer rigs sitting motionless on the interstate.

"What's the advantage of binoculars over the rifle scope?" Macie asked as she peered through them.

"You're using two eyes with binoculars and your field of vision is greater." She picked up the binoculars and after only a moment she grinned.

"I found one!" she said excitedly. "Oh, I found another one. **They're** sitting in cars. One of them is sitting in a semi."

"Are they still moving?" I asked.

"A little bit," she looked at me. "Can I shoot them?" she asked hopefully.

I made a quick scan for any threats nearby. Seeing none, I nodded. "Sure. You know what to do, right?" She nodded at my question, swapped the binoculars for the rifle, and laid it across the bridge railing. I put my fingers in my ears a mere second before she fired. I saw the starburst explosion of the semi's windshield, grabbed the binoculars and looked.

"Right in the forehead, nice shot," I complimented. She looked at me and grinned before finding her next target.

"Oh, my God, what a rush," she said breathlessly after she shot the last one. I stored the rifle behind the back seat and we both got in. When I got seated, Macie took her jacket off and straddled me. She kissed me passionately, her tongue probing deeply. Then she started working at my belt buckle. "Let's make love, Zach."

"Right now?" I asked between kisses.

She huffed, grabbed my face, and kissed me. "Yes, Zach, right here, right now."

I didn't need to be told three times. Somehow, I got my jacket off and we crawled into the back seat. We tore at the rest of our clothing and went at it with an urgent fury. I was glad I had taken a power nap.

Afterward, we were lying together in the back seat breathing heavily. When our pulse rates returned to normal, I leaned closer and kissed her.

"How are you, Macie?" I asked.

"Wonderful," she responded.

"Well, I guess what I was wondering is, we've not talked much about your baby. I mean, I've no idea what to say or a tactful way to ask you how you're coping with his death. If there is anything I can do…" I was interrupted by Macie. She grabbed my hand and squeezed.

"You and Julie have been good to me, Zach. I love you both. You know that, right?"

I nodded. She rubbed my chest and was quiet for a long minute before she spoke again. "This may sound cold or cruel, but the first time I held my baby, I somehow knew he wasn't going to live. When I'm alone, I think of him and cry. When I'm around you two, I'm happy. It's a different life now, but I'm happy, Zach."

I kissed her again. I was happy too.

"Is it wrong for wanting you to myself, without Julie, just once?" she asked.

"I don't know. I guess not," I said quietly.

Chapter 27 – Fred

Los Angeles Air Force Base was a ghost yard of aircraft. Some had crashed and burned. Many more were parked in military fashion, but otherwise, they sat silently. Major Sarah Fowkes pointed, but Fred had no idea what specifically she was pointing at. He leaned forward and looked anyway.

"Do you see? There is one landing strip relatively clear."

Fred looked hard, but he didn't see it.

Sarah began a descent. "The great thing about a C130, they don't need much room to land." She looked over at Fred and grinned mischievously. However, in only a brief moment, her expression quickly changed back to her game face and she concentrated on landing.

Fred watched in growing concern as she lined up on a runway with multiple wreckages all around it. She touched down smoothly and brought the plane to a stop without a spot of trouble. She began the step-by-step process of powering down the engines while she talked.

"If we find any fuel, we can take on several pounds and still be able to take off. I'll have to make some calculations."

When she shut down the engines, it was quiet again. Fred took his helmet off. "I can't thank you enough."

"Don't mention it, cowboy. What are you going to do for transportation?" she asked.

"I'll try to find a car with a little fuel in it and a good battery," he replied.

"Are you going to ignore the Humvee stored in the back?" she asked sarcastically. "Why do you think I had them load it up?"

Fred looked at her in appreciation. "I don't know what to say. Thank you, Sarah." She scoffed and made her way down the ladder.

"Alright, you two, make a perimeter sweep of the area, and then find a fuel truck." She looked back at Fred. "Help me get the Humvee unloaded," she said with the voice of someone used to issuing commands.

Fred looked at a map of Los Angeles and found the street. He backtracked the route with a pen, measured it, and pointed it out to Sarah.

"It's not far from here, about ten miles as the crow flies. I'll take the Humvee. If I'm not back by dark, go ahead and leave without me."

"Fred, do you actually think I'm going to let you go by yourself?" she asked. Fred looked at her blankly. "I'm going with you."

"I can't let you do that," Fred replied.

"Quit being all macho on me, Fred. It's a major turnoff." She tossed the map back at him. "I'm driving."

Chapter 28 – Secret Notes

"How did it go?" Julie asked when we arrived home.

"The Captain showed up with Andie. It seemed to go well. He's going to set up at the truck stop. Oh, and Andie passed a note saying she needed to meet with me," I said with a small smile. Julie chortled.

I let out a short sigh. "For your information, Miss Smart-Aleck, I have no intentions of going alone. You and Macie are free to join me."

Julie snorted again. I blew her a kiss.

Macie changed the subject. "There is some bad news," she said. Julie looked at us questioningly. "Toby and his sons are gone. They weren't home when we got there and there was a lot of dried blood on the back porch."

"We drove around looking for them, but no luck," I added.

"Oh shit," Julie said. "But, there were no bodies, right?" she asked. Macie and I both shook our heads.

"Well, the only good news I have is the new radio antenna is working. I made contact with Howard and Macie's boyfriend."

I looked at her questioningly. "The old dude who lives on the Cumberland Plateau. He seemed really excited to know there was another live woman on the planet." Macie laughed.

"Anyway, we chatted for almost an hour. He's had a cold winter as well, but he had plenty of food stocked up. He said he's only seen one other live person in the last three months, and to tell you he can't wait to meet you."

"What's his name?" I asked.

Macie laughed again. "He only calls himself Hillbilly."

Julie grinned briefly, but then looked downcast. "I tried raising Fred," she said and then shook her head slowly. We understood.

Later, we had dinner by candlelight and discussed tomorrow's meeting.

"I'm thinking the two of you meet with Andie in the morning instead of me," I said while we ate. "We'll head out early and you two drop me off. I'll find a good sniper position and watch out for you. We'll use the standard hand and radio signals. Afterward, we'll pay Bernie a visit and check on him. Then, if there's enough daylight left, we'll do some scavenging. What do you girls think?" They nodded in agreement."We always like it when you do the planning. Will you be wearing a diaper?" Macie asked with a coy smile.

We went to bed early, got up well before daylight and worked up a plan where the girls would meet with Andie and I'd be their security.

The girls dropped me off a couple of miles from the store.

"I'm going to walk my way in and find a spot to set up a decent distance from the store but I'll stay close to the road," I said. "If you hear gunshots, it means I've encountered zombies or those assholes who tried to ambush me." They nodded. "I can't risk leaving the radio on. We really need to find some earpieces for these things. But anyway, if you girls have any problems while we wait, fire some shots or use the hand signals."

I made my way toward the store and finally chose an abandoned car in which to hide. It was approximately three hundred yards from the store. I positioned myself so I could sit in the back seat and aim the rifle out of the passenger side. Adorned in my newly fashioned ghillie suit, a casual passerby would only see a clump of rags in the back seat.

Looking at my watch, I was satisfied to see I was in place two hours early. It seemed futile to go through this precaution at this point, either they had no cause to try to set us up, or whoever their guy was, George maybe, was really good. If he was out there, he was better than I was, because I never saw him.

The girls drove by me promptly at sunrise. I watched as Andie arrived from the opposite direction.

*****

"There she is," Julie said as she pointed at Andie driving up in her jeep. Macie nodded and parked. All of the girls got out. Andie was startled and flinched when they hugged her.

"How've you been, Andie?" Julie asked.

She shrugged. "It could be worse I guess."

"We've brought some food. Are you hungry?"

Andie nodded. The three of them ate cold hard-boiled eggs dipped in honey while they talked.

"Where's Zach?" Andie asked.

"Oh," Julie said between mouthfuls. "He's around. He left out early this morning and said he'd catch up with us later."

Macie spoke up before Andie could respond. "Your note said it was urgent to meet with us. What's up?"

Andie fidgeted, pulled out a joint, and lit it. "I wanted to talk with Zach privately."

"Andie, we're your friends," Macie said quietly. Julie burst out in sudden laughter.

"Hell, we have to be friends. All of our names are the same. Andie, Macie, Julie. Get it?" Julie laughed again. "Do you not like us?" she asked. Andie stammered and puffed on her joint.

"Well, we like you," Macie said. "We worry about you tremendously.""Why?" Andie asked warily.

"Because, the three of us are kindred spirits," Macie replied. Andie scoffed.

"So says Miss Cheerleader with the blue eyes and big perky tits. You were probably the most popular girl in school. Most of the boys in my school were assholes toward me. Girls like you turned their nose up at me," she scoffed again and smoked her joint. Macie grabbed it and took a puff.

"You're right. Well, mostly. My eyes are hazel, but you're right. There was a time when the three of us would have probably never been friends, but it's different now. You know that," Macie puffed the joint again, coughed, and handed it back. "We're now more alike than ever."

Andie thought about Macie's statement a long minute before she slowly nodded.

"Can I come live with you guys?" she suddenly blurted out. "I promise I won't be a burden." There were sudden tears in her eyes and her voice cracked. "I can't take it anymore."

Macie and Julie looked at each other. Zach had told them this might happen.

"Sweetie, if you leave and come live with us, will your uncle come looking for you?" Macie asked. Andie nodded reluctantly, and then looked up.

"What if we fake my death or something?" she asked.

"I think that's cool!" Julie said and giggled again. Macie and Andie smiled.

"I think it's cool too," a man's voice said from inside the abandoned store. The girls looked in shock as Barry emerged from the front door. He was armed with an assault rifle.

*****

I saw the girls startled expressions and knew something was wrong. They turned toward the front door of the abandoned store. There was someone standing there. Unfortunately, the vehicles were partially obstructing my line of sight. I watched helplessly through my scope wondering what was going on.

*****

The three girls were stunned when they saw Barry. Julie started to reach for her handgun, which was holstered in her tactical vest. Barry stopped her with a gesture of his rifle.

"No, no, no. You go for that gun and I'll shoot." He grinned malevolently, showing a fresh gap between his discolored teeth. "Remember Eli? He's on the other side of that window with a rifle aimed at you two bitches. Now you may be able to get a shot off at me, but he'll surely kill you."

Julie stopped, and realized what needed to be done. "Please don't hurt us," she said, and slowly raised her hands. Macie did the same.

*****

I saw the signal, but I had no shot. Macie and Julie stood there with their hands raised, and probably waiting for me to start shooting. I moved my scope quickly to Andie. She was frozen in place. I moved it back toward the front door when my eye caught something in one of the windows. I could see the outline of a figure, but not much else. I knew I only had a scintilla of a second to decide. I aimed center mass at the shadowy figure in the window and squeezed off a shot.

*****

"You two bitches thought you were funny when you left us a canteen of piss to drink. Before I'm through with you, you'll be begging to drink my piss you..." His diatribe was cut off by the crackle of window glass breaking, followed quickly by the sound of a gunshot. Barry looked at the window stupidly, and heard his companion fall. When he turned his attention back to Julie, she saw her opportunity, grabbed her handgun and shot Barry at the moment he turned back toward her. His expression was of surprise and pain. As he fell, he squeezed the trigger on his rifle. The fully automatic weapon fired off ten rounds in rapid succession as he hit the ground.

Julie instinctively crouched, shot Barry again, and ran to the rear of Andie's jeep. "Macie!" she yelled. Macie drew her handgun and held it on Andie as she backed toward Julie. "Are you hit?" Julie asked.

"We need to get out of here," Macie said quietly. "Where's Zach?" the two of them walked backwards toward their truck. As they got in, Andie yelled out.

"Wait!" she said and ran toward them. She stopped short when Julie pointed her gun squarely at her head. Andie held up her hands. "Please take me with you!" Andie pleaded.

"Let's take her," Macie said. "Zach will know what to do with her."

Julie looked over at Macie. She seemed pale and out of breath. Macie looked across the seat to Andie, who was standing near the driver's side door.

"Get over here," she said gruffly. Andie complied and ran around to the passenger side. Macie opened the door.

"Get down on the floorboard. If you try to look up, I'll shoot you." Andie hesitated only a moment and crouched down on the floor. Julie started the truck. As she sped away, she turned her radio on.

*****

I watched them through my scope as Julie did a quick draw and shot whoever it was confronting them in the doorway of the store. I could see the barrel of a rifle and the telltale smoke coming out of it. Whoever it was, they had fired on full auto before they fell. I smiled in pride knowing Julie had hit her target. I refocused on the window in case there was another target or I had missed my first target. The girls got themselves back into the truck, and much to my surprise, Andie got in the truck with them.

I covered them as they drove away and then turned on my walkie-talkie. Julie was calling me.

"We're coming," she said breathlessly. I clicked the microphone and waited quietly until they were close.

"Stop the truck," I said. Julie slammed on the brakes and came to a screeching stop. I crawled out of the car and jumped in the backseat of the truck. Julie took off as soon as I got in.

"She set us up!" Julie said angrily. I looked around and then realized Andie was crouched down in the floor at Macie's feet. When she looked up at me, she looked like a frightened little girl.

"I didn't, Zach, I swear," Andie said.

"I said, keep your head down," Macie chastised. She looked back at me. She didn't look good and she looked frightened as well.

"Macie?" I asked questioningly.

"I'm cold, Zach. Can you hold me?" she said feebly. The blood drained from my face.

"Julie, find a good spot to pull over." Julie heard the urgency in my tone and stopped beside the on ramp to I-840. I got out and opened the passenger door.

"What's wrong, Macie?" I began looking her over. It was then I noticed a distinctive hole in the front of her jacket. I hurriedly unbuttoned it. Julie and I saw the blood at the same time. Her front was covered and it was spreading. It looked like she was hit in the liver. I vaguely heard Julie screaming.

I grabbed Andie by the collar and dragged her out. I slung her against the truck as if she was a rag doll, frisked her, and found a revolver secured in a holster on her hip. I took it from her and tossed her to the ground.

"You stay right there," I said coldly and turned my attention to Macie. As gently as we could, Julie and I got her out of the truck and laid her on the ground.Macie looked up at us.

"Do you know how much I love you two?" she said softly. I retrieved the first aid kit out of the truck and hurriedly began trying to staunch the flow of blood. I knew it would not be enough, but tried anyway. I kept glancing in her eyes and saw the life slowly drain away. She gurgled once and her head listed to one side. Julie screamed in anguish.

Julie cried uncontrollably as she held Macie's head in her lap. I realized I still had the ghillie suit on. Standing up, I began disrobing until I was down to my shorts and a tee shirt. There was a change of clothes in the back seat. I put them on, laced up my boots, and then directed my attention to Andie. She had pulled her knees up to her chin and was rocking herself. I pulled my knife out and locked the blade open. Her eyes widened with abject fear.

"Macie was my first love. Did you know that, Andie?"

She was shaking uncontrollably and stammered out an illegible response.

I gestured at Julie. "We both loved her very much. And you killed her."

"Zach, I swear, I had no idea they were there. I wanted to meet with you so I could ask you if I could come live with you guys."

"No, I don't think so. I think you were in on the ambush a while back and you were a willing co-conspirator today." I grabbed her by the hair and yanked her up. She was crying freely now.

"Please, don't hurt me, Zach," she pleaded.

"Why shouldn't he?" Julie said. She still held Macie's head in her lap. Her face was red and her eyes were swollen from crying.

I turned to face Andie. She was crying as well.

"Zach, please! Just let me show you something," she said shakily. Her voice was on the edge of panic. I let go of her hair, but I was about ready to slit her throat. Andie stepped back and took her coat off. She then pulled her shirt off and the tee shirt underneath. My eyes widened and Julie gasped at what she saw.

There were bite marks on her shoulders and breasts. Andie instinctively folded her arms over them. I stepped toward her. She flinched as I turned her around. There were several additional bite marks on her back. Some appeared to be days old, some were fresh.

"Did you get attacked by zombies?" I asked.

"No," she sobbed. It took me a moment to understand.

"Did the Captain do this to you?" I asked quietly. Andie nodded and continued sobbing. I put my knife away. "Put your clothes back on."

We carefully put Macie in the backseat, and I directed Andie back down on the floor. We rode home in silence. Mostly. An occasional sob was heard.

Chapter 29 – Fred

The side streets were fairly clear of traffic. Sarah occasionally scraped the fenders when she drove in between cars or hopped sidewalks as Fred directed her with the map in his lap. There were zombies aimlessly standing or sitting everywhere, but most of them did not seem to have the energy to follow us.

"If I'm reading the map correctly, it is the next street. Turn right and the apartments should be on the right hand side," Fred said.

There was a traffic jam in the middle of the intersection. She hopped the curb and went around them. Fred pointed at the apartments. The sign on the front identified them as Valley Grove. Fred eyed them. They weren't in the best shape. He was struck with worry about his daughter. What had she gotten herself into where she had to live in a seedy apartment?

He shook it off. "Her apartment is numbered 201, which I assume is on the second floor. I'll go take a look."

"Make it quick, cowboy. I have a feeling we're pressing our luck," Sarah said.

Fred nodded curtly, grabbed an M4, and walked through the courtyard. The grass was overgrown, and it looked like at one time somebody had tried growing roses around the arbor leading into the courtyard. He carefully made his way toward the interior stairway and made his way up.

Sarah watched Fred as he made his way into the apartment. She noticed that even though he had a slight awkwardness to his gait, he moved fluidly. She began scanning the neighborhood, silently urging Fred to hurry.

The apartment was at the top of the stairs. This was one of those old apartments, the kind where all of the entry doors were in a common hallway. He looked up and down. There were no signs of life, no noises. He quietly tapped on the door numbered 201.

After a moment, he heard something inside, or maybe it was his hopeful imagination. He tried the doorknob.

Major Sarah Fowkes, who prided herself on her stamina, was tired. Flying a C130 by oneself was no simple matter. She caught herself yawning, and wished desperately for a Red Bull, or even a cup of the General's awful coffee. Then, she saw them. It looked like approximately a hundred of them. They were about eight blocks away and slowly making their way toward her. She grabbed a pair of binoculars, looked them over, and gasped. They seemed to know she was looking at them. It appeared they were actually staring at her with those dark eyes, all the while ambling toward her.

She started to get out and run get Fred, when she heard two gunshots. Fred appeared a minute later, paused in the doorway to reload his revolver, and slowly started walking toward her. She also noticed a waft of smoke coming from the breezeway and wondered what was causing it.

"Hurry up," she whispered loudly and pointed at the closing horde. Fred looked up and saw the horde of zombies. He casually walked into the roadway, and then, instead of getting into the Humvee, he unslung his M4. Sarah watched in disbelief.

Fred stopped a few feet away from the Humvee, shouldered the M4, and started firing, rapidly, accurately. He went through all four magazines quickly. Fred knew they were loaded with twenty-eight rounds each, and silently told himself he had killed one hundred and twelve of them, not counting the two he had dispatched in the apartment. When he was out of ammunition, he gently placed the M4 on the asphalt and squared off. There were perhaps thirty left.

They were close now, less than fifty feet. It was time for some quick draw practice.

Sarah watched with incredulity at the speed in which Fred would take turns drawing one of his revolvers, shoot a zombie, and then return it to his holster in the blink of an eye. She looked around anxiously, wondering when, not if, the sound of gunfire was going to attract more zombies and possible hostile humans.

She paused a moment in her own shooting and shouted at him. "Fred! What the hell is wrong with you? Let's get going!" Fred ignored her. Did he have a death wish? She grabbed Fred's M4, got in the Humvee and started it. "Fred! Get in damn it! We need to get out of here!"

Fred acted as if he didn't hear her and calmly reloaded.

In exasperation, Sarah jumped back out of the Humvee and began shooting the remaining zombies. When they were all lying in the roadway, some of which were at Fred's feet, Sarah ran over beside him, grabbed his shoulder, and shook him roughly.

"I'm leaving! You better get your ass in my Humvee right fucking now if you don't want to be left behind!" she shouted. She ran and jumped in. Fred seemed to be broken out of his daze and looked her in the eyes. He knew she was serious. He followed her as she jogged back to the Humvee and got into the passenger side.

Neither of them spoke as Sarah tore down the streets, all attempt at stealth abandoned. Fred sat silently. As they neared the airport, Sarah calmed down enough to talk.

"Listen, we'll go back, get the other two, and keep searching, but no more gosh-danged John Wayne antics, you got me?"

Fred stared straight ahead. "There's no need to keep searching. Let's go back to Tinker."

Sarah hastened a look over at him as she drove. She thought she saw him quickly dab a tear out of the corner of his eye. She stopped the Humvee.

"What happened, Fred?" she asked quietly.

"Let's just say I found her and leave it at that," he pointed. "Let's move out."

Chapter 30 – For Macie

We gently wrapped Macie in a blanket and put her in the barn until we could prepare a grave. I suggested getting something to eat, but instead of eating, we sat at the kitchen table and brooded in silence. I only had an appetite for water.

We sat unmoving for several minutes, and I found myself drumming my fingers incessantly. Andie would glance at us from time to time, but was afraid to break the silence. Finally, I couldn't stand it anymore and stood up.

"I'm going back," I said. Julie looked at me as if I were speaking in tongues. "I've got to know what happened."

"Do you want me to go with you?" Julie asked. I shook my head and pointed at Andie.

"She's going. I have questions I want answered," I said. Julie was staring at me somberly. Her clothing was covered in Macie's dried blood. It was a depressing sight. When I stood, she stood suddenly and hugged me tightly.

"Come back to me, my love." she whispered in my ear and then looked at Andie balefully.

The sun was below the horizon when we set out. When it was fully dark, I donned the night vision gear. After a few miles, I looked down at Andie. I had her sitting on the floor with a blanket over her.

"You can sit up now," I said curtly. She tentatively pulled the blanket off of her and looked at me for confirmation. When she was satisfied I wasn't joking, she sat up in the passenger seat.

"No. In answer to your unasked question, the answer is no. I don't trust you and therefore I don't want you to know where we live." She bit her lip and nodded in understanding.

I parked on the side of the road and we hiked the last half mile to the store. When we got within eyesight, the two of us crouched down beside a wrecked car and I used a pair of binoculars to scan the area. There was a body lying beside the front door, the person

Julie had shot, but otherwise it did not appear to be anyone there. Still, I was cautious, it had also appeared unoccupied earlier when those two miscreants were hiding inside. Andie's jeep was still there as well, unmoved.

"Is that Barry lying there?" I asked. Andie used the binoculars and nodded her head.

"It was Eli who was inside. I'm pretty sure you shot him. I have no idea if there was anyone else."

We approached cautiously, ducking between cars as we made our way closer. With Andie in tow, we worked our way around to the rear of the building, and finally worked our way to the front. Satisfied there was not another ambush awaiting us, we made our way to Barry's corpse. He had died where he fell of multiple gunshot wounds to the chest. There was a spark of pride when I noted the tight grouping of the shots.

I picked up his weapon and inspected it. It was a fully automatic military issue M4 assault rifle.

"Where did this come from?" I asked.

"They found the Murfreesboro Police SWAT van and broke into it. There were a few of those guns in it, along with the two machine guns they mounted on the bus." I nodded and continued inside with Andie following so close she bumped into me when I stopped suddenly. There was another body lying on the floor in a fetal position. I heard raspy breathing and an occasional whimper. When I was sure there was nobody else in the store, I removed my night vision apparatus and used my flashlight for a better look. I pointed my rifle with my free hand, kicked his rifle away, and rolled him over with my boot. He groaned in agony. It was indeed Eli.

"I can't walk," he lamented. I looked him over. He had a bullet hole in his jacket about where his belly button would be.

"Yeah, looks like my aim was off. The bullet must have gone through your spine. I'm surprised you're still alive."

He whimpered again.

"Search him," I said to Andie. She went through his jacket and found a small caliber handgun. She looked at it a moment and handed it over to me. I held the flashlight under my armpit and stuck the gun in my jacket pocket.

"What the hell were you guys thinking anyway?" I asked in a friendly tone.

"Barry wanted some payback. When we got back to the compound, everyone made fun of him getting beaten up by a teenage boy." He had a coughing fit. I slung my rifle, dropped down on one knee and gave him some water from my canteen. Most of it ran down his face, but he managed to drink a little.

"Thanks," he said. "Are you going to help me?"

"We'll see. Tell me what the plan was," I said in the same friendly tone. Eli coughed again and I helped him with some more water.

"I'm dying for a cigarette, haven't had one in forever." He looked at me. "You got one?" I shook my head. Andie pulled out a joint, lit it, and put it in between Eli's lips. He took a draw and smiled gratefully.

"It's almost as good as a Marlboro." He puffed on it again and coughed.

"I personally didn't care you kicked Barry's ass. He was always strutting around like a banty rooster and needed to be taken down a notch." He looked at me. "We found Andie's diary. She had written down all kinds of shit about you, including meeting you here."

I glanced at Andie. She looked down at her feet.

"Barry asked George how to set up an ambush. He drove us up here last night and told us what to do. We spent the night in here freezing our balls off just so Barry could get even with you."

He smoked some more of the joint and had a coughing fit before continuing. I wondered if George was on his way back to check on his comrades and glanced out of the window.

"So, instead of you showing up, it was them two bitches. They thought they were clever with filling that canteen up with piss." He coughed again.

"So you had a taste?" I asked with a sour smile on my face.

Eli nodded his head. "Yeah, it made me throw up."

Good, I thought.

"Well, when we saw the bitches, we looked at each other and kind of agreed to take them." He looked at me with sudden worry. "We weren't going to do anything, just scare 'em a little bit."

I smiled condescendingly, as if I actually believed his bullshit.

"I guess you know the rest," he said and involuntarily groaned in pain. "You didn't have to shoot me."

I looked at him with loathing. If I had not shot him, had Julie not have shot Barry, there is no telling what they would have done to my girls. I thought of Macie staring at me as she slowly died.

Not bothering with a response, I stood and looked around. The store was pretty much the same as the last time I inspected it. Gutted, nothing left but trash. I made a pile of trash next to a wooden counter and lit it on fire.

"Hey, man, what are you doing?" Eli asked. I ignored him. When the flames were going good, I grabbed the weapons and walked out. Andie followed in silence.

"Are your keys in the jeep?" I asked. She nodded. "Come on, we've been here too long."

The sounds of Eli screaming in agony were echoing in our ears as we drove away.

"Do you want me to follow you?" Andie asked when we arrived back at my truck. I took the keys to the jeep and put them under the floor mat.

"Nope. You either ride with me with the blanket over you, or get in your jeep and go your merry way," I said. I looked back toward the direction of the store. There was a faint orange glow which was growing rapidly. The smoke was hanging low in the air.

"Make up your mind I think we're going to have company soon and I'm not hanging around."

I walked to my truck. Andie hurried after me and hopped in. She sat down in the floor and pulled the blanket over her without being told. I took a roundabout route back home.

The next morning, we buried Macie beside her child. She would have liked the gesture, and Rick would no doubt enjoy the company of a woman. While we were gone, Julie had cleaned her up. She'd washed out Macie's hair, brushed it carefully, and applied makeup to her pale face. She looked beautiful.

The Allen family joined us for the makeshift funeral. Everyone cried. I held up well, all things considered, but I was numb from the neck down. I could not even feel the shovel in my hands as I threw the dirt on top of the coffin.

It was a sunless day, overcast and dour.

After the burial, we went back to the house and shared lunch. Lashonda made everyone coffee as we sat in the den making small talk. Andie sat off to one side looking awkward and out of place. She was wearing one of Macie's pullover sweaters. I thought of how Macie's breasts filled out the sweater nicely, and how it hung loosely on Andie.

"Howard," I said. "Would you be willing to move your family closer to us? There are a couple of good houses nearby. They're large enough for your family. We can protect each other better."

Howard looked at me somberly. "You think the Captain will try to pull something?" he asked. I nodded.

"Yeah, you're probably right. He's going to blame everything on you guys, I'm betting."

"He'll twist it around somehow. Never mind that his two boys started it, he'll blame us for their deaths," I said, and then pointed at Andie. "He'll eventually figure out she's with us and he'll want her back."

Howard rubbed his face and lowered his voice so Andie could not hear. "Maybe you should send her on back. He *is* her uncle."

I shook my head quickly.

"Out of the question," I hesitated a moment before continuing. "He's done terrible things to her. She's nobody's property. She's free to leave here of her own accord anytime she wants, but I'm not going to give her back to him if she doesn't want to go." Howard rubbed his face some more. "I suppose I understand." He motioned Lashonda over and filled her in on the plan.

"I think that is an excellent idea," she said. "Do you have a house in mind?"

I nodded. "Yeah, the Parson's home. You leave the driveway, turn right, first house on the right. It's a nice four-bedroom home with two fireplaces. I think they have a wood stove in the basement as well. Oh, and there is a four car garage," I added. Howard smiled.

I thought a moment more. "It still has all of the furnishings and I winterized it, so there are no busted water pipes. I think it'll be a good home."

"It sounds wonderful," Lashonda said. "When do you think we should move in?"

"I think y'all should move in as soon as possible. When you guys leave here, take one of the trucks. I'll hook up a trailer to it and you guys can begin packing. I'll get some firewood over there later today and get a fire started." I looked around for Julie to see if she had any thoughts on the matter. She wasn't around.

"Anybody know where Julie is?" I asked.

"I saw her walking to the barn," Lashonda answered. I nodded and excused myself.

Julie was brushing Prancer when I walked into the barn. I walked over to the stall and watched her quietly.

"I've been neglecting her lately. Maybe I'll take her for a ride," she said.

"It's awfully cold out," I replied.

"It'll feel good. It'll feel good to ride out and never stop." There were fresh tears in Julie's eyes as she brushed.

"Did you know I wanted to kill Macie once? When they came that one day and tried to ambush you at the bridge, and you had me set up in the sniper hole. I sat there thinking, if they pull any shit, Macie is the first one I'm going to kill."

She wiped away a tear and pulled a carrot out of her pocket. Prancer eagerly nibbled it out of her hand.

"Sounds stupid, doesn't it?" she asked. "She wasn't with them of course. She wasn't that kind of person." I walked over and put an arm around her. Julie buried her face in my chest and sobbed. After a long while, we walked together back to the house.

"Tell me who your uncle met with," I queried. The three of us, Julie, Andie, and I, were sitting at the kitchen table, the Allen family having left after dinner. We had been grilling Andie for the past two hours. She had given us a complete list of names of those living in the Captain's compound, as well as a detailed map. I took notes as Julie mostly glared at her.

"They were soldiers," Andie said. I stopped writing and looked at her questioningly.

"They're up at Fort Campbell. We happened upon them one day at the airport in Smyrna." She fidgeted in her seat while we stared at her. "They're creating a provisional government. The Captain told them he was the leader of this area." She leaned forward. "He plans on setting them up and killing them. He thinks they're going to take over and leave him out of the loop,"

"When and where?" I asked. She spent the next fifteen minutes giving me the details while I wrote as fast as I could. When I was finished, I sat my notepad down and leaned back. Julie was nodding off and I suddenly realized how tired I was as well.

"Can I ask something?" Andie asked. I nodded. "What's with the bucket of water in the bathroom?"

"The well water is run off of an electric pump. It is also run through a filter and is treated. It's more prudent to use buckets of creek water whenever we use the toilet. And by the way, we're on a septic tank, so no foreign objects are flushed, if you get my drift."

Andie nodded in understanding.

"Is that the only thing you wanted to know?" I asked.

"Um, well, what are you guys going to do with me?" Andie looked at us worriedly. If I find out you were involved in my girls' attempted kidnapping and Macie's death, you're going to experience a slow painful death, I thought while looking at her. I glanced at Julie. She appeared not to be listening.

"You can stay here for now. You'll be expected to pull your weight with the chores. We'll discuss it more at a later time. In the meantime, we're going to bed, you should do the same."

Andie started to get up. "Oh, if you get any ideas of wandering around during the night, I sleep with a gun and am very paranoid. Consider it a warning."

"What if I have to pee?" she asked.

"You better take care of it before you go to bed would be my advice," I answered curtly. Andie hung her head and walked off to the bedroom.

"Do you trust her?" Julie asked sleepily. We were in bed holding each other, intentionally avoiding talking about Macie, even though we were on one side of the bed, as if we were saving a space for her.

"No," I answered bluntly. I lay there in silence for a moment. "But I didn't trust Macie at first."

"She's not Macie. She'll never be Macie." Julie's voice cracked a bit. She was right; Andie was no Macie.

"I love you," I said quietly.

Chapter 31 – Carry Your Own Water

I poked my head in the doorway of Macie's bedroom. "Get up," I said. Andie stirred sleepily. She had slept in her clothes. She was probably convinced we would wake her in the middle of the night and kick her out into the cold night.

"Breakfast in fifteen," I said. "Get cleaned up and wash those bite marks. I'll have Julie take a look at them if you want. Make sure they're not getting infected."

I walked back to our bedroom without waiting for a reply. Julie was still lying in bed.

"Hey, sweetheart," I said softly. She cracked one eye open and a sad smile made its way onto her face.

"Is this going to be the speech where you tell me to get out of bed and keep going with my life?" I nodded. "It won't bring Macie back," she said glumly. Before I could respond with an inspirational cliché, she crawled out of bed and headed to the restroom. I couldn't help but notice her toned legs and baby bump as she walked by.

We had breakfast in silence. Julie was in a somber mood and Andie was too worried she might say the wrong thing.

"I don't want her sleeping in Macie's bed," Julie suddenly said. "She can sleep on the couch."

I started to respond, but Andie spoke up.

"It's okay, I understand. It'll be nice sleeping in front of the fire," she said. I looked at Julie. She ignored me. The rest of the meal passed in silence.

"I'm going to help Howard with moving," I said as we cleaned the dishes. "You want to tag along?"

Julie shook her head. "Take her with you. I don't have any desire to hang out with her all day." She looked sidelong at me. "Why do you trust her? What makes you think she had nothing to do with the ambush?"

"They had no way of knowing it would have been you and Macie showing up. They thought it was going to be only me. Eli said Barry was planning on getting me. When it was you two who showed up instead, they opted for plan-B," I said.

"Wait, you talked to Eli?" Julie asked.

"Yep, he was still alive when we got there. Gut shot. It went through and hit his spine, effectively paralyzing him. He said they found Andie's diary. Apparently, she had written about meeting with me, so they came the night before and set up inside the store."

"Are they dead now?" she asked. I nodded.

"Zach set the store on fire. Barry was already dead, but the fire finished Eli," Andie added. Julie looked at her and then back at me.

"For Macie," I said in explanation. Julie looked at me a long moment before turning her attention to cleaning up the table.

Andie hopped in the truck sat in the seat until I glared at her. She grabbed the blanket, slunk down in the floorboard, and covered herself without comment. When we neared the tire shop, I told her she could get up.

"Thanks," she said quietly. "Is it always going to be this way?"

"I'm not sure yet, but your commentary earlier sure didn't win any points with me," I said and glared at her momentarily. We rode in silence then for a couple of miles until we neared Old Hickory Boulevard.

"Okay, we're going to get the Allen family moved as quickly as possible. You can help or sit in the truck."

"I'll help," she said.

"Good, I was hoping you'd say that. Now, here's something we need to address. If the Captain shows up, what are you going to do?"

Andie looked confused. "What do you mean?"

"I'm guessing he'll be pissed and demand you go back with him."

Andie shook her head violently. "I can't go back, Zach. I can't take it anymore."

I looked at her quietly. She was trying very hard not to cry, but it wasn't working. I reached into the glove box and gave her revolver back to her. She looked at it, and then looked at me.

"We'll encounter him one day. It is a matter of when and not if. The question is, am I the person who is supposed to be your knight in shining armor and kill him for you?" I shook my head. "In the immortal words of Max Hoover, you carry your own water."

She stared at me for a long moment before responding.

"I have no idea who Max Hoover is," Andie said, "but I think I get the idea."

Howard and Lil' H met us as we drove up. "They've been trying to call you on the radio, Zach."

"Who, the Captain?" I asked.

"Yep. I got a bad feeling. We need to get out of here as soon as possible," he said and looked around anxiously. I can't say I blamed him.

Andie and I got out of the truck and looked around. "What's left to load?"

He shook his head. "Nothing we can't come back and get later."

"Alright," I said and gave Howard a hand drawn map with directions to the Parson house. "Let's get going then. You go straight there. I'm taking a roundabout route and will meet you guys there."

Andie took her cue, got back in the truck, and lay down. We arrived at the former home of the Parsons approximately twenty minutes later. I told Andie we had arrived, and we met the Allens in the front yard of their new home. I scanned the surroundings. The surrounding landscape appeared much the same way it did the last time I was here. Hopefully, that equated to no unwelcome visitors.

"This is a nice house," Lashonda said.

"Yeah, I like it. It's fully furnished as well. Let's err on the side of caution and make sure there are no unwelcome visitors since the last time I was here, and then we'll get you guys moved in."

Fortunately, there were no surprises awaiting us. With all of us working together, it only took a couple of hours to get all of their belongings unloaded and moved into the new house. Howard got a fire started and we sat in the den recuperating.

"What now, Zach?" Howard asked.

"There is a recycle bin in the garage filled with aluminum cans. Have the boys use them and string up a perimeter around the house. Make it about waist high. It'll serve as a makeshift alarm system. We'll work on hardening up the house later. We also need to get a greenhouse built, among other things. In short, there's a lot of work to be done, Howard, but I'm very happy to have y'all as neighbors."

I pointed toward a nearby hill. "Our house is on the other side of that hill. If you ever have to bug out, just head that way and announce yourself loudly when you get to the front door."

Howard nodded in understanding. As I pointed, I saw a rider on a horse crest the hill through a grove of trees, and make their way toward us. It was Julie. When she saw us, she broke into a gallop. Lashonda clucked her tongue.

"I'm going to get all over that girl." She clucked her tongue again in the way only a caring mother could. When Julie rode up Lashonda started in.

"Young lady, you know better than to be riding a horse like that when you're pregnant. What has gotten into you?" she scolded.

Julie looked down a moment. "I just wanted to go for a ride." She then looked over at me. "You won't believe what I just saw." She had our attention. She pointed back toward the state highway.

"There is a dude parked in a bus out on the road near Fred's house. He's sitting on top of it, playing a guitar."

"The Captain's bus?" I asked. Julie shook her head.

"No. It's one of those fancy tour buses that country music stars use."

Julie dismounted from Prancer. I took Prancer's reins and stripped her of the riding tack before giving her a slap on the rump. She took off at a scamper. She'd make her way back to the barn on her own. Julie, Howard and I jumped in the truck. A minute later, we came upon the bus. Sure enough, there was a man wearing an old straw cowboy hat sitting in a lounge chair on top of the bus. He was wearing raggedy jeans, scuffed pointed-toed boots, and was strumming on a very nice looking acoustic guitar.

He paused briefly to wave, pointed to the other side of the bus, and then went back to singing a country music song about a man, a woman, and his favorite coon dog. The lyrics seemed to indicate the man had to choose, and perhaps the dog won out.

"Guys, wait here and cover me." I got out and walked around to the other side of the bus. A woman, wearing jeans, flannel shirt, and a torn goose down vest, was staring up at the man. She seemed enrapt by his singing. Her back was to me, but there was something which didn't seem quite right. She wasn't clawing up in the air at him, she was merely standing there. She wasn't aware of my presence, so I went back to the truck and got the machete.

When I approached her, the man stopped singing. "There's something wrong with her, Hoss," he said to me. "I'd be careful."

I glanced up at him a moment and then snapped my fingers. She turned and faced me. She was indeed infected, but she looked distinctly different from most of the others I had been up close with. Her eyes were almost black. Her skin coloration was slightly jaundiced and there was distinct marbling, but that was the extent of any decomposition.

She hissed at me a second before I buried the machete in the side of her neck. Her spine was the only thing that kept me from completely decapitating her. I took another swing and finished the job.

"Oh, hell Hoss, I was close to serenading the panties right off of her." He smiled broadly and used the ladder mounted on the rear to climb down. He walked over and offered an outstretched hand.

"The name's Rowdy, named after Rowdy Yates from the old TV show Rawhide, although I am much more handsome than Clint Eastwood."

I smiled and introduced myself. Rowdy was a tall, lanky man, the same height as me. He looked like he was in his mid-thirties, had long hair the color of burned brick, and a matching beard.

"You're admiring the beard, aren't you?" He grinned. "I started growing it five years ago and vowed to not shave until I had a hit song. When I finally made it, my agent told me not to dare shave it and then this damned plague hit. I think God didn't want me to be a star." He leaned forward. "He's jealous of my good looks too, no doubt."

I nodded. "No doubt. Come on, I'll introduce you to my friends."

When we came in view of the truck, I casually gave a hand signal. When Rowdy saw Julie, he whistled long and slow. He then took his hat off and held it to his chest.

"Howdy, ma'am, I'm Rowdy Thomas, also known as Rowdy Yates, of the once world famous country rockabilly band, Rowdy's Rednecks. Whichever one of these gentlemen you are betrothed to, I'm ready to fight 'em to the death in order to win your affections." He then winked, took her hand and kissed it sloppily.

Julie laughed. "You are so full of shit."

Rowdy gave a big smile. "Perhaps, perhaps. It's one of my endearing qualities."

I introduced Howard and Julie. Howard grinned and shook Rowdy's hand.

"Don't worry, Hoss, I won't kiss you," he said. Howard chuckled.

"What are you doing way out here in a tour bus, Rowdy?" Howard asked.

"Well now, the answer to your question requires me to regale the three of you with a story of my life for the last year. I suggest we do it over a bottle of some good Stoli vodka. I happen to have one in the bus. What do you say beautiful?"

Julie smiled sweetly. "Sorry, can't drink. I'm pregnant."

Rowdy's jaw dropped momentarily, but he quickly recovered.

"Well, then beautiful, I'll gladly drink enough for the both of us. I shall return shortly." He went into the bus and emerged a moment later with a bottle.

"I got enough booze to last for years." He took a swig and handed it to Howard. Howard looked around as if Lashonda was spying on him and took a swallow. He grimaced and swallowed. Rowdy chortled and slapped him on the back.

"Good shit, huh?" He tried to hand the bottle to me. I declined. He shrugged and took another swallow.

"My tale begins a little over fifteen years ago. I was a nineteen-year-old wannabe stud still living in a trailer out in the middle of bum-fuck Alabama with my baby half-brother, my alcoholic daddy, and his third wife, who was also of the dipsomaniac persuasion." He thought about what he said, and looked at the bottle with a bit of concern. However, it didn't stop him from taking another drink, although to be honest, it was more of a light sip this time.

"So, I'd been playing the guitar since I was around ten or so, and did a lot of singing in the shower. I graduated to karaoke and eventually found myself in a band. We travelled around the south playing in every roadhouse and dive bar out there. In the middle of it all, I sowed many a wild oat and pitched our songs to anyone who would listen. Somehow, a major label in Nashville liked our music and signed us on. We were scheduled to be the opening act at that fancy arena downtown, when that danged plague took over."

"How did you survive?" Julie asked.

"We had our bus parked in the underground garage at the hotel." He gestured at us with the bottle. "Now here's the funny shit. This hotel was supposed to have a five-star restaurant. Well, guess what? Most of their food was canned or frozen. Those hypocrites tried to claim all of their food was fresh, which was total bullshit, but it turned out to be a boon for us. All of that canned food didn't rot on us, so we had plenty to eat." His expression turned somber.

"How many in your group were there?" I asked.

"There were nine of us at first. We were in the bus having a little party when one of my buds comes running in and said there was a massive riot going on in the streets. We locked ourselves in the bus. It got crazy real quick like. People were running around like their asses were on fire and they were all trying to drive their cars out of the garage at the same time. All they did was crash into each other and block the entrances, which also turned out okay, sort of. We were trapped in, but it plugged up the holes enough where most of them infected things kept on walking instead of coming inside the garage." He looked at the bottle before looking up.

"The bus windows were tinted. Nobody could see in. We watched as people attacked other people and tore into them. It was awful man, just awful." He drank heavily this time.

"On the second day, four of our group decided for some stupid reason to make a break for it. Those idiots didn't even know where they were going. Well, they made it out of the garage and out of our sight." He shook his head. "We heard these ungodly screams a minute later. That was enough for the rest of us. We kept ourselves locked in the bus until the food ran out. Then we went exploring and found the service entrance to the kitchen. Like I said, everything they served was frozen or it came out of a can. We were lucky." He gave a short laugh. "Yeah, real lucky." He drank some more, remembered his manners and offered the bottle to Howard. Howard wiped it off and took a small sip.

"Here's the crazy shit. First, the electricity and the water in that hotel stayed on for about three months. But, oh yeah, here's the crazy thing. We were all fine until the second time we ventured out of the bus. We snuck out at night and took turns taking a shower in the manager's office. Then we stocked up on food, water, and booze before hightailing it back to the bus. We had a good time that night. Hell, this little groupie who was hanging out with us got drunk and did a little strip tease. She ended up in the sack with Ed, my bass player." He smiled at the memory.

"Yeah, it was a good night. The next day, she was sick as a dog. At first, we thought she was hung over, but it was worse. She attacked Ed. Ed bashed her brains in, but she had scratched and bit him several times. We knew she was infected and Ed had probably become infected too, so we kicked him off of the bus and tossed out the girl's body right behind him." Rowdy shook his head sadly.

"He stood outside the bus door begging for us to let him back in. It took about two hours, and then he started changing. He was..." he left the sentence unfinished.

"Well, let's just say that one of us put him out of his misery. After that, our congeniality with each other went to hell in a handbag. I must admit, I was probably the worst one. One day, we were sitting around boozing it up and got into an argument over something stupid. I got my gun out and waved it around. Hell, I even shot it a couple of times." He pointed at the bus. "I got a couple of holes in the roof." He snorted and reached for the bottle.

"So everyone left me. They set themselves up in a few rooms in the hotel. I tried to apologize the next day, but they banished me, I guess you'd say." He scratched his head and followed up with his beard.

"That was about six months ago. They fixed me good. You see, that hotel is full of zombies, all trapped in the rooms. They have no fucking idea how to open the doors, so they're stuck. I tried to find my friends, but every room I tried had some of those rotten sons of bitches in it. I finally gave up looking for them. For all I know, they're either still hiding out, or they took a chance and left without telling me goodbye." He chuckled without humor at the memory.

"During all of this, I would peek out of the windows and check the streets every day. There used to be thousands of those things wandering around, so I was stuck in that damned hotel for, shit let's see, a year?" he frowned at the memory.

"I never thought much of prisoners doing solitary, but man, let me tell you, it's enough to drive anyone crazy. There was enough bottled water and canned stuff to keep me alive, but when the electricity went out, most of the time, I had to eat without benefit of cooking. When the water went out, I used the water in the toilet tanks to wash, which was no fun at all." He shivered in disgust at the thought.

"Anyway, I would peek out of the windows every chance I could. After a while, I noticed the numbers of them rotten motherfuckers were significantly less every day. One day, I watched a few of them no good cocksuckers walking aimlessly, and then they fell over and didn't get back up. The next morning, I walked up the stairs to the top floor and looked out a window." He looked off into the distance.

"There were dead motherfuckers everywhere you could see. Oh, there were still some of those pus infested bastards wandering around, but not nearly as many as there used to be."

"So you made a break for it?" Howard asked.

Rowdy shrugged. "After being totally alone for six months straight, I couldn't take it anymore, Hoss. I had to get out of there." His eyes started watering up now. We found other things to look at. After a minute, he dabbed his eyes and continued.

"I stocked up as much food, bottled water, and booze as I could cram in this bus, and managed to get some of the cars moved out of the way. Now, here I am."

"But why here?" Julie asked. "Where were you going?"

"The Interstate is clogged up tighter than a constipated pig, darlin'. There was no possible way to maneuver a bus through all of those trucks and cars. I was trying to take the back roads to go back to Alabama, but I made one big mistake." We all looked at him questioningly.

"I ran out of fucking gas," he said and then howled with sudden laughter.

"I got out and looked around, and that's when I saw the young lady there meandering down the road." He peered over at her headless body. "She looked different from the other zombies I've seen."

"So, you climbed up on the roof and started singing to her?" I asked. Rowdy grinned and nodded.

"She was the closest thing I've seen to a live human in quite a while. I know it sounds crazy, but I was enjoying the company. It seemed like the thing to do at the time," Rowdy exclaimed. Howard chuckled. I shook my head in disbelief.

"Well, there is one other thing." He pointed at one of the trees we had cut up and moved off of the road.

"When I saw those trees, I told myself, somebody had cut them up recently. Now, I might not be the shiniest piece of corn in the manure pile, but I realized there were some live people somewhere around here. All I had to do was cop a squat and wait." He looked over at Julie.

"And here you are. If God is especially good, you'll tell me you have an older nymphomaniac sister somewhere nearby," he said with a hopeful grin.

While the three of them talked, I walked over to the decapitated head, rolled it over and looked at the eyes. To my chagrin, they opened and she gnashed at me with her teeth. It caused me to flinch and jump back. Julie must have noticed and walked over.

"What is it?" she asked.

"The head is still alive," I said. She looked, and gave out a yelp when it looked at her.

"What's wrong with her eyes?" she asked. The zombie's eyes were an opaque shade of black. The pupils were barely discernible. Wanting to conserve ammunition and keep noise to a minimum, I found a rock on the side of the road of sufficient size and was about to bash its skull in, but hesitated. I remembered the experiments conducted by Boom-Boom. Here was my chance to conduct my own experiments. I looked over at Julie. She seemed to know what I was thinking and slowly shook her head.

I brought the rock down.

"What do you think of him?" I asked. We'd all eaten dinner at the Howard's new home and were now sitting on the couch with Andie and lovable Curly. He had given Andie a good sniffing when she first arrived and decided he liked her. I was sitting in between her and Julie, who currently had her head on my shoulder.

"He's a piece of work," Julie said. "I think he's a little off in the head from being stuck in the garage for so long."

"Is he going to stay?" Andie asked.

"I don't know. Tomorrow, I'll give him a few gallons of diesel after breakfast. He'll probably move on."

Andie looked a little sad at the thought.

Chapter 32 – Fred

They drove back to the plane in silence. Sarah would occasionally glance over at Fred. He stared straight ahead, his features a sculpture of stone, unreadable. Sarah adeptly drove around obstacles, which included wrecked automobiles, corpses, and zombies. They arrived back at the airport without further incident. The sergeant and his girlfriend were nowhere to be seen.

"I'm going to jump all in their ass," Sarah said under her breath.

Fred seemed to come to his senses. He grabbed the empty magazines and began hurriedly loading them. Sarah stopped the Humvee two hundred yards away from the C130 and scanned the surrounding area for any signs of life while Fred continued reloading.

"What's it looking like, Sarah?" he asked quietly.

"I don't see anyone. The ramp is still down, but the start cart isn't hooked up. There's something not right here."

Fred didn't respond immediately. He finished loading the magazines and looked ahead. "If you don't mind putting up with some more John Wayne antics, I'd like for you to cover me from here while I go and check out the plane."

Fred saw Sarah about to object, but he stopped her with an upraised index finger. "I can stay here and provide cover if you like, but once you go inside the plane you will be on your own. I'm pretty decent with my six-shooters is the only reason I suggested going into the plane by myself, unless you have a better idea."

Sarah stopped before she voiced her objections and looked at Fred. She realized he made perfect sense, which surprised her, considering he was a man.

"Alright, but how will I know if you're in trouble?" she asked.

"Well, if you hear me shooting, that'll be a good indicator. Now, in case I run up on any people, I want to show you some hand signals I learned from a good friend."

Sarah drove the Humvee closer and stopped it a hundred yards away from their C130. Fred got out and walked the rest of the way with his M4 at the ready. It was a pleasant evening, with a light easterly breeze. The whole place smelled bad, which made it difficult, trying to discern any distinct odors of nearby zombies. He edged his way onto the loading ramp and stopped a moment to let his eyes adjust to the dim light.

"Sergeant, are you in here?" Fred asked the darkness. He was met by silence. He slowly worked his way through the plane and then slowly went up the stairs. He had climbed only a few steps when he heard a loud moaning. Fred thought he knew what it was, but still could not believe it when he walked into the cockpit. Both of them were buck naked.

Sergeant Fandis was sitting in the pilot's seat. His female soldier companion was straddling him. Her eyes were closed in ecstasy, and her breasts had a steady bobbing rhythm as she bounced up and down with the tenacity of the energizer bunny. Fandis looked back over his shoulder.

"What in the hell are you two doing?" Fred asked.

"Oh, hey, Fred," he replied. The young sergeant's companion stopped her bouncing and quickly covered her breasts with her arms. Her expression was that of a little girl getting caught playing doctor with the neighborhood boy.

"For the love of God, will you two please get yourselves squared away? The Major is outside wondering what's going on and we've got a long trip ahead of us." Fred turned and walked out without waiting for a response. He stood in the rear of the plane and waited for a few minutes before stepping outside and waving Sarah to him.

Chapter 33 – Rowdy

Rowdy didn't leave. In fact, he parked his bus beside the barn and declared himself the guest of honor. That was three days ago. During that time, he alternated between being drunk or hung over. This morning, he was sitting at the kitchen table with us, holding his head with one hand and unsteadily holding his cup of coffee with the other.

I watched him with growing irritation. Julie and Andie noticed my mood and made small talk with each other. I caught Julie glancing at me and gestured with my head. We were so close now it was as if we could read each other's minds.

"C'mon, Andie, let's go check on Prancer." Andie looked confused, but Julie grabbed her by the hand and they walked out.

"Rowdy, it's time you and me had a man-to-man talk," I said. He set his coffee down and groaned.

"Oh, Zach, not now," he said with a groan.

"I'm afraid so," I replied. He glared at me with bloodshot eyes.

"No offense, kid, but I'm a grown ass man. How old did you tell me you are, seventeen?" He waved me off with a flick of his hand and sipped his coffee. "You're all just a bunch of kids."

"For your information, Rowdy, if you care to take a look around you'll see that not only have us *kids* survived, but we have thrived in the face of almost overwhelming odds. Now, we're going to have a little talk. I'll do the talking, and you'll do the listening." He sighed heavily but finally nodded.

"First, no more playing your guitar and caterwauling in the middle of the night. Sound carries at night, and you're going to attract unwanted visitors to our doorstep."

Rowdy chortled. "I wasn't caterwauling. I was serenading the ladies. And for your information, they're interested. At least one of them was peeking at me out of the curtain last night."

"That was me. I was debating on whether or not to shoot you."

He looked at me and realized I was serious. He stopped grinning. "Oh."

"Second, you're going to have to start pulling your weight around here if you plan on staying, and I'm not talking about singing for your supper. I'm talking about work, ball busting work. There's always something to do around here, and plenty of it."

Rowdy set the coffee down, held his head in his hands and groaned.

"Third, you really need to cut down on your drinking. I can only imagine what you went through this past year, but believe me, we all have our own stories." He peeked at me to see if I was serious. I changed my tone. "I'm not saying quit completely, just slow it down. You drink yourself silly every night and then you feel like shit all day. It has to change. You've got to slow it down. Otherwise, you're going to kill yourself. "He groaned again. "Anything else?"

"Not at the moment, but there will be. I really need an extra hand around here, and I'd like for you to stay. But, if you don't intend to pull your weight and help out, I'll help you get your bus prepped and you can be on your merry way."

Rowdy smoothed his beard, leaned to one side, and let out a long watery fart.

I glared at him. "You think this is a fucking joke? Fine, enjoy your coffee and then you're out of here." I started to stand up.

"Oh, come on. It was a little funny," Rowdy said with a grin. I continued glaring at him. His grin faltered, he sighed again and held up his hands in surrender.

"Okay, Mister Zach, I understand. It's your way or the highway." He stood and held out his hand. I shook it with no small amount of trepidation.

"What's the first thing on the agenda?" he asked.

"Oh, let's see, feed the livestock, check the fence lines, till up a garden plot, muck the chicken coop, gather eggs, feed the chickens, feed the rabbits, all of the usual farming chores. When we get finished, we're going to build a greenhouse for the Allens."

He frowned. "All in one day?" he asked. I nodded. "Yeah, okay. I'm in, but I need to go to the bathroom first. I think I've shat myself." He leaned forward and lowered his voice. "I would be most appreciative if you don't tell the ladies." He winked and hurried off to the restroom in a peculiar duck walk.

I purposely worked hard and fast, if nothing else, to make Rowdy feel even worse than normal. I hoped it would convince him to slow down on the drinking. We worked until noon and took a quick ten minutes for lunch before starting on the greenhouse. It took until sundown to assemble it, but with all eight of us working, we got it completed. Afterward, we stood together admiring our work.

"It's real nice, Zach," Lashonda commented. I nodded. It was just the hull, but even so, I was proud of our accomplishment.

"Howard can fabricate a small wood burning stove and you can start planting stuff right away. Come over, check out our greenhouse, and get an idea of what you want to grow. We've also got Fred's greenhouse that Julie has been maintaining. He won't mind if you borrow some plants. When the weather gets warmer, we'll add some concrete footings to bolt it down to." Howard and Lashonda nodded appreciatively.

"Alright," I said. "Speaking of Fred's place, Rowdy and I are going to check on it." I looked at Julie.

"I'll see you two back home, okay?" Julie nodded and glanced at Andie without emotion. She knew what I was doing. I was trying to get them to become friends. She walked over and gave me a kiss, which was nice, but she also goosed me in the ribs, her way of telling me she knew what I was doing.

"Rowdy, there are some things I need to tell you about," I said once we arrived at Fred's. I spent the next hour bringing him up to speed as we inspected Fred's house. Rowdy listened without interrupting. When I finished, he scratched at his beard thoughtfully.

"You killed Barry and Eli?" he asked.

"No, Julie killed Barry. We took Macie back to the house, and then I went back and found Eli. He was wounded, but still alive."

"And then you killed him?" I nodded.

"Have you killed others? I mean, besides zombies, have you killed other people?" I told him about the ambush and the cannibals, but left out some of the other ones. He nodded thoughtfully.

"Okay," he finally said. "You're leaving something out. Why did Andie come back with you? Seems to me you would have killed her or left her, not bring her home with you."

I thought a moment how to phrase my answer to his question.

"The Captain, um, he had done some terrible things to her, so she asked to come live with us." Rowdy frowned and looked at me, expecting me to elaborate.

"If she wants to tell you about it, I'm sure she will," I said.

"Okay, I understand," he finally said while scratching his beard again, which he seemed to do frequently. "This Captain, is he going to blame you for his two men being killed?"

"I've no doubt he will. He's also probably going to figure out that Andie is with us, and he'll not be happy about it."

"And this Fred guy, he's off somewhere searching for his daughter, and y'all don't even know if he's still alive?" I nodded. He scratched some more.

"I'm having some difficulty getting my head wrapped around all of this," he finally said.

"I understand, but I want to make sure you are aware of what is going on. It's a different world now. I could use your help, but I totally understand if you want to move on and try to get back to Alabama."

"So, what are you going to do about the Captain?" Rowdy asked.

I shook my head. "I honestly don't know. Andie said he is meeting with some soldiers in a couple of days. I really want to be there ahead of time, stake it out and listen in on the meeting, but there are wild dog packs roaming around here. I'd hate for them to find me out in the open."

Rowdy grimaced at the thought. "Yeah, that'd sure ruin your day."

I snapped my fingers at a detail I'd forgotten and motioned for Rowdy to follow me to the barn. Fred had traps hanging on the wall.

"As much as I hate to do it, we're going to need to set these out. We ran into a pack of those feral dogs not too long ago. It was pretty large, large enough to take down two or three of us. We need to kill them off." I thought about Moe and it tore at my heart.

Rowdy held up one of the traps and nodded approvingly. "I understand. Okay, I just have one other question. Is Andie single and available?" He looked at me with a hopeful grin.

I couldn't help but chuckle. "Yes, she's single. But, as for being available, she's probably not in a good place emotionally right now. My advice would be to take it slow and be nice to her. She deserves to be treated nice." I felt no need to tell him she had hit on me a couple of times. If Andie wanted him to know, she could tell him herself.

"Do you think she'd be interested in me?" Rowdy asked. "I mean, I'm fully aware of how devilishly handsome I am, and most women find me irresistible, but some women are funny, and I don't mean ha-ha funny." I shook my head and walked to the truck.

Julie and I had our usual bedtime conversation while lying in each other's arms. I told her of the two conversations with Rowdy.

"How do you think he's going to work out?" she asked.

"I think he'll be okay, although I strongly suspect one day he'll get itchy feet and bid farewell. Knowing him, he'll do it with a song." Julie chuckled quietly.

"He's certainly a piece of work," she said.

"He asked me if Andie was available."

"What'd you say?" She asked. I told her my response. She snuggled closer to me. "Good. Maybe she'll take an interest in him and stop with this crush she has on you."

"I don't think it's that bad," I said. Julie scoffed. "Okay, so, we can help play matchmaker then."

"Good idea," she said.

"Julie, I've never asked directly, but I've always wondered why you were okay with me and Macie. You even encouraged it."

"That was different."

"But how?" I asked.

"Because, I was in love with her too," she whispered. "All three of us were in love with each other, Zach." I listened as her breathing changed, indicating she had fallen asleep, and thought of what she said. I realized that it made sense in its own quirky way.

Chapter 34 – A Most Unpleasant Radio Conversation

"Zach!" Andie shouted. I came running out of the barn and met Andie, who was running toward me. She was out of breath and frightened. Rowdy emerged from the front door and stood on the porch. He shrugged unknowingly.

"I swear, Zach, I didn't do anything," Andie said. "I was just showing Rowdy the radio."

"Alright Andie, calm down and tell me what's going on."

Julie peered out of the barn with her M4 in hand.

"The Captain, he's on the radio calling for you," she said.

"Did you say anything to him?" I asked pointedly. She quickly shook her head. Julie came up beside me.

"What are you going to do?" she asked. Andie looked at me expectantly. Rowdy was rubbing his belly as if he was wondering when lunch was going to be served. My watch showed me it was right at noon, the time we used to speak to each other. I looked at Julie and shrugged.

"I guess I've got to speak to him sooner or later, may as well be now."

We went inside and I sat in front of the radio.

"Go ahead, Captain," I said into the microphone.

"Well, there you are. Is there a reason why you've been avoiding me, Zach? Perhaps you've done something wrong toward me?" His tone was unfriendly, condescending.

"On the contrary, it is you who has done me a terrible wrong. Quite frankly, I have nothing to say to you, nor do I care to speak to you anymore."

"You killed two of my men, you fucking ungrateful punk," he growled.

"They were planning to ambush me, you pompous ass," I responded.

"I had nothing to do with that."

"Your men, your responsibility," I said curtly. He didn't quite know how to respond to my assertion, so he changed the subject.

"Where's Andie?" he demanded.

"Wherever she wants to be. For your information, she's nobody's slave, especially not yours."

"You listen to me close, boy. You owe me for the deaths of two of my soldiers and you better tell Andie if she knows what's good for her, she'll get her ass back home."

"And you listen to me, Captain," I said in a low tone. "You owe me for your boys murdering Macie." There was a long moment of silence before he responded.

"You're lying," he waited. When I didn't respond, he continued. "I didn't authorize them to kill anyone."

"It sounds to me like you don't have very good command of your boys," I retorted. "They were planning on ambushing me when I was supposed to meet with Andie. Out of respect for you, I sent Julie and Macie to meet with her instead." Okay, the respect part was a small lie, but he had no way of knowing it.

"So, Macie and Julie meet with Andie instead of me. Your boys see the two girls, *my* two girls, and they attempted to kidnap them. Macie was shot and murdered by your boy, Barry. Because of that, they paid the price, *Captain.* They were under your command, and therefore their actions are a reflection of you. You're responsible."

"You should have reported this to me rather than taking the law into your own hands," he said evenly.

"And in the meantime, let them do God knows what to Julie? You must be out of your fucking mind." I looked at the radio for a moment before continuing. "Captain, I want no further contact with you. I know where you live now and I give you my word, I will not trespass. But know this, if I see any of you or any of your boys anywhere near my property, I'll consider it a hostile act and kill them on sight. This conversation is over." I turned the radio off while he was ranting. I felt Julie's hand on my shoulder and realized I was shaking. I looked up at her.

"Well, that went well." I tried to smile but didn't do a good job of it.

Later, the four of us ate dinner in an uneasy silence. Finally, Rowdy spoke.

"Zach, I get the impression this is not good?"

"Yeah, you could say that." I played with my food a minute before continuing. "This Captain, he's got a severe ego, a lot of weapons, and they outnumber us. He's going to take this as a personal affront. I don't think it's over, but I'm not sure what our alternatives are." I ate a bite and noticed Andie looking at me.

"Andie, the Captain wants you back. It's your choice. Do you want to go back?" I asked. She stared at me somberly and slowly shook her head. Julie grabbed her hand and squeezed, then looked at me and nodded. I nodded back.

I put my hand on top of theirs. "Then that's good enough for Julie and me. This is your home now, Andrea," I said. Rowdy added his hand to the group.

"That's good enough for me too," he said and smiled as he gently squeezed. Andie looked at him deeply. Already I could see the beginning of an attraction. Rowdy responded with a flirtatious smile of his own, and then looked over at me.

"I sure do like this democratic process we have here, but what now?" he asked.

"For now, we have to be on constant guard. We don't do anything alone. All of us will be armed with a full load of ammo at all times. Andie knows every one of the Captain's group. If we spot any of them, we consider them hostile. I can only hope he chooses to go his own way, but I highly doubt it."

"Why's that?" Rowdy asked.

"It's his ego. He won't be able to let it go. The logical part of his brain is telling him to move on, but this type of man is driven by his ego," I said. Rowdy looked at Andie, who nodded in agreement.

I thought for a minute and looked at Rowdy. "If you stick with us, there may be trouble. I don't blame you if you want to get in your bus and ride on. Maybe Andie will go with you."

Andie shook her head. "I want to stay here," she said.

Rowdy looked at her a long moment, maybe hoping she'd change her mind. Finally, he spoke.

"Guys, I'll be honest. I can't be alone anymore. The thought of it scares the dog shit out of me. I'd like to stick around too if you don't mind," he looked at the three of us expectantly.

"Welcome aboard then," I said. I tried to put some warmth in my welcome, but quite frankly, I was too worried about what the Captain may do next.

After supper, Rowdy retrieved his guitar and a bottle from the bus. We sat in the den and listened to him play. He was actually quite good and had a pleasant tenor voice with a hint of a southern twang. We cheered and applauded after each song. Rowdy would smile with pride and take a sip from his bottle. I believe it was Patron tequila tonight. He offered Andie the bottle, who took a large swallow and nearly coughed it all back up. We laughed as tequila ran down her chin.

After a while, I felt Julie nodding off beside me. I was tired as well.

"Okay you two, we're going to bed," I said. "If y'all are going to stay up, please go to the barn or the bus. Be mindful of your noise."

Rowdy looked over at Andie. "Well, what do you say, darlin'? You wanna head to the bus and I'll sing you a few of the songs I wrote while I was in purgatory?" Andie readily agreed.

"You kids have fun," I said lightheartedly. Andie smiled at us as they exited the door.

"Well, that didn't take long," Julie said. I gave her a kiss and we went arm in arm to the bedroom.

The next morning, Andie quietly entered the front door as I was getting breakfast prepared. She seemed surprised I was awake and looked at me sheepishly.

"Are you hungry?" I asked. She nodded. "Get the table set and I'll see about getting something ready."

Julie came in a minute later, ordered me to sit down, and took over.

"We didn't fuck," Andie said suddenly. Julie and I looked at her and exchanged a glance.

"Andie, it's none of our business," Julie said.

"No, it is, I think." She blew some hair out of her face. "He passed out after the second kiss, and then he snored and farted all night."

Julie burst out in laughter. I had to admit it was funny. We were still chuckling when there was a knock on the door. Rowdy came in and headed straight to the bathroom. A few minutes went by before he made his way to the kitchen.

"Good morning all," he said as he sat down. He rubbed the sleep out of his eyes and made a motion to straighten his beard. "God almighty, you people get up early."

I looked at Julie as she served breakfast. She eyed me, started grinning, and burst out laughing again. It had a snowball effect. Andie and I were soon laughing as well. Rowdy looked at us as if we'd gone crazy. When we finally settled down, we ate our breakfast contentedly.

"What's on the agenda today, Zach?" Rowdy asked.

"Morning chores, and then I think you and I are going to do some scavenging."

"We want to go too," Julie chimed in. "You said we all need to stick together, remember?"

I saw the stubbornness in her stare. I knew the look well, so I did what a real man would do, I held my hands up in surrender. I had many other things planned for her and Andie, but I knew it'd be a losing argument trying to convince them to stay. We were on the road two hours later, riding in Rick's dually, loaded with our usual equipment and several gas cans in the bed.

"What's with the gas cans, Zach?" Rowdy asked. "I thought you had plenty of fuel."

I glanced over at him and nodded as I drove. "We do, but you don't. And the way you're running the bus engine every night, you'll be out within a day or two. So, you're going to be scavenging for your own diesel. I'm not giving you anymore."

Julie giggled.

"Oh, and I have a list of other things we could use." I looked back at Julie and she handed a notepad to Rowdy. Rowdy scanned it over and looked at me.

"You seem to have a penchant for writing everything down," he said. Andie leaned forward and nudged Rowdy. He handed the notepad to her. I watched her in the rearview mirror as she went through several other pages, seemingly absorbed in everything I had written.

"Where are we going?" she asked a moment later.

"Cool Springs area. The first stop is Home Depot. If you notice, I have some out of the ordinary things, like driveway sealer. I'm betting nobody bothered taking anything like that. But, if you see other things on the list, you know what to do, and remember the golden rule. If we can eat it, we take it," I said. I thought for a moment and spoke again.

"You two haven't practiced with us in the dynamics of clearing a building, so I want you two to standby outside until we give the all clear," I said.

Rowdy cleared his throat. "Hoss, I don't mean to be arrogant, but my daddy taught me how to shoot guns when I was just a snot-nosed kid."

"I've no doubt, Rowdy, and I'm betting Andie is a pretty good shot too. But, Julie and I have trained together. We use hand signals, signals with our flashlights, code words, entry procedures, and assigned sectors of fire. We've been doing this together so long we practically read each other's minds."

Rowdy nodded. "Well, I can certainly believe that. You two are peas in a pod." Andie laughed.

"Okay, Hoss, pretty little Andie here will help me watch out. I'm guessing you'll give the word when it's okay to come inside?" I nodded. "Okay, I'm good with that, but one day, you two are going to have to teach us some of those signals."

"Trust me, he'll have us practicing together so much you'll want to shoot him yourself," Julie said. I looked at her in the mirror with mock sadness. She stuck her tongue out and licked her lips provocatively. I concentrated on the road so I wouldn't become aroused.

The windows of the Home Depot had all been broken out, which seemed unnecessary for whoever felt the need to do it, but it worked out well for us. I drove by the front and revved the engine several times. We were rewarded with two of them slowly trudging their way out.

Andie bounced in the back seat. "I want to kill one!" she said. I looked at Rowdy.

"There's one for each of you," I said. They got out of the truck and the two of them took up positions on each end of the truck. I watched as Rowdy took aim and scored a headshot within a second. Andie followed a second later. I glanced at Julie.

"Not bad," she said. I agreed.

"Good shooting," I said to them when we got out. "Something you two may or may not have seen, even when you score a headshot, they don't always instantly drop dead. Sometimes it takes a few seconds, so be careful. You might assume the threat is eliminated and just before they drop dead they'll get one final bite in." They nodded. I looked around and saw no other zombies.

"Alright, you two wait out here. Oh, and I need to emphasize to you two not to shoot into the store. If I get shot, whether it's by accident or not, I'm shooting back. Stay by the truck and mind your sectors of fire. If any hostiles approach, either sound the horn, or start shooting."

They grinned and nodded in understanding.

Julie and I did a fast, dynamic entry and cleared the path to the building materials section quickly and silently. There were no other zombies, only a few putrefied corpses. Most of the inventory was gone, the shelves empty. But, as I suspected, there was plenty of five gallon buckets of asphalt sealer, along with some swabs. I grabbed a flat cart and loaded up. Julie guarded me as I pushed it out. I stopped suddenly and saw another item we could use, termite poison. There were several five gallon cans. I loaded all of them. When I was done, the cart must have weighed over three hundred pounds. I was breathing heavily when I finally got it pushed outside. Rowdy saw me, got out, and helped me load it all in the truck.

"What's the sealer for?" Andie asked.

"The driveways," I smiled at her confusion. "We've got to keep up the maintenance of our property," I explained. "Same thing for the termite poison."

"There are some gas pumps over yonder," Rowdy said, while pointing. "I reckon we should check."

I agreed. I was going to tell him the chances were slim, but he'd need to find out for himself. Andie joined him as he walked over to them.

"Andie needs clothes," Julie observed as we watched her pull her pants up over her skinny butt. I chuckled.

"Next on the list I guess. There's a sporting goods store down the road. We'll give it a try and see if there are any hunting clothes left. I may be wrong, but I'm guessing she hasn't worn a dress since kindergarten," I said.

"I'm going to need some bigger pants as well, feel," she put my hand on her baby bump. It had definitely grown in size. I rubbed it softly.

"Mmm, that feels good," she cooed. I was interrupted by Rowdy waving at us. I sighed and stopped. "We'll continue this later," she promised. I patted her on the butt in agreement, as we got in the truck and drove to the end of the parking lot where the gas pumps were located.

"Hoss, how in the hell do you get this here gas cap off of the storage tank?" Rowdy asked.

"Yeah, Hoss, show him how it's done," Julie mocked. I gave her a look. She smiled sweetly at me.

"Okay you two, watch close. It's actually fairly simple, but you've got to be careful with static electricity," I pulled out the bolt cutters, grounded them, and then snapped the lock. The cap opened right up.

"Alright, that's step one. Andie, there is a length of string in the truck with a couple of lead fishing weights tied on the end. Grab it and bring it over here." She complied without complaint. I dropped the weighted end and it struck the bottom of the tank with a clang. I shook my head.

"Bone dry," Andie said. I nodded in agreement.

"I was afraid of that. Most of these tanks were emptied long ago." I held up the rope. "This is a simple way to check. The only disadvantage is if you find a tank with fuel, the rope gets wet, so you can't tell how much is in the next tank you check until you let the rope dry out." They nodded in understanding.

"You've seemed to have thought of everything, Zach," Rowdy said. "I'm glad I found you guys." He smiled, but I honestly thought he was about to tear up. "It was a long winter," he added quietly. Andie grabbed his hand and squeezed it.

"Alright, load up, we have other places to check and I'm going to show you two how to siphon gas out of motor vehicles."

The sun was on the horizon as we headed home. It had been a successful day. We found enough diesel fuel to fill most of the cans and new clothes for Andie. There was even a case of trail mix hidden under a pile of clothes on a shelf in the sporting goods store.

Our good feelings ended as we got closer to home. The first thing I saw was an inordinate amount of smoke in the sky. There was a pit in my stomach and it was growing quickly.

Then we saw it. Julie gasped.

"Oh, my God," she exclaimed in fear. It was Fred's home, and it was totally engulfed in flames.

Chapter 35 – Fred

They secured the plane and spent the night inside it. Even though the doors were secured, Sarah insisted having a guard on duty. Each of them took two hour shifts. Fred was the second to the last shift and Sarah was going to take the four to six. Fred opted to let her catch up on her sleep. He knew he wouldn't be able to go back to sleep anyway.

He quietly watched the three of them sleep. Sarah was sleeping fitfully, her arms and legs twitching occasionally. The two lovebirds, he finally learned her name was Sabrina Smith and she was an Airman First Class, had laid out some sleeping bags on the floor and they were now snuggled up together, blissfully asleep.

Fred's thoughts went back to the apartment. He had knocked softly on the door and heard the telltale noises a moment later. He knew there was an infected individual inside his daughter's apartment, but he had to see for himself. When he kicked the door open, the zombie caught the impact of the door and flew backwards into the room. Fred watched as his daughter, or rather, what was once his daughter, climb back to her feet. She then launched herself at him. Fred had instinctively drawn his revolver and fired. Another one emerged from a back bedroom a second later, another female. It was probably Betsy's roommate. Fred put her out of commission as well.

Fred seemed to have zoned out afterward. He didn't remember setting fire to the apartment, nor did he seem to remember his ensuing actions. His next conscious thought was Sarah yelling at him. If not for her, he would probably be still standing out there, waiting for the zombies to attack him. He heard some movement outside and snuck a peek out of a window.

"What is it, Fred?" Sarah whispered, startling him. He turned to see she had awakened and sat up. He stepped softly as he walked over to her.

"There are three or four of them wandering around out there," he observed. Sarah looked at her watch and frowned at him.

"You were supposed to wake me two hours ago."

"I wasn't tired, and you needed your sleep. There may be others out there. Are we going to need access to the outside of the plane, or can we start up and fly off?" Fred asked. She shook her head.

"I wish it were that simple. We'll need to go outside. There are pre-flight checks and procedures which are required." She pointed at the other two. "I didn't know they had a thing for each other." Fred shrugged and looked out the window.

"They're moving like molasses. Since I know nothing about flying, why don't I take care of them while you three get the plane ready?"

"What do you have in mind?" Sarah asked.

"I'm going to draw them away from the plane. They're so slow, I think I can merely walk in a big circle until I hear the engines turn over, and then I'll run back.""Why don't we just shoot them all?" Sergeant Fandis asked. He had awakened while we were talking and was listening to our conversation.

"We want to avoid making noise as long as possible. Rule number two, they're attracted to noise."

"What are these rules you keep referring to?" Sarah asked.

"A very smart young man I know wrote up a list of rules. They've come in handy," Fred said. "I'll write them down for you, if you like." He looked at the three of them. "Well, let's get this dance started."

They lowered the ramp and Fred took off at a jog. Sarah watched him as he ran with those ridiculous cowboy boots and made a mental note to get him squared away with some combat boots when they got back to Tinker. Fred jogged twenty feet away from the plane, and then stopped. He stomped his foot a couple of times, and when he had the zombies attention, he started fast walking out toward the opposite end of the tarmac. The zombies hungrily followed.

"Alright you two, we've got work to do. Did you find a fuel truck anywhere around here, Sergeant?" Sarah asked.

"We did, ma'am, but the battery is dead on it," Sergeant Fandis replied.

Sarah sighed. "Alright, get the start cart hooked up and start preflight checks. Smith, you and I are going to take the Humvee over to that tanker and see if we can jump it off. I don't need to remind you two to keep an eye out for those things."

"Shouldn't someone keep an eye on Fred, ma'am?" Sergeant Fandis asked.

"If you hear him shooting, that means he needs help. Let's get moving."

Fred stomped on the asphalt occasionally to keep their attention, and the zombies eagerly followed. They were at irregular intervals, and he noticed one of them was several feet ahead of the others. He was very tall, well over six feet, and wearing a dirty Air Force uniform. Fred increased his stride, saw a shovel lying in the weeds beside the tarmac and headed toward it. He picked it up as he kept walking and tested the handle. It was still sturdy.

"Yep, I think you'll do nicely," Fred quietly said to the shovel as he walked toward a crashed plane. He stepped around some of the wreckage, gave himself a little room, and waited. The tall soldier/zombie came near and stepped around the wreckage. Fred rightly assumed having to turn a corner was difficult for them. He reminded himself to tell Zach what he had discovered.

The zombie's rasping noises increased and he struggled to align himself to where Fred was standing. Fred buried the shovel in the zombie's skull, wriggled it free, and waited for the next one. When he had dispatched all of them, he made a wide circle back to the plane. He discovered no other zombies. The three soldiers were waiting for him.

"Where are the zombies?" Sergeant Fandis asked.

"I took care of them," Fred answered. Sergeant Fandis saw all of the goo on the shovel blade, and pointed at it.

"With a shovel?" he asked. Fred nodded. "Holy shit, Fred."

"I wanted to keep the noise to a minimum. How are we doing here?"

Sarah had a calculator out and was scribbling on her kneepad. She ignored Fred.

"We found a fuel truck, but the gas was contaminated with water. The Major is crunching the numbers. If we had a J model, this wouldn't be an issue. But, we don't." He pointed at the plane. "It's an older, E model. If we don't have enough fuel to get back to Tinker, we're going to resort to plan B," Sergeant Fandis said. Sabrina looked at him, perplexed.

"What's plan B?" she asked.

"Hell if I know," he responded with a boyish grin.

Sarah looked up and sighed. "We'll have enough, but only if we don't encounter any strong headwinds. Sergeant Fandis, be prepared to dump the Humvee, if necessary. Alright, let's get underway."

Fred kept guard while the two enlisted soldiers completed the ground duties. Once the start cart was secured and the ramp closed, Fred went into the cockpit, strapped himself in, and put a helmet on. Sarah warmed the engines, checked the numerous gauges, and slowly turned the plane around. Satisfied she was not going to encounter a stray plane coming in for a landing, she moved the throttles forward and had the plane airborne a minute later.

"Keep an eye on those fuel gauges, cowboy," she said after a minute.

"Yes ma'am," Fred replied.

They flew in silence for the next hour. At one point, Fred pointed to one of the gauges. Sarah flipped a switch, which began drawing fuel from the starboard fuel cell. Sarah had her hands full, but she occasionally looked at Fred out of the corner of her eye.

She keyed up her microphone. "Do you want to talk about it?" she asked.

"There's not much to talk about. I found her and she was infected. I apologize for wasting your time."

"What are you going to do now?" Sarah asked, after a moment.

Fred stared out at the sky a few seconds before answering. "I'm going home. I've got friends there. I never should have left them. They're my family now."

"Are there any lady friends waiting for you, Fred?" Sarah asked with a small grin.

"Julie, Macie, and Zach. They're teenage kids, although this current situation has made them grow up quick. And, there is the Allen family. Howard and Lashonda are married and they have two preteen boys, Howard Junior and Derry. They're good kids," Fred worked a kink out of his neck before continuing.

"Zach, now Zach is a special kid. He's very intelligent and tough as nails. He got shot upside the head one day and he's no worse for the wear." Fred recalled the event and shook his head in wonder.

"He and Julie are head over heels in love with each other. Macie is Zach's ex-girlfriend, but the three of them seem to get along okay. But, the answer to your question is no. There are no ladies waiting for me." Fred cast a brief glance at her.

"Are there any ladies waiting for you?" he deadpanned.

Sarah arched an eyebrow at Fred. "I've dated a few women in my time, and I've dated a few men. Hell, I was even engaged once. What do you think of that, cowboy?"

"Do you really want my opinion?" Fred asked. Sarah looked over at him.

"Fire away, cowboy, this ought to be interesting," she said.

"I think you're a very driven woman, an overachiever. When it came to a significant other, you always had high expectations. But, when you would become involved in a relationship and then see all of their flaws, they always came up short." He gave her a wry look.

"Of course, if you had ever gotten together with a cowboy from Tennessee, all of your prayers might've been answered." Fred looked back out of the window without waiting for a reply. He missed the glare from Sarah, which was slowly replaced with a small grin.

Chapter 36 – Arson Most Foul

There was no saving it; no need to even try. I floored it and headed toward the house. I knew it was no accidental fire, I'd been too careful. No, it was deliberately set, and I had a pretty damn good idea who did it. Stopping at the turn to our driveway, I motioned to Julie. She grabbed her M4, a walkie-talkie, and jumped out of the truck."Where the heck is she going?" Rowdy asked. She was heading toward her sniper hole but I didn't bother explaining.

"She knows what to do. You two lock and load." Andie reacted without hesitation and grabbed the other M4. Rowdy was having vapor lock until Andie leaned forward and punched him in the arm.

"Get your ass moving!" she shouted at him. Rowdy looked at her and began fumbling with his revolver. I stopped the truck right at the curve, slammed it into park, and shouted over my shoulder to Andie.

"Cover me! Rowdy, you stay here with the truck and kill anyone you don't recognize," I said. Without waiting for a response, I grabbed my Winchester and exited the truck. Hugging the tree line, I made my way to the bridge in much the same manner Jason's boys did not so long ago. I was much more careful than they were though, utilizing stealth and cover as I approached. Andie followed me closely, and much to my relief, she was as quiet as a mouse.

One of them was sitting on his ass near the gate and holding his arm. I could plainly see the third degree chemical burns on his face and hands. Good, my booby trap actually worked. I used my riflescope and scanned around the house. Andie's jeep was there, parked beside my truck. There was a man whom I did not recognize admiring it. I couldn't blame him. It was probably the most beautiful motor vehicle on the planet. Another one emerged from the front door, carrying a gas can. My blood ran cold.

I was just about to shoot him when a little voice in my head started screaming. I swiveled my rifle around and scanned the rest of the area. I stopped suddenly and looked closely at Rick's hill. The casual observer would never have seen it, but I knew every bump, every curve, and every nuance of that mound. There was a slight, very slight, bulge in one spot. He was well camouflaged, possibly wearing a ghillie suit.

"Well hello, George," I whispered. Anyone hidden so well and set up to provide cover for his buddies had to have been a Marine. I would have liked to have gotten to know him. Perhaps we could have been friends. It was a good thing we were well back in the trees. Otherwise, he would have immediately spotted us. I had to act quickly, for all I knew he was sighting in on one of us at this very moment.

I knew what the range my rifle was sighted in at, and I also knew the exact range to the top of the mound. I was concentrating on the crosshairs when I saw a small puff of smoke and the tree I was kneeling beside spat out a chunk of bark. He had spotted me, but his aim was slightly off.

I had to act quickly or I was a dead man. I forced myself to relax and gently squeezed the trigger. The cloth material made a slight inward indention before returning to normal, but otherwise did not move. I put another round in the same spot before swiveling the scope back toward our other two adversaries. The one with the gas can was hurriedly digging into his pocket, perhaps reaching for a lighter. I shot him before he succeeded. The other one ducked behind my truck. I should have started laying down fire, but hell, I loved that truck and didn't want to damage it.

While I was concentrating, there was a three-round burst of gunfire over my head. I looked up in fright. Andie was standing over me with the M4 pointed toward the bridge. I looked at what she was aiming at. The man with the chemical burns had a sawn-off shotgun grasped in his hands. I had not seen it. I looked back up at Andie and gave her a grateful nod. It was obvious she was scared shitless, but she smiled at me nonetheless. I turned my attention back to the house. I saw nobody else, but that one asshole was still hiding somewhere. I turned my walkie on.

"Come in, Saigon," I whispered. Julie clicked her radio. "Two tangos down, one still active, anything on your end?" I asked.

"Nothing," Julie whispered. "Is the Captain there?"

I told her I did not see him, but I felt he was around here somewhere. Andie crouched down beside me.

"Good job, girl," I said.

"Julie doesn't like me very much," she replied. I took my eye off of the scope and looked at her. It astounded me that she was thinking of Julie's antipathy toward her rather than the problem at hand. Typical female.

"I'll have a word with her."

Andie looked at me gratefully. I pointed toward the dead dude by the bridge.

"Who's the asshole?" I asked.

"Tony," she said. "He was okay, I guess. I mean, he never did anything fucked up toward me."

I nodded in mock understanding.

"There is one other man hiding behind my truck. There may be someone still inside the house, or maybe in the barn, I don't know. But I have an idea if you're up for it."

I explained what I had in mind. Andie listened without comment, and agreed. She walked out from the tree line and moved toward the gate. Squinting up at the house, she waved. After a minute, I saw a face peeking out from beside the truck. She dragged Tony out of the way, opened the gate, and walked up. At my instruction, she stopped several yards away. I got on the radio and told Julie what we were doing. She clicked in acknowledgement. I waited for him to show more of his head. It was going to be a tricky shot. He slowly stood and looked down toward the gate.

I took aim and was about to shoot. There was no need.I saw him stagger a split second before I heard a gunshot. I put my scope on Andie. She had her revolver in her hand, tucked it in her waistband, and then used her assault rifle for a three-shot coup de grace. She carefully entered the house, came out a minute later, and began jogging back down the hill.

"You killed Randy and I killed Herb. They were assholes," she said.

I stared at her with curiosity as we walked back to her jeep. She felt me staring and looked at me.

"I told him I'd just killed you and I wanted to go back to the Captain. He fell for it. You have to carry your own water, right?" she said. I gave her a wry smile.

As we rounded the curve, Rowdy raised his revolver and pointed it at us. Andie slowed and we waved at him. Recognition dawned on his face and he lowered his weapon as we drove up.

"What the hell happened?" he asked. I quickly filled him in. He looked at us wide-eyed. I got on the radio.

"We have four tangos down. Can you maintain your status while we clear the house?"

"Ten-four," she whispered. The three of us drove up to the house and carefully cleared it and the barn of anyone who Andie might have missed. There was nobody.

Both structures reeked of gasoline. We'd saved the buildings from fire, but the gas ruined any chance of habitation for the foreseeable future. I was pissed.

No, wrong descriptive. I was saddened. The Captain was right. I was naïve to believe in a utopian society where our fellow man would peacefully join together in order to survive and rebuild.

"This isn't going to stop," I said to myself. The Captain is going to keep doing shit like this until we were all wiped out. History was filled with people of his ilk.

Andie must have heard me. She walked over and touched me on the shoulder. I instinctively put my arm around her.

"What are you thinking?" she asked.

"What I have planned will most likely get me killed. I want you to stick with Julie and Rowdy. You're a lot stronger than you believe. The three of you can protect each other."

She shook her head. "I know what you're about to do. You're going to the compound, aren't you?" She didn't wait for an answer. "I'll come with you. I know the layout. I can help."

"I'm afraid it's going to be a suicide mission, Andie," I said quietly.

"I'm still going with you. You'll need my help," she said. She was looking at me seriously, deeply. I thought about it. She had already killed two of them, she just might do.

"What are you two talking about?" Rowdy asked. I stared at Andie a moment longer before focusing on Rowdy.

"He's not going to stop. He's decided we're enemies now and he's going to kill us all if we don't do something about it," I said. "Andie and I are going to pay him a visit. If we don't make it back, it'll be up to you to take care of Julie and the Allen family."

Actually, I was thinking Julie would be the one to look after them, but did not say as much.

Without waiting for him to respond, I went to the house and filled two knapsacks. One of them I filled with water, ammo, and a small amount of food. The other one I filled with some special items.

Our ghillie suits were hanging up in the barn. I grabbed both, although Julie's was going to be a little large for Andie. I explained it to Julie when we picked her up from her sniper position. Actually, I prevaricated somewhat.

"So, Andie and I will sneak in, I'll wait for the right moment, and put a bullet in him. We'll be home by dinner." In truth, I feared it would not be so easy.

"Zach, there must be another way," Julie implored.

I shook my head. Unfortunately, there wasn't.

"Then I'm going with you," she said. I immediately shook my head.

"Julie, I love you and our unborn child more than anything else on this earth. I'd never forgive myself if anything happened to either of you," I said. I also left out the part where I didn't want her killing anyone else. She was too sweet, warm, and loving. I never wanted her to change.

"Then why is she going?" Julie asked while pointing at Andie.

"She saved my ass back there. She's volunteered to go with me and she knows the layout of the compound."

Julie looked long and hard at me.

"You're a terrible liar," she accused. Without waiting for a response, she hugged me tightly, and then punched me in the chest.

"We need to check on the Allens," she finally said. It was a good point, I had totally forgotten about them. We arrived at their house two minutes later with weapons at the ready. Much to my relief, there was no ball of fire greeting us, nor were there any hostiles shooting at us. Howard came running out with his shotgun.

"Lil' H was at your house and seen them coming. He ran all the way back. I got 'em all in the basement."

"Good," I said. "Julie and Rowdy are going to stay with you guys."

Howard looked sidelong at me.

"What are you about to do, Zach?" he asked.

"With a little help from Andie, I'm going to end this shit." I looked at my friend. "He was right, Howard. He told me I was being naïve. He was right."

I held my hand out. He slowly held his out and we shook.

"You're a good man, Howard, and a good friend," I said. Howard had difficulty making eye contact, and opted instead to stare at our feet.

Andie and I drove in silence most of the way. We swapped vehicles and got into her jeep. I parked at the burned out store in College Grove and looked at her.

"How far?" I asked. She pointed.

"About four miles, I should drive from here on." I agreed and we swapped seats.

"I want a spot where we can hide your jeep and approach on foot, and we don't need to accidentally encounter them."

Andie nodded. "There is an old barn about a quarter of a mile from Ward Road. Nobody ever used it. We can get there the back way. I don't think we'll run in to anyone."

"Sounds perfect."

Andie took a hard left into a driveway of an old home with wood siding badly in need of paint. It may have been green at one time. She drove around the back of the house, continued through the backyard, across a shallow creek, and into some woods. She drove down an overgrown trail through the trees, swerving left and right. I was now lost and getting concerned. Soon, we emerged from the trees and faced the back of a barn that looked like it was on the verge of collapse. I looked at Andie.

"It was my dope smoking hang out back in the day," she said in answer to my unasked question. "On the other side of the barn is Rocky Glade Road, just a little bit down from Ward Road. Is it good?" she asked.

I jumped out of the jeep and opened the barn doors. She eased the jeep forward and inside the barn.

I looked around before I closed the doors. If one looked closely, you could see the tire tracks, but you'd have to have a sharp eye. It would have to do.

"We've cleared out most of the zombies in this area. We should be safe, from them anyway," Andie said.

"We'll leave the jeep here," I said and unloaded the knapsacks. I unloaded the contents and took a quick inventory.

"What is all of that?" Andie asked and pointed at my special goodies.

I gestured at the two plastic milk jugs with nails duct taped to the exterior. "Those contain a mixture of fertilizer and diesel fuel. The nails will add to the carnage," the tops had some detonators screwed into the tops.

"They're bombs?" Andie asked. I nodded.

"Now these should be obvious," I said as I pointed to the bottles containing fuel and rags sticking out of the ends.

"Uh, Molotov cocktails?" she asked. I nodded.

"Fight fire with fire I always say."

She nodded tentatively. I had been watching Andie the entire time. The trepidation seemed to be growing in her with each passing minute.

"Alright, it's time for a talk," I said. "I've got to ask you, are you ready to go through with this?" she started to speak, but I held up my hand.

"Before you answer, I want you to know, my intention is to kill your uncle and anyone else who I believe is a threat. If you can't go through with this, you still have a home with us. We won't hold it against you. I can only imagine how difficult it must be to go against a blood relative."

Andie looked strong, at first. Then, when the brevity of the situation sunk in, her lower lip started quivering. I set my rifle down, walked over to her, and hugged her tightly. A sob escaped her lips.

"I'm scared, Zach. I don't know if I can," she admitted weakly.

"It's okay," I said quietly. "It's okay."

We stood there a moment while Andie fought through the tears. She finally spoke.

"I'm sorry," she said meekly. I held her at arm's length.

"It's okay, really," I repeated, "so, a minor change of plans." Andie looked up at me. "I'm going to take care of this, once and for all. If you get into trouble, or if you get a bad vibe and you don't think I'm going to come back, you hightail it out of here and go back to the Allen's."

"But what if you need help?" she asked.

"Don't worry about me. You take care of yourself," I looked at my watch. "I better get going. Point me in the right direction."

Andie led me to the front of the barn and pointed to a bend in the road about a hundred yards away.

"This is Rocky Glade Road. Just around that bend is Ward Road. The compound is at the dead end, about another hundred yards." She bit her lip before continuing. "The Captain's living quarters is on the second floor of the main house. There is a trailer behind the house that some of the guys share."

I nodded, remembering the drawing she made. As we peered out of a crack in the wall of the barn, the bus drove by. We quickly ducked out of sight.

"Damn. There goes plan A," I said and furrowed my brow in concentration.

"Okay, I've got something else in mind."

We sat on the bare dirt floor of the barn and ate a snack of old protein bars while I went over my plan with Andie.

"What time do they usually go to bed?" I asked.

"Usually around twenty-two hundred hours. We rotate guard duty, but it's become a little bit of an inside joke. Whoever has duty just sleeps in the guard shack," Andie said.

"Alright, I'm going to head out at midnight. It would be best if we tried to get a little shuteye, I have a feeling it's going to be a long night," I said. Andie looked at me somberly, and retrieved a blanket out of her jeep.

Chapter 37 – Payback

I awoke with a start and quickly checked my watch. It showed a few minutes after midnight. I was shivering. It had grown even colder after the sun went down. I woke Andie, who was sleeping by my side.

"It's time," I said simply. She nodded and stood while I stretched, worked the kinks out of my stiff muscles, and put on my ghillie suit.

Andie watched me, and then stood. "I'll show you the way, it's the least I can do."

I looked at her a moment, nodded and told her to put on the other ghillie suit.

Getting my things together, Andie led me down Ward Road, stepping behind a tree when we were within site of the house. I peered around the tree and checked it out.

It was a full moon with a clear sky tonight, so I could see fairly well. The front entrance was gated and there was a guard shack made of wood with concertina wire wrapped around it. It wasn't very impressive. I would have thought, at the very least, it would have been fortified with sandbags.

The house was an old two-story structure with white wood siding and a wraparound front porch. I couldn't see the trailer from my angle, but the lack of any backlighting indicated everyone was asleep.

I saw no movement, heard no noise. Either I was going to pull this off, or I was walking into a trap.

"Okay girl," I whispered. "Sneak back to the barn and wait. If I don't show up after all of the shooting stops, you get the hell out of here. Got it?" Andie looked at me in the dark. I saw her nod her head, but could not see any facial expression. She stood on her tiptoes and kissed me, and then disappeared in the darkness.

After she was safely away, I low crawled my way closer to the front entrance, keeping an eye on both the guard shack and the house. There was no movement. I made it to the gate undetected, crouched beside one of the support posts, and listened. Turning my head so my good ear was turned toward the little guard shack I heard nothing. Now came the hard part.

The gate was a typical galvanized steel cattle gate you could buy at the farmer's co-op. There was concertina wire carelessly draped all over it, otherwise, there appeared to be nothing special about it. The rest of the perimeter was protected with a four strand barbed wire fence and concertina also strung across the top. I suspected there may be booby traps here and there. I carefully laid my rifle down and slowly, gently, caressed the entire gate with my hands. I found no wires, monofilament lines, or containers filled with burning surprises. The slide latch was located in the inside of the gate. It had a spot to put a padlock, but surprisingly, there wasn't one. I reached through and slowly, painstakingly, slid the latch. The soft scraping noise seemed to scream out, and I was certain at any moment I was going to be discovered. The resistance of the latch suddenly lessened. I had it open. I opened the gate a fraction and again checked for any tripwires. There were none. Grabbing my knapsack, I eased through.

I made a quick peek through the small slit in the front of the shack I assumed was supposed to be a firing port. All I could see was a dark blob of a figure inside. I took a longer peek this time and watched for a few seconds. I could hear deep breathing through the slit, but the person did not move. I worked my way around and located the entry door in the back. I tried the knob carefully, found it unlocked, and opened the door. The heady odor of marijuana immediately assaulted my nostrils. No wonder he never knew of my presence. He was stoned senseless. His back was to me, his feet were propped up, and he had a couple of blankets wrapped around him. His breathing was heavy and rhythmic.

The only new sound he made was a gurgling noise when I slit his throat. He may or may not have been a good guy who didn't deserve to die like he did, but it was not my concern. He chose the wrong group to throw his lot in with. I wiped my knife on his blanket and shut the door quietly.

I caressed my two milk jug bombs, I guess to subconsciously insure they were still with me. The detonators were homemade and were stuck into the tops of each milk jug. I set one of them up at the front door of the house and rigged them with a monofilament tripwire. I did the same with the second one at the door to the trailer in back. I kept looking around as I was setting them up, wondering when hear the crack of a gunshot immediately followed by mortal pain.

It didn't happen. Lady luck was on my side. Free of the extra weight, I made it quickly over to the parked bus. I tried to open the door quietly, but it started to make a horrible squeaking noise when I only got it open a fraction of an inch. I stopped and ducked around to the far side of the bus, out of sight from the house. Peeking out, I still saw no movement or stirrings. Looking up at the two machine guns mounted in this beast, I realized there was no way I could allow them to have this death-mobile in their arsenal.

I pulled out a lighter and lit all four of the Molotov cocktails. I tossed the first one through one of the open turret bays on the bus. The sound of the breaking glass was quickly followed by the distinctive sound of gas igniting. Next, I ran toward the house and slung the remaining three. Two of them definitely broke, but I was uncertain of the third one. No matter, it was time to flee. I ran through the partially open gate, pausing only long enough to grab my rifle. I was twenty yards shy of the big hickory tree when I heard muffled yelling, followed by the door opening. I ducked behind the tree a fraction of a second before the bomb was detonated. Fighting to control my breathing, I raised the rifle and looked through the scope. There was a body lying on the ground. A second later an older man, long beard and wild hair, wearing nothing but boxers and combat boots ran out of the door. He was armed with an assault rifle and fired wildly. I took aim as he started making his way toward the bus. The round took him in the right shoulder. He fell and started crawling. I shot him again. It was then I heard the second explosion, followed by an agonizing scream. Presumably, this was the bomb I had set up on the door of the trailer.

A woman in a nightgown ran outside. She had something wrapped in a blanket and I was chastened when I realized she was carrying a baby. I had forgotten all about the child when I planned this out. She ran toward the back of the house and disappeared from sight. Lady luck was still with me. I'm not sure how I would live with myself if I killed a child.

I waited for the Captain to make an appearance. In the meantime, two other men ran out from the back of the house. They were armed with assault rifles. They looked around for a target, and finding none, they tried valiantly to put out the fire. I scored a headshot with each.

I waited another ten minutes for him, my nemesis, to appear. All I needed for him to do was show his face, even for a moment, and I'd send him to hell. The old wood house was now fully engulfed, but he was nowhere to be seen. I came to the conclusion he was currently burning to death, or perhaps, he had escaped out of the back, which I could not cover. I watched the house burn.

I had no idea if I'd gotten him, but I knew I had hurt him. Badly. By my count, ten of his men had been sent to hell, and, I just burned his house down.

It felt good, but not good enough. The not knowing if he was dead was going to be bothersome. Nevertheless, my gut instinct told me to get the hell out of there. I slipped out of sight into the darkness and headed back to the barn.

"It's me," I whispered as I opened the barn door. Even though it was getting light outside, it was still dark inside the dusty old barn. I made out Andie, standing at the far wall, unmoving. I sensed something was wrong, but I did not react fast enough.

The first punch caught me on the side of the head. I partially avoided the blow, but it still struck me with enough of an impact to knock me to the ground. I was on the verge of losing consciousness, but I was still awake enough to feel the sharp impact of a steel-toed boot in my abdomen. It knocked the breath out of me. The only thing I could do was bring my knees up in time to block a kick to my groin, but not the follow-up kick to my head. Fireworks went off in my head.

While I was dazed, the Captain rolled me over on my stomach, and I felt a pair of handcuffs being snapped around my wrists. He cinched them down tight before rolling me over again. He grabbed my Kimber out of the holster and tossed it over to where my rifle was lying. He then stood over me with a sadistic grin on his face.

"When my soldiers didn't come home last night, I knew you'd be coming to pay me a visit," he kicked me again, in the side this time.

"Zach, Zach, Zach. It is time for you to pay for your betrayal," he lamented, and looked around the barn.

"It's you who betrayed me, you cocksucker," I croaked out. He laughed and kicked me again.

"Did you know this is Andie's favorite spot?" he nodded with a wicked grin. "It sure is. She would meet the neighborhood boys here in this barn after school and suck their cocks. Did she tell you that?" he asked.

I didn't answer, but I glanced at Andie. She was crying, and I noticed for the first time she was battered and bloody. Both eyes were swollen, and it looked like her nose was broken.

"Oh, yeah. They'd bring the dope, she'd bring her mouth. I caught her one day and threatened to tell her mother. Do you know what she did? She offered to suck my cock if I'd keep her secret," he laughed without mirth.

"So, Andie, what happened yesterday?" the Captain asked.

"They're all dead," she answered with a weak attempt at defiance.

The Captain grimaced, and slowly nodded. "Yeah, I figured as much. I told them not to underestimate young Mister Gunderson, but they didn't listen of course," he canted his head. "What about George?" he asked.

"I killed him. I killed them all," I proclaimed. Andie stared at me with despair.

The Captain laughed again and kicked me in the thigh. I had an instant painful charley horse to go along with all of my other aches. He waved a hand at Andie.

"You see, when I arrived home yesterday, I was chagrined. My work was not completed because your stinking ass was still alive. Yes, Zach. I knew you were a threat to me from the very moment I met you." He kicked me again in the same thigh. I grunted with pain and my whole leg became paralyzed with pain.

"When my crew did not arrive home last night, I knew you would be coming. I didn't know how, but I *knew* you were going to bring the fight to me. You were going to try something, but I didn't know what. I pondered over it all evening and well into the night. Finally, at about four, I suddenly awakened. An epiphany came to me in a dream."

He smiled and pointed at Andie. "I figured the little slut would probably help you. I dreamt of this old barn and Andie on her knees pleasing all the boys, so I snuck out the back door and made my way over here. What do you know? My instincts were right on the money," he looked down at me with a contemptuous sneer.

"But I erred in my logic. I told my soldiers to be extra vigilant, for you were coming. How did you get past the guard?"

"If you mean the dumbass in the guard shack, he was asleep." I smiled up at the Captain. "I slit his throat."

The Captain smiled back at me, knelt down and dropped his knee on my chest, putting his weight into it. I thought my sternum was going to crack and fought to breathe.

"Where are your friends, Zach? Are they around here somewhere, waiting for you to meet up with them?" I glared at him while gasping for breath and didn't answer. He clucked his tongue.

"Refusing to answer? No matter, I'll get it out of you, and then you know what I'm going to do?" His sneer was replaced with a lascivious grin.

"I'm going to pay Julie a special visit. I'm going to kill them all, but I'll save Julie for last." He brought his face even closer. "Yeah, I'm going to have a good time with her. But first, I'm going to have a little fun with you." He pulled a knife out of a sheath on his belt and locked the blade open.

"I think I'll start with your face and work my way down. Oh, and you'll be pleased to know I brought a camera along. I'm going to take pictures to show Julie." He brought the knife closer and stuck the point in my cheek. Blood spurted out. He then pulled a small digital camera out of his pocket.

"Smile!" he said, and took a picture.

I grunted, but managed to keep from screaming out in pain. It was going to happen though. I knew at some point I was going to scream out in agony, and once I did, I wouldn't stop. But, there was no way I'd ever tell him where my friends were. At least, that was what I kept telling myself.

It was a hell of a way to die. Lady luck had left me, and I was now paying the price. The Captain dragged the point of the knife along my cheek, cutting deeply. It was a searing pain. I gritted my teeth. He chuckled at me.

"You're a tough one, huh, Zach?" he chuckled some more. "Not tough enough though. You'll be begging me to stop soon enough, and maybe I will. Maybe I'll work on you a little while, and then work on Andie a little bit. What do you say, Andie? How about you telling me where Zach's friends are and I'll be nice to you. Hell, you can even come back and live with me." He chuckled as he turned to face her. He suddenly froze. I looked over at Andie. She had retrieved her snub-nosed revolver from wherever she had been hiding it, and was now pointing it at the Captain.

"Get off of him," she said. She was glaring at him, but her voice betrayed her fear. The Captain smiled at her.

"Andie, be a good girl now and put that gun down." He continued smiling but I could feel him tensing up. He was about to spring on her, and the big bastard could do it.

"Watch out, Andie!" I shouted. The Captain turned back to me and twisted the knife blade. I gasped in pain.

"Shut the fuck up," he growled.

"Uncle Charlie?" Andie's voice was cracking. The Captain looked back at her. "I loved you once," she said and then pulled the trigger.

The Captain's head flew back as the bullet struck him in the cheek. Andie stepped closer and fired again. The second projectile struck him in the right eye. He fell on top of me, which gave me a close-up of his lifeless face. What was left of his eye began to ooze out. I wiggled free and attempted to stand, but was too weak.

Andie knelt down beside me and stared, as if she didn't know what to do.

"I'm sorry, Zach," she stuttered. She was breathing hard, and looked like she was on the edge of panic.

"Andie, I need you to focus. Go through his pockets and find the key to these handcuffs," I said. She complied dumbly, as if she was in a fog. She fumbled through her uncle's pockets, came up with some keys, and slowly went through them, one at a time.

"Focus, Andie," I repeated, and gestured with my head at one of the keys. "I believe it's that one. Stay with me, sweetheart," I said, trying to calm her. She separated one and looked at me expectantly. I nodded and turned my back to her. She made several attempts before finally unlocking one side. I turned and took the keys from her. Getting my other hand unencumbered by the cuffs, I dropped them on the floor and unsteadily got to my feet. Andie instinctively grabbed my arm and put it around her shoulders.

"Help me get in the jeep."

She walked me to the passenger side and helped me get in. I was in a lot of pain and blood was gushing down my face.

"Do you have a first aid kit?" I asked. Andie looked at me blankly. "I need to staunch this bleeding. Do you have anything at all?" She responded with a look of confusion, but after a couple of seconds, she opened the glove box and came out with a tampon. It wouldn't have been my first choice, but it'd have to do. I tore the wrapper off, took the cotton material, and held it to the gash in my cheek.

"How bad are you hurt, are you able to move?" I asked. She nodded nervously. "Okay, gather up all of our stuff and let's get the hell out of here."

She complied, but it looked like she was moving in a fog. When she finished, she got into the driver's seat and looked straight ahead. She was in a daze. I had to do something.

"Hey," I said. She continued staring straight ahead until I snapped my fingers several times. She finally looked over at me. She looked like she was in shock.

"You've saved my ass twice now. You've done good," she stared at me as if my words did not register to her.

"Hey!" I yelled. Her eyes widened. "Don't be zoning out on me!" I lowered my voice.

"Listen to me, we've just been through a nightmare, but we survived. Okay?" I asked. She continued looking at me, but finally nodded her head. "Good girl. Now, let's go home."

Andie nodded and started the jeep.

Using the mirror on the sun visor, I took a look at my injuries. I had a knot on the side of my head the size of a softball. The cut to my cheek looked to be less than an inch long, but it was deep. I could see my cheekbone through the gash. I worked my jaw, and although it was swollen and ached, it didn't seem to be broken. I knew my leg was going to have a large bruise, but my main worry was when he kicked me in the gut. I was having a lot of pain there.

We arrived at the Allen's new home approximately twenty minutes later. Julie and Rowdy jogged outside to greet us. I saw Howard standing inside the doorway with his shotgun at the ready. Julie gasped when she saw us.

"Oh, my God, are you two alright?" she asked as she helped me out of the jeep. I smiled at her. It was only an hour ago I thought I'd never see her again.

"We got our asses kicked, but I think we're okay. Help me inside and I'll tell everyone about it."

I put my arm around Julie, and Rowdy practically carried Andie inside. Everyone gathered around as I was assisted to a chair at the head of the kitchen table. Lashonda hurried about fixing a meal while Julie fussed over me. I was in too much pain to eat.

"You should eat," Rowdy said to Andie. "Put some meat on that skinny butt."

Andie tried to smile, but couldn't bring herself to do it.

Julie looked worriedly at the gash on my cheek. The bleeding had almost stopped now, but I had no doubt it was a pretty ugly wound. I tried out a carefree smile while I offered advice.

"I would suggest pouring some peroxide in the wound and then sealing it with super glue. If we have any ice or anything cold, I sure would like to put it on my head. Andie can use some as well."

Julie gave me a condescending look, but did as I suggested while I told them of the encounter with the Captain. Rowdy got a wet rag and began tenderly cleaning up Andie's face.

I told them everything, except for the remarks the Captain said about Andie. When I had finished, everyone seemed to be in stunned silence.

"So this Captain fellow, he's dead now?" Rowdy finally asked. I nodded, and then felt the need to speak further.

"I want y'all to know something. Andie came through. If not for her, I'd be dead." I looked over at her and patted her hand. "It was a very hard decision for her to kill her own uncle, so I hope you guys understand and not pester her with questions about it."

Everyone nodded in understanding.

"Are all of them dead, Zach?" Howard asked.

"I'm not sure. There are three unaccounted for, not counting the baby. One of the women ran out of the house with the kid, so they may be okay. The others may have escaped or they may have burned up in the fire. Either way, I don't believe they are a threat, not anymore."

"What are we going to do now?" Julie asked. She had finished with the gash on my cheek and began wiping the blood and dirt off of my face with a washrag.

"I want to go to our old house and take stock of how much is ruined," I said.

"We'll do it first thing in the morning," Julie said.

"I really want to do it now. Tomorrow, I would like to get everything that is undamaged loaded up and moved into the Riggins' home. Besides, we need to get those bodies burned."

Rowdy grinned broadly. "For once, I am one step ahead of you Mister Gunderson, sir," he said smugly. I looked at him and then at Julie. She was smiling too.

"Rowdy has already stacked the bodies by the sinkhole and pulled everything out of the house that was doused in gas," she said. "He was going to burn them, but we thought you might want to look them over first."

"Yeah, we were going to wait a day or so, and if you didn't come back I was going to go ahead and burn them," Rowdy said, and then realized what he implied.

"Sorry," he murmured.

I shook my head, which sent a minor wave of nausea over me. "No need to apologize, your reasoning is perfectly logical. Alright, let's go look them over."

Even though Julie was very much against it and demanded Andie and I straight to bed, my stubbornness won out and we rode in the jeep over to the sinkhole. Secretly, I wished I had listened to her. Every bump sent waves of pain through me.

Andie pointed at one of the corpses. "That's Eddy, he must have been the sniper you shot."

"That was some pretty good shooting Hoss, you put two holes in his head, side-by-side," Rowdy said. "Oh, here's what he had on him." Rowdy went to the truck and returned with a sniper rifle. It was a Remington model seven hundred with a scope, fluted stainless steel barrel, and a black synthetic stock.

"That is a nice looking rifle," I commented. Rowdy grinned. I pointed at the bodies. "So, none of these are George?" I asked Andie. She shook her head. So, George, the Marine, was still out there somewhere. It was cause for concern.

We were interrupted by an unusual sound. All of us looked around and then saw something none of us had seen in quite a while.

A helicopter flew overhead.

Chapter 38 – A Message From Above

It was a military helicopter, a Chinook by the looks of it, although I was no expert. It was painted olive drab, and it was flying low, maybe five hundred feet.

"What are they doing?" Julie asked as it went into a banking maneuver. We watched as someone standing at the rear of the helicopter threw an object out. Whatever it was, it was small. There were a couple of long white pieces of cloth attached to it and they were furling in the wind as the object descended. It landed about a hundred yards from us.

Andie ran after it. It looked small, not much larger than her hand. She jogged back to us a minute later.

"It looks like a small tube," she said and handed it over to me. I opened it while everyone peered closer. It was a typed memorandum and looked like it had been photocopied many times over, with the exception of a handwritten paragraph at the end. I read it aloud.

"Attention to orders: The Provisional Government of the United States of America is hereby requesting all surviving personnel to report to the nearest military facility in order to receive care and treatment. Upon arrival, personnel will be processed accordingly. We offer housing, health care, food, and most importantly safety." I looked at my friends.

"The rest is handwritten. It says the nearest military facility is Fort Campbell, Kentucky, and there will be a military transport plane waiting at Smyrna airport the rest of today and tomorrow to pick us up," I finished. Julie took the memo out of my hand and reread it. Rowdy shook his head slowly.

"I don't know about this, Hoss. Now don't get me wrong, I'm glad there are other people still out there, but I surely don't like that word – processed. That's the word they use when they lead cows to the slaughter house."

"What do you girls think?" I asked.

"I think I'm with Rowdy on this one," Andie said. I looked at Julie. She had her head down and was looking at the memo.

"Julie?" I asked. She looked up at us.

"They said they have medical care. I'm just thinking about the baby," she said. "But I'm not overly fond of abandoning everything we've done here."

"Okay. We'll show this to Howard and Lashonda. In the meantime, let's get this shit burned."

We dumped all of the gasoline soaked items from the house and used it to burn the bodies. The ruined items included Rick's old chair, which didn't help my sour mood. We watched them burn for a while and then headed back to our home. I did a walk-through in silence. Although Julie and Rowdy had opened all of the windows, the house still smelled of gas. Julie and I went down into the root cellar. Everything was intact, but I could still faintly smell the gas odor. She stood close and I instinctively grabbed her butt. She slapped at my hand.

"Don't get something started you won't be able to finish. You really need to be in bed right now, for rest, not for sex," she chided. She was right. I was sore as hell.

"I agree, but I knew I wouldn't be able to sleep if I didn't get a firsthand look at all of this," I responded.

"So, what do you think?" she asked after a minute.

"If we try to live in here I'm afraid the fumes will make us sick. Not to mention we won't be able to use the stove or fireplace. I think it's time to move into the Riggins' home," I said.

"I like that house. The master bedroom is big enough for us and the baby."

"They have well water and a generator hookup, but no barn or greenhouse. It'll be a lot of work," I said.

"So what else is new?" she asked sarcastically. "You thrive when there's hard work. In the meantime, I'm getting you to bed. No arguing with me, you look awful." I smiled at her reassuringly, but she was right, I felt awful. I explained to Rowdy what I wanted to do on the ride back to the Allen's house.

"Don't you worry about a thing. I'll get right on it," he said with a wide grin. "I'd like to play around with this rifle though."

I shrugged. "It's yours. I hope you can shoot."

"Thank you kindly, Hoss," Rowdy said and caressed the rifle lovingly. "Yeah, I can shoot. I was raised in southern Alabama, so of course I can shoot," he said.

Julie insisted I eat. I forced down a couple of boiled eggs while Howard and Lashonda read the memo.

"It seems promising," Howard said. "I mean, we didn't think anyone in the government was left."

"It'd be nice having a semblance of society again," Lashonda added. "A hospital to go to when you're sick, a school for the kids, Sunday church, that'd be real nice."

I didn't blame her sentiment, but still, I was wary.

"Alright, why don't a couple of us go pay them a visit in the morning and see what they have to say?" I suggested. They readily agreed. I was thinking about the last time we encountered soldiers. It did not end well.

I awoke in the middle of the night. The four of us were sleeping in the den of the Allen's new home. It was like a slumber party and I was the one who had eaten too much candy. My gut was still hurting from the kick the Captain gave me, may he rest in hell. In truth, I was hurting all over. There must have been a few punches and kicks I didn't remember receiving.

I went to the restroom and shined the flashlight in the bowl. My urine had an orange tint to it, indicating blood. Not a great deal, but enough to concern me. I went back to the den and lay beside Julie. Andie's eyes opened and she watched me, as I got comfortable. She was snuggled up beside Rowdy, who was snoring contentedly. Her face was bruised and swollen, but Julie had managed to straighten her nose. I gave her a small wave, a simple hand gesture to let her know I cared and was glad she was here. A little smile crept across her face. I closed my eyes.

The next day, Howard, Rowdy, Lil' H, and I took the truck and drove to the Smyrna airport. I had Howard drive and directed him to take a route down Rocky Fork Road, which was stupid because we had to stop and cut up three trees that had fallen across the road. I was hoping to see Toby and his kids, or even Moe. The only thing we saw was a zombie with its peculiar, distinctive amble, walking down the middle of the road. We had the windows protected with hardware cloth, so I saw no immediate threat.

"Howard, drive up close to it on the passenger side and take a look. Get ready to pop it with your handgun, Rowdy." He nodded in agreement.

When we approached, the zombie suddenly stopped. It must have heard us, but it didn't turn around. It only stood there with its back to us. I drove up beside it and stopped.

It was a female, wearing jeans and a torn beige jacket. She slowly turned her head and stared at us. I had several encounters with zombies over the past year, but this one made the hair on the back of my neck stand up. She stared at us with black eyeballs while slowly gnashing her teeth. Suddenly, she lunged at the jeep and clawed at the window. Rowdy jerked back in fright, but then stuck his handgun through the hole in the mesh and fired. She continued staring at us for another second before falling to the road.

"Wow. That was weird," Rowdy said. Howard and I agreed.

We elected not to spend the time burning the corpse, and instead hurried toward the Smyrna airport. Surprisingly, there was only one crashed plane off in a field. The hangars had a few planes tethered down, but many others were empty.

The olive drab cargo plane on the tarmac was easy to spot, and a cadre of soldiers milled about near a hangar. I stopped the truck on Fitzhugh Road a hundred yards away from the hangars, looked at Rowdy and pointed at the M4 assault rifle.

"Would you mind staying here by the truck with that M4 handy, just in case? I asked.

Rowdy gave a curt nod. "I understand. But if they're friendly, and there're women around, you better give me a whistle."

I chuckled and confirmed he knew my hand signals before Howard and I walked toward the group. They saw us coming. Two of the soldiers approached.

"Welcome, before we proceed, you will need to surrender your side arms," one of them said while holding his hand out. The other soldier had an M4 with a front sling. He held it casually, but I had no doubt he could swing it around in action quickly. I shook my head and gave the warning hand signal. His rank showed he was a corporal. He was in his early twenties, clean shaven, and clear blue eyes. He didn't look at all like Corporal Leon Hart, but the rank and attitude reminded me of him all the same.

"That's not an option," I replied calmly, but deliberately.

"I'm afraid it is," he replied in the same tone.

"Then we'll leave," Howard said. He was getting a little miffed as well. Howard motioned to me and we turned to leave.

"Hold up just a moment," he said. We turned back toward him. "It's just a precaution," he continued. "We don't want anyone playing around and having an accidental discharge."

"I see. Why are you and your fellow soldiers armed? How do I know one of you won't have an accidental discharge, hmm?"

He looked at me incredulously, and then sighed. "Will you do me a favor and wait here while I get my sergeant?" I looked at Howard. I was done with these guys, but I knew Howard was going to have to answer to Lashonda when we got back.

"Okay, please make it quick," I said. He smirked at me, as if to say, okay smart ass, and jogged off to another group who were standing by a couple of rectangular tables. There were soldiers sitting there and four people in civilian clothes on the other side. They were all looking at us curiously.

I watched as the corporal spoke to a short Hispanic soldier, who I assumed was the sergeant, before pointing at us. The two of them walked back toward us. He was a compact man. His torso made a V shape down to a narrow waist, indicating athleticism. His uniform was clean and even appeared to be starched. He walked up to us, stopped, and assumed a parade rest position.

"I'm First Sergeant Santiago. I'm Puerto Rican, so don't you dare call me Mexican unless you're ready to fight," he said with a distinctive accent.

"I'm Howard Allen and this is my friend, Zach Gunderson," Howard said. We shook hands formally. He looked at both of us for emphasis. "This is Corporal Alexander." The corporal nodded at us with a pleasant smile. "He advises me the two of you are refusing to relinquish your weapons."

"He is correct," I said.

"May I ask why?" The First Sergeant asked.

"Certainly. The last group of soldiers I encountered tried to kill me." I pulled some of my hair aside, pointed to the scar on the side of my head, and looked at the corporal. "I certainly don't believe it was an accidental discharge," I said. First Sergeant Santiago eyed us both closely and reached a decision.

"You've been in another recent altercation, it would appear," he observed. I didn't respond. "Very well, but keep those side arms holstered at all times. If you will follow me I would like to introduce you two to the commanding officer." He came to attention, did a smart about face, and marched off without bothering to see if we were following.

He led us into a hangar, told us to wait a moment, and then walked over to a man who was sitting at a table reading something. The man looked up in mild irritation, listened to the First Sergeant, and said something. First Sergeant Santiago waved us over.

"I guess the Captain feels you are worthy enough to have an audience with him," the corporal said under his breath. We walked over together and stopped in front of the table, whereupon we were pointedly ignored for several seconds. He was in his forties, balding with a little stubble sticking out on the sides. He used store bought glasses to read with. He looked more like a book editor or a college professor than a soldier. He finally looked up, glanced at us, and then glared at the First Sergeant.

"First Sergeant, I thought I made myself clear. When rounding up these people, they are to be disarmed for purposes of safety."

Maybe it was because I was not feeling the best, but I was instantly irked. First Sergeant Santiago started to speak, but I interrupted him.

"First Sergeant, tell the arrogant Captain we will not disarm for anyone." I heard the corporal snort behind me while his captain looked over and glared at me. He spoke while still staring at me.

"First Sergeant, inform this young man that I am to be addressed as sir, Captain, or Captain Steen. Anything else is unacceptable and may lead to charges," the first sergeant eyed me.

"First Sergeant! Please please inform the arrogant, bald headed prick that I am not in the military and therefore don't give a shit what his rank is!"

To my surprise, the first sergeant snapped to attention, clicking the heels of his boots loudly.

"Sir! The young man says you're a bald headed prick and he does not care what rank you are!"

Howard erupted with one of his belly laughs. The Captain's face turned red and he stood so quick his chair flew backwards.

"Escort these two off of the premises," he said curtly, turned and walked off, disappearing into an office within the hangar. The corporal was now chuckling out loud, as he escorted us outside.

"Holy shit, I haven't seen him that pissed off in a while." He slapped me on the shoulder. "I like you kid," he said. The goodhearted slap sent a shockwave of pain through me, but I didn't show it.

"Come on," the First Sergeant said. "We need to get you two out of sight before he does something stupid, like order us to arrest you two. Follow me." We followed the first sergeant out of a side door.

"Corporal, let's escort our guests back to their vehicle," the First Sergeant directed. I looked around, scanning the area as we walked.

"What happened to you kid? You get in a fight or something?" Corporal Alexander asked.

"A douchebag who liked to call himself Captain tried to kill me," I said.

"Ah, that's why you took an instant disliking to Captain Steen," he mused.

I shrugged. "I guess so. He sure is an arrogant prick though."

Corporal Alexander shrugged as we walked. "Yeah, he is, but otherwise he's not so bad. When it comes to running the unit and the civilians, he's pretty competent."

When we reached the jeep, we introduced the soldiers to Rowdy.

"Howdy boys," he said while shaking their hands. "Do you fellows like country music?"

Corporal Alexander peered closely at him and then his eyes widened in recognition. "I know you," he said. "You're Rowdy Yates. I'm from Alabama too. I got your CD, man, it's awesome!" He pumped Rowdy's hand again. "My name's Terry, Terry

Alexander. Man, oh man, I never thought in a million years I'd be meeting you."

Rowdy grinned and the two of them started talking about music. I saw First Sergeant Santiago watching. He shook his head in mock disgust. I caught his attention and pointed to the group of soldiers and a couple of civilians. They looked familiar.

"What are they doing over there?" I asked.

"That is the in-processing station. All incoming personnel fill out a questionnaire. Most of it is standard data, name, gender, age, ethnic origin, what trade skills you have; the usual. Then, the questions go into more detail, as in surviving family members, who and how many in your family were infected, and then there are questions about your health," First Sergeant Santiago said as he looked at the process with satisfaction.

"Then, all incoming personnel are given a briefing on the transition to Fort Campbell. They are advised on what items they may bring and the weight limit."

"Let me guess, weapons are not allowed," I said. The First Sergeant jutted his chin out.

"There is no need for personal weapons. I have a company of highly trained soldiers who are more than capable of providing protection of all of the citizens. In the event we need additional armed personnel, we have more than enough firearms secured in our armories. We can arm the citizenry as needed."

"Kind of sounds like Stalinist Russia," I commented dryly.

"Alright, gentlemen, why are you really here?" First Sergeant Santiago asked pleasantly. I looked at the two civilians who were meandering around the soldiers. I recognized them now. They were the ones who tried to ambush me. I turned to the First Sergeant.

"We got one of your messages from the Chinook and thought we'd come check you out," I responded.

"I'm getting the impression you two have no desire to be relocated," he said. I scoffed.

"I don't, but Howard here has a wife and two kids. He might be more receptive, but we've not even heard what you guys have to offer yet."

First Sergeant Santiago resumed his parade rest posture. "We have cleared Fort Campbell of all infected individuals. Displaced families will be relocated to the on base housing. Single civilians are housed in the barracks." He paused a moment as Captain Steen made a reappearance. He saw us, and then walked over to the table of other soldiers. They stood immediately and saluted.

The First Sergeant continued, "I'm very pleased to say we have housing, health care, potable water, food, and our school is scheduled to be reopened any day now. In addition to the company sized unit of military, we currently have ninety civilians whom we have rounded up from as far away as Louisville, Kentucky."

"And then what?" Howard asked. "Tell me what you guys are doing up there? What do you have the survivors doing?"

"We have work crews. Everyone works, everyone has a purpose. We are constantly striving to improve our living conditions and way of life. Do you have any kind of specialty?" Santiago asked.

"I do. I'm a mechanic. I can fix any kind of automobile you got, and my wife is one hell of a cook," Howard said proudly.

First Sergeant Santiago nodded thoughtfully. "We have a sizeable motor pool and a severe shortage of skilled mechanics, and we can always use another chef. You'd fit in very nicely, Mr. Allen," he then turned his attention to me.

"What about you, Mr. Gunderson? Do you have any special skills?"

"None at all," I replied with a slight shake of my head. "What would you do with a person who has no skills?" I asked sarcastically.

"There is no shortage of work involving manual labor," he said without hesitation.

"Don't let him fool you, First Sergeant," Howard said while chuckling. "If it wasn't for Zach, my family and I probably wouldn't have survived." Howard gently squeezed my shoulder. "He's meant a great deal to us."

First Sergeant Santiago looked me over closely in renewed interest. I watched over his shoulder as Captain Steen along with two soldiers, started walking toward us. I gestured with my head. First Sergeant Santiago turned around.

"I wonder what the hell he's up to," he asked himself. He waited until Captain Steen was close, came to attention, and saluted, as did Corporal Alexander. Captain Steen responded with a crisp salute.

"Carry on, First Sergeant," he said.

"Sir, I was filling in the three gentlemen on our operation and relocation process."

Captain Steen nodded at the First Sergeant and peered over our shoulder.

"Who is the armed gentleman over there talking to the corporal?" he asked.

"He is our back up, along with another one of my friends about three hundred yards from here surreptitiously hidden." I cast a glance down the road in a vague direction, hopefully giving the impression I was indicating the position of an imaginary sniper. His eyes widened slightly.

"Mister Gunderson, do you have a sniper deployed?" First Sergeant Santiago asked. I nodded. "That is totally unnecessary, sir," he replied tersely.

"I believe it is," I said. "Let me tell you about the last encounter I had with you military types."

Rowdy stopped talking as I told the story of the group of National Guard soldiers, culminating in the fatal encounter with Corporal Hart and his crew. All of the soldiers listened with intent interest.

"This is a constant reminder, gentlemen," I said as I pointed again to the scar on the side of my head.

Captain Steen pointed at my face. "It would appear you have recently been involved in another violent encounter," he said.

"I have." I briefly told them about the Captain. "I'm not a very trusting person these days, so you can see why I will never allow myself to be willingly disarmed. And, I certainly don't like anyone with the title of captain."

"That's a lot of people you've killed, Zach," The First Sergeant said quietly. I gave him a slight nod. He didn't know the half of it.

"Which reminds me, one of these civilians behind me said you murdered his wife. I am duty bound to take you into custody pending an inquiry," Captain Steen said somberly.

"If you want a response, all I have to say is they attempted to ambush me one day on a lonely country road. They failed."

"So, you murdered his wife," he said.

"I believe the legal system, when it was still around, made a clear distinction between murder and justifiable homicide. I've never murdered anyone," I responded. I hoped I was right, and not merely rationalizing. I continued.

"However, I understand your obligation to duty. May I edify you for the record, at this point all you have is an unsubstantiated allegation. You do not have any physical evidence, including a *corpus delicti*. Simply put, you have not met the burden of probable cause for taking me into custody. I submit to you, anyone who is serious about reconstructing society must adhere to the bastion of justice." I studied him a moment before continuing.

"Of course, some people believe justice is nothing more than a commodity which is a more or less adulterated condition the State sells to the citizen as a reward for his allegiance, taxes, and personal service."

Captain Steen looked at me long and hard. It was difficult to tell what he was thinking, but I believed he was digesting what I had just said.

"Noted for the record," he finally said. "But we will have to conduct an investigation. Oh, and I believe it is the first time anyone has ever quoted Ambrose Bierce to me, touché."

I arched an eyebrow. I didn't think anyone read Bierce anymore.

"Nobody recognizes my quotes from Bierce. I am dutifully impressed." I waved toward my friends. "Sometimes, I'll say something which I believe is steeped in witticism and all I get are some very odd looks."

"Me as well," Captain Steen quipped. I chuckled before I could help myself.

"As for this allegation of murder, I assure you I will give you some amount of cooperation, about seventy-five percent worth. I doubt it'll go any further than that," I said cheerfully. Rowdy and

Howard burst out in laughter. Even the soldiers joined in. Captain Steen furrowed his brow momentarily.

"I'd like to ask a few questions, if I may," I said. Captain Steen made a gesture with a hand.

"Have you had any contact with any government entity, NORAD, anybody?"

Captain Steen shook his head slowly.

"Not with any of those entities, but we have been in contact with some personnel. It would seem that several of the naval ships and submarines weathered the plague, but the Continuity of Government plan apparently did not materialize. We have also been in contact with personnel at other military installations, both in this country and in others. I cannot be more specific due to operational security. I hope you understand."

"Do you have an estimate of a survival rate?" I asked.

"The numbers are incomplete, but the raw data suggests twenty percent," Captain Steen replied. I nodded in understanding. Howard looked at me.

"What does that mean, Zach?" He asked. Numbers were not his strong suit."When the outbreak occurred, the population of the United States was roughly three hundred sixteen million. With a twenty percent survival rate, roughly sixty-three to sixty-four million people survived the initial pandemic. If one were to speculate about the ensuing aftermath, approximately fifty percent of those survivors will die due to starvation, violence, pestilence, and other health issues in the ensuing year. Also, with societal breakdown and the lack of proper neonatal health care, the growth rate will plummet to near zero. In all probability, there are about thirty-two million Americans left living, for now. The number will no doubt drop severely before it starts growing again."

Captain Steen nodded. "So, you can see the need for what we are doing. Mister Gunderson, I'm getting the impression you are a knowledgeable person. You would be a welcome asset to our community."

I was instantly irked by being called an asset. It reminded me of the other Captain. He said the same thing of me not so long ago. I shook my head slowly.

"No," I said quietly.

"We have a lot to offer," Captain Steen pressed.

"Before I respond, I don't care for your title and calling you Mister Steen doesn't feel right. Would you mind if I called you by your first name?"

"It's Jack. Jack Steen," Captain Steen said.

"Alright, Jack. The First Sergeant makes a good sales pitch, shelter, food, water. However, I never once heard him specifically say your group has doctors, dentists, pharmacists, or veterinarians. Let me ask you, I believe the hospital at Fort Campbell is called Blanchfield?" he nodded. "Is it operational and staffed?"

"Not at the present time. We have a clinic being run by one physician's assistant and three nurses. You must understand, Zach. This is a work in progress. It is a slow, painstaking process. The First Sergeant and I regularly put in sixteen hours a day, sometimes, more."

I looked over at the First Sergeant. He nodded in agreement at Captain Steen's statement.

Captain Steen peered at me closer. "Your group can help in this endeavor. What was your major?" I stared at him blankly. "In college, what was your major?

"Jack, I was a sophomore in High School when the outbreak happened." The three of them looked surprised. Howard chuckled.

"He's the smartest, most resourceful seventeen-year-old you'll ever meet," Howard said and beamed at me. I stood there as the three soldiers looked at me with renewed interest.

I finally broke the silence. "Jack, would your group excuse us for a minute? I'd like to talk to my friends," I requested.

"Certainly," he replied. The cadre of soldiers waited by my truck and the three of us walked down the road. I stopped when I believed we were out of earshot and told them what I wanted to do. They readily agreed. We walked back to them.

"Jack, First Sergeant, you are both cordially invited to our home for lunch. If you can requisition a vehicle around here, you can follow us and be back in time for lights out."

"Can I go, sir?" Corporal Alexander immediately asked. Captain Steen glowered at him. "Sir, you'll need security," he added belatedly.

"Are you sure you just don't want to hang out with your new friend?" the First Sergeant asked. Corporal Alexander grinned bashfully.

Rowdy patted his new buddy on the shoulder. "Yeah, bring him along, Captain. Howard's wife is one hell of a cook and I might even sing a song or two."

Chapter 39 – A Family Dinner

We radioed ahead, let the women know we were coming, and gave them an ETA.

"Howard, take a detour over to the truck stop. I'd like to see if anyone is there or if the Captain ever made any improvements to it."

He nodded and we were there ten minutes later. It remained unoccupied and unchanged. I explained to the soldiers what we had planned to do. Captain Steen looked around with his brow furrowed, much as it was earlier.

"Jack, I've a gut feeling there is something you're not telling us," I said.

He looked at First Sergeant Santiago before responding. "We've met him before. He solicited us for resources in order to create an outpost, or trading post. I assume this was going to be the location for it."

"I don't think you were aware of it, but he was planning on setting you guys up and killing you," I said. He looked at me questioningly. "His niece told me. She's living with us presently."

"Ah, yes, I remember her, a skinny little girl with a butch haircut. Do I understand correctly, you and the Captain were friends at one time?" Captain Steen asked.

"Yes, we were, but an incident involving his men ruined it all." I told them of the incident with Barry and Eli, and the death of Macie.

"Even though they were the instigators, the Captain blamed me. Oh, and he was abusing his niece, so she came to live with us. He blamed me for that as well. He was bent on vengeance for this misperceived injustice."

Captain Steen nodded in seeming understanding. "Where is this Captain now?" he asked.

"Dead," I responded.

"Did you kill him?" he asked. I didn't answer. "I'd like to hear the story," he said.

"Maybe I'll tell you when I get to trusting you better. In the meantime, let's go eat," I said. Our conversation was interrupted by Rowdy giving a short whistle.

"I see somebody," he said, and pointed down the road. I got the Remington sniper rifle out of the jeep and looked at them with the scope.

"Zombies," I said. I took aim and started to shoot them, but stopped and handed the rifle to Rowdy.

"You said you can shoot, Hoss. Well, let's see what you've got," I said with a smile. Rowdy grinned back, shouldered the rifle, and squeezed off a shot. He worked the action as the first zombie fell and shot the other one quickly. I took my fingers out of my ears and slapped Rowdy on the back.

"Good shooting, for an Alabama boy," I commented. He grinned again and scratched his beard. "Alright everyone, this area has not been completely cleared. The noise is going to attract more of them. Let's get out of here."

Lashonda had a large meal prepared, including steaks, and the house was fixed up to receive guests. The Parsons had a nice, family sized walnut table in the dining room. Even so, it was a tight fit seating all eleven of us. Lil' H and Derry peppered the soldiers with questions about military life while we ate. They in turn profusely expressed their admiration of the cooking to Lashonda throughout the meal. Afterward, we all sat in the den. Much to their credit, none of them mentioned Andie's bruised and swollen face. She looked like she'd been beaten with an ugly stick, but I probably didn't look much better.

After dinner, Rowdy retrieved a bottle of twenty-one-year-old Balvenie Scotch and poured everyone a glass. Well, with the exception of Derry, Little Howard, and of course, Julie. I had never drunk Scotch before, but I found it very smooth and tasty.

"This is a very nice home," Captain Steen commented.

"Thank you," Howard said. "Zach found it for us. It was already furnished."

"It had a layer of dust an inch thick and cobwebs everywhere, but other than that, it was ready to move into," Lashonda said.

"The homeowners were my employers at one time. They were vacationing in Florida when the outbreak occurred," I said.

"Where do you live?" he asked.

"We're currently living here until we get a new house readied. The Captain's boys burned down our friend's house and were about to do the same to our house before we caught them. They doused everything with gas, so it's uninhabitable now. We should have the new house ready within a day or so." I waved my hand around. "I had done some prep work on this house earlier, but I'd like to get it hardened against intruders.""He has a list," Julie said. The group laughed at the inside joke while the soldiers looked at us questioningly. Howard explained my propensity for creating lists. First Sergeant Santiago burst out in laughter.

"It sounds like someone else I know, although I won't mention any names," he said while jerking his head at Captain Steen.

"It's a good way to organize your thoughts," Jack said defensively. I understood, but it didn't stop everyone from laughing some more.

"Why aren't you drinking, Julie?" Corporal Alexander asked.

"Julie is expecting her first child," Lashonda said.

"How wonderful, congratulations," Jack said with a smile. "Julie, we have a health care facility with a physician's assistant and two nurses on staff. We can provide you with prenatal care."

"What is a physician's assistant?" Julie asked. "Is it a doctor?"

"Um, no. It is the title of a person who has had some medical training, but has not yet completed medical school," First Sergeant Santiago said. "The rank is a warrant officer. Mister Jones is well qualified."

"But they have been trained to rely on pharmaceuticals, which are no longer viable. Do they have any knowledge of homeopathic care?" Julie asked. I looked at her in surprise. Captain Steen tried to phrase an answer, but ceded a shrug of the shoulders instead. I changed the subject.

"Your fuel is over a year old," I asked. "How are you still able to fly a plane?"

"We have a fuel technician who monitors our reserves. He tests the fuel frequently. Nevertheless, the amount we have left at our disposal can be measured in a finite amount," Jack said. "We've decided to use it before it goes bad and search out survivors."

I continued with questions. "Why did you use the Smyrna airport, why not the Nashville airport?"

Captain Steen shook his head. "BNA is completely blocked with crashed and abandoned planes. Our pilots did a fly by and said it was too unsafe. There are even cars parked on the runways."

We continued to enjoy the Scotch and talked at length, sharing our individual stories of survival. Captain Steen seemed to have found them particularly fascinating. He took a small notepad out of his shirt pocket and took fastidious notes while everyone talked. I watched and listened. Although I had heard them before, I did not tire of hearing my friends relate how they had survived. When it came my turn, I told them of Rick.

"He was Army?" First Sergeant Santiago asked.

"Yes he was. He was an Airborne Ranger and served time in Vietnam," I said, and was lost in memories for a moment. "He was a hell of a man," I said quietly. "Everything I've become, everything I've achieved, I owe to him."

Rowdy raised his glass and we all saluted the memory of Rick. First Sergeant Santiago broke the awkward silence that ensued.

"When it became apparent what this plague was doing, the post commander ordered the base locked down and everyone put on alert. Even so, the base was infested with people who were already sick," he said, and paused a moment.

"I lost a wife and four children." He wiped his face and quickly continued. "Everyone has lost loved ones. The Captain had a fiancé. Corporal Alexander's entire unit became infected. We managed to band together and eradicate the infected people, which was no small feat. We were at battle stations for days on end, killing those things."

He wiped his brow. "A lot of them were wearing uniforms, so we knew we were killing things who used to be fellow soldiers.

We lost a lot of troops." He shook his head ruefully. "It was tough." He looked at his glass of Scotch, raised it silently, and we joined him in a drink.

All of us talked at length, each telling their life story, until the sun started to set. The First Sergeant glanced at his wristwatch and nodded at Captain Steen. They stood.

"Ms. Allen, thank you for the wonderful meal. It was delicious," Captain Steen said. First Sergeant Santiago and Corporal Alexander quickly voiced their agreement. They said their goodbyes. Howard, Rowdy, and I walked them to their vehicle.

"Zach, Howard, I'm impressed. Each story I heard, whether it was Julie, Rowdy, Andie, and even you, Howard, each story centers around Zach. Your friends think very highly of you."

"If it weren't for Zach, we'd have probably all starved or been killed, or been eaten by those damned things," Howard asserted.

I shrugged. The meal was not settling well in my stomach and my head was buzzing from the Scotch. I was through talking and wanted to go to bed.

"It's been a pleasure, gentlemen," I said as we shook hands. "Jack, if you ever consider establishing an outpost in this area, let me know. I believe we can help you out." I looked up at the sky. There was a dark line of clouds in the western sky. "Looks like bad weather moving in."

I thought a moment, inhaled, and motioned to Captain Steen. When we were sufficiently far enough away from the group, I whispered in his ear.

He looked at me in surprise, and then nodded. "I'll see what I can do."

First Sergeant Santiago handed Howard a sheet of legal paper. "We're lifting off at 1700 hours tomorrow. If any of you want to join us, here is a list of the items you can bring. If you drive in tonight, flash your lights several times so we'll know you're friendly. If we don't see you tomorrow, we'll be back in two weeks. Will you guys meet us at the airport?" Howard and I looked at each other and agreed. We all shook hands again, Corporal Alexander gave Rowdy a hug, and they left.

The last thing I remember was lying down on the sleeping bag in the den. Everyone else was sitting around talking about our visitors. Having friendly visitors was a rarity these days, so naturally it was a big event for us. Everyone was asking questions of each other and voicing their opinions. Somewhere in all of that, I fell asleep.

When I awoke, my watch said a few minutes before four. I stretched the kinks out. Curly, who had nestled himself in between Julie and me, woke up as well and mimicked my actions. We thought he had been killed, but he most likely ran away in fright. He was lying on the porch, waiting patiently for us yesterday morning. I dressed quietly, holstered my Kimber, kissed Julie on the forehead, and slipped outside without a peep from anyone. Curly followed me out, did his business, and then looked at me as if to say, why are we up so early bud? I gave him a friendly scratch on the head and then started walking. When he realized I was walking to our old home, he whimpered slightly, but in spite of his fear, he followed me faithfully.

I fed the chickens and rabbits with the aid of a flashlight, and then began loading the trailer. I was tired of sleeping on the floor of someone else's home, and was determined to be in our new home by this evening. I emerged from the darkness of the cellar carrying a Rubbermaid tote bin of mason jars, when Curly started growling. I set the plastic tote bin down quietly. I had leaned the M4 beside the door, and it was too far away. I drew my Kimber as a figure appeared in the doorway.

"Whoa, hey now, no need for that." It was Rowdy. I holstered my weapon.

"You're usually sleeping off a drunk at this time of the morning," I said gruffly, as I picked up the bin.

"Yeah, very true," he replied. "When you drifted off to sleep, I knew you'd be up early and would be working on something or another. Besides, Julie threatened me with grave bodily harm if I didn't look out for you while you're still injured."

I started to interrupt, but Rowdy held his hand up. "Save it, we all know you're hurting, even if you don't complain."

"Has Andie complained of any internal injuries?" I asked.

Rowdy shook his head. "She said he gave her a few slaps, but that was it. Her nose is still tender as hell though." He looked at the tote bin. "So, what are we doing here?"

"We're moving. We got a lot of stuff here that I want to move into our new home and I want to get moved by the end of the day. I hope you're here to help." I picked up the tote bin and handed it to him. He took it with a grunt.

With Rowdy's help, we got the cellar emptied out and loaded into the trailer. Even though the morning was in the lower forties, Rowdy was sweating and breathing heavily. He sat on the edge of the trailer and caught his breath. I wasn't feeling so good myself, but I was better than yesterday.

"I need to get back in shape. I really let myself go this past year," he said. I sat next to him. "Were you always in good shape?" he asked. I shrugged.

"When I was in school I ran cross-country track. I could run all day, but I was skinny as a rail." I thought a minute. "When everything happened, I was out here with my friend Rick. There was a lot of down time, so I worked out quite a bit."

I seemed to keep referencing Rick, but I didn't want to talk about him. I talked about him with Julie, but that was different. I changed the subject.

"Speaking of Andie, how are you two getting along?" I asked. He looked at the ground a long minute before answering.

"We're getting along fine. She's a little shell shocked right now, but I think she'll be okay." As if on cue, he scratched his beard. "She's a real sweetie, but every time I look at her, all I see is a skinny little girl. I've got to tell you, Zach, I haven't got any arousal going, if you know what I mean."

I snorted. "She'll gain weight. She's only been with us a short time. The Captain had all of them on short rations. She's eating a lot better now."

"Well, I guess so. She's young though, and I'm not so young," he said, and stood up. "You think it's going to rain?"

I nodded as he looked up at the gray sky.

"Yeah, you may be right. I'm going to regret saying this, but we better get back to work before everything gets drenched." I laughed at him and stood up.

"The house is actually right across the field," I said as I pointed toward the south. "We'll have to cut a hole in a few fences and create a road. Otherwise, if we take the existing roads, it's about a half-mile."

We had all of our canned goods moved in the ample storage cupboard of the Riggins house by sunup. Julie and Andie drove up as we unloaded the last box.

"Y'all have been busy," Julie said. I nodded.

"How are you two this morning?" I asked.

"I threw up my breakfast," Julie said with a frown. "I guess that's a good sign."

"How about you, Andie?" I asked. "The swelling seems to be going down," which was true, but both of her eyes were black, along with the ridge of her nose. Andie shrugged her shoulders.

"Okay, I guess," she said and looked at Rowdy. He busied himself with emptying the box. I gave Julie a sloppy kiss, and gave Andie a peck on the cheek.

"I've been told my kisses go a long way," I said as I ruffled her hair. She smiled before she could help herself. Julie rolled her eyes.

"We've got a lot of stuff to move still, but most of it can wait. I think while you guys get the house cleaned up, Rowdy and I are going to find a generator." I hugged Julie again before I thought anything of it. She grinned; no eye rolling this time.

"Oh, I almost forgot. What do you guys think of Fort Campbell, do you want to go?"

"No!" they all said in unison.

"We talked about it last night after you went to sleep," Julie said. "All of us want to stay, but I think Lashonda wants to relocate."

"It's not too late for them to leave and get there on time," I said.

"I think they're talking about going the next time they come back," Andie explained. I nodded thoughtfully. The fact is, it would probably be better for them, but for purely selfish reasons, I wanted them to stay with us. I shook it off and motioned to Rowdy.

"Let's get moving, Zach, you're dilly-dallying. I don't have time for dilly-dallyers," he said with a mischievous grin.

We had no sooner exited the driveway, than we saw them, three people in a beat up police car. When they saw us, they stopped and the driver, a man, got out. He was accompanied by two women. I glanced at Rowdy, who readied his M4.

"How much ammo do you have?" I asked.

"Eight magazines," Rowdy answered. During the last few months, we'd not resupplied our supply of ammunition, and were starting to run low.

"Alright," I said. "I have four magazines for my forty-five. Let's hope they're friendly. As I drove closer, their features came into focus. I recognized one of the women.

Chapter 40 – George

I stopped when we were fifty feet away. Opening my door, I leaned out and pointed my handgun through the gap between the door and the truck frame. The man raised his hands. I stared at him for the first time. He was in his twenties, maybe six feet tall, about a week's worth of dark whiskers on his face, and greasy hair cut in a high and tight. He was wearing military camouflage fatigues, and they looked pretty dirty as well.

"I'm guessing you're George," I said loud enough for him to hear. He nodded.

"Let me come closer, Zach. I just want to talk," he shouted back.

"Alright, walk forward until you're ten feet from the truck and then stop. Keep your hands where I can see them. If those women make any furtive moves, you'll be the first one I kill." I lowered my voice to a whisper. "Watch the sides of the road, Rowdy. He may have a friend somewhere." Rowdy gulped and nodded. George stood in the middle of the road with his hands out.

"We meet at last, Zach." He smiled slightly and eyed Rowdy. "I don't have anyone out there, Red. It's just me and the two women, thanks to Zach."

I scowled with anger. "Thanks to Zach?" I repeated his words. "What the fuck do you mean by that? Are you about to blame me for everything? I am sick and tired of being blamed for everything that has happened to you cocksuckers." I tried to take a breath, but my anger was growing and I started shouting.

"For every action there is an equal and opposite reaction, you stupid fuck! It's obvious all of you are so fucking stupid that you don't think there should be consequences for your actions, but there are," I snorted in disgust. "Look how fucking pathetic you look now! Did you see the Captain? Did you?"

"I did," he said quietly. "Did you kill him?"

"Andie killed him. He suffered the consequences for his actions. Barry and Eli suffered the consequences. Tony, Randy, Herb, Eddy, and every one of you retarded fucks who hung your hat with the Captain. You all turned on us and suffered the consequences." I thought of Macie and felt my finger depressing the trigger. George saw it too.

"Newton's third law," he said quietly. I continued scowling at him, but relaxed the tension in my finger. "Newton's third law, for every action there is an equal and opposite reaction. You're right, Zach. All of my so-called friends are dead. The Captain's dead. Now, I have nothing but a couple of trailer park whores and an infant kid who may or may not belong to me. You're right about me being stupid too. I'm nothing but a stupid Marine who was trying to find his place in life." He kept his hands out in the open and looked at me plainly.

"Why are you here, George?" I asked quietly.

"I came here to ask for some food. The fire burned up all of our stores. I was going to lay a guilt trip on you, but..." he shrugged. "I know you don't owe us anything," he continued after a moment. "But, if you can find it in your heart to give us enough for a few days, we would be most appreciative. We'll leave the area and won't cause you any further trouble."

"Take your jacket off and toss it over here. Then lift your shirt up and turn around in a circle," I ordered. George obeyed without complaint.

"I'm not armed," he said. "There are weapons in the car, but they're unloaded and I've told them don't dare touch any of them." I picked up the jacket, searched it, and tossed it back to him.

I looked at him a long moment and sighed. "Why the fuck did you guys convince yourselves we were your enemy?"

George rubbed his face. His expression was one of pained sorrow. "Because the Captain said you were," he said quietly.

Rowdy and I fixed them up a supply of food and told them about Fort Campbell. George surprised us when he retrieved a surplus ammo can out of the trunk filled with ammunition. He handed it over.

"It's a mix of different calibers. I think it's a good trade," he said simply. He held his hand out and I reluctantly shook it. Rowdy shook his hand and gave him a hug.

"You take care of your women and kid, bro," he said. "And be careful who you hang your hat with."

We watched quietly as they drove away.

Rowdy and I drove in silence to Home Depot. The streets were bereft of any kind of humans or zombies. There was nothing but vacant automobiles, vacant buildings, and trash being blown about by the wind. I stopped on the Moore's Lane overpass of I-65, and got out. Rowdy got out with me.

"What're you thinking about, Hoss?" he asked. I pointed at the mass of vehicles sitting silently along the Interstate.

"We need to figure the most efficient way of scavenging those cars and tractor trailers," I said while rubbing my stomach. Rowdy saw me doing it.

"You got a gut injury?" he asked.

"Yeah, the Captain gave me a pretty hard kick in the stomach. He got me pretty good. I don't think I've got any internal injuries, but I'm still hurting all over."

"Yeah, but you won in the end," he said.

I scoffed. "I don't feel much like a winner. We lost Macie and Fred's family home. If he ever comes back, everything he had, everything reminding him of his family, is gone. It seems like this all could have been avoided somehow." I sighed at the thought.

"All true," Rowdy said. "There have been losses, but don't sell yourself short, Zach, you won." He pondered a minute before speaking again.

"Those six months when I was locked in my bus with absolutely nobody to talk to. I think I went crazy. I started seeing people that weren't there and even started having conversations with them. If I hadn't of stumbled upon you guys when I did..." he wiped his brow. "I don't know, man. I think I was pretty close to eating my gun."

I looked at him, but he pointed down at the Interstate before I could respond. "I'm seeing some zombies or something."

"Yeah, a lot of them turned while in their vehicles. Their higher level functions went on the fritz, so now they don't know how to open the door and get out. A lot of them are still in their seatbelts. I covered it in rule number seven, by the way," I said. Rowdy chuckled.

"Let's go see if there are any generators left. The shelves were pretty empty, but there were a few items still there. We'll grab what we can, and then we're going back to the compound. There may not be anything left, but I bet the tanker is still there."

"You need to paint your rules around here too," Rowdy said. "I tell you what; I'll paint them for you on the front of Home Depot."

We struck out with finding a generator. Even though we found some small items we could use, but we didn't make any major discoveries.

"We'll find one, just gotta look harder, or we can move the old generator over there to the new home," Rowdy said.

"It's an option, but I kind of wanted a generator at both houses." I sighed. "Oh well, you can't have everything."

I experienced no small amount of anxiety when I stopped in front of the barn where we had left the Captain. His body wasn't there. George must have moved it. All that remained were some dark stains on the dirt floor.

We drove up to the remnants of the Captain's infamous compound. The trailer was still standing, but the siding was charred and melted. There were fresh graves in the far back corner of the yard. George must have buried them, but he did not mark them. Looking at the farmhouse in full daylight gave it a different perspective. The yard was large, muddy, and without a hint of grass left. The fields behind the house had cattle peacefully grazing. There were garden plots fenced off. The barn had a fresh coat of whitewash. The tanker was parked beside it. I pointed it out to Rowdy and we looked in it. It was about one-quarter full, maybe a hundred gallons.

"I guess it's a bit ironic, but the tankers are what brought us together," I said and told Rowdy about Operation Gas. His eyes lit up.

"I heard you guys that night! I thought it was thunder at first. I was going to try to run out and find you guys, but I was too damned scared y'all were unfriendly or would mistake me for a zombie and shoot my ass."

"They used the bus," I said, pointing at the burned out hull of the bus. "They were shooting at everything they saw, so yeah, it was probably best you stayed put." I peered closely at the two M60 machine guns.

"Let's take those bad boys home with us. Howard may be able to restore them," I said. Rowdy agreed. We got soot all over us, but we got them dismounted and strapped down in the back of the truck. Hooking up the trailer was a little more challenging. The wheels had sunk down in the soft ground and we ultimately had to dig them out. By the time we got back on the road, the sun was setting.

"I surely don't want to be out here after dark," Rowdy said.

"We're okay. The hardware cloth is effective in keeping those things out, and I have some night vision equipment I can use to drive with." I grunted and slapped the steering wheel.

"What's wrong?" Rowdy asked as I reached over and turned the radio on, and then figured it out. "Oh, we forgot to call the girls," he said. I nodded in agreement, as I tried to reach them. There was no answer.

"We may be out of range. It'll be the excuse we'll use anyway, right?" I looked at Rowdy pointedly. He chuckled.

"I'm game. I don't want to catch hell from them either." We sealed our conspiratorial lie with a fist bump.

Chapter 41 – Fred

Sarah was still feeling the pangs of fatigue. Flying a plane like the C130 was no easy task, especially when one had to do it without a co-pilot or flight engineer. Nevertheless, she flew expertly and had Tinker in sight within a minute of her flight plan. She switched the radio frequency to Tinker approach and tried calling them. She repeated it several times, but there was no response. She switched back over to the intercom where all of them could hear.

"There may a problem. Nobody is responding on Tinker approach frequency. I'm switching to Tinker guard." She saw Fred looking perplexed. "It's the emergency frequency. Do me a favor and make a continuous visual scan for any other aircraft flying nearby," Fred nodded as she switched frequencies and adjusted the flaps. She switched back a minute later.

"It's no good. Nobody is answering. Alright people, I don't like it, but we're going to land. Let's hope there isn't something going on that'll get us killed."

Fred felt the landing gear being lowered and he watched as Sarah increased the flaps. Watching the large aircraft descend from the vantage point of the cockpit was somewhat unnerving to Fred, but he kept a poker face. Besides, he was having an increasing level of respect for Sarah's skills as a pilot, as evidenced by her perfect three-point landing. She reversed thrust on the engines and the plane slowed dramatically. When they had slowed sufficiently, Sarah killed the reverse thrust of the engines and taxied to a stop on the runway.

"It's too risky taxiing this bird around on the tarmac without a ground guide. We'll park it here and worry about it later," she said in explanation. After shutting the engines down, they exited out of the rear ramp door. There was nobody waiting to greet them.

"There's something wrong," Sarah said under her breath. Sergeant Fandis jogged out with the wheel chocks and put them in place while Airman Smith stood guard with her M4 at the ready. The air base was eerily quiet.

"Let's unload the Humvee and drive over to the General's office."

The four of them quickly unlashed the military vehicle from its lashings. Fred climbed in back and scanned the area. There was no movement, no sound, other than some birds chirping. Sergeant Fandis drove quickly to the squat office building which housed the command staff of Tinker. The door to his office was open. The room was dark, with the exception of the daylight shining through the dirty windows. There was someone sitting in the General's chair. It wasn't General Shoemaker though. It was the Master Sergeant, the General's aide. He swiveled in the chair as we walked in. He gave a halfhearted salute to Sarah. His crisp uniform was soiled and he had not shaved.

"Sergeant, report!" she said crisply. The Master Sergeant stood slowly and assumed a loose parade rest position.

"Well, Major, there have been a few changes since you left."

"Where is General Shoemaker?" she asked.

He turned and pointed. "He's right out there, ma'am. Do you see him?" They looked where he was pointing. Sarah was the first one to see the simple cross sticking into the ground of freshly turned dirt, and gasped.

"I buried him beside the flagpole. I think he would have liked my choice. What do you think, Major? Should I have buried him in a cemetery instead? Or should I have burned him?"

"What happened?" Sabrina asked. The Master Sergeant looked at her as if it were the first time he had ever laid eyes on her.

"He shot himself in the head. Right here in this very chair. It happened about an hour after you left," he said quietly and sat back down. "There's nothing to worry about, Major. I cleaned everything up and filed a report indicating his weapon accidentally discharged as he was storing it."

"Where is everyone else?" Sergeant Fandis asked.

"I tried to talk to them, but they had their own ideas. As far as I know, everyone has left. Curious though, where does one go when they leave? There is nowhere to go to, not anymore." The

Master Sergeant swiveled in the chair and resumed staring out the window, much like General Shoemaker had done the day before.

With the aid of a Coleman lantern, Fred took a cold shower in the windowless gym locker room. Sergeant Fandis said they occasionally had hot water, but not today. Cold water notwithstanding, Fred enjoyed washing the accumulation of a few days of grime off of him. Per the sergeant's advice, he also took advantage of the laundry room while they still had running water. He was sitting in a plastic chair in front of the dryer wrapped in a towel watching the dryer turn round and round, when Sarah walked in. She had battle dress utility pants on and a black tee shirt with a military logo on it.

"Well, well, cowboy, looks like you've run out of clean things to wear," she teased. Fred suddenly felt self-conscious. He remembered his first meeting with Sarah and her six-pack abs. He self-consciously sucked in his gut.

"I figured I'd get everything washed before heading out," he said.

"When are you leaving?" She asked.

"First thing in the morning."

"You could stay here," she said after a moment.

"You could go with me," Fred responded.

She jutted her jaw out. "My place is here. There are millions of dollars in assets here. I cannot simply abandon them."

Fred nodded. "Your sense of duty is admirable, but there's nothing left here for you, Sarah. The two lovebirds have been talking about leaving. The only one left is that Master Sergeant, and who knows how long it'll be before he completely goes off the deep end."

"I can't simply abandon my career, Fred," she said plaintively. Fred understood her position. He found himself attracted to Sarah and he was torn. They sat together in silence. Fred looked at Sarah. He leaned over to kiss her, but was startled by the dryer's buzzer going off.

"Your clothes are dry, cowboy. You better get them out before they wrinkle."

They stared at each other a moment longer, then Sarah abruptly stood and walked out. She walked back in right about the time Fred had dropped the towel and was starting to put on a clean pair of underwear.

"Listen up, cowboy. Do you know how risky it is to land a large airplane on an unmanned and unsecured airstrip? I stuck my neck out for you and I have no idea why. I guess you struck a soft spot with me when you told me what your mission was. But now I need help, and I'm asking you to help me."

"I have a question for you," Fred said quietly. Sarah stared into his eyes. "Is Major Fowkes asking me, or is Sarah asking?"

Sarah took a step closer. "Would it be okay if I said both?"

Fred nodded. "Fair enough, I'll give you a week, and then we'll have this discussion again."

Sarah nodded gratefully. "Thank you," She turned to go, but stopped. "Did your cowboy friends give you a nickname like Bull, or Horse, or Big Tex, anything like that?"Fred frowned. "No, just Fred. Why?"

Sarah glanced at Fred's crotch. "Surprising," she said and walked out of the laundry room.

Fred felt his cheeks redden as he hurriedly pulled on his underwear and finished dressing.

Little did he know his promise of one week would turn into seven months.

Chapter 42 – Bernie

I could see the light of candles through the windows as we drove up. I made a mental note to get the girls to sew some blackout curtains as soon as was feasible. Julie opened the door as we parked and trotted up. She seemed upset and hugged me immediately.

"What's wrong?" I asked.

"It's Bernie. Andie and I went to check on him. He was dead in his bed. He'd been there a while, Zach. We should have checked on him more often," she said with her voice cracking. She hugged me again and held me.

"It's okay love. It's okay," I said, trying to comfort her. She was right though, we should have checked on him more often. It was another item to add to my list of regrets. We ate a late dinner while Julie and I described Bernie. Rowdy howled with laughter when we told the story of Fred's encounter with him and the fixation with women's panties.

"Did you tell Howard and Lashonda?" I asked. Julie nodded.

"We went and got Howard. He buried Bernie behind his house." She saw me frown, and clarified. "Behind Bernie's house, not Howard's house," she sighed and wiped her eyes. "He was quirky as all get out, but he was a good person. Kind of like a crazy family uncle who spent some time at the nervous hospital."

Our new bedroom was the master bedroom located in the back corner. The bed was a king size, with an elegant walnut frame in a canopy style. We'd be able to hang mosquito netting off of the frame, which would be nice. The sheets were clean, although the house still had a little bit of a musty odor. I gave Julie a back massage while we talked. She occasionally gave a moan of pleasure, which encouraged me to keep massaging.

"That feels wonderful. I had no business digging a grave while pregnant," she said.

"You did what you thought was right," I replied. "But you're going to have to limit yourself to light physical activity. We want a healthy baby boy."

"Listen to you. Maybe it'll be a baby girl," Julie retorted.

"Either way, I want our baby healthy," Julie agreed with a pleasing moan.

"Did Rowdy say anything about Andie?" she whispered.

"Yeah, at the moment he sees her more as a skinny little girl than a romantic partner. I think his brain is still messed up a little bit from practically being in solitary confinement. It'll take time. What did she say?"

"She's a little confused. She said when they go to bed at night, Rowdy holds her close, but doesn't do anything else. He's very kind to her, so she said it'll have to do for now." Julie rolled over and pulled my head close to her in the dark. "That was a wonderful massage," she said, and kissed me. "You're very kind to me too." After a moment, she spoke again in the darkness.

"I'm going to miss that crazy old man," she said.

Howard made clucking and grunting sounds as he inspected the machine guns. After poking and prodding them for five full minutes, he finally spoke.

"I can fix them. The plastic butt pieces and heat shields will have to be replaced, but I think I can fabricate something. All of my tools are at the tire shop. Do we have time to go there today?"

"Yeah, I want to find a generator, so we'll kill two birds with one stone."

I found one sitting behind a biker bar located on Antioch Pike, but it was not a freebie.

"Be careful, Rowdy," I chided under my breath as we worked our way to the rear parking lot. He had gotten anxious and moved ahead of Howard and me. As we rounded the corner of the building, we spotted six of them standing around a barbeque smoker. I've no doubt the remnant aroma of burning meat attracted them, but now they stared at it dumbly, as if the lid was going to magically open and a fresh pig or something would jump out.

They were all still wearing their cuts, which identified them belonging to a local outlaw biker club. When we exited the truck, they headed right for us. Rowdy shot one immediately, but his gun apparently jammed. He tried to run backwards, but he stumbled and fell. The five of them were within a couple of feet of him immediately. Howard and I shot as quickly as we could while Rowdy slithered backwards. Two of them fell on top of him and he let out a shriek.

"Get them off of me!" he shouted, while Howard and I watched him wiggling around like his pants were on fire. He managed to free himself of the bodies and got to his feet. He was breathing heavily.

"Holy shit, that was close!" he exclaimed. Howard chuckled. I shook my head.

"Rowdy, you've got to learn to move as a team. You got out ahead of us and you were in our line of fire. We could have accidentally shot you, and it's not like we can carry you down to the local emergency room and get you patched up."

He hung his head, duly chastened.

"Since you're already grimy with zombie goo, check them out and see if they have anything we can use," I instructed. Rowdy looked at me as if I had just asked him to eat a fresh pile of shit. Howard and I worked our way to the back, and found it.

"How'd you know it was back here?" Howard asked.

"A couple of years ago, there was a wreck down the road. I had driven by and all of the power was out except for the lights in a tent behind this bar. When I started thinking about where to find a generator, the memory popped up in my head."

I looked down at the generator. It was a Honda portable, capable of 6500 watts, and ran on gasoline.

Howard tried to lift it. "It's about three hundred pounds I'd guess. Good thing we're all here. It'd be hard getting it into the back of your truck by yourself," I agreed. After getting it on the truck, I found some hand sanitizer for Rowdy.

"Did you find anything?" I asked.

"One of them had a Bowie knife," he replied and showed it to us. It was a simple looking knife with a wooden handle and brass haft, but the blade was at least ten inches long and lethal looking.

"I've got some sharpening stones at the house," Howard said. "I can put an edge on it so sharp you can shave with it."

Rowdy grinned with delight.

Before leaving, we checked the bar. There were no zombies, but there was nothing else either. Even the beer kegs were empty. We left them there, but I made a mental note of their location. They may come in handy for something later on.

"We better get moving," I said. "Those gunshots might have attracted some more friends for Rowdy to play with."

Howard chuckled, but Rowdy was not amused.

Chapter 43 – A Sad Goodbye

There was the sound of a vehicle approaching as I sat at the kitchen table drinking coffee and watching my beautiful love cooking breakfast.

"It looks like Howard," I said, looking out the window. I fixed a mug of coffee and had it waiting for him when he came in. Lil' H was with him.

"What are you guys up to this morning?" I asked as we walked into the kitchen.

"I gots something I want to tell you guys," Howard said as he sat down. He nodded gratefully at the coffee. Andie came in and sat down.

"Rowdy is in the bathroom," she said. "I've learned to give it about thirty minutes after he's been in there." Julie and Lil' H laughed.

"What's going on, Howard?" I asked, but I felt like I already knew the answer.

"We've talked about it every day since Captain Steen and the First Sergeant visited. I think we're going to move to Fort Campbell."

There was a stunned silence from all of us. Well, with the exception of Rowdy coming into the kitchen. He scratched himself, and then belched loudly before sitting down. He looked us over.

"Good morning, have I missed something?" he asked.

"Howard just told us they're leaving," Julie said. We all looked at him in surprise, and an awkward silence ensued.

"What are you thinking, Zach?" Howard finally asked.

"I think you should do what you believe is best for your family, Howard," I said. He nodded quietly. "I want you to know, if it doesn't work out, you and your family will always be welcome back." He nodded again in gratefulness.

"What do you think, Julie?" Howard asked.

"I don't want you guys to go," she said simply. "But, I'm with Zach. If this is what you think is best for you guys, I have to agree." Her eyes watered up then, which caused Howard to tear up as well.

"How many pounds are each of you allowed to carry on board?" I asked. He showed me the list. I read it over and nodded.

"Clothing can take up a lot of weight, so minimize those. I would go with specialty food items, extra shoes, hygiene items. Oh, don't forget firearms and ammunition," I said.

Howard shook his head. "They don't allow that."

"Conceal it, big guy," I said. "Don't allow yourself to be disarmed, Howard. Put a handgun in each of the boy's waistband with their shirts hiding it, and hide the ammunition in your luggage. Trust me on this, Howard, you may never have use for them, or you may need to protect your family. Better to have them and not need them rather than the other way around."

"You think so?" he asked. I nodded. "Alright, then," he said quietly.

I sighed, and on impulse, got up and hugged the two of them. "We'll keep the house ready for you guys in case you ever want to come back," I said again. I have to admit, it was tough. I didn't want them to leave. They were the last of our original group. It was going to hurt when they left, but I kept it to myself. I didn't want them to feel guilty.

"Don't those soldier boys fly in tomorrow?" Rowdy asked. Howard nodded. "Well, that don't give us much time to throw a going away party, but we'll sure get started." He scratched his beard, started to hike his leg, and then remembered he was in mixed company. His face took on an expression of a person trying desperately to squeeze his but cheeks together.

We all rode to the Smyrna airport together. Beforehand, Howard insisted I inspect their baggage to insure they had packed the proper items.

It was a cool, but sunny day. We sat at the hangar and awaited the arrival of the Chinook. The pleasant day had a calming effect. I was leaning against the truck tire and found myself drifting off when Andie spoke up.

"There's someone coming," she said. We all stood and watched as an older model Olds Cutlass approached. Other than being dirty, it looked like it was in good shape. I recognized the two in front immediately and stood.

"Those are the two who tried to ambush me. I don't know about whoever it is in the back seat," I said. Everyone followed my lead and stood.

They drove up slowly and stopped twenty feet away in a parking lot beside the hangar. I watched them warily. It was time to nip this problem in the bud.

"You guys stay back. I'm going to have a little talk with them."

I could see the apprehension on their faces as I approached them. The passenger in the backseat was a woman whom I did not recognize. She appeared to be in her early thirties, and with the exception of questionable hygiene, was actually quite attractive. I walked purposely up to the driver's side. The two of them seemed even skinnier, but to be honest, the last time I looked at them up close was through a riflescope.

"I believe it's time for us to have a little talk," I said through the open window. The driver glared at me and tried to raise a revolver. I yanked my Kimber out and stuck it against his head.

"Don't you fucking move or you're a dead man," I growled. He wasn't totally stupid, he froze. I reached in with my left hand and grabbed his revolver. "You three get out of the car slowly with your hands where I can see them or else my friends and I are going to start shooting."

They didn't like it, but they complied. I ordered them to stand beside the car while I searched them and the inside of the car. I found one additional revolver and tucked it in the small of my back.

"Remember what I told you two the last time we met?" they looked at me without answering. I continued staring at them until the passenger finally nodded.

"Explain yourself," I said in a low snarl.

"Explain what?" the driver responded.

"The last time we were all here, you accused me of murdering your wife."

"You did! You murdered my wife and my buddy Vernon," he responded. I hit him with a short punch with my left. He yelped and grabbed his nose.

"You're lying. I don't like liars. Were you there on that day?" I asked the woman in the backseat. She shook her head in confusion.

"What are you talking about?" she asked.

I waved my gun at the two men. "These two idiots, along with his wife and another man, tried to ambush me a few weeks back. I reckon you shitheads thought I should have bent over and surrendered, rather than defend myself, right?" They stared at me, but didn't say anything. I punched the driver again. It was a soft punch, meant only to sting his nose a little bit.

"Am I right?" I asked again.

"Fuck you, man," he whined.

"Yeah, fuck me. So many of my friends have died and you two pieces of shit are still alive," I said.

"What are going to do?" the woman asked.

"Why did you come here? Are you going to relocate to Fort Campbell?" I asked.

"We are," the passenger said. "We don't want any trouble here."

"Fair enough," I said. "I didn't want any trouble when I was driving along the road minding my own business, but y'all had a different idea, didn't you?"

"We weren't going to hurt you," the passenger claimed. "We were hungry and just wanted food."

I sighed. "You dumb shits. All you needed to do was wave me down and ask. I had plenty of food that day. Y'all could have had all you wanted." The passenger hung his head. The woman looked at me curiously. The driver continued glaring at me. I pointed at the passenger.

"Go ahead and get your bags out. I'm going to search for any other weapons, and then y'all walk over to the other end of the hangar. You can wait there for Captain Steen and his helicopter," I said, and looked at the driver.

"Personally, I want you to try something so I can kill you without remorse," I said as I glared at him. He returned my glare.

There was a trickle of blood seeping out of his nose, and I fought the urge to finish the job. I searched their baggage while they watched quietly. They had new clothing with tags still on them. They had been shopping somewhere. I noted the store name on the tags. If they were able to go in there, we could do so as well. There were few hygiene items, which probably explained their dirty appearance. There were no weapons. I closed the bags and stood.

"Satisfied?" the driver asked sarcastically. I ignored him.

"What are you going to do with our guns and car?" the passenger asked.

"We have no interest in your car. Leave it here in case you don't find Fort Campbell hospitable, but I'm going to hold the firearms for Captain Steen." I pointed to his friend. "You two have already tried to kill me once, why should I make it easy for you? Besides," I said. "There is at least one person over there that will feed you your testicles if you try anything stupid, so I'm doing you a favor."

I looked at the driver, who had snorted and spit on the ground in front of me. "I don't know your name, but I know you. You may have been a good man once, but now, you're nothing more than a lowlife piece of shit. You put the life of your wife at risk in order to waylay someone whom you believed was helpless and vulnerable. If you guys don't like Fort Campbell and come back here, take your car and drive away. Don't hang around here."

"Fuck you," he responded, and spit on the ground again. He was out of the car now, and standing approximately five feet from me. Well within striking range. I stepped toward him and struck him squarely in the nose with a hard left cross. He dropped to the ground.

"No, no, no. Fuck you," I said without emotion. I walked back to my friends.

"Well, even though I said I would do it, I decided not to kill them," I said, sat down on the concrete, and displayed the two handguns I took off of them. "They had these on them." Andie picked one up, began inspecting them as I watched the passenger pick up his friend, and helped him walk toward the hangar.

Rowdy chuckled. "Zach, you sure are full of piss and vinegar."

I shrugged.

The Chinook arrived promptly at noon. The pilot circled the airport once, and then landed. When the engines were shut down, the tail ramp lowered and a squad of soldiers exited. Each soldier seemed to have a specific task to perform. Two soldiers chocked the wheels, while three other soldiers carried equipment out of the helicopter. I recognized Captain Steen and Corporal Alexander as they exited the plane. The Corporal grinned and waved as they walked over to us.

"Good afternoon, ladies, gentlemen," he said while shaking hands. He glanced over at the three I had ordered to sit off to the side. They looked back with no friendliness. "Any trouble?" Captain Steen asked.

"Nope. I made my opinion of them known and that was it," I said.

"One of them has a bloody nose," he observed. "He must have fallen down while you were giving your opinion." He looked at me expectantly. I shrugged.

"Oh, that reminds me," I gestured at Andie. She brought the two revolvers over. "I took these off of them." Andie handed them over to Captain Steen.

"I'll log it down and keep them in the armory for them. So, you guys are here, does this mean you're going to relocate to Fort Campbell?" Captain Steen asked.

I gestured at Howard and Lashonda. "The Allen family has decided to join you, yes."

"But, not the rest of you," He surmised.

I shook my head. "We value our freedom too much." To my surprise, Captain Steen smiled.

"Yeah, I figured as much," he said, and looked around. "Looks like a small group for today's activities." He looked at me pointedly and gestured to Corporal Alexander. The corporal grinned and ran over to the group of people setting up tables and chairs. An older looking man, maybe in his sixties was standing with the group. He was no more than 160 pounds and a couple of inches under six feet. He was wearing jeans, a white button down shirt, tie, and a blue blazer. He smiled at the corporal and walked with him back to our group.

Captain Steen cleared his throat. "Everyone, I'd like you to meet Fort Campbell's unofficial chaplain, Don Dexter." He said hello and we took turns introducing ourselves. I introduced myself last.

He looked me over and cast a glance at the rest of my group. "Are you the young man who is going to be an expectant father?"

"I am sir," I replied. I motioned to Julie, who was standing beside me. "This is my beautiful girlfriend and the future mother of my child."

"What are your intentions with her, Mister Gunderson?" he asked somberly. Julie frowned and I saw the hint of her anger starting to surface. I squeezed her hand briefly before answering.

"That is an excellent question, Father Don." I looked around as if confused and then reached into my pocket before dropping to one knee.

"Julie," I said as I displayed the diamond ring I held in my hand "I would be honored if you would marry me."

Julie, Andie, and Lashonda all gasped in unison. She looked at me a moment, and smiled as a tear broke free.

"I told you once, Zachariah Gunderson, treat me right and I'll be with you until the end. I still mean it."

Father Don married us in front of everyone. We set up the grill and Howard cooked steaks. Lashonda had already prepared side items of vegetables and her special corn casserole. It was the best we could do under the circumstances, but everyone was enjoying themselves. I even invited the trio to eat with us. They readily agreed, even the driver, though he still glared at me from time to time.

"Where is the First Sergeant?" I asked while we ate.

"He had duties back at HQ," Captain Steen said without elaborating.

"Are you going to sing for us?" Corporal Alexander asked Rowdy with a wide grin.

"Of course I am," Rowdy replied. We chitchatted with each other throughout the meal, and of course, Rowdy sang.

"I'd like a word with you, if you don't mind," Captain Steen said to me. "Let's walk over to the Chinook. I have something to show you."

We walked up the Chinook's rear ramp and he showed me a pallet of supplies. "The First Sergeant and I discussed it, and we'd like you to begin the process of creating an outpost. You'll find various items which you may need, including ten thousand rounds of ammunition."

Chapter 44 – Big Mac

"I have a plan," I said to everyone. We had stopped working for a noon time lunch.

They looked at me quizzically. "Well, Hoss, is this the part where we ask what your plan is?" Rowdy asked with a grin.

"Yep," I answered.

"Zach?"

"Yes, Rowdy?" I responded.

"What's your plan?" he asked.

"I am so glad you asked. It concerns the outpost we're going to create."

"Do tell," Rowdy said.

I washed down the remainder of my lunch with a glass of water. "Yep, we're going to scrub the idea of the truck stop for now, and instead use the radio station located on Concord Road."

"Why the change?" Julie asked.

"The radio is the biggest factor. We'll be able to communicate to anyone out there listening. Plus, there is a large generator on site. We'll need to get fuel to the location, so I'm thinking we need to find a fuel truck and fill it up at the reservoir. Then, we get that generator running, and start broadcasting radio messages."

"If only we had a list to show us what to do," Julie lamented sarcastically. There was much laughter at my expense, but I didn't mind.

After the laughter died down, I held up a finger. "That reminds me. I found all of my notepads spread out all over the basement floor. What gives?" I asked.

Everyone looked at me questioningly. Except Andie, she was looking at her plate.

"What's up, Andie?" I asked. "I mean, I don't mind you reading my notes, but is there something in particular you wanted to know?"

She looked up at me uncertainly. "Um, I hope you don't mind, but I'm writing a journal. Well, no, that's not the proper word. Maybe more like a biography of our lives, what troubles we've encountered, how we've survived, people we've encountered. I thought it might be important." I thought about it, and she was right. It could be important.

"That sounds pretty cool," Julie said. I nodded in agreement.

The four of us loaded up and made our way, but we were stymied as we approached the intersection of Nolensville Pike and Concord Road. Julie was driving and stopped suddenly.

"I hear gunfire," she said. I heard it too. We all readied our weapons as Julie slowly started driving toward the intersection.

Andie suddenly pointed toward the Publix store. "There!" she exclaimed. Julie moved toward the Publix store and stopped on Concord, about thirty yards west of Nolensville Pike. There was a miniature RV, surrounded by at least fifty zombies. There were at least a dozen more lying dead, scattered around the RV, and there were more than a few stuck under the vehicle, rendering it unmovable. I watched as a rifle barrel poked out of the window vent, shoot another one, and then disappear quickly. Then, I watched in consternation as one of the zombies started trying to open the door handle of the RV's passenger door. They weren't supposed to be able to do that. I opened the door and placed my M4 in the usual spot. The others quickly exited and took up their own firing positions.

I led off the first volley, which resulted in four zombies dropping to the asphalt with an almost simultaneous thud. The remaining zombies turned toward us in tandem, as if they were operated by remote control. Rule 13: They're easily distracted. They forgot all about the RV. Our disciplined shooting made short work of them. Well, I suppose there was a minor lack of discipline. It seemed Rowdy, even though now he stayed with the team, had developed a proclivity to yell out, 'Boom, head shot!' each time he fired. I watched with satisfaction, the repeated explosions of the back of each zombie's heads as each 5.56 full metal jacket bullet exited the skull.

"Green!" each one of them yelled after reloading their weapons. I looked at them and smiled in satisfaction. Julie returned with a knowing smile. The four of us were working well together, like a well-trained team of soldiers.

"Alright, guys, this is weird. I saw one of them actually trying to open the door to the RV," I said. "Let's see who the survivor is and then I want to check out those damned things."

We drove up, and after circling the swath of bodies, parked in front of the RV. I got out while the rest covered me. There was a person crouched down in between the driver and passenger seat. I waved. After a moment, they waved back. I set my M4 on the hood of the truck and began walking slowly toward the RV. The driver's door opened as I was maneuvering through the corpses, and a person stepped out.

She was over six feet tall and most assuredly weighed over the two hundred pound mark. She was wearing a green flannel shirt with a leather vest, jeans, and boots. To top it off, she had long, flowing, grayish-white hair.

"I appreciate the help," she said. "I was out of bullets and I'm running low on gas."

I assumed she was talking at a normal level, nevertheless, she could probably be heard for three blocks.

"I'm Zach," I said as I extended my hand. She shook my hand with a grip every bit as strong as the late Captain's.

"The name's Mackenzie, but everyone's called me Big Mac ever since I was a little girl, only I wasn't very little." I smiled as I introduced everyone else.

"What brings you to this area?" Julie asked.

"I was making my way back to my Grandpappy's farm. When God unleashed his wrath, I was stuck down in Birmingham. I lived down there a while with some folks, but they got more and more fixated on religion. The last straw was when the menfolk insisted I start wearing a dress." She slapped her thigh and laughed, which sounded like a dying bull.

"I ain't worn a dress since I was in kindergarten. Anyway, I figured it was time to leave. It was a straight shot up I-65. It took some doing, but I got this little RV through all of them stalled cars. The 840 turn off was completely blocked off, so I got off at

Concord road and was making my way back to the farm when I ran out of gas. So here I was, sitting here figuring out where to find some gas when I was surrounding by these things. What about you folks?"

Julie explained while I began inspecting the dead zombies. I was not surprised to see the black eyes, but the decomposition was nowhere near the level it should have been. I looked closer at one man, and gasped.

Andie walked over and stood close. "What is it, Zach?" she asked.

"Look," I pointed. "Everyone, come here and look." I waited until everyone was close. I squatted down and pointed again. "Look at this one's face. That's not decomposition. Those are scabs."

"Well, what the hell does that mean?" Mac asked. I stood.

"Scabs are a healing process. The question is why does he have scabs? Was he healing from being scratched up before he turned, or is there something else going on? I'm not sure I have an answer, but I'm going to cut this one open. You might want to go sit in your RV if you're squeamish, Mac," I said, but did not bother waiting for a response as I got some nitrile gloves out of the truck. Her only response was a snort.

Pulling the dead zombie's shirt up, I opened my lock-blade knife and made a Y-shaped incision. A dark colored goo oozed out as I peeled the skin back. The putrid smell was nauseating but I kept at it until I had a clear view of the insides. I pointed with the blade of the knife.

"His guts should be completely dried up and rotted away by now, but they're not. Alright, stand back a little bit," I said as I slit the stomach open and jumped back. Pus, or bile, spewed out. Everyone made their own little noises of repulse. I leaned forward and inspected the contents. It looked like this one had eaten some type of small furry animal recently. It was enough for Julie. She ran a few feet away and heaved. Rowdy decided it was a good time to retrieve the magazines we'd dropped on the ground and reload them. Andie and Mac stood there watching.

"Anybody got any opinions?" nobody commented.

"Okay, I've seen enough for now. We've made a lot of noise, and it's time to get out of this area." I looked at our new acquaintance. "Mac, we were on a mission to find a tanker truck. We are going to attempt to establish a trading post at the radio station on Concord Road."

"Do any of you know how to drive a truck? In case you can't, I've been a truck driver for the last ten years," she said. I looked at her and smiled. "I think I'm going to like you, Big Mac." Mac grinned at me broadly. To my surprise, she had all of her teeth.

We got the RV unstuck, and followed Big Mac to her family's farm, which surprisingly, was only a few miles from College Grove. Unfortunately, there was nothing left. The homestead, barn, and outbuildings had been burned to the ground. There was a large W.E. spray painted on the road in front of the house. I looked at Andie, but she didn't make eye contact. We went up to the remains of the house and looked around. Mac gasped, and pointed at a skeleton mostly obscured in the ashes.

"Who would have done such a thing?" Mac questioned sadly. "He was a sweet old man who wouldn't have harmed anyone."

"It could have been anything," I said. "Maybe a chimney fire or a lantern knocked over in the night. He might have been infected. Some of the survivors used fire as a means of attempting to eradicate the infection." I looked around at my friends. "Would you like us to help you bury him?" she nodded as tears ran down her cheeks.

Big Mac did most of the shoveling. She worked as hard as any man, and had a hole dug in little time. We used an old blanket to wrap up the skeletal remains and carefully placed them in the ground.

Chapter 45 - The Radio Station

Big Mac pointed with her meaty finger. I noticed she was a nail biter before I looked down I-65 with my binoculars.

"Do you see it?" she asked. The tanker truck was stuck in a long line of other cars and trucks. I answered in the affirmative. "I noticed it as I drove by it. The driver left about ten feet between his truck and the truck in front of him. Some little weasel tried to wedge his Audi in between them, but with a little work, we can get it free and drive it home."

"Do you know if there is any fuel in it?" I asked. Mac shook her head. No matter, I knew where we could fill it up.

"The good thing about those big diesel truck engines, charge the battery and they'll most likely start right up," Mac said. "If it don't, I know how to work on them."

Rowdy smiled. "I bet you do." Mac responded with a cool look. Rowdy stopped grinning and directed his attention to the Interstate.

"Alright, we'll get back to it," I said. "Let's go have a look at the radio station."

The radio station in question is located on Concord Road beside the Interstate. When you get close, the first thing you notice is a very tall tower painted red and white. The wire cables holding it in place were still intact. The station itself was a plain white building, and doubled as the caretaker's residence. It was nestled on approximately twenty acres, which now consisted of overgrown grass and weeds. It was surrounded by chain link fence with a couple of strands of barbwire on the top.

"The fence looks intact and I see a large generator beside the station." I scanned some more, looking for any signs of life. "I'm not seeing any threats, but there may be something inside. Are you guys ready?"

"I was born ready!" Rowdy said enthusiastically. Mac looked at him, as if she was wondering if he were firing on all cylinders.

The station was locked, which was not an issue, and devoid of life. Upon entry, we were hit with a stale, musty odor. Nobody had been inside in quite a while. The radio room itself was smaller than I had imagined it would be. Most of the room was taken up by the equipment. There was a small kitchen, two equally small bedrooms, a full bathroom and a small half-bath in the radio room.

"It looks like all of the radio equipment is intact, and it doesn't look too difficult to figure out how to use it," Rowdy said. "Let's get that tanker over here and fire this sucker up."

"I'd like to see this thing running as well," Mac said. "But I was hoping we could eat first."

Julie quickly turned away, but not before I saw her grinning.

Getting the semi started only took twenty minutes. Getting the tanker truck maneuvered through the half mile maze of vehicles took another hour. Nevertheless, with teamwork, and not less than a dozen zombie encounters, we got the truck parked at the radio station. The tanker indeed had fuel in it, and Big Mac knew precisely how to transfer the gasoline to the generator's tank.

"We got two choices," she said. "Give the engine a good tune up first, or fire it up and see if she runs."

I wanted to give the engine a thorough going over first, but I was out voted. After I bitched about it a minute or two, they agreed at least to at least let me clean the spark plugs and air filter. There was a spray can of ether sitting beside it, which told me this thing would probably be a bear to start. We hooked up the jumper cables, put a squirt of ether in the air filter inlet, and gave it a try. This time it only took ten minutes before it roared to life with a thick puff of black smoke. Everyone cheered in delight. Rowdy ran inside the station ahead of us, hooting the entire way.

"Good afternoon, ladies and gentlemen. This here is Rowdy Yates, lately of Brentwood, Tennessee. The time here in Brentwood is high noon, give or take a few minutes, and this is my very first radio broadcast since the world went to hell in a zombie infested bread basket." Rowdy paused to take a drink of some Patron tequila. Andie rolled her eyes and took the bottle away from him.

"It's only noon, for Christ's sake," she said. Rowdy looked at Andie like a whipped puppy dog, drew a deep breath, and continued.

"Well, I have just been informed that there is no drinking allowed until sundown. I know friends, it is a terribly unjust law, but if you care to visit, we'll make arrangements." Andie rolled her eyes again.

"Anyway, let me tell anyone who is listening about us. We are a group of survivors. Hopefully, you're just like us. We're not like some people we've encountered. We're friendly and are always willing to help others. If you're good people and you can hear this radio transmission, come visit us. We're in Williamson County, Tennessee. Come on down Interstate 65 until you get to the Concord Road exit. Look for the big red radio tower. Oh, and if you're so inclined, the provisional government of the United States has a refugee center in good old Fort Campbell, Kentucky. Tell Captain Steen I sent you. Now, don't go assuming that we're some kind of socialist community where everything is free for the offering. Our resources are limited. Don't come empty handed. We're always open to trade."

Rowdy continued speaking nonstop for over an hour, until I reminded him of the generator's fuel consumption.

"Alright, folks, I'm signing off for the day. We should be back on the air this time tomorrow. In the meantime, be safe, and always remember rule number one, shoot 'em in the head. This is Rowdy Yates signing off." He flipped the switch and the 'on-air' light went out. He looked at all of us expectantly.

"How'd I do?" he asked.

"Rowdy, you're a natural," I said. Everyone voiced their agreement. He grinned broadly.

"We can make this work, guys, but it's going to take a lot of blood, sweat, and tears." I gave a wry grin and pulled out a folded sheet of paper from my shirt pocket. I heard a collective sigh from Julie and Andie. Mac looked perplexed.

"Oh yes, it's a list. First, we're going to move one of the stills out here. Second, we're going to need a couple of outhouses dug, otherwise you'll have people crapping everywhere. Third, Captain Steen provided us with a few thousand sandbags. They'll need to be filled and stacked around the facility. I'd start with four foot high walls and then go from there. Oh, and here is a big one, zombie pits."

"What the hell are zombie pits?" Mac asked.

"I'm glad you asked," I responded with a grin. "Zombies are so stupid they'll walk right into a hole in the ground without the forethought of how they're going to get out. I think if we dig a trench around the fence line, say about six feet wide by eight feet deep, any zombies wondering up from the Interstate will fall into them and they won't know how to climb out. Hopefully there is a backhoe nearby. Do you know how to use one, Mac?" I asked.

Mac scoffed. "Does a hog like slop? Of course, I can run a backhoe. I can run a bulldozer too," she grunted, as if this were something I should have already known. I nodded without any smart assed retort.

"And then, we'll need to create an airstrip for the soldiers. This little task will require a lot of work, including knocking down the power lines around here."

"You're right about one thing, that's a lot of work," Rowdy said.

"It is," I said. "However, if we have any survivors dragging themselves in with nothing to trade, we can put them to work in exchange for food. But, I'm thinking we're going to need to round up a whole lot of cattle and start planting more crops," I frowned for a minute and rubbed my face.

"I know that look," Julie said. "What's wrong?"

"Sometimes, I'm like totally stupid," I said. "There is a large horse farm within a mile from here and we've never checked it out. Let's go have a look."

We shut the generator off and loaded up in the truck. We crossed over Interstate 65 on Concord Road, heading toward Franklin Pike. I pointed to the right. There was a large farm surrounded by a wooden green plank fence.

"This is, or was, an active horse farm owned by a family who made millions in retail. I think it's somewhere around eight hundred acres." I informed them as we drove to a gate and stopped. In the distance, there was a large mansion facing Franklin Pike.

"Let's go in and check out the barns. I bet there may be some horses still alive," Julie said.

"I bet you're right, look at the field. The grass isn't overgrown, something has been eating it," I continued scanning the area and frowned.

"Guys, this area looks like there's been some human activity. It may still be occupied."

"What do we do then, Hoss?" Rowdy asked.

"We're going to drive in slow. If we encounter anyone, just remember, this isn't ours, we're visitors here."

Julie drove through the gate and I closed it behind us. Instead of getting back into the passenger compartment, I jumped in the bed of the truck and kept the M4 out of sight. As we neared the barn, my suspicions proved correct. A man walked out of the barn and stopped near the door. He was a white man, mid-forties, an untrimmed salt and pepper beard, somewhere around six feet tall. He was wearing bib overalls and a well-used John Deere ball cap.

I leaned my head toward Julie's open window. "Stop about twenty-five feet away," I said as I waved at him. He returned the wave with a single, slow nod.

"Good afternoon," I said pleasantly.

"Yes sir, it is. Looks like the weather is finally turning for the better," he replied. "The name's Bo McClendon."

I introduced the others and myself. He nodded at Rowdy and addressed the women as ma'am as he tipped his hat. I was growing to like him already.

"Where are y'all from?" he asked.

"We live over by Nolensville. We've taken over the old Parson's farm."Enlightenment dawned on his face. "I thought your name sounded familiar. You're Rick Sander's buddy," I nodded. "How is the old fart?" he asked.

I slowly shook my head. "He died a year ago. He survived the plague, but I think his heart gave out."

Bo shook his head and spat. "I'm sure sorry to hear that. He was a good man."

I gestured at the farm. "Do you live here?" I asked.

"Nope. I could never have afforded a place like this. I have a small spread a few miles from here. I'm a farrier by trade and used to tend to these horses back in the day. I come by every so often to make sure they're doing okay." He hooked his thumb back at the mansion.

"There are a few corpses back there in the mansion, but I have no idea who they are. I had to kill about forty or fifty of them infected things over the last year, but otherwise, it's pretty quiet in these parts. Y'all are the first people I've seen in four or five months. The last group I came upon was a married couple with a couple of children. They were half starving to death. I fed them and put them up for the night. Then they stole the rest of my food and took off," he spit again. "I see cars driving by once in a blue moon, but I haven't cared about interacting with anyone since then."

"I can assure you, we're not here to steal your food or anything else of yours. We're doing okay in that regard," I said.

Bo nodded. "I'm glad to hear it. What brings you folks out here?"

We took turns explaining everything to him. He was especially interested in turning the radio station to an outpost.

Chapter 46 – Bo

The six of us sat in front of the barn until late afternoon, chatting about our individual experiences.

"I'd been divorced about ten years, although my ex and I still fooled around from time to time. I had gone to her house one evening for dinner. When I got there, both her and our two daughters were infected. At the time, I had no idea what was wrong with them. Looking back, I was lucky I didn't get bitten and infected." He frowned a moment.

"One night, back when we were married, I came home a little late from the VFW. I was drunk and in a surly mood. We got in one of those heated arguments, she called me a foul name, and I slapped her pretty hard. The police got called, I got arrested, and we got divorced. She and I never really stopped loving each other though. I was set in my ways, she was set in hers, but we actually got along better after we divorced." He smiled a little bit at some private memories.

"When they attacked me, I got a little violent with them and managed to get away." Bo rubbed his face and decided it was better to omit the part where he fought them off by bashing their heads in with a croquet mallet. "I was certain the law would be coming to arrest me again, so I hurried back to my house, grabbed food and camping gear, and hid out for almost three weeks. When I ran out of food, I went back. I guess you guys know the rest. Things that were once people were wandering the streets, attacking any living thing in sight." Bo bit his lower lip and shook his head.

"Yeah," I said. "This infection, or whatever it is, has apparently hit the entire world," I looked at the horses in the stalls, contentedly eating grain. I wondered where he got it. "Bo, we've got a horse that probably could use a new set of shoes."

"I'd be happy to do it," he replied.

"Prancer will love you for it," Julie said cheerfully. Bo suddenly looked at her sharply.

"Would Prancer happen to be a pretty Appaloosa?" he asked.

Julie nodded. "She belongs to a man named Fred."

Bo stared at her. "Fred McCoy?" he asked. Julie nodded. "Is Fred okay?" He then looked at the rest of us. "He and I go way back."

Julie told him about Fred going to find his daughter. Bo's face clouded up. "If anyone can find Betsy, Fred can." We echoed the sentiment. I looked at the setting sun and stood.

"Bo, we need to get home. You're welcome to join us for dinner."

"I believe I'll take a rain check. I got some things to do. How about I meet you at the radio station tomorrow?" We agreed and bid our goodbyes.

As we made our way along Concord Road back toward Nolensville Pike, Andie sat up and pointed. "Well, I'll be damned. Rowdy is drawing them like flies." Looking south along the Interstate, there appeared to be a caravan of two vehicles slowly making their way along. I estimated they were about six hundred meters out. Unfortunately, there was a line of zombies ambling along behind them, and they were driving slowly enough where the zombies did not have much trouble keeping up.

"Those yahoos are going to bring all of those zombies right to our doorstep," Rowdy said. "We sure didn't think anyone would be so stupid, did we, Hoss?"

"Nope," I said simply, silently cursing myself for the oversight. "Get your Remington out, Hoss," I said, as I retrieved my Winchester from its carrying case. I looked over at the girls. "Hold off on shooting with those M4s until they're within three hundred meters. Rowdy and I will try to pick off as many as we can."

Rowdy grinned with delight as he hurried over to the edge of the bridge. He took his jacket off and used it as a buffer between the metal railing of the bridge and the stock of his rifle. We each took a moment to put in our earplugs. Julie watched us and readied a pair of binoculars. Andie walked over and stood beside Rowdy.

"I sure wish I had me a deer rifle or something," Mac lamented.

Rowdy fired first and then he watched through his scope a second before announcing, "Boom! Head shot!"

"You know, you're a pretty good shot, when you're sober," Andie quipped. Rowdy pretended not to hear and took aim at another target.

We killed a dozen before they got within range of the assault rifles. I picked up the empty cartridges and pocketed them, hoping they were in good enough shape to use for reloading. Thanks to Captain Steen, we had plenty of ammo for the assault rifles, but our supply of our other calibers of ammunition was dwindling quickly. It was time for us to start doing some serious house-to-house salvaging.

Julie and Andie adjusted their ACOG sights and started firing. They took their time, ensuring a good aim, and firing a single round for each target. I watched through the binoculars as they repeatedly made headshots. It made me warm with pride. Rowdy glanced at me, grinning in pride as well. I handed the binoculars to Mac, who thanked me with a smile. I looked over to see Bo riding up on a horse.

"I heard the gunfire. What's going on?" he asked. I pointed out the two vehicles approaching and the zombies following them. He started to pull a rifle out of a scabbard, but stopped when Julie stopped firing and turned around with a grin.

"We got 'em all. Do you want us to start shooting the ones stuck in the cars?"

I shook my head. "We'll take care of it later. It's getting too dark now."

Bo looked Julie and Andie over. "You girls sure can shoot," he commented.

"My husband taught me," Julie said with a grin and slapped me on the butt.

"My Uncle taught me, but then I had to kill him," Andie said without a grin, only a blank expression. Bo looked at Rowdy and me. We both nodded.

"We'll tell you about it sometime. In the meantime, let's see who these people are," I said.

"Yeah, and ask them why they didn't kill any of those things," Andie added as she slapped a fresh magazine in.

We watched as they finally made their way to the Concord Road exit and slowly worked their way toward us. The lead vehicle was a Toyota Tacoma truck, followed by a blue minivan.

"It looks like all women and some kids," Mac said as she eyed them with the binoculars. Julie turned and waved, which caused Andie and Rowdy to wave. The cars crept forward, which seemed silly at first. Then, I realized we were all armed. It might have been intimidating looking. I put my Winchester back in the case.

"Rowdy, hand your weapon to Andie and walk with me," I said, but Mac interrupted.

"I believe I know those people. They were with the religious sect I told y'all about." She walked with us toward the small caravan, which had stopped on the exit ramp. We stopped about halfway and waited, but they didn't move. It was getting darker now and my patience was wearing thin. Mac waved them in, which seemed to be the invitation they needed. They finally drove up and stopped beside us.

Mac smiled and walked up to the driver. "Well, I'll be! Y'all went and did it. Y'all left them." The driver, a haggard looking woman, perhaps in her late forties or fifties, got out of the Toyota and hugged Mac.

Rowdy walked up to the passenger who happened to be a rather attractive woman in her twenties.

"Howdy, I'm Rowdy." I watched as he typically held out his hand and instead of shaking, he kissed her hand instead. I walked up to the driver and Mac.

"This is Wanda," Mac said.

"My name is Zach." I didn't bother holding out my hand. "While I can appreciate your caution, you ladies burned precious daylight by taking so much time to drive up here." I pointed to the radio station. "Why don't you ladies park your vehicles there and close the gate behind you. The fence will afford you some degree of protection."

"Where are you going?" the driver asked. I looked closely at her. The tone in her voice seemed to indicate I had breached some form of protocol.

"We're going home. We'll be back tomorrow and get acquainted then."

"But we've got hungry children here," she snarled at me.

"Hush, Mama," I heard the passenger say as I walked off before I said something rude. Rowdy tipped his cowboy hat and hurried after me.

"Let's get moving," I said, and walked over to Bo. "If you want to talk to those people, be my guest, but we're going home. We'll be back around noon tomorrow. Depending on the amount of chores I have waiting on me, I may not be with them, but we'll see each other again." We shook hands and I headed to the truck. The rest followed. Mac jogged over to me as I squirted my hands with sanitizer.

"If you don't mind, I think I'll spend the night here and get these people settled in," she said. I nodded in understanding.

"There's a cooler in the back of the truck with some food. Take it with you," I said. Mac nodded gratefully. "Oh, I guess you better take one of the M4s with you too. These women don't seem to know how to protect themselves."

"I am much obliged, Zach. You won't regret it. I'll see y'all tomorrow." Big Mac waved and walked toward the group of women carrying the cooler over her shoulder.

Chapter 47 - The Women of Birmingham

Everyone was dying to go back to the radio station the next morning, except me.

"You guys go ahead. I'll get the chores done and join y'all later," I told them. Julie wanted me to go with them, but I shooed her away with the promise I'd be there by noon.

I accepted the fact none of them, with the exception of Fred and Howard, had my work ethic. So, I toiled at the daily chores by myself, took the clothing off of the clothesline and folded them. Well, I took care of my clothing and Julie's, the rest stayed put, and then spent a few hours reloading bullets. It was time-consuming work reloading a bullet by hand, one at a time. After a while of it, I finally grew frustrated, jumped in Andie's jeep, and headed out.

Andie was sitting by the gate with an M4 cradled in her lap. She looked up as I approached, but didn't smile when I stopped at the entrance.

"Where is everybody?" I asked.

"They're inside. Everyone watched Rowdy talk on the radio and now, who knows what the fuck they're doing. They're swooning around him like he's some kind of fucking star."

I got out of the jeep and sat down beside her.

"I've been sleeping next to him for almost a month and he's never tried anything. But, as soon as other women show up he's flirting with every one of them. Hell, he's been eye-fucking Cindy all day," she said bitterly.

"I take it Cindy is one of the women in the group," I said.

Andie chortled. "Yeah, she's the brunette with the big store bought tits." Andie stood suddenly. "I'm taking my jeep and leaving."

I stood with her. "Where are you going, home?" I asked.

"No. I'm getting the fuck out of here. Julie doesn't like me. Neither you nor Rowdy will fuck me. There's no reason to stay here," she had the same scowl on her face from when I first met her. I grabbed both of her hands. She struggled against me briefly, but I held on tight.

"Listen to me a minute, would you?" She stopped struggling and glared at me.

"If you want to leave, I won't stop you, but I'll certainly beg you to stay," I said.

"Why?" she asked angrily.

"I can think of two very important reasons off the top of my head, you've saved my life twice already. I'd be dead if not for you. Julie and I consider you a very valuable part of our team. I have a lot of admiration and respect for you, Andrea." I looked around and lowered my voice. "If I didn't have Julie, I think things might have been different between you and me, you know?"

She lowered her head and reluctantly nodded.

"But you're in love with her," she said.

"Yep, very much so. I think you'd be surprised to know, I love you as well, but more like a little sister." She looked up at me. "Is that a bad thing?" I asked.

"I guess it's okay," she said quietly.

"Good, I never had a little sister," I said.

"Zach, what is it with Rowdy? Does he like me or not?" Andie asked.

"I know he likes you and cares for you, but I think he views you more as a little sister as well."

She nodded in sad understanding. I looked toward the station building, nobody seemed to be watching. I gave her a kiss on the forehead. "C'mon, let's go inside and listen to Rowdy's bullshit."

I introduced myself to each woman. Wanda was the self-proclaimed matriarch of the group. She struck me as a bitter old woman. She didn't bother thanking me for the food, and instead criticized me for leaving them alone and vulnerable the night before.

Cindy was her daughter. She had obviously taken the time to clean up. She was wearing clean clothing which consisted of tight fitting jeans with an equally tight fitting bright red polo shirt. She even had some makeup on. Andie was right. She was pretty, and had a very nice set of breasts which were stretching her shirt to its limits. She was unabashedly flirting with Rowdy and it was driving him nuts.

Rhonda was an eighteen-year-old redhead with lots of freckles. She was attractive in a unique way, but very quiet. She would answer you if you asked her a direct question. Otherwise, the only time she spoke was to the three children. She was wearing the same plain print dress she was wearing yesterday.

The children, I didn't even bother remembering their names. They were all little girls around two to four-years-old, and poorly behaved. Julie told me all of the girls were orphans.

Finally I met Kelly. She was raven headed with dark, smoldering eyes. She was the same height as Julie, and had the movements of a woman who maybe did a lot of yoga, which probably explained the yoga pants she was wearing. I guessed her age at no older than twenty. When Mac introduced the two of us, she hugged me close, and I mean close as in she pressed her entire body up against me. She ran her hands along my back and whispered in my ear.

"It's nice to meet you, Zach. Thank you for the food last night." She held the hug a moment longer than necessary before letting go. I caught Julie looking at me with an arched eyebrow.

"It is certainly a pleasure to meet all of you. Could you tell me what led you to come up here from Birmingham?"

"We've already told that story," Wanda said. "If you were here this morning instead of sleeping in, you would have heard it."

I shrugged. "I guess I'll have to speculate then. Let me guess, you were run off because of your caustic attitude." Andie burst out in laughter. Wanda glared daggers of poison at me.

"They all belonged to the same church which evolved into a Christian survival group." Julie said. "The men, and especially their leader, became more and more radical. They were expected to be subservient to the men and submit to polygamy." Julie pointed. "Cindy and Rhonda were going to be married to one of the men in the group, who happened to be thirty years older than them. They finally had enough, packed up, and left while the men were off hunting."

"Who was the poor bastard that was going to marry Wanda?" I couldn't help myself. Andie laughed again. Even Rowdy chuckled.

"The preacher was my husband. He insisted on marrying Kelly. That was the final straw with me," Wanda said with another cold glare. "I'm not a woman to be trifled with, young man," she admonished harshly.

Cindy continued the story. "We knew Big Mac was coming here. She had drawn a map for me. When we heard Rowdy's sexy voice on the radio, we had to come see this man in real life." The girls giggled. Wanda made a derisive snort.

I was growing tired of her attitude and decided to change the subject.

"Okay, ladies, I'm glad you're here, but if you want to stay, you'll need to earn your keep. Freeloaders are not welcome." I focused my attention on Wanda. It was obvious she was the one who was going to cause problems. "Do I make myself clear?" She continued glaring and scoffed.

"We're not freeloaders, and we don't answer to you. Who do you think you are?" Wanda said. I stared at her pointedly.

"I'm the person who provided you with food last night, and now, Miss Attitude, I'd like to know how you intend to pay." They all looked at me as if I'd asked them to solve Fermat's last theorem.

Wanda chortled. "Pay? We have no money, or anything else."

"Not a problem. Since you don't have anything of value to trade for, you can work it out in labor."

Wanda chortled again. She seemed to think this was a joke or something. I ignored her and turned to the other women.

"Rowdy and I set up a still out back which can be used to distill water. We put a storage tank in the kitchen. There are some buckets in the shed out back. Two of you get those, and go down to the creek, which is a couple of hundred yards east of here," I said pointing. "You'll need plenty of water and firewood. You have a day of distilling water ahead of you. You other two can use some of that water to clean up this station." Rhonda and Kelly immediately stood up and began walking toward the door.

Wanda stood and snapped her fingers. "You two sit back down." She turned her head and glared at me. "I don't know who you think you are, boy. We're not your slaves."

"And we're not a welfare agency. Keep in mind, you have no claim to this property," I retorted immediately. "We used precious ammunition shooting zombies who were chasing you ladies. You've got shelter here and a full belly, thanks to our efforts. None of this is free, especially with such a disrespectful attitude." She continued glaring at me. "You don't want to work?" I pointed at the door. "Then get the hell out of here."

Wanda looked around and fixed her attention on Rowdy. "Is this how you let boys act around here?" she asked him.

Andie jumped up. "You stupid woman, he's no boy." Julie stood as well.

"And I'm not going to sit here and listen to you speak in a disrespectful tone to my husband." She looked at me. "I'm going outside, but she better get a quick attitude adjustment before I shoot her." Julie and Andie walked out together.

Rowdy held up his hands at shoulder level and shrugged. "Zach is in charge around here, Miss Wanda, I accepted that when I signed on, and I haven't regretted it for a minute. He's a smart kid – eh, I mean, he's a smart young man."

"Momma, he's right," Cindy said. "We're not freeloaders." She looked at me. "I've done my share of distilling water. Show me where the creek is and I'll get right on it. I'm not very strong though. Maybe Rowdy can help me with the hauling," she said as she smiled coyly at him.

"Yeah, sure!" Rowdy said, almost a little too eagerly. As they started for the door, I heard a gunshot. I pushed by them as I ran outside.

"Fucking zombies," Andie said as she pointed. We had forgotten to close the gate. Eight of them were currently walking in.

"Where the hell did they come from?" I asked as I grabbed Andie's M4.

"No idea," Andie said and reached for the rifle. "I can shoot them." I ignored her. Wanda's disrespectful behavior pissed me off. I needed to vent, and I could think of no better way than killing a few zombies. I fired eight rounds to their heads in a little over twelve seconds. I had a long way to go to achieve the level of Fred's marksmanship level, but I was getting better.

"Wow, Zach, you're a good shot!" I looked over. It was Kelly. She was looking at me in wide-eyed wonder. "Were you the one shooting all of them yesterday?"

"It was all of us," I said. "Which reminds me, why weren't you guys shooting at them?"

Kelly shook her head. "We don't have any ammunition." She pointedly looked at Wanda. "We owe them our lives Wanda. We shouldn't be disrespecting them."

Wanda gave Kelly a hard look. It looked like a toxic retort was on the edge of her lips, but she managed to hold it in.

"The house could certainly use a good cleaning," she finally said.

Julie and I went back to the Interstate in our truck. I wanted to see where the hell those other zombies came from. It didn't take much brain power to figure out. There were infected bastards up and down the Interstate. They were sitting, standing, leaning against cars, in cars, under cars; you name it. Most of them were dead, but there were plenty still living.

"When you drive up beside these cars, give me enough room so I can open the door and jump in, if necessary," I said.

"You got it, babe."

She slowly drove beside the multitude of abandoned cars as I walked along. There was a mixture of empty vehicles, vehicles with corpses, and vehicles with zombies.

"Zach, why are the southbound lanes more congested than the northbound lanes?" Julie asked.

"I can only assume everyone was fleeing Nashville when the plague went viral," I replied. "There was a chain collision, everyone was stuck, and then people started turning. I imagine it was pretty horrific."

"Just think, you're stuck in a traffic jam, and all of a sudden there are these fucking zombies everywhere. You don't dare step outside of your car, but you look in your rearview mirror and your children are infected. You watch in horror as they jump over the seat and rip your throat out. Your last conscious thought is ruing the fact you let the little bastards ride without their seatbelts on," Julie spoke as if she was narrating a horror movie. I looked at her.

"You have a vivid imagination," I said. She grinned at me.

In the interest of expediency, I only made a quick peripheral search of each vehicle before moving on to the next one. If a car was occupied by a zombie, I'd dispatch them with a head shot. Luggage was opened and unceremoniously dumped out, although I took the time to dump everything inside the car. After all, dumping them on the side of the road would be a tremendous waste. Anything we thought was useable I tossed in the bed of the truck. We kept it up for most of the day and were able to clear approximately three miles on both sides of the Interstate.

I checked my watch. "Okay, let's head back. This time I really want to be home before the sun goes down."

Andie and Kelly were keeping watch and waved as we drove up to the radio station. I saw the zombie corpses piled together and burning steadily. Julie started chuckling.

"Look," she said, pointing. The side of the radio station was painted with my rules in neat, block lettering.

"Kelly and I put them up. What do you think?" Andie asked when we parked and got out.

"That's fucking awesome," I said with a grin.

"Oh, wow, you guys really scored," Kelly said as she looked in the bed of the truck. There was an assortment of toothpaste, soap, shampoo, hygiene products, first aid kits, boots, shoes, underwear, gas cans, canteens, and most importantly, assorted firearms and ammunition. Cindy and Rowdy walked up while we were inspecting our loot and looked it over. The others saw we had returned and began filtering out of the house.

Cindy gasped. "What do I have to do to get some toothpaste and dental floss?" she asked slyly. I grabbed one of each and tossed it to her. I tossed some to Kelly as well.

"On the house," I said. The two of them smiled warmly. Kelly gave me another hug, which earned her no points with Julie. I looked over at Rowdy. "How's everything here?"

"We've gotten ten gallons of water distilled. Rhonda insisted on giving the kids a bath, so we have around seven gallons left."

"Okay, we'll discuss it when we get everyone together," I said. Rowdy seemed to interpret my statement as some type of order. He put his fingers in his mouth and gave a loud whistle. I frowned, but didn't say anything. Somehow, I needed to emphasize the point to him to refrain from unnecessary loud noises. Anyway, it had its intended effect. Everyone gathered around expectantly.

I looked at the women. "There are eight of you altogether, so you've got roughly one day's supply of water. Tomorrow, you'll need to distill at least ten more gallons, and I would strongly suggest distilling three times that amount." I looked at Rhonda. "I'm sure you had good intentions, but don't use distilled water to bathe with. The distillation process takes longer and requires more heat. You can boil creek water for bathing purposes. It doesn't take as long and uses less wood."

Rhonda nodded, but stared at my feet rather than making eye contact. "How did the cleaning go?"

"Both the house and the station are clean enough to eat off of the floor, Zach," Big Mac said. Wanda looked on in insolent silence.

"That's awesome," I said. "Alright, Julie and I talked at great length about the current situation. We want you to know we're glad you're here and you're welcome to stay, but our food supply is limited. Since you have kids, perhaps it would be a good idea for you to relocate to Fort Campbell." I held up a hand before anyone responded. "You ladies have three days to talk it over amongst yourselves, so there is no need to make a decision at this time." I paused while they murmured among themselves.

"Okay, you know how to secure water for yourselves, next is food. You guys don't seem to have a hell of a lot, and like I said, our supplies are limited. After our crops are harvested later this year, we should have plenty, but last year, we only harvested enough to feed ourselves."

"What do you suggest, Zach?" Big Mac asked.

"I'd suggest first thing in the morning that you go hunting. There are plenty of deer around here, and stray cattle."

"You expect us to do the hunting?" Cindy asked.

"Yes, ma'am, and the butchering. You ladies need to be self-sufficient." I looked over at Mac. "Mac, we've discussed our plans for this radio station. Do you want to live here and run it?"

Mac slowly nodded. "I'd like that a lot, Zach."

"Excellent. The main thing for you to keep in mind when encountering new people is trade. Always think of commodities to trade."

"Don't give anything away for free," Wanda said.

"Exactly," I replied, and pointed across the street. "Use the churches across the street for staging areas. You don't want people setting up camp inside the perimeter. Sanitary conditions will become a major problem if you do. Also, if you ladies decide to stay here, you're going to need to work out security protocols. We'll be glad to help, but the first thing to start with is reinforcing this building and creating the zombie pits we discussed." Mac nodded and started to ask a question, but our conversation was interrupted by a truck approaching on Concord Road.

Andie looked through her ACOG scope. "It's Bo," she said. Bo entered through the open gate, parked beside us and got out. He had a German Shepherd dog with him.

"This is Lucy," he said. "She looks mean, but she's a spoiled baby." Lucy hopped out of the truck with a well-worn tennis ball in her mouth and ran around sniffing everyone.

"I killed a deer and brought some venison. You ladies look like you could use some meat on your bones." He glanced at me wryly. "Besides, maybe some good meat will improve Wanda's disposition." I wholeheartedly agreed. Wanda ignored me a minute in order to glare at Bo. It seemed to be her natural facial expression.

The ladies, with the exception of Wanda, thanked Bo graciously and he in turn helped cook the venison. I helped myself without asking and ate a large portion. Julie and Andie knew exactly what I was doing. Rowdy paid no attention and flirted shamelessly with Cindy.

"Stop the truck a minute, sweetheart," I said, and pointed. "Pull in right there." Julie stopped at the entrance to the Governor's Club, an exclusive gated community on Concord

Road. Most of the houses in the subdivision were well over a million dollars in value. I casually walked over to the rock wall and urinated while I looked around. The wrought iron gate across the entrance was chained and padlocked. There was a hand painted sign posted on the gate saying 'keep out.' The street into the subdivision was completely devoid of cars and corpses. There were cars in driveways sitting silently. I saw no movement or any telltale wisps of smoke coming out of chimneys, but still, I had a feeling. I walked back to the truck and got in.

"Feel better?" Julie asked.

"Yeah. Someone is living there. Maybe several people, I don't know." I explained my logic. "I think I'll leave a note on the gate.

Later, after everyone had turned in, I lit a solitary candle and put it on the nightstand.

"What are you doing?" Julie asked.

"Get naked and lay on your stomach," I directed. She looked at me questioningly, but complied. "I'll be right back." I hustled out of the bedroom and came back in a moment later with a bottle of baby oil.

"What are you fixing to do, big boy?" Julie asked amusedly.

"I'm going to give you a massage from your neck all the way down to your toes, and you're going to lay there and enjoy it." I opened the bottle and squirted some between her shoulder blades. Julie chuckled and moved her hair out of the way. I worked slowly and methodically. Julie sighed in delight as I worked all of the knots out of her muscles. When I finally finished, Julie was moaning in ecstasy. I leaned forward and spoke quietly in her ear.

"Happy birthday, love," I said. Julie gasped.

"You remembered!" she exclaimed, turned over, grabbed me and kissed me passionately.

It was a great night.

Chapter 48 - Departure Aborted

Since Murfreesboro Road had a few snarls which we had not cleared, I kept us to the back roads until we reached Sam Ridley Parkway. Then, it was a clear shot to the Smyrna airport. We turned left on Fitzhugh Boulevard and stopped at the back of the hangars. We had a caravan of three vehicles. We were in the dually, the Birmingham clan were in their vehicles, and Bo and his dog decided to tag along. Rowdy opted to ride with Cindy and Wanda, which caused Andie to pout in silence the entire ride. Lucy sensed Andie's melancholy and tried to cheer her up by dropping her tennis ball in her lap.

We brought plenty with us. Bo helped us round up a few heads of stray cattle and we butchered one of them. We had a full assortment of food and we were going to make a day of it with cooking out. I found myself actually looking forward to Captain Steen and the rest of the soldiers.

"What a beautiful day!" Julie said. She was right. The sun was shining and there wasn't a cloud in sight.

"I bet it'll get up in the mid-sixties today," Bo commented. I agreed. We unloaded tables, food, a grill, and other supplies out of the truck. Julie started to drag a table out of the truck bed, but before I could intervene, she was quickly stopped by Bo.

"I'll be damned if I let a pregnant woman do any lifting while I'm around," he said with a grunt. Julie smiled and moved out of the way.

"Julie, would you supervise setting everything up? I want to ride around the airport and make sure there are no surprises lurking around."

"You got it, sweetie," Julie replied cheerfully. Why don't you take Andie with you?" she suggested with a wink. I looked over at Andie. She shrugged noncommittally.

I handed Julie a walkie-talkie. "I'll give a SITREP every ten minutes," I said. I slowly drove down Fitzhugh Road, weaving in and out of the various buildings.

"This place is bigger than I thought," Andie finally said.

"Yeah, in the sixties it was a military airbase. When Johnson became President, he ordered it shut down and moved the operation to Texas."

"Why?" she asked.

"Oh, I assume it was a purely political decision and had nothing to do with logic and reality."

Andie grunted. "Some things never change. Do you think political shenanigans had anything to do with the plague?"

"I have no idea," I said as I slowly circled around a building.

Andie started. "What? Are you saying the all-knowing Zach Gunderson in fact doesn't know everything?"

I gave her a look. "Smart ass," I quipped. She chuckled. "I'm glad you're in a better mood." Wrong thing to say. The smile left her face immediately.

"Back in high school when Macie dumped me, I was devastated, but I got over it. You'll find someone else. I bet Corporal Alexander is single. He seems like a pretty good guy."

"I bet they've fucked already," Andie said. I chuckled. She looked at me. "Well? Have they?"

"Now you've found two things the all-knowing Zach Gunderson does not know. Why don't you ask him yourself?" I asked. Andie turned away from me quickly.

"That Corporal hardly looked at me the last time they were here," she said while staring out of the window.

I stopped the truck and gave Julie a quick negative SITREP on the radio. Then I reached over and pulled the passenger side visor down. "Look in the mirror."

Andie glanced at me and then did so. "Remember the last time the corporal saw you? Your face was black and blue, and your nose was so swollen it looked like an overgrown tumor. Now look at you. Your face is almost completely healed, your hair has grown out a little bit, which makes you a lot sexier by the way, and your nose only has a small hint of crookedness, which adds character. You've put on some weight in the right places too, and if my eyes don't deceive me, your boobs have grown," I said and sat back in my seat. Andie looked over and her face brightened.

"They have! Do you want to see?" she asked.

I laughed. "No, I better not." I started driving again. "If that corporal is not hooked up with somebody, I'd bet a dollar to a donut he'll be looking you over real good.

"You better be right," Andie said threateningly. I laughed again.

The Chinook arrived shortly after noon. The two pilots, whom I hadn't yet met, kept the rotors running. Captain Steen walked out of the rear, with Corporal Alexander following, carrying his M4 in one hand, a duffel bag in the other, and wearing a rucksack. Jack's posture was a little stooped. He didn't have his usual military bearing as he walked over to me. When the two soldiers were clear of the rotors, the Chinook powered up and lifted off.

"How are you, Zach? That wound on your cheek is healing nicely," Captain Steen said as he shook my hand. He was right. Julie had done a wonderful job of aligning it properly when she glued it together.

"I'm doing well. You look like a man with a lot of weight on his shoulders," I replied. He smiled tightly and looked around.

"You've brought a lot of company," he commented.

"I have, and we've brought some fresh fish, venison, and vegetables. Bo over there said he's pretty good on the grill. I hope you brought an appetite with you."

"It sounds much better than army chow," he said.

Corporal Alexander hurried over to us as quickly as the extra weight would allow him. We shook hands and then he leaned forward.

"Holy shit, Zach," he said in a loud whisper. "Where did all of these women come from?" Julie had walked up beside him and overheard him. She giggled.

"Come on, I'll introduce you to all of them. Leave your gear here." She hooked her arm through his and led him off.

"Julie," I said, stopping her in her tracks. "Maybe Terry would like to say hello to Andie first?" I gestured in an expression I hoped she would understand. She did, and nodded at me.

I turned my attention back to Captain Steen. "You don't have the usual complement of soldiers today. Where'd the pilots fly off to?"

"I have a makeshift office set up in that hangar," he said, pointing at the first of three hangars. "Why don't we go check it out?" He waited until we were in his office before speaking.

"Zach, there's no way to say this diplomatically. We will be unable to relocate any people to Fort Campbell at this time." He looked at me somberly.

"Has something happened?" I asked.

"There have been some social unrest among the civilians, and some desertions," he sighed. "It hasn't been pretty. In fact, there have been several we have banished."

"I see," I said. "Julie and I pumped these women up about relocating. They're going to be disappointed. Rowdy will be ecstatic though, because he's got a thing for one of the women." Some of the women were pleasant to be around, but I couldn't wait for Wanda to get the hell out of my neighborhood.

"There is some more unpleasant news, I'm afraid," he said. I looked at him closely. "Howard was killed in an unfortunate set of circumstances." He looked at me somberly.

"What happened?" I asked.

"It would seem his two sons were concealing handguns. When they got to their new home, the youngest one pulled the handgun out of his pants and handed it to his father. The weapon discharged, striking Howard in the chest."

Captain Steen could have punched me in the gut and it wouldn't have been any worse than what he had just told me. He looked at me hard.

"Mrs. Allen blames you. She said you insisted they keep their firearms," Captain Steen said, and continued staring at me. I reluctantly nodded. He took a long deep breath before speaking again.

"Zach, you are a remarkable young man. You have a highly ordered mind and the adversity we face has brought out the natural leadership ability in you. If the world was a normal place, I'd get you enrolled in an ROTC scholarship program. You'd be a great officer, with the right tutelage. But your major problem is inexperience. You assumed these kids would handle those weapons in a safe manner. You assumed Howard would have ensured those handguns would have been unloaded." Captain Steen took his glasses off and rubbed his eyes.

"You seem to be indirectly saying I fucked up," I said.

"Yes, I am," he replied.

The rebellious teenager in me wanted to stand up and tell him to go fuck himself. I couldn't do it though. He was right. If I had inspected the weapons myself, or if I had personally taken the time to train Derry...

"Point taken," I said quietly.

"The point I believe you are missing is my order of no firearms possessed by civilians. Howard would still be alive if you guys had deferred to my doctrine and to my wisdom."

"You'll be pleased to know, none of these women are armed, as far as I know. Maybe you better search them," I retorted sarcastically.

Captain Steen sighed. "It doesn't matter. They won't be going to Fort Campbell, at least not anytime soon."

"What happened?" I asked.

"Some soldiers and civilians basically conspired to take over. It was an ill-conceived plan concocted by a few idiots who thought they knew how to run things better. It was doomed from the start. Nevertheless, a few people were killed. Fortunately, Corporal Alexander was our inside mole. He exposed the plot and we were able to contain collateral damage."

"How many were involved?" I asked.

"Five soldiers and about a dozen civilians." Captain Steen looked me in the eye. "The soldiers were tried for treason and executed. The civilians were banished. I directed them to head north and get out of this area altogether, but I've no idea where they've gone." We were interrupted by Julie and Andie. They had fixed us a plate of food and brought them in. They seemed to sense the tension in the air, so they left, knowing I'd tell them everything later. Captain Steen waited for them to leave before continuing.

"Although we were successful in quashing this ill-conceived act, there is a growing discontent among the remaining civilians. Until we can bring things under control, I'm not comfortable accepting any new incoming personnel." I heard the sound of the Chinook returning.

"There is something else I'd like to talk to you about. Due to Corporal Alexander's role in the whole affair, he has received death threats, and someone took a shot at him last night while he was on guard duty." Captain Steen paused a moment before adding. "If you don't mind, I'd like to leave him with you people for a little while."

"Of course," I said. I knew of at least one person who was going to like this situation greatly. "Is there anything else?" I asked.

"No, I think we've covered it for now." He stopped as he was putting his glasses back on. "Oh, let's go talk to the pilots. When we were flying down here, one of them thought he saw some signs of life along the I-24 corridor. Let's eat and then we'll see what they have to say."

We ate our lunch, mostly in silence. I was still trying to wrap my head around the death of Howard, and the more I thought about it, the more intense the feelings of guilt. By the time I walked out of the hangar, I was in a deep funk. Julie saw it immediately of course. I put my arm around her and walked her over to the truck.

"I don't want to ruin your day, but I know you're going to pester me until I tell you."

"You got that right," she said. So, I told her. Her response was predictable and she started crying. I held her tightly. I saw Rowdy walk over and stop tentatively. I shook my head. He understood and walked back to the main group.

The Birmingham women, especially Wanda, did not take the news well when they were told they would not be going to Fort Campbell. Frankly, I didn't care. I'd already decided my contact with them was going to be limited. I didn't like Wanda, and Kelly was going to get me into trouble. Andie was excited that Corporal Alexander was coming to live with us though. Julie and I exchanged a glance. We'd let her enjoy the day and tell them about Howard's death later.

Chapter 49 - Memory Lane

We had three days of drizzling rain, which is not unusual for March. With the daily temperature hovering in the mid-sixties, it was great weather for planting certain vegetables. Our garden plots were much larger than last year and we'd added to the number of vegetables. With the five of us working, we transferred the seedlings from the greenhouse and got them in the ground in record time. Corporal Alexander, or Terry as we now called him, proved to be a hard worker. He helped with the chores and had no trepidation about getting down in the mud and individually hand planting each seedling. He got along well with both Andie and Julie, but I had not spoken to him very much. Julie chastised me about it the night before.

The truth of it, I was not in a sociable mood since the latest meeting with Captain Steen. Howard's death upset me greatly. It was yet another person whom I cared for deeply who was no longer with us. I felt guilty about Rick's death, Macie's death, and now Howard's death. It ate at me and was yet another topic of my nightmares.

"What is everyone going to do today?" I asked as we cleaned off the table.

"Well, Hoss, I told Cindy I'd take her squirrel hunting," Rowdy said.

"Is that what it's called these days?" Julie quipped. Terry and I chuckled. Andie didn't say anything, only stared out the window.

"What is my husband going to do today?" Julie asked.

"I thought I'd go over to Bernie's and get some honey, and then maybe do some scavenging." Julie gave me a look. I knew what it meant. "Terry, how about going with me? I'll show you around and you can get an idea of how we do things."

"Sure, sounds good, Zach," he replied.

"I want to go!" Andie exclaimed.

"Have you finished your reading assignments?" I asked. Andie frowned and stuck her tongue out at me.

"We'll go another time," I promised.

"Terry, I've no idea what kind of training you've had, but we have a certain method of clearing houses," I said as we parked in front of Bernie's house. "This house belonged to a friend of ours. He's dead. We can do some practicing here so we'll be on the same sheet of music."

"Sounds good, Zach. We did a hell of a lot of house clearing back at Fort Campbell, so I should be good to go."

Surprisingly, Terry and I worked well together. I watched him as we went through the motions of clearing Bernie's house. Even though it was filled with clutter, Terry moved fluidly through each room. Satisfied, I found a tote bin in the utility closet and began loading up Bernie's beekeeping equipment. Terry saw several jars of honey sitting on the kitchen counter.

"This old man was a beekeeper, huh?" he asked. I nodded. He pointed at the honey. "How old is this stuff? Is it good anymore?"

I stopped a moment and was tempted to wow Terry with my vast knowledge of honey, but I held off.

"When honey is stored under proper conditions, it can last for years. It's still good, let's load it up." We carried the stuff to the truck and I looked around outside.

"He sure did have a lot of junk," Terry commented.

"Yeah, one day we'll go through it all with a fine tooth comb and see if there is anything worth taking."

"We can do it now," he suggested. I shook my head.

"I'm not up for it now," I said. "His death reminds me of Howard's death, which reminds me of other people who have died."

Terry nodded somberly. "I know the feeling. I take it he was a pretty good dude?"

I let out a short laugh. "He was downright crazy, but crazy in a good way I'd say." I pointed at the protective headgear. "He didn't even use any protection when he harvested the honey. The bees wouldn't sting him. He'd say they were his friends and would never hurt him." Terry laughed. "Well, let's get going. I've got a few places I'd like to check out."

Terry spoke to Andie on the radio as I drove. He told her we were leaving Bernie's. Andie asked where we were going. "Tell her the Woodbine and Glenrose area," I said. "We'll be home before sundown," Terry repeated what I said and signed off. I was content to drive in silence, but decided I needed to be friendly, and get to know Terry a little better.

"What happened up at Fort Campbell? Are you allowed to talk about it?" I asked.

He sighed. "I'd been in a bad mood and got into the habit of bitching and complaining a lot. One day, First Sergeant Santiago had enough of me and a couple of other soldiers, and he put us on guard duty. We stood around gate six, one of the entrances to Fort Campbell, all day long doing nothing but swatting flies. I bitched and complained about everything under the sun. So, these two privates tell me about a plan a few of them have cooked up. They intended to kill the Captain, the First Sergeant, and a couple of others, and then take over." He stopped a moment to look out the window.

"So anyway, I go to the First Sergeant and tell him all about it. He went straight to Captain Steen. They decide for me to go along with this group and gather intel. When we thought we had identified everyone involved, we arrested them and I gave testimony in the court martial. But, instead of the other soldiers praising my actions, I was labeled a snitch. Someone fired a few rounds into my barracks window one night. The Captain and First Sergeant felt it would be safer for me to get out of Fort Campbell. They figured you wouldn't mind me hanging around. So, here I am."

"I see," I said. "Well, personally, I'm glad you're here. The girls are hard workers, but there is so much to do, we always seem to stay behind."

"How's Rowdy?" He asked.

"Oh, he's enjoyable to be around, but his work ethic is fleeting. Now that he's chasing after Cindy…" I left the sentence unfinished. Terry chuckled. I drove into the parking lot of Walmart where there were a few cars I'd not siphoned gas out of yet. I showed Terry my siphoning apparatus and we started going at it.

"How do you know which cars to siphon from?"

I pointed toward other cars. "What do you call the fancy lid that closes over the gas cap?" I asked.

Terry frowned and looked. "The fancy gas cap lid?" he replied. I laughed.

"Yeah, I guess. Anyway, take a look at the parking lot. See all of the open lids?" Terry looked and nodded. "Those are the ones I've already siphoned gas from."

"Ah, makes sense."

The first car we came to seemed to have a full tank. We siphoned half of it out and into the truck. "I'm going to leave the fancy lid closed because there seems to be a half of a tank of gas still in here," I said as we got back in the truck. Terry nodded in understanding.

"Where to now?" he asked.

"I believe we'll stick with the Nolensville Pike corridor today. One day, I want to venture out further. The police department's evidence warehouse is over in east Nashville. I think we have the numbers with us now to enable us to do so. I've not gone very far before because we didn't have the numbers to be able to defend against a sizeable number of hostiles we may encounter."

"Nashville has to be a treasure trove of stuff," Terry said. I agreed.

"What do you think of Andie?" I finally asked. I hoped my question seemed one of boredom rather than inquiring.

"She's a cute kid," he frowned momentarily. "I thought she and Rowdy were hooked up."

"Who, Rowdy? Nah, they're friends, nothing else. I thought they were going to hook up one day, but now Cindy is here and Rowdy is like a tomcat on the prowl."

"Oh," he said. I started to add more, but decided against it.

"Cindy sure is a looker. So is Kelly."

I nodded silently. I guess he wasn't interested in Andie. "You know, Rhonda is pretty in her own way too, but she doesn't talk."

I nodded. "Yeah, she's very quiet. I thought one of those kids belonged to her, but I think they're all orphans they took in."

"Ah, so none of them have kids," Terry opined.

"I don't think so."

"What was up with you making Andie read?" he asked me.

"She's a smart girl, but like Julie and I, she never finished her education. She and Julie are reading all of the books we have. When they finish one, we discuss it."

"Which one are you reading?" he asked.

"I've read them all, so I need a few more. If you spot any books, point them out to me." I drove around two zombies standing in the middle of the road. Terry looked at them.

"You don't want to shoot them?" he asked.

"No, we need to conserve our ammo. Besides, I'm still convinced they'll eventually die off. I said it would happen last summer, but there are a lot of them still around" I was looking at them in my rearview mirror as I spoke and then suddenly came to a stop. Corporal Alexander looked at me and turned in his seat quickly.

"What is it, Zach?" he asked. I continued looking in the mirror for several seconds before answering.

"One of those sons of bitches just squatted down and took a drink from the water puddle," I said quietly.

"Huh? Are you sure?" Terry asked.

I turned the truck around, slowly approached them, and stopped about thirty feet away. They stared at us with those evil looking black eyes for a full minute, and then started ambling toward us.

"Well?" Terry asked while rubbing his assault rifle. I turned the truck where his window was facing them. He grinned at me as I stuck my fingers in my ears.

I stopped the truck in front of a house on Southlake Drive, and for some unknown reason, I suddenly realized this house was less than two miles from the National Guard Barracks on Sidco Drive.

"What are we doing, Zach?" Terry asked. I gestured at the house.

"One of my best friends lived here. His name was Felix. You know, over the last eighteen months, I've been within a mile of this house more than a few times, and never checked on it."

"Do you want me to check inside?" Terry asked. "You can wait here."

I put the truck in park, turned it off and got out. "No, let's get this over with."

What was left of his parents were in the master bedroom, but Felix was nowhere to be found. There was no food in the kitchen and it appeared some of his clothing was gone, but otherwise there was no indicator where he may be. I found a sharpie and wrote a note for him on the door.

"We'll leave everything on this block, just in case he's around here somewhere."

My next stop, as much as I wanted to avoid it, was the National Guard Barracks. The steel doors were all locked, with the added insurance of chains and padlocks, but otherwise it seemed bereft of life.

"I'd say everything is intact. I'm sure Captain Steen will be interested in this," I said. Corporal Alexander agreed.

We worked our way over to Harding Place and picked houses at random. It was high-risk work with iffy reward. Most of the houses we searched had nothing more than skeletonized corpses, moldy furniture, dead pets and rotten food. Terry found some civilian clothes for himself and we found a few odds and ends we could use, along with some dog food. I also found a box of condoms and gave them to Terry.

"Thanks brother!" he said with a grin. "Do you happen to have some inside information where I may have need of these anytime soon?" he asked. I shrugged noncommittally.

"I know of one in particular who has her eye on you," I said. He looked perplexed.

"Are you talking about Andie?" he finally asked. He grinned when I nodded.

Chapter 50 – The Long Road Home

Fred woke up to see Sarah looking at him.

"I'm surprised you don't snore," she said. Fred sat up, stretched, and gave her a kiss.

"I'm surprised you do," he responded. Sarah playfully slapped him on the chest.

Fred washed up and dressed. Sarah had apparently been up a good thirty minutes before him, as she had already cleaned up and was dressed in utilities. They opted to eat a couple of packets of MREs, even though they both hated them.

"Today is the day," Sarah finally said.

"Yes, Major, it is. Have you changed your mind?"

"I have a duty," she responded curtly. Fred nodded. They had this discussion many times over the past month. Sometimes, there was yelling. Actually, Sarah was the only one who yelled. Fred would sit across from her silently, which sometimes angered her even more.

"So, you're going to leave then?" she asked, even though she knew the answer. Fred did not respond. He wiped his mouth and began cleaning up the packaging.

"I suppose I can fly you," she finally said.

"I think I'd rather drive than risk jumping out of an airplane. Besides, you're the one who has said more than once how foolish it is to fly a big plane by yourself. Too many things could go wrong, your words, not mine."

Every soldier left had eventually drifted away over the past couple of months. Sarah and Fred were the only ones left.

"You're being stubborn." Another awkward silence followed and Fred methodically started packing his belongings.

"I can't just leave, Fred," she finally said.

He stopped and looked at her. "I understand, and I hope you understand why I have to go. There are people who depend on me."

"I depend on you," she retorted. Fred looked at her a moment and then resumed packing.

"Well, fuck you then, you fucking hick!" she shouted and stormed out of the small apartment the two of them had been sharing for the past six months.

Fred watched her as she slammed the door. It wasn't their first argument. She was very passionate in bed and very amicable otherwise, as long as everything went her way. However, at the slightest inkling something was happening beyond, or out of her control, she reacted with anger. Fred's personality type was actually a good match for her. He never reacted angrily. He waited in silence for her to get it out of her system and then he'd talk. Only then would she listen to him.

She would be content to live the rest of her life being the curator of all of these aircraft, Fred thought sadly. A caretaker, for machinery that would probably be never used again.

Fred closed the backpack and hefted it over his shoulder. He closed the door quietly and headed to the parking lot where the trusty VW was waiting for him.

He tossed the backpack in the backseat and looked everything over for the fourth or fifth time. Several days ago, Fred figured out the fuel problem by crafting racks from some angle iron. He bolted them on each door, which allowed him to mount two five gallon jerry cans on each side. He looked at the two cases of bottled water sitting in the front seat, along with two cases of MREs. He sure hoped Lashonda would fix him a good meal when he got home. He made one last cursory inspection of his gear and car. Everything seemed good.

Fred fought the urge to look around, perhaps hoping he'd see Sarah running to join him with her own duffle bag. He knew it wasn't going to happen. On impulse, he took a sharpie and wrote his address on the hood of the nearby car. Satisfied, he got into the VW and started it.

He was going to miss her.

Fred drove nonstop, fighting fatigue with energy drinks, and only stopping to refill the gas tank or answer the call of nature. Once, he swore he saw headlights on the Interstate, going in the opposite direction, before they quickly went out. He wanted to speed up, but there were far too many obstacles to go very fast.

If one were to ask, Fred would have been hard pressed to tell how he made it back to West Memphis without any incidents or encounters. All he could say for certain, the sun was cresting the horizon when he made it to West Memphis.

Fred was close to his truck now, just a few thousand feet away. However, he knew he was too spent to walk across the bridge. His reflexes would be too slow.

He parked in the same spot where he found the VW so long ago, turned it off, and fell asleep with his head resting against the window.

Fred awoke suddenly when he heard the handle to the car door being pulled on. He grabbed one of his pistols that was lying on his lap and pointed it at the window. A frightened, dirty face greeted him before stumbling back and falling down.

Fred slowly got out with his pistol at the ready. The frightened face was a boy, maybe eleven or twelve. He had a shotgun leaning up against the fender of the VW. Fred grabbed it and did a quick circle, looking for anyone else.

"Where are your friends, kid?" he asked. The kid shook his head. He was still frightened. "What were you doing?"

"I thought you were dead," the kid responded. Fred looked around some more and glanced at the sky. The positioning indicated it was noon. He focused back on the kid.

"Are you hungry?" Fred asked. The kid had risen up on his elbows, but was still lying on the ground. He nodded his head. Fred holstered his weapon, and looked at the shotgun.

"Browning sweet sixteen. It's a fine shotgun, but it needs a good cleaning." Fred unloaded a single shell out of it and leaned the shotgun back against the fender.

"Let's have a bite to eat and we can talk." Fred reached in and pulled out the case of MREs. "These things are not very tasty, in fact, they're downright awful, but they tell me if you eat everything in the packet you'll get a full day's worth of nutrition. Let's dig in."

Fred used a Case pocketknife to cut open the plastic packets. The boy watched Fred start eating and quickly joined in.

"My name's Fred. What's your name, kid?"

"Joe," he said.

Fred held out his hand. "It is a pleasure to meet you, Joe."

Joe looked at Fred and tentatively shook his hand.

Joe continued looking at Fred while he ate. "That car was here a while back, and then it was gone. Did you take it?"

"Yes I did, but I'm returning it now. Is it yours?" Fred asked. Joe shook his head.

"Where did you go?" Joe asked.

"Well, Joe, I drove the car to Oklahoma City, and then hitched a ride to Los Angeles."

"Why?"

"I was trying to find my daughter," Fred responded.

"Did you find her?" Joe asked.

Fred ate in silence for a moment before answering. "I did. She had turned."

Joe nodded in understanding. They finished their meal in silence. When they were finished, Fred stood and stretched. Joe aped his movements.

"Alright, Joe, I've got a cleaning kit. Let's see if we can get your shotgun cleaned up a little bit." Fred showed Joe how to disassemble the shotgun and they began wiping the pieces down.

"Where do you live, Joe?" Fred asked, as he watched Joe wipe the breech face with a scrap of rag and some cleaning solvent.

"Here and there. I have some cars I sleep in, depending which part of the city I'm in."

"I take it your family is dead?" Joe nodded. "What about friends, you got any friends around here?"

"A couple. We see each other every once in a while. Are all your family dead too?"

"Yes, they are."

"What about friends?" Joe asked. "Do you have any friends?"

Fred looked at Joe and thought about Sarah before he thought about everyone back home. "Yeah, I have some friends back home. That's where I'm going. Let me see how good of a job you've done."

Joe handed the shotgun to him. Fred looked at it. It was still dirty, but significantly cleaner than it was. Fred dug the shotgun shell out of his pocket and handed both items back to Joe.

"Good job, buddy. If I had any shells, I'd give them to you, but I don't have any in this particular gauge."

"What kind of guns are those?" Joe asked, pointing at Fred's pistols.

Fred gave him a small grin. "They're Ruger forty-fours. They're tough, reliable guns and I've had some custom work done to them."

"Why'd you do that?" Joe asked.

Fred chuckled. "You sure are full of questions." He looked at the bridge in the near distance. "I've got to get across on the other side of that bridge, Joe. I'm going to take a few of those MREs and bottles of water with me, and you can have the rest, okay?"

"Fred?"

"Yes, Joe?"

"Can I go with you?"

Chapter 51 – Prancer

"Are you sure?" Julie asked me, for maybe the fourth or fifth time. "Kelly's going to be disappointed." She drew out the word 'disappointed.' Andie grinned.

"Very tempting, but no. Now stop asking," I said. They were all going over to the radio station. I had tried to get along with Wanda, but honestly, I couldn't stand the sight of her. She was derogatory, opinionated, ignorant, and an all-around unpleasant person to be within a hundred yards of. And the women, they'd sit around and talk about something they saw on Oprah two years ago. I'd rather muck the horse stall, which was exactly what I was going to do. I said as much to Julie.

"Oh, yeah, that sounds like fun. Take Prancer some oats." She hugged me and gave me a kiss. "I'll see you later, I guess." She leaned in and whispered in my ear. "If you're going to be playing around in horse shit, take a bath before bed. I'll make it worth your while." She then nibbled my ear.

I worked on the usual stuff, mucked out Prancer's stall, and then concentrated on reloading some bullets for the sniper rifles. I reloaded the remaining cartridges I had left. Fortunately, Terry and I had found a box in one of the houses we searched, so that added twenty more bullets to the inventory.

I stopped long enough to eat some jerky for lunch and walked around the barn. I looked at the old house and secretly wished we still lived there. Prancer walked up and nuzzled me while I was reminiscing.

"What are you doing, girl?" I said as I rubbed her on the neck. "You need some attention?" She nudged me again and snorted.

I looked around. "How about we go for a ride?" I asked her. To my surprise, she responded with a short nicker. She followed me to her stall and stood patiently while I put the bit in her mouth.

Getting a blanket and saddle on her, I shoved a rifle in the scabbard and mounted up.

I let Prancer have her head as she took off at a gallop down the field. I guess she liked the new shoes Bo had put on her. She continued running, and I guided her in a circle, eventually running toward The Parson house. She seemed to know where I was guiding her and I held the reins loosely.

When we reached the house, I slowed her down and had her slowly walk around it. Everything looked good, but all it did was make me think about Howard's death. While I was beating myself up mentally, Prancer continued walking. I didn't attempt to guide her. Of her own accord, she had made her way to the road and was heading toward Fred's house.

"You want to go to your old home, girl? Is that where we're going?" Prancer flicked an ear at me. "Yeah, sure, let's go look it over. It's another thing to add to my list of regrets."

Prancer walked in a slow, easy gait. It was comforting. I could see why Fred and Julie liked to ride. I was lost in my own thoughts as I watched for hostiles. I started using the term to include zombies and predatory animals, both the four-legged and the two-legged kind.

We came upon a red ribbon tied to a tree limb. It was where we had placed a trap. As I neared it, I saw a dead dog trapped in it. It may have been a friendly pet at one time, but no more. I made a mental note to take care of it later. Prancer kept walking and I kept thinking.

We rounded a curve in the road. This is where Fred's house would have come into view. That is, if it hadn't been burned to the ground. Prancer suddenly whinnied and started trotting. I looked quickly around, thinking she had caught a scent of something. Then, I saw it. A black Volvo semi-truck was parked in the driveway where Fred's house once stood. There was a man and a boy standing beside it. Prancer was in a full gallop now. They were too far away for me to get a good facial recognition, but I did not doubt Prancer's eyesight. The tall man was Fred.

Prancer leapt over the fence, which almost caused me to fall off, and came to a sliding stop inches from Fred. She was breathing hard and blowing froth, but Fred did not seem to mind.

"Hello, pretty girl, did you miss me?" he said while scratching her behind the ears. The first thing out of my mouth should have been something like, hi Fred, it's so good to see you. But no, I spoke before thinking.

"We thought you were dead!" I shouted in wonder. Fred looked at me and grinned. I stared at him with my mouth hanging open a moment, and then looked at the kid standing beside him.

"Hi," he said timidly. "I'm Joe."

"Hi, Joe, I'm Zach," I said and dismounted. Prancer broke away, ran around the truck, and then almost knocked Fred down as she ran up and nuzzled him. I shook Fred's hand, and then hugged him. I felt tears in my eyes, but held them back.

"Did you make it to LA?" I asked. Fred nodded. "And your daughter?" I asked tentatively. Fred shook his head.

"We have a lot to tell each other, but for now, I just want to know what happened to my house," he said.

I briefly told him the story.

"How are the girls?" Fred asked.

He saw my face darken. "One of them killed Macie. That was before they burned your house down. Julie and I took care of them. It's a long story and I know Julie will want to be there when I retell it." I hugged him again. "Damn, it's good to see you!" Prancer agreed. She took Fred's hat and began gleefully running around with it clinched between her teeth.

I got the generator going and the two of them took turns in the shower. From looking at the kid's face, I was guessing he had not had a hot shower in quite a long time. I cooked up steaks, eggs, and a strong pot of coffee. Fred came out with a fresh set of clothes and looked at the meal.

"Do you know how to cook anything besides steak and eggs?" he asked.

"Nope," I said, grinning.

"I'm glad. I haven't had one of these meals since I left. Where's the honey?" he asked. He found it sitting on the kitchen counter before I answered, sat down and waited on Joe. I poured us a cup of coffee while we waited.

"Where'd you find the kid?" I asked.

Fred chuckled. "He actually found me in West Memphis. He doesn't have any family, so I brought him along." I nodded.

"There's so much to tell you, but I better wait. In the meantime, we'll get you two set up here."

Joe came wandering in, freshly showered, but wearing the same dirty clothes. He looked around and I think his mouth started watering when he saw the juicy steak.

"Hey, Joe, before we eat, I think I can find some clean clothes for you. Hang on." I went into Andie's bedroom and grabbed some clothing. She wore boy's clothes, and even though she was bigger than Joe, she was the closest one in size. The pants were a little long for him, but after Fred rolled the pants legs up a few inches, they were fine.

"Alright, guys, dig in for Christ's sake," I exclaimed. Fred ate his meal with the control of a man attuned to self-discipline. Joe devoured his meal and asked for seconds. I refilled his plate and heard the truck driving up.

"It sounds like they're home," I said with a grin. "Julie is going to be beside herself. Oh, and by the way, we've picked up a couple of people. I'll introduce you to them. One of them you'll recognize."

Julie was the first person through the door. "I hope you didn't dirty up the kitchen," she said as she walked in. She saw Fred, stopped in her tracks, and held her hands to her face. Rowdy bumped into her as he walked in, which caused him to belch. Julie ran over and threw her hands around Fred.

"Oh, my God, we thought you were dead!" she wailed between sobs. Fred wrapped his arms around her and for the first time since I had known him, I saw tears falling down his cheeks.

I introduced Fred and Joe to everyone. We sat up well into the night talking to each other and telling our stories. I had to shut down the generator, but I fired up a couple of lanterns so we could continue seeing each other while we talked. Joe stayed quiet the entire time and fell asleep somewhere in the middle of all of it. Rowdy unrolled a sleeping bag and gently placed him in it. Finally, even I was yawning.

"Let's go to bed," Fred said. "We've got all day tomorrow to talk." I agreed and got some blankets. Fred fixed himself a bed on the couch. Rowdy had started sleeping in his bus again and did so tonight. Terry rolled out his own sleeping bag and was out within seconds. Julie and I were about to head to our bedroom when Fred stopped us.

"I want you two to know, I've missed y'all, and I'm sorry I left."

Julie reached out and hugged him again. "But you're back now. That's all that matters."

Chapter 52 – A Sentimental Return

For the first time in a long time, Julie was up before me. I awoke to something I hadn't smelled in a while, the aroma of frying bacon. I hurriedly cleaned up and went to the kitchen. Fred was sitting at the table drinking coffee, listening to Julie talk while she cooked.

"Where did the bacon come from?" I asked, as I walked up and kissed Julie.

"Bo had butchered a hog. I traded him some canned vegetables." She directed me to a chair with a spatula and fixed me a mug of coffee.

"Who is Bo?" Fred asked.

"Bo McClendon, he said you two know each other," I said. Enlightenment dawned on Fred's face.

"Bo is alive? Well, how about that," Fred said, with the same excitement as watching cars rust. I looked at Julie and grinned thinking, same old Fred.

"I believe I'd like to go see him sometime today," he added.

"Sure, but I hope you know where he lives. We've never been to his house," I said.

"I do," Fred responded. "He and I go way back."

Everyone else started waking up then, and soon we had a table full of people. Rowdy was full of himself and had everyone laughing at his antics. I caught a glance from Julie. She was probably thinking what I was thinking - a man in such a good mood had to be getting laid.

"What are you and Joe going to do today?" Julie asked.

"I'd like to go see Bo, and then, I'd like to hang out with y'all for a spell. Now keep in mind, Prancer may demand I take her for a ride." I smiled. It was good having him back home.

I figured Bo might be at the horse farm, so we headed there first. Andie and Terry followed in their jeep.

"Let's stop at the radio station and introduce Fred to the Birmingham girls," Julie said.

"Sure, but why don't you tell Fred about them so he'll know what to expect," I replied.

"Do you mean should I let him know Wanda is a bitch?" Julie said and then suddenly gasped. I glanced over at her and looked around. "We forgot to tell Fred something very important."

"I think we told him pretty much everything," I said.

"If you're referring to the ring on your finger, I'd say you two got married somewhere along the line," Fred said. Julie and I laughed while she told him about the wedding.

"I'm sorry I missed it."

As we approached the radio station, the first thing we saw was Big Mac on a backhoe. We stopped at the locked gate and waited for her to come over. Today she was wearing bib overalls with a plain white tee shirt underneath. Her hair was held back by a blue bandanna.

"That is one heck of a large woman," Fred commented dryly.

We introduced Fred to Big Mac, and to my surprise, Mac was a bit on the giddy side.

"I think she likes Fred," I whispered to Julie, who giggled in agreement. Wanda was her usual self, but the rest of the women gave Fred a warm welcome. Mac excused herself and went into the restroom, emerging a couple of minutes later with freshly brushed hair. Julie nudged me and giggled again.

"Zach, did you see the pits I dug?" Mac asked, while casting glances at Fred.

"Yes, I did, they look awesome. You've been busy. Have y'all had any problems?"

"We had a few people drive up yesterday. They didn't stay long," Mac said.

"They were a bunch of freeloaders who tried to bully us," Wanda interjected.

"Yeah," Kelly added. "They told us they needed food and tried to get inside the house. Mac knocked one of them out," she said with a grin. We looked over at Mac in surprise.

"I used to be on a roller derby team," she said for explanation. "Of course, Wanda and Kelly had rifles aimed at them too. I told them to come back when they had stuff to trade, but we haven't seen any zombies in a while."

As much as I wanted to, I refrained from commenting about Wanda's remark concerning freeloaders. Hopefully, she understood now. I looked around and noticed two people were absent.

"Where are Rowdy and Cindy?" I asked.

"Oh, they went scavenging," Kelly said. I frowned but withheld commentary. I hoped Rowdy had picked up enough about clearing houses to keep from being surprised.

As we were leaving, Wanda pulled me off to the side. "I don't feel comfortable with that little colored boy around the babies," she said in a hushed tone. She was referring to Joe, of course. It was bullshit. Joe was very polite when introduced to everyone, and well behaved the whole time. He gave nobody any cause to be concerned. Even so, Wanda had an issue with him. It was pathetic.

"He's a good kid, Wanda," I could have said a lot more, but I held off. Instead, I bid my goodbye and left.

I tried the horse farm first, and found Bo mucking the stalls. He met us at the barn door with a pitchfork. Lucy saw us, disappeared inside the barn, and came back out with her tennis ball and a wagging tail.

"Hello, Bo," Fred said when he got out of the truck.

"Hello, Fred," Bo replied. The two men shook hands, and then hugged.

"I'm glad you're alive," Bo said.

"Same here."

"My, what an emotional reunion," Julie said. We laughed while Fred and Bo looked at us.

"Have you two known each other long?" Corporal Alexander asked.

"We grew up together," Bo answered. "Did any of the rest of the family make it?" He asked. Fred slowly shook his head. Bo sighed. "Mine neither."

Fred looked at us. "If you all don't mind, I'll take that thermos of coffee and spend a bit of time with Bo. We have some catching up to do. He'll give me a ride back."

Joe looked anxious. "Can I stay?" he asked Fred. Fred looked at me.

"Hey, Joe, let the old men talk about the weather while we go find you some new clothes and stuff." It was obvious Joe wanted to stay with Fred, but he quietly assented.

We went back to the Lennox Village area. I had previously cleared over half of the condominiums, and remembered seeing kids' bedrooms in a few of them. I insisted Julie stay in the truck. I explained it was due to her pregnancy, but she called me a chauvinist anyway. I pulled Joe off to the side.

"Alright, big guy, we've cleared houses together before, so I want you to hang out with Julie until we get a house cleared. Then, you can come in and pick out what you need."

Joe agreed quietly, although I think he wanted to help out. He had survived on his own, so I knew he was pretty tough for an eleven-year-old kid.

We located the units which obviously had children at one time and checked them out. Joe found several articles of clothing he could wear and we loaded up. We also looked for more clothing for Julie. Her baby bulge was growing daily.

"Alright, the third bedroom in our house is empty. I was thinking we can get it set up for you and Fred," I said to Joe. "So, I want you to pick out a bedroom suite for the two of you. We'll need two beds and furniture. I think we have room in the bed of the truck. If not, we can make two trips."

Joe's eyes lit up and he ran into one of the condos before I could say anything else. He ran out a minute later.

"I found some!" he shouted.

Chapter 53 – Oh Rowdy, Where Art Thou?

The weather was so pleasant, we opted to eat outside at the picnic table which was set up under an old oak tree. Terry had shot a turkey and Fred helped him dress it. We complemented it with some of our canned vegetables.

"How is Bo doing?" I asked Fred while setting everything up.

"He's doing okay, been a bit lonely, but now I think he's fine. He's going to help me build a new house."

"That's awesome," Julie said. "With no costs to consider, you can build a mansion."

Fred shook his head. "Nope, it's going to be something simple, concrete block walls and a roof. Nothing fancy."

Julie made a raspberry sound. "You'll do nothing of the kind. We're going to make it pretty." Fred glanced at her, but said nothing. "I'll talk to Mac tomorrow and get her over there with a bulldozer. She'll have the lot cleared in no time." She grinned mischievously at Fred. "She'll be glad to help you."

"We've actually got the numbers now to get things done," I said. "If you want, I can start drawing up some plans."

Fred nodded. "You should create a boiler plate design, something simple to build and easy to fortify. You also want to take into consideration the utilities, so electricity from a generator, or better yet, solar, and a water storage system."

"There has to be a business around here somewhere that built water tanks," I said, more to myself than anyone else.

I started with some notes, but kept getting distracted by Julie playing footsie with me under the picnic table. I'd frown at her, but she'd smile at me playfully, which totally prevented me from getting mad. She had been in a great mood ever since Fred came back. We all looked up when we heard a vehicle approaching.

"I believe that's Big Mac," I said.

"Well, you're girlfriend didn't waste much time coming to call," Julie teased. Fred looked at her with an arched eyebrow. As they got closer, I saw Wanda sitting in the passenger seat.

"Shit," I muttered. Julie giggled. The two women got out of the truck and walked over to the picnic table.

"Hello, ladies," I said with mock cheerfulness. Everyone else said hello as well.

"Hi everyone," Big Mac responded. "Is Cindy here?" she asked. Julie and I looked at each other.

"I don't think so. Isn't she with Rowdy?" I asked.

"They left out early this morning and were supposed to be back at noon. We were getting a little worried," Mac said. I looked around. The dually was missing. I got up and looked in the tour bus, just to make sure. It was empty. I walked back to the picnic table and sat down

"I wouldn't worry about them. They're probably out enjoying this pretty day and lost track of time," I said. Wanda shook her head vigorously.

"There's something wrong. I know it."

"The dually had a full tank of gas. I think they're okay," I tried to say reassuringly, but Wanda shook her head vigorously again. I sighed. "Okay, did Rowdy say whereabouts they were going?"

"He only said they were going shopping," Mac replied. I immediately thought of Cool Springs and voiced my suspicions.

"He wouldn't be stupid enough to try going inside the mall with just the two of them, would he?" Julie asked. I looked over at Andie.

She sighed as well. "Yeah, he would. He was talking about the two of us doing it a couple of days before the Birmingham women rolled into town."

"Oh, shit," Julie said. I groaned.

"What's wrong?" Mac asked.

"The mall is full of zombies. We tried going in several months back. It was like a zombie black Friday in there," I said, and immediately regretted it. Wanda went pale and started hyperventilating. She started to swoon and Mac caught her. Picking her up as if she was a small child, Mac carried her over to a chair and gently set her down. She looked at Fred and me with worry.

"Okay, okay, let's not all get worked up. We've got plenty of firepower here, so we'll go look for them," I knew an argument was about to start as I looked over at Julie.

"Don't you dare suggest I stay here, Mister Zach Gunderson. I'm going with you!" she declared sternly. I looked at Fred. He was very dramatic as he tilted his head about a quarter of an inch.

"I'll be damned if I sit here on my ass while a pregnant woman goes huntin' zombies," Bo said as he stood. I nodded in thanks.

"Andie, how about you and Terry get the 5.56 ammo cans. It's the ammo we have plenty of, so everyone take one of the M4s or an AR-15," I looked at Fred. He stood up.

"Bo and Joe will ride with me in the semi," he said. "I believe you and Julie should ride in the truck." He gestured at Andie. "Andie and her soldier boyfriend should ride in the jeep." Terry looked startled at being described as Andie's boyfriend. "What CB channel do you think Rowdy would be listening to?" Fred asked.

"The last time I drove the dually, I had it on channel nineteen," I said.

Fred nodded. "Nineteen it is then."

We followed the large Volvo down Concord Road. I looked over at the gated entrance to the Governor's Club as we drove by. My note was gone. Someone lived in there, I was sure of it. I didn't see a red dually anywhere in the neighborhood, so I hoped we weren't going on a wild goose chase. Fred opted not to try I-65, and instead turned on Franklin Pike before turning back left on Moore's Lane. At Wanda's insistence, they followed us. I hoped Mac took care of her, because she was worthless.

"Come in, Zach," I heard Fred calling me on the radio.

"Go ahead," I responded.

"Is it Rick's red dually they're in?" He asked.

"Roger. I figure when we get close, we spread out and search the parking lots for it. I'm guessing he'll park close to one of the entrances, if he's even there."

"I copy. In the meantime, why don't y'all continue trying to raise that knucklehead on the radio? I'd suggest trying all channels and we'll stay on nineteen."

I did as suggested, but to no avail. It became evident why when we turned onto Galleria Boulevard. Julie suddenly pointed. "There!"

The dually was parked in front of one of the main entrances on Galleria Boulevard. She drove up beside it and stopped. I jumped out with my M4 at the ready, and ran up to it. There was nobody in it, nor was there any damage, or anything else out of the ordinary. I ran back to the truck and radioed the information.

"Zach, do you think he's in the mall?" Andie asked.

"He's got to be," I said. "They didn't park right at the front entrance in order to go somewhere else."

"Zach," Fred said over the radio. "Would you move your truck out of the way? We have an idea." Julie looked at me perplexed and backed the truck up. About the time we were clear of the entrance, the big Volvo zoomed by. The steel cattle catcher busted the concrete flowerpots which were supposed to act as barriers, and crashed through the glass doors. As Fred entered into the mall, he laid on his air horns repeatedly.

Julie followed the Volvo in and slid to a stop beside it. "You will keep your ass in the truck or I'll spank you so hard you won't be able to sit for a week!" I yelled at Julie as I exited. Andie and Terry jumped out and took up firing positions.

It didn't take long before we had company. There had to be over a hundred of them. Most of them were horribly decomposed and could hardly move, but a few of them seemed to be moving without a great deal of difficulty.

"Don't rush your shots! We have plenty of firepower for a change!" I yelled as I took aim at a male zombie in a security guard's uniform and dispatched him with a clean headshot. The others followed my lead and began methodically picking them off. I felt a presence by my side. It was Julie. I glared at her.

"I can't wait for my spanking," she said, and stuck her tongue out at me before she started shooting. At least she had her earplugs in. Mac ran up beside Julie, stood over her protectively and started picking off targets.

I concentrated on the ones who seemed to be in better shape, and the whole time I was wondering if they were people who had recently become freshly infected. Julie seemed to pick up on what I was doing and started shooting them as well. She knew what I was thinking more than I knew what I was thinking.

"Red!" I shouted while I ejected the empty magazine and slapped a full one in, locking it in place and releasing the charging handle.

"Green!" I shouted right after Julie shouted red. I glanced at everyone before resuming shooting. Fred and Bo looked like twins. They were relaxed and casual as they shot into the horde. Bo reloaded without saying anything. I'd get Fred to say something to him later. Little Joe was standing behind Fred with an arm full of magazines, handing them to Fred and Bo when they needed them. Terry and Andie were crouched down beside each other, their shoulders touching, shooting in tandem. There was nothing like a firefight with zombies to bring two people together. I grinned and resumed firing.

Suddenly, I heard a horn honking behind me. I turned in irritation. Wanda was still in the Toyota truck and she pointed frantically to her right. There was another wave of zombies coming from the opposite direction.

"Andie, Terry, six o'clock!" I shouted. They turned together and started firing without missing a beat. I ran back to our truck, retrieved an ammo can, and slid it across the floor to Joe. "You know what to do, big guy!" I shouted and resumed shooting. After a minute, I glanced over at Joe. He was crouched down beside Fred's legs, loading empty magazines. I grunted in satisfaction and continued shooting.

When the last one fell, I reloaded quickly, pulled my earplugs out, and looked everyone over.

"Is everyone okay?" I asked. I looked at Julie first, she blew me a kiss. Fred gave a curt nod. Andie and Terry gave us a thumbs up and then traded a fist bump. Mac looked harried, but otherwise okay. I made a quick count. There were one hundred and sixty-seven. Too many for comfort, it seemed to defy logic. I shook it off and looked around.

"Aright, where is our dumbass friend?" I asked, more to myself than anyone else. As I was looking around, Julie pointed.

"What do you think?" she asked as she pointed out a woman's boutique halfway down. It had a broken window, and although I can't say how freshly broken glass was different from old broken glass, it looked freshly broken.

"Yeah, maybe." I looked at her with I hoped was a stern expression. "This time, please stay with Fred and provide us cover. I can only spank you so much," I said. Mac heard me and frowned questioningly. "Andie, Terry, let's check out that store," I said, pointing. Fred gave me another nod and stood watch.

We found them in the back, locked in a restroom. There were four or five dead zombies lying around, and five more scratching at the door, totally oblivious to the massive firefight that just occurred. We killed them quickly, efficiently. Andie ran toward the door.

"Careful, Andie, he might shoot through the door." She looked at me in understanding, stood to the side, and knocked.

"Hey, dumbass, are you in there?" she said loudly. After a moment, the sound of the door unlocking was heard, followed by it being opened a crack. We could see someone peeking out, and it opened wider. Rowdy emerged.

"What the fuck, Rowdy?" Andie asked in exasperation. "Where's Cindy?"

"She's in here. She's not doing very well," he said anxiously. I pushed passed him and walked in. Cindy was lying on the bathroom floor, semiconscious, covered in sweat and ashen faced.

"What the hell happened?" Terry asked. I already knew the answer. I could see it on her neck and arms. There were at least three distinct bite marks. Trickles of blood oozed out of them.

"We got jumped," Rowdy replied. "I fought them off as best I could, but Cindy got bit."

"Oh shit," Terry muttered as Andie gasped.

"Rowdy, help me carry her. We've got to be quick," I said, and looked at Andie. "Run ahead and get every cigarette lighter going. Tell them what happened." Andie took off at a run. Rowdy grabbed Cindy by the shoulders and I grabbed her legs. Terry covered the rear as we made our way back to the trucks.

Fred leaned forward with a red-hot lighter as we sat Cindy down by the Volvo.

I looked at Rowdy. "Hold her down," I said as I grabbed her legs in a bear hug. Fred jabbed the red-hot coils into the wound on her neck, and held it there for a few seconds. The smell of burning flesh permeated my nostrils. Cindy began screaming as Bo jabbed another one onto one of the wounds on her arms. When Wanda saw this, she began screaming and tried to pull the two men away from her daughter.

"You're hurting her!" she screamed. I let go of Cindy's legs and grabbed her.

"Listen to me," I said calmly. "She's infected. We have no idea how to treat her. Either we take a chance that cauterizing the wounds will help, or we put a bullet in her head right now, your choice." Wanda looked at me and began crying. "It's the only way, Wanda," I said quietly. "If there is any chance of saving her, this is it. She'll have a couple of scars, but she'll be alive."

Mac came up beside Wanda and put an arm around her. Joe ran up with another hot lighter. Fred took it and continued cauterizing the wounds.

I rode in the bed of the dually with Cindy as the convoy made its way to the radio station. I had no emotional attachment to Cindy. If she turned in my presence, I'd not hesitate to kill her. Rowdy drove, and kept looking back at us. At one point, he almost rear-ended Julie.

"Pay attention to the road, Rowdy!" I yelled. He nodded quickly, but adjusted the rearview mirror so he could watch me.

We made it back to the radio station and Big Mac gingerly lifted Cindy out of the bed of the truck. She was still semiconscious and sweating profusely as Mac carried her inside. All of us followed. When Mac gently laid Cindy on a bed, I motioned to her. She followed me outside. Fred and Bo followed me.

"I don't need to tell you what to do if she turns, do I?" I asked. Mac slowly shook her head.

"You want one of us to stay here, so you won't have to do it?" Fred asked.

Big Mac shook her head, but stopped and looked at Fred. "I'll be the one to do it, if it comes to that, but I'd be most appreciative if you'd keep me company," she said. Fred looked at her, and then us.

"It looks like I'll be staying here tonight," he said.

Chapter 54 – Punishment

I slapped Julie on the butt as we got undressed. She let out a yelp and looked at me in wonder. "That's for disobeying your husband," I said and finished undressing. We got in bed and snuggled up against each other.

"Aren't you going to spank me some more?" she asked provocatively.

"No," I said. "You'd like it too much and I'm punishing you."

She snorted and wiggled her butt up against my crotch. "Are you sure?"

"I'm sure," I said harshly, even though I could feel myself getting aroused. "You're supposed to listen to me. You could have provided firepower from the safety of the truck. You know I worry about you and our unborn son."

Julie sighed, reached back, and began stroking my thigh. I instinctively kissed her on the nape of her neck.

"Okay, I can understand the concern you have for our unborn *daughter*. I'll try to be a better wife," she said, and wiggled up against me some more. "I think you should punish me now," she cooed.

I didn't see how it was punishment, but agreed anyway.

I sat on the opposite bunk watching Rowdy snore. An empty bottle was loosely gripped in one hand. When we got home yesterday evening, he skipped dinner and locked himself inside his bus. It took me almost ten minutes to jimmy the lock. It was obvious he was feeling guilty, but it was no excuse. After trying for several seconds to wake him, I grabbed his arm and pulled him off of the bunk. He landed in a heap.

"What the fuck, Hoss?" he said when he looked up at me.

"Get yourself cleaned up. Julie has breakfast going and then we're going to go visit Cindy." Rowdy groaned loudly at my directive.

"I can't go back there, Hoss. Those women are going to kill me after what I did."

"You might be right, but you've got to face the music, no pun intended."

"You're a funny boy," Rowdy mumbled as he struggled to stand.

I went back inside and peeked inside Andie's bedroom. Andie and Terry were naked, and intertwined in each other's arms. I quietly shut the door back, and then knocked on it loudly.

"Breakfast in ten," I said through the door and walked down the hall to Joe's room. I repeated the announcement. He was sleeping on the top bunk of his new bunk beds, and had his head under the pillows. Fred had taken one look at the bunk beds and advised us he would be sleeping in the Volvo's sleeper until he got his house built. Joe stuck his head out when he heard my voice. I gave him a wink and walked back into the kitchen.

"I don't think you have to endure Andie making goo-goo eyes at me anymore," I said with a grin. She looked at me questioningly and I told her what I saw. She nodded in approval.

"It's about damn time. I thought you were the one who was going to have to give her a good fucking from the way it was looking," she said glibly. "Now we need to find someone for Kelly, or I'm going to have to stud you out to her as well."

I stared at her, perplexed. Sometimes, it was hard to tell when she was serious and when she was messing with me. She smiled sweetly and continued cooking. I set the table while we waited for everyone to make their way to the kitchen. Joe was the first one to walk into the kitchen.

"Good morning, buddy. Did you sleep well?" I asked.

"Zach, I think Andie was having bad dreams last night," he said. I looked at him. "She was screaming, a lot."

Julie burst out in laughter.

"Yeah, that must be it, Joe," I said. "Don't worry though, I bet she's all better now."

A minute later, Terry and Andie came into the kitchen. They sat down quietly beside each other. Andie looked at Terry and smiled. I grabbed the coffee pot and poured everyone a healthy dose.

"What do you need me to do?" I asked Julie.

"Sit on your butt and stay out of my way," she replied as she cooked some eggs. "You can wash the dishes after I'm through."

"Okay. Don't forget to make Fred a plate. I'm going to pick him up after breakfast," I said. Julie looked at me as if I was two steps behind, which I'm sure I was. I looked over at the others.

"Yesterday, y'all were awesome, especially you, Joe." Everyone voiced their agreement.

"Can I go with you to get Fred?" Joe asked, as Rowdy came inside. He looked awful. I hoped he was merely hung over and not getting sick. He poured himself a cup of coffee.

"Ah, Joe, not this time. I need to talk to Fred and Rowdy about some stuff, but don't worry, we're coming right back home." He looked dejected, but didn't say anything.

"Say, Joe," I said. "Terry there is a soldier. If you ask him, I bet he'll give you some military training on his Army rifle."

Joe's eyes lit up and he looked at Terry.

"It would be my pleasure," Terry said. "But, you have to help me with some of the morning chores first, okay?"

Joe nodded his head vigorously.

Rowdy and I rode to the radio station in silence. He was very pale, and I had to stop once for him to lean out of the truck and throw up.

I stole a line from Andie Griffith. "You beat all, you know that?"

"Not now, Zach," he said, in between groans.

"If not now, when? When do we have a talk about your actions, Rowdy? Should we wait until after someone else gets all fucked up?" I asked rhetorically. Rowdy held his head in his hands and groaned.

"All you had to do was ask me. Hell, I would have gone with you guys. We could have found somewhere else besides that big mall with all of those fucking zombies."

"You don't get it, Zach. I was trying to get some alone time with her, and impress her," he coughed. "Pull over!" he managed to choke out. I stopped immediately. Rowdy barely got the door open before he heaved again. When he was finished, I reached into the glove box and retrieved a tube of toothpaste. It was almost empty, but it was all I had.

"Here, squirt some of this in your mouth."

He did as told without complaint. I found a canteen in the backseat and handed it to him. He took it gratefully, took a big gulp, and squished it around in his mouth before spitting it out.

"Much obliged," he said quietly.

"Rowdy, are you merely hung over or are you getting sick?" I asked quietly. He looked at me when he understood the implication.

"I wasn't bitten or anything," he responded. "When Cindy got bit, we didn't do anything, like sex or kissing. I just tied one on last night. More than I've drunk in a long time."

"Alright, wipe your face off. When we get there, you probably shouldn't say anything. I'll do the talking and maybe those women won't castrate you on the spot." Rowdy looked at me and nodded dejectedly.

Fred met us outside as we drove up. He waited until I shut the truck off, and the two of us got out.

"The young lady didn't make it," he said. Rowdy looked at him a moment before running back to the rear of the truck and dry heaved.

"Did she turn?" I asked. He nodded somberly.

"Mac was true to her word," he said. "When the young lady turned, she put a bullet in her head. The ladies refused to burn her, so we buried her down the road at a church." He gestured over at Rowdy.

"Do him a favor, and take him back home. That mother is blaming him for everything."

"You want to ride with us?" I asked. Fred nodded. I headed back toward the truck, but before I took two steps, Kelly burst out of the door to the house and ran up to me. She grabbed me in a hug and held me tightly.

"Oh, Zach, this is so terrible," she lamented. "I feel so vulnerable out here."

I patted her on the back and consoled her. Fred gave me his typical arched eyebrow before walking back to Rowdy and helping him into the truck.

"I want to come live with you," she said quietly in my ear.

"Uh, well, we've got a full house currently. It'd be a little cramped." I felt her waist press against me.

"I don't care. It can't be more cramped than here. I'll sleep on the floor if I have to. It'll be safer living with you, and I'll earn my keep, I promise," she said plaintively.

"I'll see what my wife has to say, okay?" I said, while attempting to gently pry her off of me.

She looked at me deeply with her dark, smoldering eyes. "Okay. I'm counting on you, Zach," she said, and then she kissed me on the cheek, the one with the scar.

"Zach, check this out," Terry said. He turned to Joe. "Answer the following for Zach. When using an M4 assault rifle, what is a malfunction and what actions should you take?"

Joe looked at me. "A malfunction is when the weapon stops firing because of a mechanical failure of the weapon, the magazine, or ammo. There are two types of actions you can take, immediate action and remedial action. For immediate action, you slap on the magazine, pull the charging handle, observe a bullet come out, release the handle, tap the forward assist, and shoot. If that doesn't work, you apply remedial action, and that is, you pull the magazine out, lock the bolt to the rear, put the weapon on safe, and then find out what's wrong."

I raised my eyebrows. "The kid picked it up within minutes, Zach," Terry said. "Hell, I did hundreds of pushups in basic before I got it right," he said with a chuckle.

"Awesome, Joe," I said. Joe looked over at Fred expectantly.

"I suspect we have the makings of one hell of a soldier," Fred said. Joe beamed with pride.

I poured a thermos of coffee and carried it to the bus. Rowdy was once again curled up in the fetal position on one of the bunks. The interior was rank smelling.

"If you throw me off of the bunk, I'm going to throw up on your shoes," he muttered.

"Nope, I'm not going to touch you. I've got some semi fresh coffee here, if you feel up to it."

Rowdy eventually rolled over and sat up. "Yeah, I'll try some. It can't make me feel any worse."

I poured some into the plastic cup. He blew into it and took small sips.

"Is it helping?" I asked.

"A little," he replied between sips.

"Good," I said and unfolded a piece of paper. "You need to do some work to keep your mind occupied. When you're able to get up and moving, I need you to do this."

He looked at the piece of paper.

"What is it?" he asked.

"It's a design for an open top crate. I need a dozen of them to store the vegetables and stuff in the basement. Here is a scaled drawing with the dimensions. I've got lumber and tools in the barn, everything you'll need."

Rowdy looked at it a long moment before answering. "Okay, I'll get started on them. I don't know if I can get all dozen of them finished today, but I'll do what I can."

I nodded and left quickly, it stunk in there.

Chapter 55 – The Mother Lode

It probably would have been better if we had tried this in the dead of winter, when the zombies were frozen, but back then, there were only a few of us. Today, there were eight of us. Mac insisted on driving the Volvo. Fred, Bo, and Joe were with her. I convinced Julie to stay home, so it was Terry, Andie, Kelly, and me in the truck behind the Volvo. For reasons I don't know, Julie had invited Kelly to live with us. That was three weeks ago, and she unabashedly flirted with both Terry and me whenever she got a chance. She flirted with Terry one night and Andie immediately stuck a knife to her throat. That ended that.

Rowdy was by himself, driving the utility work truck Rick had found last year. We had it loaded with equipment we were sure we'd need, along with one of the tankers. Only Andie and I were wearing tactical vests. The rest were dressed casually in jeans, tee shirts, and windbreakers.

Our destination was on Trinity Lane. Specifically, we were going to loot the police department's property and evidence warehouse. It was a nondescript building located behind the East Precinct. First, we were going to take a minor detour to the reservoir.

I probably never would have known about it, but I had to drive Rick there one day after bailing him out of jail. For some reason, they had taken all of his property out of his truck, and turned it in to the property unit. I was rather perturbed at him on that particular day. I had to miss a day of school to pick him up from the jail, and then we had to drive across town to the property room. To top it off, we had to drive over to the other side of town in order to get his truck out of the impound lot. I gave him hell the entire day, and he retaliated with a nonstop barrage of beer farts.

I missed him terribly.

The walls of the building were concrete block and the doors were reinforced steel. The main entrance was a double set of doors, with bulletproof glass separating the citizens from the police personnel. I was hopeful the reinforced structure had kept everyone out. I had a plan to get us in.

The Volvo, with its modified steel cowcatcher, made for easy travel. Whenever Big Mac encountered a traffic jam, she simply pushed the cars out of the way. We made a straight path down Nolensville Pike, crossed Broadway, and turned onto James Robertson Parkway. The bridge had its share of abandoned cars, but we had little trouble clearing a path, and made it to the reservoir with little trouble.

There were no new zombies roaming about the property where the reservoir tanks quietly sat, and the ones we killed back in August were now nothing more than skeletal remains. I stopped the truck, and as we rehearsed, everyone got out and formed a defensive perimeter while Rowdy unhooked the tanker. He fumbled with it for a moment, but got it unhooked within a minute. Everyone loaded up and we headed out.

"Why did we leave the tanker there?" Kelly asked.

"We're going to return here on our way back, fill it up, and haul it home. We have no idea what we're going to encounter in the east Nashville area, so I didn't want Rowdy to be trapped with towing that tanker."

"I see, I think," she said as she smiled at me. "Do you think we'll find some good stuff?"

"If nobody has looted it before us, I'm cautiously optimistic."

"There better be some good weed in there," Andie said. "I haven't had any since I don't know when." She looked at Terry and grinned. "Weed, that is."

"I haven't had any of anything since I don't know when," Kelly quipped. I glanced at her, and she grinned coyly.

"What kind of work did you do, Kelly?" I asked.

"I was a night auditor at a hotel and was going to school part time. I wanted to be an accountant," she touched me on the thigh as she spoke. "What about you?" she asked.

"I worked on the farm we're living on, but I was still in high school," I said with a grin. Her mouth dropped open at the realization she was older than me. "Yep, I'm only seventeen."

"Holy shit, I thought you were at least twenty-one."

It seemed to shock her, but it didn't stop her from touching my thigh.

When we turned onto Trinity Lane from Gallatin Pike, I got on the CB radio and advised them it was only a couple of miles more. We drove under the railroad bridge and turned left. Now was the high stress moment. Would the building be unoccupied? Or, would a group of people be living there and start shooting as soon as we drove through the entrance?

The East Precinct building had a public parking lot in the front. The back had a fenced in area where police personnel parked their marked and unmarked vehicles. Someone had cut some holes in the fence, and more than one of the marked police cars had been vandalized, which seemed a stupid waste of time to me. Why would someone take the time out of their quest for survival to spray paint derogatory terms on a cop car? The thick layer of grime on them, along with the vandalism, indicated they hadn't been moved in a while.

We drove past, and immediately behind the precinct was the plain white building with a separate parking lot. We pulled to the side and Rowdy drove around us. He backed up to the edge of the building, jumped out, and immediately began unlashing an aluminum extension ladder. He had it leaned against the building and bounded up the ladder quickly.

"Damn, he's firing on all cylinders today," I commented.

We parked and jumped out. Fred and I walked up to the main door. There were numerous pry marks and indentations in the door, probably from a sledgehammer, but the door was still secure.

"Let's drive around the entire building and check it out," Fred suggested. We jumped into the Ford truck and slowly drove around the entire perimeter. There was no evidence of any kind of entry being made. It was a good sign. We drove back, and lined up the vehicles in case of a need to flee quickly. Rowdy, was dutifully up on the roof, scanning the area with binoculars.

"Explain to me why we don't simply hammer through one of the walls?" Bo asked.

"It'll take longer and make more noise," I replied. "We run a higher risk of attracting attention. Plus, if we put a hole in the roof, it can't be seen from anyone at ground level."

Bo nodded in semi understanding. I knew he thought we were exercising unnecessary caution, but I disagreed.

"If the roof is fortified, it might be easier to hammer through a wall, but I'm betting they didn't bother with it," I said as we got out and approached the group.

"Are we ready, Hoss?" Rowdy asked from the top of the roof. His Remington was slung over his shoulder. He was acting all giddy, which made me wonder if he had a bottle stashed in the truck somewhere, like Rick used to do. I nodded to him.

I went up next, and then the rest of them formed a line. They handed me the tools we were going to need, including another extension ladder, a gas operated commercial grade Sawzall, bolt cutters, pry bars, and flashlights. We walked around, eventually finding ourselves in the middle of the building.

Fred pointed at the roof. "It would appear you're right, Zach. I don't see any means of fortification of this roof. It's nothing more than wood, tarpaper, and hot tar poured over the top." He squatted and rapped the roof with his fist. "We can start here. If it's no good, we'll cut another one."

I agreed. I pulled out a pair of large hearing protectors, some goggles, and put them on before I started the Sawzall. The rest of them held the tarp over me to help mask some of the noise.

I got carried away and broke a blade, but I had three more. Still, I was much more careful with the second blade. It took about fifteen minutes to cut a proper sized hole. We extended the ladder to its maximum length and carefully lowered it into the hole. It hit the ground with two feet left sticking out. Fred looked at me and I grinned.

"So far, so good. Let's see if there are any inhabitants," I said and started tapping on the ladder with a pry bar. The intent was to create enough noise to attract any zombies which may be lurking around inside.

I kept it up for five minutes while the rest of them aimed their flashlights through the hole, watching for the appearance of any zombies. Finally, Fred looked at me.

"I think we're good," he said.

Fred, Andie and I went down into the hole. I went first. I bypassed the ladder's rungs, grabbed the sides, slid down quickly, and landed in the dark on a hard concrete floor. I grabbed my flashlight and made a quick circle.

"All clear," I said. I stepped aside as Andie slid down. Fred was the last one to come down. He casually stepped down on the rungs as if he were on a Sunday stroll. Bo lit a lantern and lowered it on a rope. It wasn't as bright as the flashlights, but it provided decent ambient lighting. We all looked around, shining our flashlights down the aisles of shelves.

"Zach, you continue to amaze me," Fred finally spoke.

"How's it looking down there?" Bo shouted down.

Fred looked up at Bo. "We've hit the mother lode," he said, with a small iota of excitement in his voice.

There was everything imaginable, but I had prepared a list the night before with instructions only to concentrate on certain items. It went without saying any viable food products were going with us, along with all ammunition. When I broke into the gunroom, Fred let out a low whistle. I conservatively estimated there were barrels containing at least a thousand firearms of different makes, models, and calibers.

"It'll take a while to sort out the good ones from the junk," I opined.

"I agree. We'll do a cursory search through these piles of weapons, and concentrate more on ammunition. We can come back again at a later time."

I couldn't argue with Fred's logic. I left it to him to sort through the weapons while Andie and I walked down the many aisles, conducting an overview of the various and vast amounts of wares. There was a little bit of everything. Andie focused her flashlight beam on a bin containing multiple evidence bags. Obviously, it was marijuana, a lot of it.

"Can I?" Andie asked with a hopeful grin.

"You want all of it?" I asked in disbelief. "There has to be twenty or thirty pounds there."

"Well, maybe a pound, or two?" she asked. I shrugged and Andie squealed with delight. She dragged the bin to the ladder while I continued looking.

I could not get over the wide variety of items. The first aisle I came to was a large quantity of alcoholic beverages, probably confiscated on a tippling house raid. I had no intention of telling Rowdy and left it behind.

I also bypassed all electronic items. There was no need for them now. Instead, I focused on items more important to us. I found reloading supplies, black powder, blasting caps, squibs, and various assorted tools. I loaded them up in plastic tote bins the police seemed to favor for storing evidence, and had them hauled up out of the hole. Fred walked over to me while I loaded up a couple of cases of Coca Cola in a bin.

"We've been here almost six hours now. I think we should head out and get some gas while we still have daylight," he said.

"Okay, I found a couple of cases of dog food. Let's get those and get out of here," I said. "Oh, I have a present for you," I said as I tossed a pair of brass knuckles to him.

He caught them in the air and looked at them. "Are these for protecting me from Big Mac?" he asked dryly. I laughed.

We climbed out of the warehouse, tacked the tarp over the open hole, and helped load the last of the property we had retrieved. About the time we lashed down the ladders to the work truck, a black utility van approached. Three men got out. They were all wearing black vests with a cloth badge sewn over the left breast. They approached us warily. Their weapons all appeared to be Glock semiautomatics, and they were wearing nylon thigh holsters. Each man had their hand on their side arms. Fred and I walked out and met them halfway while the rest of our group stood by the vehicles, weapons in hand. They were muscular, late twenties or early thirties. Two of them looked like bulldogs. The third one was my height with a swarthy visage. He had a sour expression, as if he was constipated. None of them had shaved in a while.

"Hello," I said. "My name's Zach. We haven't seen any other survivors around in quite a while." The taller one stepped forward. He didn't offer his hand.

"I'm Detective McElroy with the Metro Police Department. We just observed you people burglarizing our property room," he replied with no hint of friendliness. Bo snorted in contempt.

"I beg your pardon," I said with as much diplomatic tact as I could muster. "We were under the impression this building had been abandoned."

"On the contrary, dumbass, this is Metro property, as well as all of its contents," he sneered. Before I could respond, Fred spoke up.

"Watch your mouth, young man." He stared at the self-proclaimed detective with coldness in his eyes. His friends puffed up their chests, much like gorillas do. I didn't like these guys, but I tried to be diplomatic. I held my hands out in seeming placation.

"Hey, not a problem," I said. "We certainly didn't mean to impose on your jurisdiction. Why don't you fellows unlock the front door and we'll gladly put everything back."

They didn't expect my response. I picked up on it, and I'm sure Fred did as well. The two bulldogs looked at their peer with uncertainty.

"You fellows are full of shit, aren't you? You have no keys, nor do you have any claim on this property, right?"

"Listen up, cocksucker, we're..."

He never got a chance to finish. Fred stepped forward in a blink of an eye and cold cocked him with his new pair of brass knuckles. I drew my weapon quickly.

"Don't move!" I shouted. "You're outgunned. Either of you make a wrong move, you're dead!" They froze in place, but stared at us angrily.

"You guys call yourselves cops, but y'all don't even see the man on the roof, do you?"

Now they looked up. Rowdy was still up there, and even though I wasn't looking at him, I could tell by the expressions on the men's faces he was currently pointing his rifle at them. "Now, very slowly, you two take your handguns out and drop them on the ground."

"Like hell I will," one of them said. I aimed my handgun at him.

"I won't say it twice," I said.

"Do it now!" Bo yelled. They saw the predicament they were in, and reluctantly placed their weapons on the ground.

"This is our territory," one of them said haughtily as Andie went around and gathered up their weapons. Detective McElroy was conscious now and rubbing his jaw. He sat up slowly. Fred continued staring at him.

"Check the van," I said to Andie, and then looked back at the man who thought we were in their territory. "What's your name?" I asked.

"Chet Henry," he said after a moment.

"Well, Mister Chet Henry, if you're claiming this as your territory, that means all we have to do is kill the three of you and this will now be our territory, right?" I asked. Chet stared at me silently. "Do you see how stupid your statement sounds now?" He nodded slightly. I lowered my weapon. Andie exited the van and looked at me.

"They have three assault weapons," she reported.

"Unload them and bring the bullets," Fred said. Andie ducked back in the truck.

"You three strike me as nothing more than bullies." I motioned toward the tall one sitting on his ass. "He meets us for the first time and, let's see, calls me a dumbass and a cocksucker. There's no way y'all used to be cops. You're bullies," I said.

"You got that right," Bo added.

Chet shook his head. "No, really, we were cops." He pointed back behind him. "We worked out of the East Precinct."

Bo spat in disgust. "That makes it worse. You men are supposed to protect society from bullies, but that's all you are, bullies." He spat again, "Fucking punks."

"I have to agree with my friend," I said. They stared at us sullenly. I shook my head. "We always try to start a positive relationship with survivors we meet, but you guys are not people we want to be friends with. Otherwise, we'd love to get to know you guys and hear your stories of survival. But, we have things to do. Y'all get in your van and leave. We'll leave your weapons here. You can come back for them after we're gone," I said. "Please don't follow us. If you do, we'll consider it a hostile act."

The one who called himself Chet, and his buddy who chose not to identify himself, turned to walk toward the van. The one who called himself McElroy started to get up and stumbled toward me. It seemed odd in the manner which he staggered. Before my mind could process it, he suddenly lunged and grabbed my tactical vest. He turned me where all of my friends were behind me. Then, he grabbed my handgun and attempted to wrest it away from me.

I used my left thumb and jammed it in his eye. He grunted in pain and loosened his grip. I turned it toward him and pulled the trigger. The gun didn't fire. He had managed to move the slide just enough to cause it to go out of battery. The only way to make it fire now was to rack the slide. I chose instead to hit him in the head with it. He staggered to his knees and punched me in the groin.

It hurt, and it probably would have taken me out of the fight, but I was in a rage – again. I hit him with the butt of my handgun, and continued battering him until someone grabbed me from behind in a bear hug. I desperately fought to get away.

"Easy, Zach, easy."

I recognized Fred's voice in my good ear and stopped resisting. Fred walked backward until there was some distance between us and McElroy before let go of me.

"Holster your weapon, Zach. It's over," he commanded. I did as he said, and looked at the other two cops. Chet and the other one were pale, but didn't look any worse for the wear. I watched as Bo jogged up and checked on the downed man. He checked his pulse before looking up at me and then at Fred. He slowly shook his head. I looked at the cop closely then. His head looked like freshly ground hamburger. For some reason, it took me a moment before I realized I was the one who did it.

"Alright people, load up and move out," Fred said in his usual deadpan tone. I caught my breath, walked over to my beautiful Ford Raptor truck, currently overloaded with newfound wealth, and got in the back seat. Fred pointed at the two men and pointed at their van. They picked up their friend and without commentary.

"Andie, you drive," I said.

Terry jumped in front, and Kelly jumped in back beside me. The windows were down and I overheard Bo speaking to Fred.

"Holy shit, Fred, that kid is a terror when he has his dander up."

Fred nodded without comment and they got into the Volvo.

We arrived at the fuel reservoir without any complications. I got out, but instead of helping get fuel, I walked over to the riverbank. I knew they'd figure out how to fill the tanker without me. Kelly followed me.

"You've got blood all over you. Are you hurt?" she asked. I shook my head, and pulled a bandanna out of my back pocket. I fumbled with my canteen, wet it down, and began wiping my face. Kelly took it from my hand.

"Here, let me do it." She wiped my face off, rinsed the bandanna, and began wiping my hands.

"That guy outweighed you by twenty or thirty pounds and you beat him to death," she said quietly. "I knew you were tough, but damn."

I didn't respond. I was emotionally spent. I didn't want to talk. I only wanted to look at the Cumberland River. It was quite a bit higher than normal, which led me to believe at least one dam had finally given way.

Probably the Percy Priest Dam. It had been damaged back in the eighties when a couple of idiots had set off a case of dynamite in the bowels of the dam. They had hoped to flood downtown Nashville. Then, they were going to go in with scuba gear and loot the numerous businesses. Unfortunately, for them, the dam held and they went to prison.

I watched as various type of debris floated by, along with an occasional corpse. Kelly wrapped herself around one of my arms. I felt her breasts pressing against me. My thoughts were interrupted by a jostling. Andie had approached and pushed Kelly.

"If you want to fuck him, you're going to have to go get permission from Julie, you dumbass," she said. "Go get in the truck."

Andie was three inches shorter, and probably twenty pounds lighter than Kelly. Nevertheless, Kelly was quite intimidated by her. Without a word, she walked back to the truck. Andie took her place and interlaced her arms through my right arm. She was wearing her tactical vest, so I didn't feel any breasts this time.

"So, what are we doing here, big guy?" she asked.

"I'm just enjoying the view, Miss Andrea," I said. "Why didn't anyone shoot that asshole?" I asked.

"Hell, Zach. You and Fred were moving so quick, nobody had a good shot." She pressed her head against my shoulder. "Who would have thought that old man could move so fast."

"Really? You've seen him with those pistols, right? He's like a rattlesnake, don't underestimate that man."

"I certainly don't underestimate you."

"It looks like you and Terry are doing pretty good," I commented, changing the subject.

"You don't mind that I'm sleeping with him?" she asked.

"I want you to be happy. If Terry makes you happy, I'm happy for you." I reached out and put my arm around her shoulders. "I want my little sis' to be happy."

"Are you happy, Zach?" Andie asked. It was a long minute before I answered. These days, whenever I felt threatened, I went into a cold rage. It didn't seem normal.

"I don't know," I finally said.

Chapter 56 – Weak Moments

When we got home, Fred and I sorted out and inventoried our loot. Everyone had the compulsion to pick stuff up and play with it. It was very irritating and I wasn't in a pleasant mood anyway.

Rhonda, Wanda, and the three little girls drove up. Rowdy was standing with us by the truck, so they pointedly ignored us and went inside, hopefully to help Julie cook. I found myself on the edge of snapping at a few people, so I went into our bedroom, stripped, and took a cold shower. Changing into some clean clothes, I waited in the bedroom and massaged my temples until I felt like I was civilized enough to rejoin everyone.

There were so many of us, some sat in the kitchen, others sat in the den. For some reason, we never used the dining room.

Even though we had scored a major haul of loot, the conversation was hushed. I didn't feel like talking, Fred didn't talk much anyway, and Rowdy was worried about saying the wrong thing. I finally broke the silence.

"All of you did great today," I said, without any real emotion.

"Yes, you did," Fred added. "It was unfortunate about those cops, if they were really cops."

"Fuck those assholes," Kelly said.

"Kelly!" Wanda chided.

Fred looked over at Wanda. "We found some good stuff. I believe we can now get you ladies properly armed, right Mac?"

"Hell yeah!" Mac responded.

"I hope you ladies are up for some firearms training," Fred said.

"We'll do whatever you say, Fred," Mac replied, with a little bit of eagerness in her voice. Julie grinned at Fred. He responded with an arched eyebrow.

It started the conversation. Everyone was now talking about all of the riches we found, and I ate my meal in silence. Julie looked at me occasionally, but I didn't respond.

Afterward, I shooed everyone out of the kitchen and cleaned it up by myself. Eventually, Mac took the women and girls back to the radio station, Bo went home, and Fred retired to the sleeper of the Volvo. I finished up and walked out onto the back patio. Andie and Terry were smoking a joint, while Julie and Kelly were still talking about the day's events. When I walked outside, they stopped talking, which told me they were talking about the fight. Joe was sitting there quietly.

"Where's Rowdy?" I asked.

"He's in the bus," I walked over and knocked on the door before opening it and going inside. Rowdy was in complete darkness. I could barely see him propped up in his bed.

"Howdy, Hoss, you come here for a drink?" he asked.

"What are you drinking?"

"This evening, I am enjoying a delicious and slightly expensive brand of Vodka. Svedka, I believe is the name of it." He reached up, turned on a small reading light, and looked at the label. "Yep, Svedka," he held it out. I stepped closer and reached for it. Taking a small swallow, I handed it back to him.

"When are you going to stop beating yourself up?" I asked.

"When are you?" he responded, and took another drink.

"Touché." I grabbed the bottle and took another small swallow.

"It was an unfortunate situation today. I would have taken care of that dude but I didn't ever get a clear shot."

"Was I justified, Rowdy?" I asked.

"You did what you had to do," he answered.

"I've had a couple of people try to kill me. They came pretty close. I guess I overreact now whenever I feel threatened."

"Perfectly understandable, I suppose." He eyed the bottle's label. We sat in silence a moment before Rowdy spoke.

"It looks like Andie and that soldier are hooked up now," he said, changing the subject. I nodded.

"His name is Terry, Terry Alexander," I said.

"Well, good for her, I reckon. I guess I should have stuck with her rather than chase after Cindy. Andie kept me straight."

"You weren't romantically attracted to Andie," I said. Rowdy scoffed.

"Does something like that really matter?" he asked. I shrugged and took the bottle from him before he drank again.

"I'm going to bed. Before I do, I want to leave you with a thought. We need you, Rowdy. You're a part of our family." I took one last, very small swallow, handed it back to him, and walked out. I heard him sobbing as I shut the door.

Everyone got quiet again as I walked up to the porch. "I'm going to bed, goodnight everyone," I said. Julie followed me inside. We stripped to our underwear, got in bed, and snuggled up together.

"I've been looking forward to this all day," she said.

"Me too. It started out as a good day, but kind of went sour."

"Yeah, they told me about it. I hope you're not feeling guilty."

I shrugged beside her. In fact, I *was* feeling guilty. It seemed like yet another needless death. I didn't want to talk about it, so I changed the subject and told her about Kelly.

"Andie has become quite protective," she commented.

"Yeah, she cares about both of us. She still thinks you don't like her."

"Oh, she's okay I guess. I'm still getting used to her. Now, about Kelly, are you going to have a weak moment and do her?" Julie asked after a long moment of silence.

"With the exception of kissing Andie, the only weak moments I've had in the past year and a half have all involved you. You seem to have a spell on me," I replied. Julie snuggled closer to me.

"Good," she said smugly.

Chapter 57 – Evolvement

We got Fred's new home built in a little over a month. The most time consuming part was driving around finding building materials, but we got it accomplished. Putting up a brick veneer over the plain concrete blocks, which Julie insisted on, took an extra week. The finished product was roughly a thousand square feet of the main living space, and a thousand square foot basement. The roof was metal, effectively making it almost impossible to set on fire.

Fred was pleased. At least, I caught a slight tic under his right eye, which was a very telling clue.

"I've got an idea, and am surprised I didn't think of it sooner," I said. Fred looked at me. "We should put some gutters on the eaves, and then fabricate them so they drain into barrels. We can collect rainwater."

Fred nodded in agreement.

"We still have plenty of daylight, why don't we run into town and see what we can find?" Terry suggested. Fred and I agreed. I raised Julie on the radio, told her what we had in mind, and we took off.

There was a Home Depot on Bell Road near I-24. We had only been there once, and although there had been a lot of looting, it was not totally empty. We drove up to one of the broken out front doors and gave a short toot on the horn. Only one came staggering out. He was so rotten he could barely walk. I used the twenty-two pistol on him.

We got out of the truck and stretched while looking around. "Hey," Terry said. He pointed down to the far end of the parking lot, over by an Italian restaurant I could never afford to eat in. There was another pair of zombies in the parking lot, slowly making its way toward us, or maybe just walking aimlessly.

"Hey, Fred, do you think you can shoot them from here with your pistols?" I asked. Terry cocked an eyebrow.

"They're what, a hundred yards away? There is no earthly way that you can shoot them with a fast draw from this far away," Terry said with a chortle.

I looked at Fred and grinned. "The gauntlet has been thrown," I teased.

Fred grunted, walked away from the truck a few feet, and squared off as if he was in a western movie. He drew with his right hand, fast as lightning, and fired two shots. He was walking back toward us reloading his pistol as they fell.

"Boom, head shot," he muttered as he walked by us.

"Holy sheep shit!" Terry said, with his eyes wide. I couldn't help but chuckle.

We found a couple of barrels and some generic plastic gutters. They had a modular design where the individual pieces could be snapped together.

"It's not as fancy as custom made guttering," I commented.

"The only person worried about fanciness is Julie, and she's not here," Fred said. "Let's load up."

We'd loaded up as much as we could and lashed it down tight. "We need anything else while we're in this neck of the woods?" Fred asked.

"You guys know where a maternity store is anywhere around here?" I asked. Terry laughed.

"Is she outgrowing her clothes?" he asked.

"Oh, yeah, lately all she's been wearing are sweatpants and my shirts," I replied.

"How far along is she?"

"We think she conceived on Christmas Eve, so a few days shy of five months. Her belly's growing, along with her breasts, which is not such a bad thing."

Terry laughed. Even Fred smiled a little bit.

There was another Walmart nearby we had never explored. We drove over there and discovered a strip mall across the street from it with a couple of women's clothing stores.

"These little stores will be easier to clear. We can clear Walmart on another day," I said as I drove into the parking lot. "Maybe something will be here Julie will like."

Fred grunted in agreement but suddenly straightened.

"We might not get a chance," he said. I looked around and spotted them in the parking lot of the Walmart. There were maybe one or two hundred. They spotted us about the time we spotted them.

"Where the fuck do these things keep coming from?" I asked nobody in particular and sighed. "Alright, let's just get the hell out of here. We can load up with everyone later and come back."

Terry and Fred agreed. As we drove away, Terry gave a start.

"What's wrong with you?" Fred asked.

"I swear to God I just saw one of them point at us!" he exclaimed with incredulity. He looked out of the back window as we drove away. I scoffed.

"They do that when they see you. They reach out as if they can grab you from a distance."

Terry shook his head at my analysis.

"No, dude, that thing pointed his index finger at us," he emphasized. "It was strange guys, very strange."

I saw Fred glance at me out of the corner of his eye.

"Back in March, I think I saw one of them bend down and drink some water out of a puddle," I told Fred.

"Yeah, I remember that," Terry said.

"The clothes can wait. Let's go home." I doubled back down Murfreesboro Road and was about to turn west on Bell Road when Fred grabbed one of his pistols.

"This day is turning out to be full of surprises," he said. I looked down Murfreesboro Road. A black van was approaching.

"It looks familiar," I said. I heard Terry click the safety switch on his M4.

"Are we running or standing?" he asked.

I stopped the truck. "I'm in no mood to run, how about you guys?" Terry and Fred shook their heads. I jumped out with my assault rifle, chambered a round, and waited.

"I got rear security," Terry said, and jogged to the rear of the truck.

The driver of the van spotted us, and stopped about a hundred yards away, well within our range. After a minute, they approached slowly. I eventually recognized them. It was the two cops, Chet and whatever his name is. Chet was driving. He got close and then turned perpendicular to us before stopping. He stared at me a moment before rolling his window down.

"Hello, Chet," I said amicably.

"Hello, Zach," he replied. "What are you guys up to?"

"Picking up some gutters for a house we're building," I replied. Chet frowned.

"You're building a house?" he asked.

"It's already built. We're merely putting on some finishing touches."

"You've been busy."

"Chet, you don't know the half of it. We've planted over a dozen garden plots. We recently harvested some winter wheat, and I taught Corporal Alexander here how to plant sweet corn last month. I won't even get started on the cattle we've rounded up. We've been busy as hell."

Chet looked at me in wonder, glanced over at his partner a moment, and stared at me again. "Are you bullshitting us?" he asked. Fred snorted.

"Chet, we work hard. We're building a life for ourselves. How about you guys, how are y'all doing?"

"After you killed McElroy, my friends wanted to hunt you down and kill you," he replied.

"Why is that, Chet? Because I chose to defend myself rather than let a bully hurt me?" I shook my head slowly. "I thought cops were proponents of justice."

"You don't understand, I told them exactly that. That's why you're still alive," Chet said. He put the van in park and turned it off before speaking some more.

"We've got a couple of garden plots going, but we haven't been doing anything with cattle other than killing one when we're out of steaks."

I nodded. "How are you processing your water?"

"We filter it and boil it," Chet replied. "How about you guys?"

"A few of our homes have well water. We have filters and chemical treatment systems. Our radio station has no well, so we distill the drinking water."

He looked at me quizzically. "Y'all have a radio station?"

I nodded. "Yep. It's actually run by a group of women. They broadcast every day at noon."

"Women?" the passenger asked. Chet chuckled.

"We've not seen any women in a while, so forgive our interest."

"If you show up and behave like gentlemen, you'll be welcome. If you act like bullies, much like the way you three acted the day we met you, you'll be dead before you hit the ground."

"Fair enough," Chet said, nodding his head.

"Heads up, ladies!" Terry suddenly shouted. I didn't take my eyes off of Chet and his partner. I watched as they looked toward the outbound lanes of Murfreesboro Road and their eyes widened.

"Oh, shit!" Chet said, and he started the van. He looked back at me, and realized I'd never stopped staring at him. "There's a shit load of them coming this way."

"Time to go then," I said. "We'll see you gentleman later, I suppose."

Chet nodded, made a U-turn, and sped away. Only then did I break eye contact with them and jumped in the truck.

"Zach," Terry said as I sped down Bell Road, avoiding cars and potholes with practiced expertise. "Those things were operating together, I'd swear to it."

"What do you mean?" Fred asked.

"They were walking in a column of twos, and when they got close, they started spreading out. It was weird, guys, it was kind of like a military maneuver."

I didn't answer. There was a rough spot in the road where Bell Road crested a hill. I was wary of busting a tire and navigated carefully. I caught Fred looking at me.

"What are you thinking, Zach?" he asked.

"I have sort of a hypothesis," I said after a minute.

"I'd certainly like to hear it."

"Okay, it goes like this. Last spring, I said these things would completely die out by the end of the summer. As we can see, a hell of a lot of them did in fact die, but not all of them. Why are there still zombies roaming around? Why are they not dead?"

"Yep, good questions," Terry commented.

"So, here's my hypothesis, some of them, the infected people, they're evolving," I declared.

Fred looked at me, perplexed. "How so?"

"Think of it like this. When syphilis infected a person back a couple thousand years ago, the entire body was consumed by sores called chancres. The infected person suffered horribly and soon died. By the time the second millennium came around, the human body was able to resist the disease to an extent. Oh, you'd still get chancres, go crazy and eventually die, but there was an element of resistance. The same goes for other illnesses." I took a deep breath.

"Now, apply it to this infection. We know nothing of it, hell, there's probably nobody left alive who can say with authority what the fuck it is. It is very destructive to the human body and lethal, but my hypothesis is that some people are actually developing some type of resistance and their bodies are somehow starting to function again." I took another deep breath. When I put it into words, the more I was convinced I was right. And it scared me.

I repeated my hypothesis to everyone else after we had eaten supper. They listened in rapt attention as I listed out each clue. Andie pointed at me.

"Is that why you cut open the zombie a while back?" she asked.

I nodded. "Yeah, I was trying to figure out why it was still alive. His organs should have totally rotted away. Instead, they were still intact and even appeared to be functioning."

"That's scary," Kelly said worriedly.

"Yeah, it is," I said. "A while back, when the plague first appeared, some of the infected people were still able to run. I don't know if these critters are able to run again or not, so don't take them for granted. Always be aware of your surroundings and always be armed."

"That reminds me," Julie said. "Mac came by earlier today. She was asking if you wanted a zombie pit dug around the house." Then she grinned mischievously. "And she said she'd come by later tonight and pay you a visit, Fred. She said the two of you can christen the new house."

Everyone chuckled. Fred pointed his fork at her, but said nothing.

"By the way, Fred, you've never told us if any of those people at Tinker were women?" Rowdy asked.

"There were a few women," Fred replied.

"Did you find a girlfriend?" Julie teased. Fred hung his head. Julie gasped. "Oh, my God, you did find a girlfriend! Tell us about her." It was a long moment before Fred spoke.

"Her name was Sarah. She was an Air Force pilot. Very smart, very feisty," Fred pointed his fork again. "Like you."

Julie smiled.

"Well, where the hell is she, Hoss?" Rowdy asked. "Why didn't you bring her home with you?"

"She refused to come," Fred said quietly. "I suppose it was for the best. She was a bit high strung," Fred wiped his mouth and looked at Joe.

"Are you finished with dinner?" he asked. Joe wolfed down another bite and nodded. "Okay, we best be getting home. We have a full day tomorrow." He stood and looked at us. "We'll be over for breakfast in the morning and help with the gardens."

They bid us all goodnight and left.

"Wow, he never said anything about a girlfriend," I said after they left. Kelly helped me clear the dishes and began washing them.

"It must have ended badly," she opined. "I had a similar experience, right about the time everything went bad."

"What happened?" Julie asked.

"I was engaged. One day, he gave me the speech about needing some space. I thought he only needed some time and he'd get his head clear. One Sunday he showed up to church with a new girlfriend."

"Ouch," I said.

"Yeah, I was devastated, especially when I found out it was the preacher's daughter. So, I lost my future husband and my church, all at the same time. A co-worker invited me to go to her church, which was Wanda's. The infection swept through and I was trapped with the group. It was a blessing at first, but then

Wanda's husband started getting more and more radical. He even claimed he was having visions from God," she chortled.

"Anyway, Wanda got us out of there. I never talked to any of them about the man who broke my heart, so I guess I can see why Fred never said anything either."

I nodded in understanding.

"You haven't been laid since then?" Andie asked. Terry tried to hide a grin.

"No," Kelly said wistfully. I nodded without responding verbally, and was about to add some commentary, but I caught Julie in my peripheral vision. She was looking at me for whatever reason. I excused myself, grabbed a lantern, and went into the basement. Julie came down a few minutes later.

"What are you doing?" she asked.

"Going through my note pads. I want to make sure I haven't missed anything about these zombies. I'm going to put a list together and have Mac put out some kind of warning advisory on her daily radio broadcast."

I looked up at her standing over me and patted the floor beside me. She sat with a little awkwardness. It reminded me of Macie when she was pregnant. Julie picked up Andie's journal and read a little of it.

"She's written quite a lot," she commented. I agreed. "I have to admit, she has a nice writing style. Her spelling is as bad as mine, but it's easy to read."

"What's the rest of the gang doing?" I asked.

"I believe they're sitting on the patio getting high," she said.

"Andie has turned Corporal Alexander into a stoner," I said with a sigh. Julie chuckled.

"Isn't he worried about getting court martialed or something?" Julie asked.

"Nah, I don't think they have the means to test for drugs anymore. Besides, he said he's not going back. He seems to think he won't be charged with desertion. His time of service was almost up when the plague hit."

"I hope he's right," Julie said. "Let's go join them. We don't socialize enough."

"Sure. But I don't want you giving me a hard time when they start talking about sex, which you know they will."

Julie chuckled. "Help me up, stud muffin." She held her hand out.

Chapter 58 – Bath Water

Rowdy and I sat on the tailgate of my truck at the Smyrna airport under a shade tree. The flies were terrible. We had our respective Boonie hats on with the mosquito netting, but it didn't stop the little bastards from buzzing all around us.

"Do you think they'll show up today?" Rowdy asked.

"I don't know," I replied. We had missed a few dates, and we had not seen Captain Steen and his soldiers since March. I looked at my watch.

"It's 12:30. They were always prompt before," I said. "I guess we wait a little while longer."

Rowdy shrugged indifferently. I looked at him. "How've you been?" I asked nonchalantly.

"Not too bad. I won't try to tell you I'm straight and sober, but I've slowed down quite a lot. Needless to say, my bowels are very pleased," he said with a grin. I nodded. "I wonder why there are no zombies around here," Rowdy said while he looked around. I shrugged. I didn't know why either.

"Did you and Cindy ever do it?" I asked, mostly out of boredom. Rowdy chuckled.

"Oh, hell yeah, we fucked like bunnies, but we had to do it in secret though. She didn't want her mother to know, and I didn't want to hurt Andie's feelings, so we had to sneak away to secluded spots before we could bump uglies." Rowdy scratched his beard. "Yeah, we had some good times. I sure do miss her." He then looked over at me.

"I tested the waters with Kelly the other night. She made it clear she wasn't interested. I don't know what I'm going to do, Hoss, but this ole boy needs a woman."

He stood and stretched. I understood how he felt, but I didn't know how to rectify the situation.

"What about Rhonda?" I finally asked. He glanced at me.

"You know, I happened to catch a peek of her coming out of the bath tub one morning, and let me tell you, Hoss, she has one fine looking body on her. Fine enough to declare you'd drink her bath water just for a taste of it, if you know what I'm saying."

I laughed at him. One thing was for certain, you never knew what was going to come out of Rowdy's mouth.

"But, she's like a broody hen over those kids. It's kind of weird how she obsesses over them." Rowdy looked around again. "How much longer are we going to wait on them?"

I stood and stretched as well. "I guess they're not coming. Let's get the hell out of here."

We got in the truck and I looked at him out of the corner of my eye. "Let's run by the radio station and see if Rhonda needs a bath."

Big Mac. How do I properly describe the woman? She worked as hard as any two men did. The radio station now had a zombie pit completely surrounding the property. There were gardens planted, and four truck trailers parked behind the house, which were being used for storage. Somehow, she had located multiple types of construction equipment, anything from a bulldozer to a road grader. They were now neatly lined up beside the trailers. And she'd done it all herself, while the Rhonda and Wanda duo did a lot of sitting around the house.

"Let me show you something, Zach," she said, and led me to the trailers. She opened them. "I've been going through all of those trucks abandoned on the Interstate and found all kinds of stuff." The trailers were full of goodies.

"I'm totally impressed," I said with a chuckle. Mac grinned broadly.

"Have you had any visitors lately?" Rowdy asked.

"We've had a few people stop in," Mac replied. "They don't have much to trade. They're mostly interested in a free meal, and then they drive on. I've caught a couple of zombies in the pits. I shot 'em and burned 'em, just like you said to do."

I smiled at her with pride. She continued talking to Rowdy, and I walked to the house. The two women were hanging up wet clothes, while the three little girls were running around the yard playing.

"Hello, ladies," I said.

"Hello, Zach," Rhonda said with a warm smile. Wanda glanced at me and grunted a hello.

"Are you here to help or chew the fat?" she asked gruffly as she secured a pair of pants on the clothesline. I grabbed some clothing and handed articles to her as she pinned them to the line. "I don't know why you brought *him* here," she complained as she nodded toward Rowdy.

"Are you ever going to forgive him?" I asked. She gave me a look and scoffed.

"He's miserable over what happened. He was quite smitten with Cindy, you know," I said and handed her a pair of large panties. She snatched them out of my hand and hung them up.

"He should be miserable. He killed my only daughter," she huffed.

"It was a mistake, Wanda. Was it shortsighted? Yes, but he had no ill intent," I offered. She responded with a brief glare. We worked through the rest of the laundry basket in silence.

"What kind of work did you do for a living?" I asked her. She gave me a look.

"It's about time you got around to asking," she said. I looked at her and waited for a response. "I was a midwife."

I think my jaw dropped. Wanda glanced at me with a hint of a smug grin.

"I got your interest now, I bet," she said. "Up until now, you've been thinking all this time I was worthless."

"Not at all, I just thought you were a bitter old woman," I said before I could help myself. She responded with a chortle.

"You'll want this bitter old woman's help when Julie gives birth, I'm betting."

"You would be correct," I said simply. She gave me a look with her lips spread. Some people might have called it a smile. I would've disagreed with them.

"Nothing's for free around here," she said. Rhonda looked over at me and rolled her eyes.

"I understand. Think about what would be an appropriate payment and consider yourself hired," I said.

Wanda quickly pointed at Rowdy. "His head on a platter."

"Wanda!" Rhonda said, and shook her head in disgust.

"Something reasonable, Wanda," I replied. She looked at me as if her request was perfectly reasonable. "Think it over. Now, changing the subject, I'd like to buy a radio ad."

Wanda stopped hanging up clothing and looked at me.

"Hang on," I said, went to the truck, and came back with a large plastic bag of peppermint candy canes. I had found them in one of the cars we searched. I handed it to Rhonda.

"We've not seen anyone from Fort Campbell since March. I want you guys to ask in your daily broadcasts if anyone has been to Fort Campbell or have been in contact with any of their personnel. If they have, ask them to contact us and tell us how they're doing. Also," I pulled a sheet of paper out of my pocket, "I want you guys to warn people about the zombie's change of behavior. I wrote down the changes we've observed.""We can do it for free, Zach," Rhonda said quietly as she looked at my notes. Wanda glared, but Rhonda ignored her. I smiled.

"I know, but I bet the kids will love those."

Rhonda returned my smile warmly and gave my arm a squeeze. "Thank you, Zach." She walked off to where the kids were playing. I watched her walk away and found myself looking at her backside.

"Does she ever wear anything besides those plain dresses?" I asked Wanda. She looked at me as if I asked some sort of perverted question. "Forget it," I said.

"Are you bedding Kelly now?" She asked. "If you are, there's no need looking Rhonda over. You'd think two women would be plenty for you."

I looked at her and sighed.

"We're never going to have anything other than this acrid relationship, are we, Wanda?" I asked. She responded with a grunt.

"Yeah, that's what I thought. Are y'all coming over for dinner?"

"We'll be there around four," she said curtly, and started in on a second basket of clothes.

"Okay, I'll tell Julie. You two can talk over her upcoming birth. Think over how much it's going to cost me," I said, and walked away without waiting for a response.

Chapter 59 – Frederick

Us men were summarily ousted from the house for the duration of the birth. We sought solace on the back patio. Rowdy broke out a bottle of something, but I was in no mood to drink. Bo was having a good time cooking some barbeque on the smoker. Fred had Prancer tied to a tree in the backyard. She was contentedly eating grass while Joe brushed her.

"How long has it been now?" Rowdy asked. I glanced at my watch.

"Her contractions started right after breakfast, so about eight hours now," I answered, and looked over at Fred and Bo.

"You two were fathers. How much longer should it take?" I asked them. Bo grinned and shrugged his shoulders.

"It's hard to say, Zach," Fred said. "Some women give birth quickly, some women take a while."

"Yep," Bo added. "My first child took all day. The second one popped out in no time."

I resisted the urge to start pacing, and sat silently, but I was getting the urge to go out and shoot something. Rowdy went to his bus and came out a minute later with a guitar.

"I thought I'd play a little to pass the time. Do you have any requests, Hoss?" he asked.

"No, I can't think of anything," I said.

"Do you know Classical Gas?" Bo asked. "My ex-wife really loved that song."

"In fact, I do," Rowdy replied. He took a minute to tune the guitar and then launched into a flawless rendition of Mason William's timeless masterpiece. He moved his fingers along the fret board smoothly and seemingly without effort. When he was finished, we applauded.

"That was beautiful, Rowdy," I complimented.

"Why thank you, Hoss," he replied with a grin. We were interrupted by the back door opening. Andie popped her head out and told me to start the generator. She started to duck back inside, but I stopped her.

"What's going on?" I asked.

"We need hot water to clean up," she answered. "It'll be about thirty more minutes." She grinned at me. "Everything is fine, Zach, you're a daddy."

Then she ducked back in the door before I could ask any further questions.

It took a long half hour before she stuck her head out again and motioned me inside. I jumped up and hurried in.

All of the women stopped talking and looked at me when I walked in. Julie, sitting in bed, looked like she had been rode hard and hung up wet, but when she saw me, she gave a glowing smile. She was holding a little bundle of something swaddled in a baby blanket.

"Would you like to hold your son, Daddy?" Julie asked teasingly, and held him out. Wanda immediately stood up and took the baby before gently handing him over to me.

"Now, you hold him exactly like this," she chided, and showed me how to place my hands. I'm pretty sure I knew how to properly hold a newborn, but I held my tongue. I held my newborn son as Andie rushed into the room with a hairbrush.

"Everyone wants to come in and see," she said. "So we need to get you looking good."

Julie smirked, but didn't protest as Andie brushed out her hair.

Everyone came in and circled the bed. There were the usual sentiments said and I nodded in thanks.

"Well, Hoss, you've never told us what his name's going to be," Rowdy said. I looked around at them all.

"Julie and I had a pretty good idea from the start what our baby's name would be if it was a boy." I held up my child. "Everyone, please say hello to Frederick Zachariah Gunderson. And, by the way, I'll most likely call him Rick."

Everyone voiced their agreement and patted me on the back. I looked over at Fred. He gave me one of his patented nods, and even grinned a little bit.

Chapter 60 – An Overdue Reunion

I glanced at Tommy as I drove. His face was covered in acne, his hair was unkempt and stringy, and he looked malnourished. He stared blankly out of the window, as if in shock.

"How are you doing, Tommy?" I asked. It was as if he didn't hear me. He kept staring out of the window. I drove past the charred remains of a mound of bodies, found a safe spot, and stopped the truck. "Tommy, look at me." He slowly turned his head, stared at me a second, and then burst out in tears. I put the truck in park and held him tightly. The realization of being raped was hitting him with full force now.

"It's okay, buddy. It's going to be okay." I continued holding him while he cried long and hard. It lasted for well over thirty minutes. I held him quietly, letting him get it out of his system. His crying was only interrupted when Julie's voice came over the CB radio.

"Come in, Saigon," she said. Tommy looked at the radio, and then looked at me in confusion.

"They're calling us." I picked up the microphone. "I'm here, heading back."

"I need you here in forty-five minutes. Don't be early, and you better not be late, or else," she said. In spite of Tommy's pain, I couldn't help but grin at Julie's menacing ultimatum.

"10-4," I acknowledged. "I've got to stop by Fred's place first and then I'll be there."

"Fred and Joe are over here," she said.

"I just have to pick something up and I'll be right there, in forty-five minutes," I said and signed off.

"Who was that?" Tommy asked. I gave him a look to see if he was serious.

"That's Julie, your sister," I said slowly. Tommy looked at me in troubled confusion.

"Mom said she was dead," he finally said.

That bitch, I thought. She probably said it to Tommy so he'd stop asking about her. It was a cruel thing to do.

"No, Tommy," I said quietly. "She's very much alive, and she's going to be thrilled to death to see you."

"You're taking me to see her?" he asked, wide-eyed.

"Damn right I am. You two have been apart far too long. But first, we're going to stop by a friend's house and get you cleaned up."

Tommy took a quick, cold shower and toweled off. I gave his backside a look and handed him a tube of Neosporin.

"Alright, buddy, you'll need to use this for a couple of days. It'll help you heal up."

The Neosporin would, hopefully, prevent any infection, but I had nothing to prevent any possible STD exposure.

"Why did he do that to me?" Tommy asked plaintively.

"Because, he was an evil person, they both were," I answered. "You don't have to worry about either one of those assholes anymore, right?" I asked.

Tommy nodded. "You killed them and set them on fire."

"Yep, and they never had a chance to tell anyone what was done to you. So, we're going to keep it between us. Nobody else knows, and nobody else needs to know," I asserted. Tommy nodded gratefully, and thanked me when I handed him some of Joe's clothes. "These should fit you. They're some of Joe's clothes. I'm sure he won't mind. You'll meet him shortly. I bet you two will turn out to be good friends."

"Where is Joe?" Tommy asked as he started getting dressed.

"He's at my house with everyone else." I looked around conspiratorially. "They're throwing me a surprise birthday party. I'm not supposed to know about it." I grinned at Tommy and winked. He grinned back.

"I won't tell anyone," he promised. "Is Julie there?"

"She is, and we're going to surprise her when she sees you. How does that sound?"

"It sounds awesome," Tommy said. I put an arm around his shoulders in a brotherly hug.

"There's a lot to tell you, buddy. For one thing, I'm now your brother-in-law," I said. Tommy looked at me blankly. I explained. "I married Julie, so that makes me your brother-in-law."

"Oh, cool!" he responded.

"It gets better. You're an uncle too," I said with a smile.

"How'd that happen?" he asked.

I took a deep breath. "I'll let Julie explain it," I looked at my watch. "We better get going, or else we'll catch hell."

Everyone shouted the customary 'surprise' when we walked in the door. I dropped my jaw and acted as if I were truly surprised. Simultaneously, everyone seemed to see Tommy at the same time and a hush came over the room.

"Oh, my God," Julie gasped, handed little Rick to Rhonda, and rushed over to where we were standing in the doorway. Grabbing Tommy by the shoulders, she looked at him a moment, and then burst out in tears. This caused Tommy to burst out in tears as he grabbed his big sister in a tight hug. Curly ran up to him with his tail wagging in recognition. I spoke up.

"Everyone, this is Tommy, Julie's little brother."

There was a collective gasp as everyone murmured their surprise, gathered around, and welcomed Tommy. I slipped out of the way and stood off to the side. Andie walked over and stood beside me.

"I didn't know Julie had a brother," she whispered. I glanced at her.

"Yeah, it's a long story," I whispered back. "So, what birthday present did you get me?"

"A blowjob," she whispered and grinned mischievously at me. I laughed and put my arm around her shoulders. "When is Julie's birthday?" she asked.

"March seventh," I replied.

"Did you do anything for her?" she asked.

"Oh, yeah," I replied with a grin. Julie broke her embrace with her little brother long enough to looked at me with tears of joy in her eyes. I gave her a wink.

We had a large dinner, and afterward, I sat in a chair holding my son while everyone chitchatted. Julie, understandably, devoted her attention to Tommy. She peppered him with questions about where he had been and what their mother was up to.

Little Rick decided to go boom-boom at some point, so I quietly walked into the bedroom and changed him. I started to walk out when I saw Wanda standing in the doorway watching me.

"I thought you might need some help," she said.

"I was a little clumsy at it, but managed to get it done," I replied.

"You did better than I thought you would," she said and disappeared down the hallway. I guess it was her way of complimenting me.

When I walked back to the den, everyone was waiting on me. Julie directed me back to the chair. "Time for your presents," she said cheerfully.

"We're doing something a touch different," Rowdy added. "A physical present from each of us to you was too hard to figure out. Whenever you want something, you just go out and find it, which can be damned annoying."

Everyone chuckled in agreement.

"So, we decided to do testimonials instead," Julie said. "I'm going first," she looked around. "When I first met Zach, I'd gone without a bath for a few days, so I was a little self-conscious. Later, even though Tommy loved him from the very first, I thought he was an arrogant prick."

Everyone burst out in laughter.

"Ditto," Wanda added. Everyone laughed again.

"In fact, he and Rick summarily kicked us out of their house with the threat of bodily harm," she said smiling. "So, I hatched an evil plan to make him find me on the streets and fall in love with me. And it worked!" She smiled sweetly while everyone laughed.

"I'm next," Andie said. "When I first met Zach, I called him an idiot and a dumb shit."

More laughter. "Now, I'm convinced he's the smartest person I've ever met, and I'm eternally grateful to him for everything he's done for me."

"When I first met Zach, he'd recently been in an unpleasant disagreement with some folks who meant to do him harm," Fred said. "I was very impressed with him and how protective he was toward Julie. I grew to love them both as my own family. Now, I consider all of you my family."

Everyone agreed and clapped. Rowdy spoke next.

"When I first met Zach, he chopped off the head of a zombie and then spent several minutes inspecting it." Everyone laughed again, except Wanda. Rowdy pretended not to notice, and continued. "Julie's first words to me was that I was full of shit." There was much more laughter. "I had gone through a rough time before meeting up with the two of them. We've all had a rough time I suspect, but Zach has helped me out tremendously. He's been a good friend."

"I first met Zach and company when I was surrounded by zombies," Big Mac said. "They came to my rescue. It was obvious Zach took a liking to me immediately. I've lived a lifetime with people looking at me strangely, or saying things behind my back. Zach didn't do any such thing."

"I haven't gotten to know Zach as well as I'd like," Bo said. "But, in the short time I have known him I've found him to be a unique and resourceful young man."

"I think he's handsome," Rhonda said sweetly.

"And a tough mother fucker," Kelly added. Everyone laughed again.

"When I first met Zach, he was beat all to hell," Terry said. "When I heard the whole story, I thought, wow, he's a pretty tough kid. When I was told the story of how he got shot in the head and lived through it, I knew one thing for certain. He *is* a tough you-know-what."

I smiled or chuckled at the appropriate moments, but to be honest, they were making me out to be a lot bigger than my britches. I looked over at Fred. He seemed to sense my discomfort and gave me a fatherly nod.

It was after eight when everyone left, which was far later than normal. Julie fixed Tommy a bed on the couch and he promptly fell asleep while we were talking.

"Where are we going to put him?" Julie asked.

"I can fix up a bedroom for him in the basement. The wood stove down there will keep him warm. Or, he can be bunk buddies with Joe."

Kelly smiled in relief. "Oh, good, I thought I was going to be booted from my new bedroom."

"Where on earth did you find him?" Julie asked. Andie, Terry, Rowdy, and Kelly looked at me attentively. I was hoping to avoid the story until a later time, but saw no way out of it. I only omitted Tommy's assault, and did not feel the least bit guilty about it.

"Damn, Zach," Terry said. "If you take a disliking to someone, they sure don't live very long." Andie punched him in the arm. Rowdy chuckled, and then poured everyone a glass of violet colored liquid.

"It's a fine cabaret wine," he said. "Now you need to give a speech."

Everybody voiced their agreement and soon joined in a hushed chorus of 'speech, speech, speech.' I held up my hand and they became quiet.

"There are a lot of things I can think of, but I'll only say this. My grandmother bought me a truck on my fifteenth birthday. As you can imagine, I was ecstatic. When I thanked her, she said, when you encounter a happy moment in your life, you should savor the moment for all it is worth, that way you'll never forget it. This is indeed a moment to savor. I'm glad y'all are here," I held up my glass and we toasted.

Epilogue

Even with an occasional missed shot, and people shooting at the same zombie, our kill efficiency was very high. We'd shoot them until they got to within fifty meters, then we'd hop in our vehicles, drive another quarter of a mile away from them, and do it all over again. We'd done it four times now.

Our strategy was working, but I hoped we killed them all before we ran out of ammo. The horde had grown somewhat when we first encountered them. Stragglers seemed to be everywhere and joined in with the equivalent of zombiefied glee."Everyone, sing out with your ammo count," I shouted. When everyone had given their number, I did a quick mental calculation.

"Alright, we have about two thousand rounds left. Try to stay within your sectors of fire." I ducked inside my truck and retrieved some binoculars.

"How many, do you think?" Terry asked as I handed the binoculars to Julie."I'm estimating a couple of hundred," I said to all of them. "Hopefully, this will be all," until next time, I thought. We waited patiently for them to walk within range. Suddenly, Terry shouted.

"Hey, everyone, get your kits out and do a quick field cleaning. Otherwise, we'll start getting jams. I'll keep watch."

I glanced at him with pride. Terry had a military mindset, which was a valuable asset for our group.

We cleaned our weapons quickly, while we waited for the slowly moving horde. I looked over at everyone's progress and noticed Kelly kept fumbling with her weapon. I reassembled mine quickly and helped with hers. I motioned for her to pull an earplug out and asked her how she was doing. She glanced at me before focusing on her weapon.

"Alright," she answered, but then shook her head. "Nervous as hell. I need a Xanax."

I chuckled. "It's a hell of a way to introduce you to zombie killing, but you're doing good, hang in there." I patted her shoulder. She smiled at me tentatively and put her earplug back in.

Once they were in range, it took another forty-five minutes until the last one fell. Afterward, we reloaded, gathered around, and exchanged high-fives.

"The cold slowed them down, but we still had some close calls," Bo observed.

"Yeah, this may not be a good strategy during the heat of the summer when they're more agile," I added. "Since we now know more about them, we may have to mount some offensive operations while it's still cold." I looked at Terry. "That'll be your project, Corporal." He grinned and gave me a mock salute.

"Mac," I said, "first thing tomorrow, let's get some bulldozers down here along with that tanker full of old gas. We'll stack 'em and have some zombie bonfires. We also want to gather up all of our brass before everyone runs over it."

"Tomorrow is Christmas," Julie said with a smile. "I might have a present or two for you," I looked at everyone and shrugged.

"Maybe we can wait a day," I conceded, and grinned. "I hope y'all plan on meeting at the house. The Wanda and Rhonda duo have a big Christmas Eve dinner waiting on us."

I let Julie drive, I needed to unwind and think. As we turned south on Nolensville Pike, I looked over at a billboard near the intersection. A few days ago, I had spent a couple of hours stripping away the advertising for a new generation of mobile phone and painted my last, and possibly the most ominous rule, in bold, three-foot block letters -

Z14: THEY'RE EVOLVING.